THE

CABIN

ON

SOUDER

HILL

LONNIE BUSCH

THE

CABIN

ON

SOUDER

HILL

**BLACK
STONE**
PUBLISHING

Copyright © 2020 by Lonnie Busch
Published in 2020 by Blackstone Publishing
Cover and book design by K. Jones

Printed in the United States of America

First edition: 2020
ISBN 978-1-982585-45-7
Fiction / Thrillers / Suspense

1 3 5 7 9 10 8 6 4 2

CIP data for this book is available
from the Library of Congress

Blackstone Publishing
31 Mistletoe Rd.
Ashland, OR 97520

www.BlackstonePublishing.com

CHAPTER 1

She waited until noon to phone the sheriff. At one point she drove down Pink Souder Road searching for Cliff, calling his name out the window, then returned to the cabin and waited. She pulled her mat from the closet and tried to do yoga but went to the freezer for the open carton of ice cream instead, then stared past the glass doors at the gray sky.

The sheriff arrived shortly before two o'clock. He had the sturdy look of a man who'd spent the greater part of his life working outdoors. He introduced himself as Sheriff Louden Fisk.

"And this here's my deputy, Elmer Bogan," the sheriff said. Even though Bogan was much younger, he was heavier, and sweating as if the eleven steps up to the cabin had been taxing.

"Hello, Sheriff," Michelle said, extending her hand. She nodded at the deputy. "My husband didn't come back last night. Cliff. That's his name."

"Where did he go?"

"Down the mountain." Michelle pointed over the railing. "Around midnight. I was in bed. He walked out on the deck to get air, then came back in saying he saw a light down the mountain. Down there through the trees."

"A light?" the sheriff said. "What kind of light?"

"One of those dusk-to-dawn lights," Michelle said, feeling nervous talking to the police. She wasn't sure why. "You know, like people have in their driveways. The kind on telephone poles."

The sheriff nodded. "You say he went down there in the middle of the night? With a flashlight? Is he an experienced hiker? Or outdoorsman?"

"No, he's a used car salesman." She hadn't intended for it to sound flip. "What I mean is . . . he's never hiked. He's not outdoorsy or anything."

Deputy Bogan stood by without a word, a sprinkle of perspiration on his upper lip.

"You folks just come up on weekends and such?" the sheriff asked. "Or you live here year round?"

"No, mostly just weekends. We bought the cabin last fall," she said. The truth was, she'd had little to do with the decision. Cliff had come home from a car auction in North Carolina with a contract for a cabin in the mountains, less than three hours' drive from Atlanta. That had precipitated another argument. Michelle liked the idea of the cabin—they could use some time together—but she hated that Cliff hadn't consulted her first.

"What was he wearing?" the sheriff asked.

"Uh . . . a red cap, jeans . . . and a tan jacket," she said.

The sheriff walked to the far edge of the deck. Rain clouds stacked along the mountain peaks like enormous gray ships. A misty breeze wet the boards and railing.

"He kept saying there was a house down there and that there wasn't supposed to be one," she continued "Then he said he heard noises or something. I was already in bed . . . I should have paid closer attention to what he was going on about . . . but I was exhausted from the drive up."

"I don't see anything down there," the sheriff said.

"I don't either, but that's where he said it was," Michelle said, zipping her coat. "Down there, through all those trees and rhododendron."

"Why would he go down there in the middle of the night?" Sheriff Fisk asked, seeming confused. "Why go down there at all? Was he vexed about something?"

Michelle tried to explain again, the entire episode sounding so ridiculous she was embarrassed recounting it—Cliff standing at the edge of the deck pointing toward noises drifting up through the bare oaks and poplars, doors shutting, wood on wood, dull shadows of sound. "Down there," Cliff had told Michelle. "The real estate agent said there wasn't another house in any direction for a mile," Cliff had said, pointing down the hill. "That's no mile. I'm not driving three hours to listen to people banging around all night. I can stay in Atlanta for that."

Cliff's mushrooming impatience with people, customers, and even her over the past several years had become taxing to Michelle. Cliff had never been unflappable, but it now seemed nothing could satisfy him. His irascibility worried her. It had been responsible for conflicts among his sales force, his lenders, and on one occasion, the Highway Patrol over a broken taillight.

"Can you send out a search party or something?" Michelle said.

"Well, why don't the deputy and me take a ride down there first and see if we can't find something," Fisk said, adjusting his hat. "You're welcome to join us."

She shook her head. She'd already driven down that road several times. There was nothing there. "I'll wait here," she said. "In case he comes back or calls."

The police car backed out of the driveway, made a slow arc onto the road, and headed down the mountain. As she slid the glass patio door closed, Michelle wondered what her life would be like if they didn't find Cliff. She stood by the window recreating her days without him. Everything she'd ever wanted had involved him—family, a home, children—but her pristine vision of a perfect family life vanished as she'd learned over the years to settle. Cliff had agreed to a big family—she'd wanted at least three children—until they had Cassie. Then everything changed. He said one was enough, that he didn't have room in his heart for another child, that Cassie was his entire world. "Remember how unsure you were before Cassie was born?" she'd told him. "And how that all changed in the delivery room, Cliff. Remember? That overwhelming rush of love you felt for our beautiful girl? Your heart has plenty of room for more children. The heart doesn't set boundaries on love." Cliff hadn't responded, just turned away from her.

Boundaries on love. What a queer notion that had seemed to Michelle. Maybe she'd been wrong. She certainly felt like she'd set boundaries on her love for Cliff since his affair.

The sheriff and deputy returned shortly, but this time the sheriff came to the door by himself. The deputy waited in the police car. Sheriff Fisk shook his head. "Nothing. I was fairly certain there was no house down there below your place, only Mattie Souder's old shack at the end of the road. But the way things are building up so fast I wasn't sure anymore."

"Who's Mattie Souder?" Michelle asked, recalling the dilapidated house. She had stood outside calling Cliff's name, afraid to go in or even knock on the door.

"Mattie hasn't been there in years," the sheriff said. "Not since her and Pink disappeared—Pink was her son. I thought maybe your husband might've holed up there if he was hurt, but there wasn't nothing in Mattie's old shack but mice and ringnecks." The sheriff gave Michelle the gas pump version of the Pink Souder story.

"Pink and his wife, Isabelle, were having some marital problems. One night, Isabelle just up and disappeared. Never even said anything to her sister, Claire. So when Claire reported her missing, we put on a countywide search. State police pitched in when we came up empty. Widened the investigation. But there wasn't much to go on, since the last person to see her was Pink. According to Claire there'd been a big argument or something, but that was it. Isabelle was gone. No witnesses. No phone call. No note. Nothing."

Fisk tightened his mouth and stared at the rain.

"Not sure why, but the state police boys were convinced Pink had killed Isabelle and buried her on the property. But they never found her. Wasn't long after that Mattie and Pink disappeared."

"The property?"

"They had this whole place dug up," the sheriff said. "Holes everywhere."

"What place?" Michelle said.

"This place. Your yard out there, all the way to the road. This was Pink's place," the sheriff said. "Built it himself. Isabelle was gonna move over here soon as it was done."

Michelle was dumbstruck. Cliff hadn't said anything about a murder. Maybe he didn't know either.

"I never believed Pink could kill anyone," Fisk said. "Especially Isabelle. He loved that girl like crazy." The sheriff smiled. "There aren't any bodies buried here. I guarantee it. Folks make up some wild tales in these mountains. I heard one that had Mattie turning her boy, Pink, into an ass and riding him out of town like the Virgin Mary headed for Bethlehem." He chuckled. "I don't believe any of that hokum—spells and runes and whatnot. Those Wicca folks are no different from you or me . . ."

"Wicca folks?" Michelle asked. "What's Wicca?"

"Uh, well . . ." Sheriff Fisk paused, scratching behind his ear. "They're witches, I guess you'd call them. Maybe you've seen some of those signs on the outskirts of town for Wiccan supplies and such. It's not like a secret society or—"

"Witches?" Michelle asked. "Like, you mean . . . ?"

"No, they don't wear pointy black hats or ride around on brooms or nothing," the sheriff said, chuckling softly. "You don't need to worry none about any of that."

"I've never heard of—"

"Pretty common in these hills. Well, maybe not *common*, but . . . You wouldn't know them if you passed them in the grocery store. They're no different than you and me."

Michelle felt momentarily transported back in time. Or to a time unknown to her. It was curious. Witches?

"Tales spring up around these parts for God only knows what reason," Fisk continued. "Probably reading too many of them Stephen King novels. Or drinking too much moonshine. Lulu—that was Mattie's best friend—Lulu said Mattie had people in Virginia and went to stay with them for a while. She never came back, though." The sheriff's expression darkened, as if his mind was wrestling with something troublesome.

"What about my husband?" Michelle said. "What do we do now? He could be lying somewhere unconscious."

"He's probably all right, ma'am. Had us a twelve-year-old boy a few years back got separated from his scout troop over there in the Nantahala Forest. Gone four days. Everybody was out looking for him. Parents were worried sick. When we found him, he wasn't a hundred yards from where they'd been camping. Walked in big circles for days. And he was just fine. A bit tired and hungry, but A-OK."

Michelle was not comforted by the story, imagining if it were Cassie lost in the woods. Cassie was only fifteen and Michelle couldn't bear the thought of her being scared, alone, hungry.

"I'll round up some of the boys with dogs. We'll search the area," Fisk said. "Could be your husband got turned around in the dark. Can't go too far round these parts anymore without coming to a road or highway. We'll find him." The sheriff tweaked the brim of his hat. "I need for you to stay close to the phone in case he calls though. Need anything from the grocery store?"

"No, I'm fine," she said, crossing her arms, not sure if she agreed with the sheriff's assessment of the area, about the abundance of roads and highways. To her the area was damn remote. That's what Cliff had loved about it, that their property was supposed to be surrounded by thousands of acres of national forest land, no one else for miles.

"You better go on inside," the sheriff said. "Chill's setting in. And don't you worry, we'll find him."

*****

Rain slashed at the deck as seven men started down the hill, three of them struggling back against leashes, their dogs burrowing close to the ground, seemingly barking at ghosts. Michelle watched from the back door until there was nothing left of the men and their hounds but the howling. An hour or so later, a helicopter rumbled past the cabin and Michelle thought they might have found Cliff until it cut down over the trees and out of sight. The sheriff knocked on the door around six that evening.

"Howdy, ma'am. Any news?"

Michelle shook her head, searching the sheriff's eyes for answers. Rain dripped from the collar of his yellow slicker.

"Well, we haven't had much luck either. Bogan and me figure to wait until dark and see if we can't locate exactly what you folks were looking at. Distances can be deceiving up here. Maybe the light was further away than you thought."

"How about the dogs?"

The sheriff's jaw clenched. "They had a scent for a while . . . but then . . ."

"What?"

"They spooked," the sheriff said. "Started howling like they'd treed a coon . . . and we thought they'd found something. But then they commenced to whimpering. They were pretty scared over something . . ."

Fisk walked down to the men in the driveway, told them they could go on home. They packed up their dogs, slamming tailgates and doors, spinning gravel as they left the driveway, taking—it felt to Michelle—all the hope with them. Encouraged earlier when the men arrived with the dogs, she'd been certain they would find Cliff. Watching them leave erased her optimism, left her anxious and guilty, even ashamed for taking a moment's satisfaction in the notion that Cliff might be dead. Over the past few years she'd pictured Cliff's overturned Cherokee, the wheels spinning, the phone call from the police. "What kind of person would imagine such things?" she thought. She was too embarrassed to even tell her sister, Darcy, about her morbid reverie.

"We don't need all that manpower tonight," the sheriff told Michelle when he came back up.

"Do you and Deputy Bogan want to wait inside?" Michelle asked.

"No, ma'am, we'll wait in the car. Won't be long 'fore dark."

Michelle washed dishes, glancing out at the horizon, trying to speed the night. She decided to call her sister.

"Hey, Darcy, it's Michelle."

"How's the getaway going?" Darcy said.

"You have a minute to talk?"

"Yeah, sure. What's going on?"

Michelle's mind kept bouncing between things Sheriff Fisk had told her about Pink, and his wife. Was Isabelle her name? Michelle wasn't sure. "It's Cliff. He's missing."

"Missing?"

Michelle told Darcy about the night before.

"When I woke up, he wasn't here," she said. "I thought he'd gone for a walk this morning like he usually does, but when he wasn't back by noon I got concerned. I called the sheriff."

"Do you want me to drive up?" Darcy asked.

"No, thanks. I'm okay. The sheriff's here."

Michelle couldn't understand why, but her mind kept drifting back to Pink Souder, why *he'd* left town. And Isabelle? If she wasn't dead, where was she? Something must have happened for authorities to think Pink had killed her.

"Darcy, the sheriff told me the wildest story about the cabin, about this Pink Souder guy who built it," Michelle said. "He was supposed to have killed his wife . . . and buried her here somewhere."

"That's creepy."

"Yeah," Michelle said, unable to understand her own interest in Pink Souder and his wife, and why was she making them her business? There was no need to find a place in her life for their drama. She had her own.

"Anyway, the sheriff and a bunch of guys were up here with dogs looking for Cliff."

"Dogs? Wow. Are you worried?"

"Well, yeah, Darcy. It's like a fricking Brazilian rainforest up here. Don't you remember how remote it is?"

"You know he'll show up. He probably found some chick hiking in the woods and—oh shit, Chelle, I'm sorry. That was fucked up. I'm so sorry."

Michelle said nothing. She hadn't considered that. Maybe Glenda had driven up and Cliff's whole light-down-the-hill chest-pounding and bluster bullshit was nothing more than a ruse to go to some motel in town so they could fuck their brains out. He could be there right now.

"Chelle? Are you there? I didn't mean to be such a bitch."

Michelle went to the nightstand and pulled out her emergency pack of Chesterfields. She fumbled with the lighter a moment then drew hard. She'd questioned her decision to stay after the affair. Had it grown from a desire for the marriage to work or merely the lack of courage to end it? Worrying about him now brought up a tangle of emotions she lacked the energy to unravel.

"Yeah, no, I'm fine," Michelle said, exhaling, the hurt rushing back.

"You aren't smoking again, are you? Michelle, you're not a smoker."

"Fuck, Darcy, if he's back with Glenda, I mean it . . . I . . . ."

"He's not. Even Cliff's not that screwed up."

Michelle drew hard again. "If he is, Darcy, I'm serious, Cassie and I are buying fucking Harleys and driving to California. And you can come with. You'll get one too and—"

"Harleys, Michelle? Really? Cassie's only fifteen, so she can't even drive one. And when I was dating Tank, you wouldn't even take a ride on the back of his."

Michelle was only half-joking about the Harleys. But the thought of Cliff's cheating provoked some renegade inside her. The idea of the motorcycles sounded freeing even though she was petrified of them.

"Yeah, Tank," Michelle said, feeling the smoke leave her chest. "He was a real winner."

"I can sure pick 'em, can't I?" Darcy said,

"It's in our genes, Darcy." Michelle heard a loud rumble outside the cabin. She dropped the cigarette into her coffee cup. "Hey, Darcy, I need to call you back. I think they sent the Army."

"Okay, call me later, Chelle."

Michelle went to the door and saw the deputy standing outside the car talking on the radio, above them a police helicopter. She was surprised it had gotten dark in the short time she'd been talking with Darcy. The craft hovered so close to the roof she could feel the thumping blades pounding in her chest. The rain had turned to a misty drizzle and Michellle wished she'd slipped her coat on over her sweater.

"Where is it, ma'am?" the sheriff shouted, coming up onto the deck holding his hat on his head.

Michelle walked to the rail and pointed down through the trees. She held her hair back from her face with her other hand, the rotors churning out a stiff wind. "Right there," she shouted over the noise. "I know that's Pink Souder Road. See the driveway? It's not that far away."

The sheriff looked over at the deputy. "All righty then," the sheriff shouted, walking to the rail. "Elmer, ask Dell if he can see that light below us." Michelle glanced toward the chopper lights against the black sky.

The deputy spoke into the hand-held microphone. He yelled up to the sheriff that Dell could see it. The helicopter sliced down the mountainside and paused above the curious light.

"Have Dell turn on his searchlight," the sheriff yelled to the deputy. "See if he can land."

A bright light snapped on, burning the trees in a glassy white light, as if the branches were neon. The deputy stood for a long time talking into the radio, shaking his head. "Trees are too thick to land, but . . ." The deputy looked down at the ground, then back up at the sheriff.

The sheriff walked to the rail. "What is it, Elmer?"

"Maybe you should come talk to Dell." Elmer hunched down, his yellow rain slicker a beacon in the fog.

Michelle heard the sheriff sigh. Fisk went to the police car and stood in the driveway next to Elmer, walking as far as the cord of the mic would stretch. A few times the sheriff glanced over at Elmer, but mostly he toed gravel and listened. The chopper's searchlight went off, darkness returning to the forest, but Michelle could still hear the thrum of its rotor.

"Do you want to come, ma'am?" The sheriff said, fixing his hat on his head.

Michelle was glad he'd asked. She was tired of waiting and feeling helpless. "Let me grab my coat."

In a few minutes they were easing along Pink Souder Road, the headlights cutting a path through the dark woods. Michelle sat in the back seat, leaning forward, her arms resting on the top of the front seat. Static on the radio made it difficult for her to understand what was being said.

"Another hundred yards or so," Elmer said to the sheriff, pointing ahead. As the police car passed the trees, a liquid blackness slid in behind the glare of the headlights, sealing the night behind them.

"Stop here," the deputy said.

The car rocked when the sheriff tapped the brakes.

"Why?" the sheriff asked.

Deputy Bogan looked around, then over at the sheriff. "This is it," he said in a low voice, as if he hadn't wanted Michelle to hear. Sheriff Fisk leaned toward the windshield, looked up, then let his eyes drift across the deserted road. "This is what?"

"This is the house," the deputy whispered. "Dell says we're sitting right in front of it, but . . ."

"But what, Elmer?" the sheriff asked, sounding frustrated with Elmer's fragmented reporting.

"Dell doesn't know how long he can stay," Elmer said. "Said he got sick all of a sudden, like the flu or something."

The sheriff looked around then got out of the car. The deputy stayed with Michelle.

"What's going on?" she asked Deputy Bogan.

"Nothing yet, ma'am," he answered, never taking his eyes from the sheriff.

The sheriff walked over to Bogan's window. "Hand me that microphone, Elmer." Fisk held it in his palm and took a few steps toward the front bumper.

Michelle couldn't hear what he was saying. The searchlight switched on again. The sheriff talked on the radio then leaned in and told Elmer to turn on the police car's emergency roof flashers. Blue and white light splashed across the tree trunks and branches. A second later, the helicopter peeled off and was gone. She saw the sheriff grimace. When he got in the car, he switched off the emergencies and drove to the end of the road, turning around in front of the dilapidated house. Michelle's eyes searched the front yard, the empty windows, the broken pickets.

Fisk drove back up the mountain to Michelle's cabin. Elmer waited in the car while the sheriff escorted her to the door, rain hissing across the deck.

He removed his hat. "I don't know what's going on, but I didn't see any house down there," the sheriff said. "Dell swore we were sitting right in front of it . . ."

Michelle could tell the sheriff was leaving something out. They walked to the deck railing. "Maybe tomorrow night we can get those fellers together again and go down there with the dogs. We'll take the same path your husband did, straight down through them woods," he said, nodding his head sideways toward the trees. Michelle could still see the light. She turned back to the sheriff, noticing that he wouldn't look down at it.

"I think Elmer and me'll take another ride down there. Maybe something we missed. If you hear anything by morning, you give me a call. We'll be back tomorrow evening."

Michelle recalled the uncertainty in Cliff's voice when he'd come back with the car the previous night. She'd been in bed while he stumbled around in the dark.

"Cliff? What are you doing?" she'd asked, sitting up to see him.

He had turned toward her and even in the dark she could see the pallor in his face. Peeling the blankets back, she asked what was wrong. He glanced toward the door, then back at her. "It's not there," he'd told her.

"What's not there?" she'd asked.

"That house. I can see the light from up here, I can hear people down there, but when I drove down, it wasn't there."

Michelle had never bothered to tell the sheriff what Cliff had said. She figured Cliff had been driving on the wrong road. She was about to tell Fisk when he gave her an empty smile, placed his hat on his head, and turned toward the walkway. There was a new reticence in his step; he wasn't nearly as confident as he'd been earlier.

"What happened down there?" Michelle said. The sheriff turned back to face her, his body bent against the rain. "You're not telling me something. I know it."

The sheriff tugged at his chin then sighed. "Dell said he could see the house till he turned on the big beam. Then, well . . . he said the house just up and disappeared." The sheriff's eyes hardened, looking at nothing for a few seconds before the life came back to his face.

"Disappeared?" Michelle said, pulling her coat together at her chest. Her breath caught for a moment.

"Probably because of the rain," he finally said. "A reflection or something. Plays tricks on the eyes. Lot of big boulders on this mountain, big as houses. That's probably what he saw." The sheriff fixed his gaze on the deck boards for a second, then turned away from Michelle and hurried down the steps. The police car backed out of the driveway, the taillights vanishing down the road. Michelle walked to the rail and stared at the light down the mountain. Just then she thought she spotted a person in the driveway. She eased along the rail to get a better look through the trees, watching the shape walk beneath the dusk-to-dawn light. It was a man in a red cap and tan jacket.

"Cliff?" she yelled. "Cliff?"

The man stopped, looked up for a moment then disappeared behind a tangle of limbs and trees.

CHAPTER 2

Michelle rushed inside and rummaged through the cupboard and drawers for a flashlight but couldn't find one. She figured if she kept her eyes on the dusk-to-dawn light as she picked her way down the slope, it would lead her directly to the house. "Screw the flashlight!" she said to herself. "I'll just fucking go down there. It can't be more than a couple hundred yards. I'll keep my eyes on the light and follow it down." She switched on all the lights in the cabin, including the porch light, so she could find her way back. Then she had to pee. She took off her coat and tossed it to the floor.

The thought of going down through those woods in the dark left a catch in Michelle's chest. "Jesus, I'm about to do exactly what Cliff did, follow some ridiculous light down a dark mountainside! Fuck!" Her heart was pounding. But that *had* to have been Cliff, she reasoned, even though he didn't seem hurt or scared. But why hadn't he responded when she called his name? Could he not hear her? Or was that some trick of light, the figure she thought she saw? After all, the chopper pilot thought he saw an entire house until he turned on his spotlight. Now Michelle started to doubt she'd seen anything at all. Sitting on the toilet, she figured there must be another road down there. Her mind started spiraling back on itself, a dizzying replay of everything Fisk had told her, everything Cliff had said the night before.

Michelle flushed the toilet and zipped up her jeans then jerked out the bathroom drawers hoping to find one of the disposable flashlights they'd bought for emergencies. One of the drawers got away from her and crashed to the floor, jars and tubes and bottles scattering along the tiles. That's when the toilet started overflowing. She quickly jiggled the handle, water spilling over her tennis shoes, then reached behind the tank for the plunger. Cliff had promised to repair it on their last trip but never did. She jabbed the plunger up and down in the toilet until the water sucked away with a *whoosh*.

As Michelle placed the plunger back behind the toilet, she noticed something shiny on the floor there. Metallic, like one of those chains inside a toilet tank but finer. She squatted and reached behind the tank, stretching her fingertips toward the object until she could scoot it toward her. It was a necklace with a peculiar pendant. It looked to be silver, old. She'd seen the symbol before—a five-pointed star inside a circle—but had no idea what it represented if anything. The clasp on the chain was broken. Michelle tucked it into the pocket of her jeans and was going for the mop when the phone rang. She ripped a bath towel from the rack and flung it at the wet floor as she ran from the bathroom.

"Cliff?" she said, pressing the phone to her ear. She paused, waiting for someone to speak. "Cliff, is that you? Are you okay? Say something!" The phone sounded dead. Michelle was about to say his name again when she thought of Glenda. Even though Cliff promised he'd stopped seeing her, Glenda had called their home in Atlanta several times and said nothing, hanging up after a few seconds.

"Is that you, Glenda? Don't pull this crap. Not tonight."

Michelle had suspected the affair wasn't over even though Cliff insisted it was. Cliff had moved out for two months, then came back professing his mistake, "A midlife crisis," he finally said, throwing out the expression like a punchline.

"Midlife crisis? That's it? That's your reason?" Michelle had said. "Are you in love with her?"

Cliff insisted he wasn't, that he was sorry. Michelle agreed to try again, conflicted by her decision. She wanted it back, what they'd had before his affair. She wasn't even sure that was possible.

Two months later, they bought the cabin. Cliff claimed it would give them time alone and a chance to work things out. "It'll be great, just you and me and the birds." Cliff had been right about the birds, and at first, it was wonderful. Michelle felt a renewed vigor for their marriage, for Cliff. But their getaway time soon devolved into Cliff complaining about his business, how if he expanded the lot to hold a hundred more vehicles he could increase sales by 20 to 30 percent. She wasn't sure the marriage could withstand the new debt and headaches.

"Dammit, don't just sit there! Say something!" Michelle slammed down the phone. She was putting on her coat when the phone rang again.

"Who is this?!" Michelle screamed.

"Mom? You okay?"

"Cassie," she said. "I'm sorry, I just—"

"I called a few minutes ago," Cassie said, "but couldn't hear anyone on the other end. You sound upset."

"No, no, baby. I'm fine. I uh, had just spilled something on the stove and . . ."

"Mom?"

"Yes, sweetie. I'm here," Michelle said, zipping her coat. "Hey, uh, can I call you back in a few minutes? Your father and I were in the middle of something." She hated lying to Cassie.

"Geez, Mom! I'm sorry. I didn't mean to interrupt."

"No, nothing like that," Michelle said, unable to remember the last time she and Cliff had had sex. She had stopped thinking about it months ago. "No . . . we were trying to stop some water coming in by the door. It's raining like crazy up here."

"I'll let you go, but let me tell you the big news real quick—not only did I make varsity swim team . . . but they voted me captain!"

"Cassie, that's wonderful!"

"Call me back, and I'll give you the details," Cassie said. "Oh, and . . . Molly and Kara are over. We ordered pizza and rented movies. They're going to spend the night, okay?"

"Yeah, sure," Michelle said, wishing she were back home, a cup of hot tea cradled in her hands, watching movies with Cassie and her friends.

"Is Dad behaving?" She laughed. "Tell him I love him. But don't tell him the news. I want to tell him myself."

"I'll call you in a little bit," Michelle said. She could hear Cassie's friends laughing in the background, yelling that the pizza was getting cold. Cassie never knew about Cliff's affair. They told Cassie the separation was just about them needing some time to sort things out.

"Bye, Mom."

"Bye, sweetie." Michelle hung up the phone. At the verge of tears, she sat on the bed. "How did things get so fucked up?" She pushed herself off the bed and turned toward the sliding glass doors and the blackness outside.

*****

The deck was over twenty feet square and extended over a steep drop from the back of the cabin, providing a panoramic view of the mountains. During the day, the abrupt slope was all rhododendron, pines, vines, poplars, sourwoods, and oaks. At night it was a jumble of jagged black, unrecognizable shapes. It was early April and all the hardwoods were still bare, but the rhododendron, even in winter, was so thick you could barely see the ground.

Rain sizzled along the hood and roof of the Cherokee as Michelle walked down the edge of the driveway, touching branches, stepping lightly, wishing she had gloves. She couldn't see anything along the ground, the sticks, leaves, and rocks a black sheet beneath her shoes. She waited for her eyes to adjust to the low light—would snakes be out in weather like this? Or other creatures? In the few months they'd owned the cabin, she and Cliff had already witnessed a bear on their property once. It woke them. At the time, they'd both been amazed by the sight, the bear lying on its back on the deck shaking sunflower seeds into its mouth from the bird feeder. Now it didn't seem so charming and cute. Even though Cliff had assured Michelle that black bears weren't dangerous, she remembered how big it was, could still picture its claws shining in the moonlight.

The dark woods folded around her, growing blacker the farther Michelle ventured from the cabin. She could see the light below, as well as the lights of the cabin above through the fabric of branches and mountain laurel. There was a fragile aspect to the night, as if something could break at any moment. She stepped carefully, steadying one foot before moving the other on the shifting floor of decayed leaves and mud. The rain was not as heavy under the canopy of rhododendron, yet everything was slick. Michelle had just placed her foot down when a root caught her ankle. Her other foot slid out, sending her down the slope head over knees, branches whipping her cheeks and forehead, ripping her palms as she tried to break her fall. A poplar tree ended her tumble, catching her in the ribs.

"Shit!" Michelle was almost to her feet, when the dirt and rocks gave way again, tossing her down through the bracken. She crashed into a boulder and landed facedown in the muck. The earth smelled of mold. She pushed herself up and leaned against the rock, her elbow burning, the air cold on the exposed skin of her knee. Her jeans were ripped. She glanced up the slope to find the cabin lights, only to see nothing but twisting blackness. Looking down, Michelle saw the light below, but it appeared to be no closer than when she'd left the cabin.

A dull pain throbbed at her ribs. Catching her breath, Michelle touched the flesh through the tear in her jeans, trying to determine if she was bleeding. She put a finger to her tongue. It tasted metallic. She couldn't tell how bad the cut was. Michelle got to her feet and brushed the dirt and leaves from her jeans. Even though the night was cold, she was soaked with perspiration under her coat. Maybe she should have stayed at the cabin and waited for the sheriff to return with the dogs. But what about Cliff? Was he lying somewhere in the woods, unable to walk, bleeding, wet, and freezing?

It was hard to picture Cliff helpless or hurt. All Michelle could think of was his intensity; he could never let anything go. She had admired his tenacity before they were married—the college jock who wouldn't quit wrestling when he'd fractured his ankle, trying to fool the coach into thinking it was a mild sprain. But over the years it had grown wearisome and felt controlling. What Michelle hated most was how effective it was against her. She had told him to forget about the light, the noisy neighbors, about going down the hill. "Maybe you drove down the wrong road," she had told him. "It's dark out. Please, just come to bed."

"There's only one road, Michelle! How could I take the wrong one?" he'd said, obviously agitated. "You pull out onto the road, drive down a half mile, then make a left turn. It said Pink Souder on the sign. How could I have been on the wrong fucking road?" He was almost yelling at that point. Michelle had looked down at the floor, then back at her husband standing on the deck and gyrating madly as he spoke.

"I can see the damn light!" he'd said, pointing over the rail. "It's right there!"

They hadn't left Atlanta until after eight that evening, and it was a three-hour drive. She was too tired to argue further.

"Go to sleep," Cliff had said, his back to her. "I'll be back in a minute."

Michelle had gone inside and was almost asleep when she'd heard Cliff rummaging through the pantry looking for a flashlight. She'd told him there was one in the Cherokee, then wished she hadn't. "Cliff! Wait!" That was the last time she'd seen him. Now she was doing the same stupid thing Cliff had done, tramping down the mountainside in the dark, too impatient to wait.

Michelle took a deep breath and steadied herself against the massive boulder, her jeans cold and muddy. The cut on her knee throbbed when she put weight on it.

Holding to trees and shrubs, she tricked her way through the cover, plotting each step cautiously. Michelle felt the burden of silence around her. No crickets, tree frogs, owls, or chirrups. No barking dogs. None of the sounds that made night tangible. Michelle's skin prickled under the warm coat. She heard something several yards away. She stopped and listened. Something walking. A bear? Should she make a sound? Or run? Maybe just stay still. Then she heard a similar sound behind her, then another to the side. "What the fuck?" She held onto the tree and tried to breathe shallow, quiet. The sounds moved closer. She stole a quick look around the tree. Hunters maybe?

"Is someone there?" Michelle finally said. "Hello?" Something loped past, a shadow, but upright, nothing like a bear.

She bolted from the tree down the hill, searching the woods for the light below. She didn't want to stop to hear if anything was following. Darting past tree trunks and branches, something caught her ankle. She stumbled, almost falling, grabbing at limbs and leaves to catch herself. Sticker bushes cut her hands, snagged her jeans. In a second, Michelle was on the ground, rolling, tumbling. Then airborne, off a cliff maybe, no sensation except drifting, flying, until her body slammed solid ground. The collision rocked her, smashing the air from her lungs. Michelle tried to sit up, gasping. She couldn't breathe. Her ribs ached. She tried to steady herself. Then she heard footsteps. She willed herself up and started running again.

After running for almost fifty yards, Michelle stopped, took a deep breath, and held herself against a tree. The woods were still. The darkness absolute. Once Michelle was able to release the tree, she eased down the slope, shifting her head back and forth to find the light below, glancing over her shoulder occasionally to see if anything was behind her. After a few minutes she found it. It was much closer now. She heard noises, like conversation or maybe a television, coming from the direction of the light.

The house came into view. It was less than two hundred feet away—though this close it was more like a cabin than a house.

When Michelle came within the glow of the dusk-to-dawn light, she looked down at her clothes. Blood stained her jeans. She could see the front door, lights in the window. She picked leaves from her hair and used her fingers to comb out the tangles. A Range Rover sat in the driveway, next to the sheriff's car. Why hadn't Fisk bothered to come back up and tell her he'd found the house?

Michelle studied the cabin, the red trim, the shutters, the herbs—sage, peppermint, basil—growing along the walk. The familiarity of the place froze her. The copper ash bucket filled with dried flowers sat to the right side of the front door. The brass door knocker in the shape of a leaping trout—exactly like the one she'd found at Kresser's in Atlanta. Michelle spun around and looked up the mountain. The lights of her and Cliff's cabin were gone, nothing but black. She was about to knock when she looked down at her shoes, at the welcome mat beneath her feet. It was the same one her sister had given them as a gag gift for the cabin. She and Darcy had laughed about the picture of the Paul Bunyan-looking hunter with his black beard shooting a musket at a fleeing turkey.

Michelle felt like a stranger about to knock on her own door, yet it wasn't hers, she reasoned. But reason and logic seemed to have no role in the events of the last twenty-four hours. She drew a breath and rapped the trout lightly against its metal base.

CHAPTER 3

"Michelle!" Cliff said, throwing open the door. "I've been worried sick! The sheriff was out with men and dogs and a chopper and . . ."

Cliff pulled her into his arms. "I was going crazy here," he said. "I was so scared." He eased back from Michelle, checking her hair, the cut at her knee, her ripped coat. "Jesus. You're hurt."

"I . . . uh . . . Cliff?" Michelle said. "You're okay. Where were you . . . ?" Finally she pushed past him, no longer able to marshal her thoughts. Her book was sitting on the coffee table, just as she'd left it. The interior of the cabin was exactly the same except for the furniture—it was completely foreign to her.

"Cliff . . . where am I? Where are we?" she asked. "What happened to . . . ?"

The mounted deer head Cliff had bought at a flea market, as well as the classic car series of prints and the rug he'd ordered from L.L. Bean were gone. So were the rustic couch and chairs that he had said would be perfect for the cabin, along with the antiques he'd bought on a trip to Knoxville. The painted duck decoy on the bookcase, the wrought iron fireplace tools—they were all missing and the new furnishings unfamiliar to her.

"You gave us all a scare, ma'am," the sheriff said, holding his hat in his hand. "I can get an ambulance up here in ten minutes if you think you need one."

"Sheriff Fisk . . . why didn't you . . . ?" Michelle could not parse the queerness of the moment. Was she still unconscious in the woods from the fall? "Bogan, right?" she said, looking at Elmer. He seemed confused and took a step back.

Michelle had recognized Fisk immediately, and Elmer, but she could tell by the way they regarded her that the recognition wasn't mutual.

"Don't you remember me?" she asked Sheriff Fisk. "How about you, Elmer?"

"I'm sorry, ma'am, but I ain't never seen you before," the deputy said.

Fisk said something to Cliff about Michelle being in shock. Then Cliff was leading her by the arm toward the couch, and they continued speaking as if she weren't there. She jerked her arm away from Cliff, and backed up, away from the sheriff and Elmer.

"It's okay, ma'am," the sheriff said, his palms opened as if to suggest he wasn't going to harm her. He turned toward Elmer and whispered something. "Now why don't you have a little rest," he said, turning back to face her. "Your husband here has some coffee on the stove. Would you like some coffee?"

"I don't want any coffee," she said. "I want to know what's going on here."

She saw Cliff nodding and smiling, agreeing with the sheriff. They spoke in tones reserved for the elderly, or the dangerous. Cliff hurried to the kitchen and returned with a steaming cup and saucer.

"Come on, Michelle," he said, setting the coffee cup on the end table. "Sit here and warm up. Let's get you out of that coat."

When he reached for her, she jerked her wrist back. "Don't touch me, Cliff."

Cliff straightened like he'd been slapped. Elmer had left the living room and she wasn't sure where he'd gone. The sheriff looked at the floor and Michelle couldn't understand why he hadn't acknowledged her, why he was acting so queer.

"Sheriff Fisk? Why don't you remember me?" Michelle asked. "I spoke to you less than two hours ago. We drove down Pink Souder Road together. The chopper? Dell?"

Fisk's eyes burst open wide. He looked at Cliff but said nothing.

"Baby, we're here to help," Cliff said. "Let me take your shoes off. They're soaked." Michelle noticed a scar across Cliff's forehead, one that had never been there before. And when he reached out to her, she saw the little finger on his left hand was missing.

"What happened to you, Cliff?" she said. "Where's your finger?"

Cliff shook his head, tears pooling along the bottom of his eyes. He looked over at the sheriff, then back at her. The sheriff took his eyes to the floor once more.

Michelle hurried past Cliff and Sheriff Fisk.

"Where are you going?" Cliff said, following her.

She ran into the bedroom and jerked drawers open on the dresser then rummaged the closet. "I want to go home," she said. "I don't know what this is all about, but I want to go back to Atlanta. Now."

"What are you looking for?" Cliff said. She heard a siren coming up the mountain, getting closer. She pushed past Cliff, headed for the kitchen. The sheriff was no longer in the living room.

"Where's my purse, Cliff? What did you do with my purse?"

"Calm down, Michelle. It's right in here." He walked back to the bedroom. "Here. You left it by the bed where you always leave it." He picked it up and handed it to her.

Michelle jerked the purse open and stirred the contents with her fingers, then dumped everything out on the floor. She dropped to her knees and pushed her hand through the pile, scattering cosmetics, deposit slips, and amber pill containers across the carpet. It didn't even seem like her purse—what were the pill bottles for? "Where are they, Cliff? Where are my keys to the Cherokee?"

Cliff looked distressed, his head cocked slightly to the side. "The Cherokee? Michelle . . . you know we don't have the Cherokee anymore."

Michelle looked up at him. "What? It was right there in the driveway when I left the cabin . . ." She pictured it clearly, the rain beating sparks along the hood, sheets of water running down the windows. She had seen it in the driveway less than an hour ago.

Cliff sat on the edge of the bed with his head in his hands. When he looked up at her, his eyes were red, his face damp with perspiration. He was about to speak, his mouth was open, but no sound came out.

"What is wrong with you, Cliff? What . . . ?" Michelle tried to speak. She couldn't tell if her words were getting out. Then, like a welcome interruption, or a desire for something familiar, her thoughts went to Cassie. The swim team.

The siren outside the cabin shut off abruptly.

"Cassie made the swim team, Cliff," Michelle said. "Not only that, they voted her captain. Did she tell you?"

Cliff shot up from the bed and left the room.

Michelle saw red lights pulsing on the branches outside the bedroom window. Then along the walls. "What . . . ?" She put her hand to her cheek, slid her fingers to her lips, and felt weak, dizzy. "I . . ." She twisted her neck to the side, as if to relieve a catch. A clatter of metal and voices rose beyond the bedroom, the sound urgent, racing closer. She ran her hand along her throat, finding a bit of dead leaf stuck to her skin, then rested her palm on her shoulder.

"What's going on, Cliff?" she whispered, then repeated it louder so he could hear. Cliff was gone from the room.

Michelle felt something inside her become unmoored, flesh from bone, organs from veins, dissolving, turning to dust.

Gentle voices coaxed her onto the gurney. Someone covered her with a blanket. She noticed a cobweb hanging from the blade of the ceiling fan as they wheeled her through the living room. "Cliff?" She thought she saw Elmer's face, distant and blank as the moon, when they lifted her into the back of the ambulance. "Cliff?" She heard crying, doors slamming, the siren coming up, drowning out the sad noises. Cliff was suddenly next to her, wiping his eyes with his sleeve. He touched her forehead. Michelle hadn't remembered taking her coat off, but it was gone. So were her shoes.

"It's going to be okay, baby," he said. "It's going to be okay."

"Cliff?"

CHAPTER 4

"Where am I?" Michelle said, looking over at Cliff. He was beside her hospital bed reading a newspaper. He put it down as soon as she spoke to him. "Where am I?" she asked again. The room smelled of rubbing alcohol and disinfectant.

"The hospital," Cliff said. He reached over and laid his hand on top of hers. Cliff looked so different to her, and it wasn't just the scar on his forehead. His eyes no longer burned with that same determination, as if life were something to be killed and eaten on an hourly basis. His eyes were soft and easy now, yet sad, flat. Nothing about Cliff had ever been flat. Even his hair was different, most of the blond now gray. He'd shaved his mustache and beard, and at first Michelle thought maybe that's why he looked so much thinner. Yet by the way his shirt draped off his shoulders, it was obvious he'd lost at least thirty pounds, almost the way he'd looked when he wrestled in college, though not nearly as vibrant. When he spoke, his voice was low and restrained, as if a baby were asleep in the next room. But in spite of all these differences, it was his hand that bothered Michelle most.

"Let me see it," she said, pointing to the one folded in his lap.

He reluctantly placed it on the blanket.

"How did that happen?" she asked.

Cliff slid his hand away from her and sat back slowly in the chair, resting it in his lap. He seemed to have trouble swallowing. He squeezed his eyes shut, as if trying to erase an image from his brain.

"What's going on, Cliff? Why am I in the hospital? Have you spoken with Cassie? Does she know everything is okay?" Michelle sat up abruptly, knocking dishes from the tray, splattering food across the sheets and floor. "Where's Cassie? Where are we, Cliff? Are we in Atlanta?"

The commotion brought a nurse to the room. Cliff motioned that everything was okay. He cleared the dishes from her bedspread.

"Sorry, Cliff. Where are we?"

"We're still in Ardenwood. Don't you remember?"

She shook her head. "How long have I been out?"

"Two days," he said.

Michelle's memory was starting to come back. The cabin, Sheriff Fisk, going down the dark mountain, falling. Maybe she had a concussion. Her side hurt. Maybe broken ribs.

"Am I okay?"

"Bruised ribs. But other than that, you're fine," he said. "At some point we need to talk about why you left the cabin in the middle of the night, Michelle. You were lost for an entire day."

That wasn't how Michelle recalled the events of the past few days. "*You* were the one who left the cabin in the middle of the night. You were the one who got lost. I came looking for you and . . ."

"Okay, Michelle. We don't have to talk about this right now."

Cliff walked to the door. "I'm going for coffee," he said. "I'll be back shortly. Do you want anything?"

They spoke no more about it.

Michelle was released the next day, the doctors believing it best she return to Atlanta. They gave her a prescription for Xanax in case she became anxious or overwhelmed by her ordeal. Cliff drove a Range Rover up to the curb. Michelle had never seen it before. She got in, shut the door, and stared out the windshield.

Michelle rubbed her neck and felt nauseous, probably from the medication, she figured. She closed her eyes and was in the backyard of their home in Atlanta, the familiar odor of chlorine and wet concrete around the pool—reassuring smells. She thought about Cassie making varsity swim team, about her being team captain, the power of her strokes as she glided from one end of the pool to the other. For a moment, Michelle felt normal, recalling Cassie, the pool, until her mind shifted to Cliff's scar, his missing finger. He had yet to explain. But those were new. Those pieces could not fit into any puzzle she constructed in her head. And Fisk. The cabin down the mountain, the one identical to the one she walked out of to look for Cliff. Had she somehow gone back up the mountain? Or gotten turned around in the woods? But what about the furniture? Fisk and Bogan? The Cherokee? Cliff's scar? Cliff's missing finger? *Stop!* None of it made sense. Michelle was suddenly engulfed in anxiety. She strained to breathe, to calm down. She shifted her attention home. Michelle pictured their pool in Atlanta, tried to recall the cool water, the sun, how it felt on her face when she sat on the chaise lounge, heat rising from the concrete. It calmed her. The fear started to subside. Michelle wondered if Cassie had told Cliff the big news yet, about being voted captain. He hadn't mentioned it. Michelle was starting to feel anxious again. She took another Xanax.

It wasn't long before everything felt vague and jumbled, as if her brain was packed in cotton. Unable to sleep, Michelle focused her attention out the window as they left Ardenwood. Fast food restaurants and gas stations swept by, along with billboards for trout fishing, canoeing, and whitewater rafting. Tire companies, insurance salesmen, and real estate brokers. One in particular caught her attention.

"Stop the car, Cliff!" she shouted.

"What?" he said.

"Stop!"

Cliff mashed on the brakes, throwing her against the shoulder harness. Cars screeched and skidded behind them, horns honking.

"What the hell?!" Cliff shouted. "What is it, Michelle?"

"Go back, Cliff! Go back now!"

Cars rushed past, drivers twisting to glare at them. Cliff turned around in a Shell station. "What's going on?" he asked.

"Make a left up there at McDonald's," she said, twisting in her seat to see the giant advertisement.

"What, you're hungry?" he asked. "You don't even like McDonald's."

"I want you to pull into their parking lot," she said. When Cliff stopped, Michelle bolted from the vehicle toward the highway. Traffic rushed past as she rounded the pin oaks at the edge of the parking lot. Cliff chased after her.

Michelle stopped in front of the sign. Letters five feet high spelled out the words NOTHING SELLS FASTER THAN PINK. Below the headline it read: *Call Pink Souder to find or sell your home FAST!*

There was a phone number and a picture of a cherub-faced man who looked to be in his forties, wearing a cowboy hat and pink shirt and a black western-style string tie. His smile seemed to be the only thing holding his heavy, round cheeks apart. His teeth were white as blocks of ice and his blue eyes followed wherever Michelle walked until she was standing beneath him. Cliff ran up behind her.

"What are you doing?" he said.

Michelle recalled the sheriff telling her the Pink Souder story, how Pink had allegedly killed his wife and buried her on the property, and how he and his mother had disappeared soon after. Had she dreamed all that? She could still hear Fisk chuckling, recounting the tale about Mattie turning Pink into an ass and riding out of town like the Virgin Mary. There was a small rip in the billboard below Pink's chin, and for a moment Michelle got lost in it.

"Sheriff Fisk told me about Pink Souder and his wife, Isabelle," she said. "She's supposed to be dead . . . and Pink is supposed to have vanished."

She turned to Cliff, but he looked worried, frightened. Some part of her wanted to drive to Pink's office to confront him, see what he would say about the cabin, the sheriff's story.

"You never talked to Sheriff Fisk," Cliff said. "How could he have told you anything about anyone?"

"Then how did I know Fisk's name?" Michelle said. "And Deputy Bogan?" Now she remembered everything and realized that talking to Cliff was futile. He teared up anytime she tried to explain what had happened or asked him a question. He couldn't listen. It was obvious he thought she was crazy. Michelle readily admitted something was amiss, but she couldn't explain it. And she didn't understand Cliff. She felt like she hardly knew him.

"I don't know, Michelle," Cliff said. "Let's just go home."

Michelle turned back toward the car, not waiting for Cliff. She missed Cassie. The rest of this could be figured out later. She glanced briefly back at the billboard, back at Pink Souder, then opened the door of the Rover.

CHAPTER 5

He would fire Clarence as soon as he got back to the office. "Put your eyeballs on that view out there, folks," Pink said, pointing at the picture window in the living room. While his clients stared out at the mountains, nodding their heads in sync, Pink brushed mouse shit off the kitchen counters. "Goddamn you, Clarence," he said under his breath.

"Hey, folks, let me show you the deck," Pink said, wedging himself between the elderly couple, guiding them out with a hand on each of their backs. "Breathe that air. None finer in all of North Carolina." The woman took a short breath, while the man ignored Pink's inducement. His attention was on the railing, more exactly, on something between the railing and the exterior wall.

"That looks like termites," the man said, taking a step closer to the dried mud trail between the board and the siding.

"Not in these parts, Mr. Hodges," Pink said. "No termites up here, not at this altitude. They can't breathe up this high." Pink had immediately recognized the telltale sign though. He knew termites, as pesky and ornery as they were, could probably survive on the moon.

"Those are mud daubers. They build their nests out of mud, on walls, just like that one. Probably got little ones in there right now. Mud daubers are good for the place, keep the mice away. Something about their scent or something. Pheromones, I think they're called."

Clarence had been reading a fishing magazine one day and told Pink how injured baitfish gave off pheromones that drove bass crazy. "If we get us some of those pheromones," Clarence had said. "We could put 'em in little spray bottles for fisherman to use on their lures. Make a million dollars. I'm not kidding, Pink. We'd become goddamn millionaires!" Pink had tried to explain to Clarence that if scientists had already figured out this pheromone business, certainly they would have bottled the shit themselves. But Pink had bigger problems right now: the old man kneeling on one leg examining the mud trail.

"Don't get stung there, Mr. Hodges," Pink said, trying to discourage the inspection. "They won't harm you most of the time, but if they got young'ins in there, they could get riled."

"Oh, Kenneth," the wife said, "maybe you better get away from there. Besides, you're getting your pants all dirty."

"Mr. Souder," the man said, using the rail to pull himself back up. "I may have spent my whole life working behind a desk, but I know a goddamn termite trail when I see one!"

Pink bent over and gave the rail a hard and steady look, even squinted his eyes and jiggled his head back and forth. He straightened slowly then nodded. "I would have swore on a truckload of gold hubcaps those were mud daubers, Mr. Hodges, but they aren't. You were right, and now that I know, I wouldn't sell you this property if you begged me. Now why don't we hop back in my Suburban and I'll show you and the missus some real properties, views that would make this dump look like swampland."

CHAPTER 6

Michelle finally fell asleep on the drive back to Atlanta. When they pulled into the driveway, she rubbed her eyes and focused on the house, the green shutters, the red rock Cassie had found in Arizona on the front porch—familiar and reassuring signs. Michelle was glad to be home. She tottered a bit, unsteady from the long nap and the Xanax, as she walked to the back of the Rover. Cliff handed her a small duffle and the Playmate cooler then lurched ahead of her, pulling the big suitcase to the front porch.

"Cassie!" Michelle called as soon as she was in the door. "We're home." She carried the cooler to the kitchen then rushed upstairs to check on her daughter. She heard Cliff at the bar making a scotch and water. Some things never changed, she thought.

"Cassie?" she called again, knocking lightly on Cassie's door. "Sweetie, are you sleeping?" She pushed the door open and padded slowly across the dark room toward the bed until she tripped over something. "Jesus, Cassie, you need to clean up this room." Michelle got to her feet and rubbed her knee, the one she'd cut out in the forest. "Cassie? Sweetie, are you awake?"

As her eyes adjusted to the dark, shapes in the room grew unfamiliar. Michelle groped empty air when she reached out to switch on Cassie's nightstand lamp. She stumbled her way back across the carpet and snapped on the overhead light. The scream that shot from her throat didn't feel like her own.

Nothing of Cassie was left in the room. "Cliff! Come quick! Cliff!" Michelle screamed. The only piece of furniture in the room was Cassie's dresser, pulled away from the wall, the drawers yawning open and empty. Michelle's first thought was that Cassie had been kidnapped. But why would they take the furniture? Her clothes?

Michelle went to the closet and threw open the louvered doors. The empty space sucked her breath away—nothing but a few hangers dangling haphazardly from the bar.

"Cliff! Hurry!" She fixed her eyes on the dresser before she felt someone behind her. She spun around hoping to find Cassie, but it was Cliff who filled the doorway, one hand in his pocket, the other hand holding a scotch. His eyes were locked on her, seemingly disinterested in the room. It was obvious that whatever had happened was not news to him. She could feel her head shaking back and forth but couldn't force a sound from her throat.

Cliff sighed and glanced at the floor. "Please come downstairs, Michelle."

"Tell me what's going on!"

"Come downstairs with me," he said, stepping toward her, offering his hand across the empty room.

"No. Tell me here. Tell me right now!" Michelle felt her legs grow cold and rubbery, her hands beginning to tremble. She shuffled in place giving the room another cursory look, hoping it had changed, wondering where Cassie's bed had gone, the nightstands, the lamp. And her books, her stuffed animals, her posters of Annie Lennox and Nora Jones—where were they? Michelle felt Cliff's hand on her arm and jerked it away.

"All right, Michelle," Cliff said, setting his drink on the dresser. He adjusted his slacks and sat in the middle of the floor between some boxes. He reached his hand up to hers and tugged gently to bring her down with him. She eased to the floor and sat facing him, cross-legged, the way she did when she meditated.

Cliff reached across Michelle's knees and took her hands in his. *Cassie is dead,* it sounded like Cliff had said, but there was no way she'd heard that correctly.

*****

It took Cliff an hour to calm Michelle down. He had coaxed her into taking another Xanax and she finally fell asleep. Checking the bathroom mirror, Cliff rubbed his fingers over his cheek where Michelle had scratched him during their scuffle. He never knew what set of memories she would operate from upon waking, if she would mourn Cassie's death or pretend that Cassie was up in her room listening to music. Cliff had assumed Cassie's death would become easier over time, but it hadn't, partly due to Michelle's lapses into denial. "Are you picking Cassie up after practice or am I?" she'd ask. He'd thought it was some cruel form of punishment, a deliberate mocking to remind him that he'd killed their daughter. But she had shown no emotion, no hostility or sorrow. Doctors said she was experiencing temporary breaks with reality, psychological schisms. Medication helped, only to leave Michelle vulnerable to the full impact of Cassie's death again, like tonight. A maddening and tedious cycle. Cliff wasn't sure how much longer he could take it.

He stood in the backyard, recalling all the times Cassie had practiced swimming laps. After a while, he went inside to straighten up the house. He thought about Michelle traipsing through the woods up at the cabin, how she'd retreated into the undamaged world she'd created, the place where she believed Cassie was still alive.

Maybe purchasing the cabin hadn't been a good idea. Cliff had hoped it would steer them away from their preoccupation with Cassie's death, using the remodeling to patch the rough spots. They'd had fun tearing down old paneling, hanging drywall, building closets, taking breaks out on the deck, snacking on chips and dip, apples, crackers and cheese. In the evening they'd order pizza or play Rock Paper Scissors to see who would drive down for Chinese takeout. One night when Cliff had put out his fist and Michelle her open palm, he had been afraid to leave her alone, but she insisted she was fine and that he wasn't going to weasel out of going into town for dinner. Loser also had to pay.

When he'd returned, Michelle was sitting on the floor, knees to her chest, staring blankly at the darkness beyond the sliding glass doors.

"How could you kill our daughter over that fucking whore!" she had said. "You killed our daughter over her!"

The memory of it left him raw.

Several times a day Cliff thought of selling the dealership, the house, everything, and moving back to Maine. He could work for his brother, sell suits. Michelle had loved Maine—beachcombing for shells, sleigh rides in winter, the gray, deserted ocean. Or they could move back to Philadelphia, where they had met when he was attending the University of Pennsylvania. She often talked of how she missed the history, the street life, the museums. A fresh start. That's what they needed. He wished they'd done it years ago, before he'd ever met Glenda.

That awful night, he and Glenda had been in the middle of a spat. Cliff—with a few beers feeding his superiority—had believed his actions would be invisible to Cassie and Michelle, that his agenda would fly undetected beneath their radar.

"Dad, where are you going?" Cassie had said. "We're going to be late for the meet!"

Glenda had turned her cell off, shutting Cliff out. Her apartment was only fifteen minutes out of the way. "I have to see a car wholesaler," he'd told Cassie. "It'll only take a minute." Cassie protested with new vigor, pointing at the clock. Speeding down the entrance ramp, Cliff never saw the truck in the outside lane. The Cherokee flipped suddenly upon impact, rolling several times before coming to a stop upside down at the edge of the median. Rescue workers pulled him from the vehicle, carried him to the side of the highway, draped a blanket over his shoulders. A fireman wrapped a towel around his left hand to stem the bleeding until the ambulance arrived. Cliff could see that the driver's side of the Cherokee was hardly damaged, while the passenger side was crushed.

Cliff leaned against the bookcase and studied the framed photo of Cassie. He would never forget the image of the upside-down Cherokee, lights from the fire engine flashing off the chrome wheels. He hated that the last thing he'd told his daughter was a lie.

*****

Michelle was tired of sitting by the pool and went up to Cassie's room. One of Cassie's dresser drawers stuck out, the one with the milky discoloration where Cassie had draped her wet swimsuit over the front. Michelle sat in the middle of the carpet. Cliff had assured her Cassie had been dead just over a year. Michelle didn't know what was happening, but she knew that Cassie's death couldn't be among the possibilities. Before she'd gone looking for Cliff that night, Cassie had been alive. Michelle remembered the phone call, the excitement in Cassie's voice over being named captain of the varsity swim team. Michelle had not imagined that call.

At breakfast, Michelle asked if Cliff wanted to go back to the cabin with her.

"Why? We just got home a few days ago."

She had to get back there, find Pink Souder. Sheriff Fisk said Pink was no longer in Ardenwood, but the enormous billboard indicated otherwise. If a logical answer were to be found, it would be in Ardenwood.

"I'm going back up there," she said.

"Can we talk about it when I get home later?"

After Cassie was born, Cliff had grown more stubborn and manipulative, pushing his version of reality over everyone else's. Over the years, Michelle had felt herself being drawn into his world, like water flowing down a slope toward an inevitable precipice. Cliff was gravity itself.

"Look, I need to go up there," she said. "I'll drive myself." She watched him fill his coffee cup, spread butter on his toast.

"We only have one car now, Michelle," he said.

She laughed. "Cliff, you own a fucking car lot! I'll ride in with you and bring one—"

"You haven't driven in months," he told her.

That wasn't true. She'd driven most of the way to the cabin this past trip.

When Cliff finished his toast, he said, "Come take a ride with me."

They rode in silence. When they passed the concrete monuments marking the entrance to Roswell Cemetery, Michelle sat up and looked around. "What are we doing here?"

"You need to see something," Cliff said.

The marble was convincing.

CASSIE

CASSANDRA ANN STAGE

BELOVED DAUGHTER OF

MICHELLE AND CLIFFORD STAGE

Michelle felt like she'd been kicked in the chest. The date on the stone had Cassie dead for almost thirteen months. It was impossible. Michelle fought to evoke every sensation from the night Cliff had disappeared— the rain slashing white trails across the deck, the water dripping from the sheriff's yellow slicker, the smell of mold and decaying leaves along the ground. She recalled the sting of the cut at her knee, the leaves and sticks tangled in her hair. She closed her eyes and made it all real, made it smell and taste and burn, felt the pain in her ribs where she'd hit the tree. She looked around at the trees in the cemetery, rows upon rows of headstones, flowers laid at the bases of some, others bare, the fresh dirt of recently dug graves. It was very convincing.

She looked over at Cliff and saw he was crying. How could they believe such different things? She was not about to bury Cassie, yet he believed their daughter already lay beneath six feet of earth. In her world there had been no car accident, no funeral, no grief and mourning, while Cliff's world was marshaled by tragedy, loss, and sadness. He was crippled with remorse over something that, in Michelle's mind, had never happened.

If she didn't accept it, what was next? Photos of the wrecked Cherokee, a police report, stacks of insurance claims and hospital bills?

"I don't know what you expect me to say, Cliff. I spoke to Cassie a few nights ago."

"Michelle . . . that's just not—"

"Stop, Cliff. Please, just stop. Why can't you just listen?"

Michelle knelt on the grass, put her palms to the ground, feeling the moisture hidden in the soil. She closed her eyes and thumbed her wedding ring. The ceremony, the music, the reception rushed back to her. Certainly, they still shared all those things, all the days before now—Cassie's birth, her first day of school, her chicken pox, the medal she won at her third swim meet—the ordinary marrow of life. They still shared the memory of buying the car dealership, the celebration they'd had that evening after putting Cassie to bed, making love out on the patio, Cliff excited over his plan for the pool, pacing it off in his robe, marking the corners with Budweiser bottles, laying the step ladder on the grass where the diving board would be. "Cassie will be an Olympic swimmer," he had told her. "And you, well, you'll just sit around the pool in your bikini looking gorgeous."

"Do you remember the night you planned out the pool?" Michelle asked Cliff, raising her eyes toward him. He squatted down next to her on the grass.

After a moment, Cliff nodded. "Yeah. I do," he said. "We were both really drunk that night. Cassie was five. I dug that stupid trench, remember? Ended up destroying half the backyard."

The recollection was so clear in Michelle's mind, Cliff filling the hole with water from the garden hose. "As I remember," she said, "you weren't content with ruining the yard. You turned the hose on me."

Cliff laughed. "God, you were so beautiful that night, standing there dripping wet, your skin showing through the nightgown. When you pulled it over your head, I thought I would lose my mind. We made love on that rickety old chaise lounge on the patio, remember? I was scared the neighbors would hear and you were so drunk you didn't care. That was a perfect night, Michelle."

She sat back on her heels, confused by how clearly they both remembered the same thing. What if Cliff was right, what if there had been an accident? Would it mean she was delusional? Or worse, insane? Surely, she would have some recollection, she thought. But the alternative was even more disturbing. What if she had spoken to Cassie on the phone that night at the cabin? Where was Cassie now? Where was everything she remembered? Michelle felt as though she were being torn in two, stretched to the point of ripping. She threw her head back and drew a sharp breath. The clouds raced across the sky above her, the tiny leaves on the branches were a new, delicate green.

Michelle felt Cliff's hands on her shoulders and heard his voice as if he were speaking from the other side of a wall.

When they returned from the cemetery, Michelle went upstairs for a nap. It surprised her when Cliff slid in behind her and caressed her shoulders. She couldn't believe he hadn't gone to the dealership. He never took naps. And after a few years of marriage, anytime he touched her it was only as a prelude to sex. She was almost asleep when he promised to drive her up to the cabin in a few weeks. She ignored his comment, too tired to fight in the moment.

Even though Cliff seemed like a changed man, Michelle wasn't convinced his word was any good. Besides, she wasn't about to wait "a few weeks" to return to Ardenwood.

*****

When Michelle woke, she rolled over to see Cliff asleep on top of the spread, still wearing his dress pants and white short-sleeved shirt, his tie slung over the alarm clock on the nightstand. He looked haggard and old. That wasn't how he'd looked the day they'd driven to the cabin, Cliff shouting orders to his lead salesman over the cell phone, hanging up and complaining about how sluggish sales were. The man lying next to her looked like Cliff's shed skin—dry and brittle and gray. Even so, something peaceful permeated his features, as if sleep gave him a release he'd never known before. He'd always fought sleep, staying up late to read or sitting out by the pool to nurse a highball, telling her he wasn't "in the mood to sleep."

She leaned over and put her lips to his, surprised by how soft they felt. He even smelled different, she thought, running her fingertips along his cheek. The side of his face was the first thing she'd fallen in love with. He'd been pinning a boy during a wrestling match, his body angled, his jaw frozen with determination. His cheeks were rosy now, the way they were when he wrestled, like he'd been sledding on a cold winter day. It gave him a boyish look that competitors often misjudged for frailty.

When she combed her fingers through his hair, his eyes opened and, for the first time in years, she desired him. Watching him wrestle, she had wondered what his hands would feel like on her skin, if his palms would be rough and hard, his touch a caress or a grip. After they married, he had been uncertain in bed, almost timid, as if he were discovering her body for the first time. It always excited her.

They had made love on their first date and almost every day thereafter for a month, as if they had invented sex and were trying to perfect it. It was at the end of their first month together when Cliff asked Michelle to marry him. She was seventeen, with braces, a junior in high school. She said no, and they ended up at a motel, her explaining why she couldn't, him telling her why they should, then fighting, crying, and making love until morning. When Michelle got home, her parents were waiting in the living room, her father as solemn as a piece of furniture. Her parents grounded her for that stunt, but like she'd told Darcy, it was worth it. Cliff waved a red rose out the window of his Impala every afternoon when he cruised by.

The only thing Michelle had ever known she wanted was a family. Cliff had used her disclosure as ammunition, insisting they should get married when she graduated from high school, that he made enough money working part-time selling suits at Famous Men's to support them until he got his business degree. He told her he was going to make tons of money, he was sure of it. "How can I marry you?" she'd said. "My parents are still paying for my braces."

The recollection vanished when Cliff reached out and pulled her close. He touched her breast, put his lips to hers and was soon inside her. She inhaled the salty wetness of his skin. Cassie's voice echoed in her head, the voice of a four-year-old screaming out in the darkness from a nightmare, the fifth grader who won her first swim meet, the worried teenager with her first period. There was no way to paste these memories together, no way to parse the reality she knew was real with the one Cliff believed. He lifted himself up to look at her. She turned away, her hair shifting across her face like a curtain.

"Are you crying?" he asked.

Michelle pushed Cliff off and left the bed, closing the bathroom door behind her. Her heart was a machine in her chest, her lungs straining as if she were trying to breathe water. She swept her hair back with her hands and leaned against the sink. Everything looked the same, yet nothing was right.

Michelle opened the door. "Who are you?" she asked, pulling her robe closed.

"I don't know what you're talking about."

"What is this? What is all this?"

"I'm confused, Michelle," Cliff said. "Ever since the weekend at the cabin you've seemed different. Not completely, but something's different about you. Like now, making love. You haven't let me touch you in over a year. One minute I think you're getting better, then the next you throw a fit. Then at the cemetery, you handled it all calmly. The last time I took you . . . you went crazy. And then Glenda."

"What about Glenda?"

"You really don't remember?" he said.

Michelle pictured Glenda, her eyes glossy with satisfaction, her smile tuned somewhere between business-pleasant and mistress-smug, as though she knew everything about Michelle—what she was like in bed, how she spent her afternoons, maybe even the kind of underwear she preferred— while Michelle knew nothing of Glenda except for her business card from the bank. Cliff hadn't bothered trying to hide it. Michelle looked at Cliff, amazed and sick once more how stupid she'd been about his affair.

"So what happened?" Michelle asked.

Cliff fiddled with the bottom button of his shirt. "A month after the accident, I drove over to her place to end it. You followed me and burst into her place. You started breaking shit, throwing her stuff at me. You messed her place up pretty bad. Luckily you never actually hurt anyone. The police came. She didn't press charges, I guess because of Cassie and all, but she got a restraining order." He leaned forward and placed his palms on his knees. "Don't you remember any of this?"

She didn't. And Cliff's suggestion of Glenda's altruism over not pressing charges irritated Michelle, as if Cliff thought Glenda had taken the "high road" in the matter. An unfamiliar brand of anger rose inside her, not the smothering, damp-wool feeling she was used to, but a vibrant aggression that burned along her skin like a new sun. But was it really anger? Maybe she didn't care anymore, about Glenda or Cliff or his lies. Maybe it was some extreme brand of proactive indifference.

CHAPTER 7

Darcy was sitting in her car reading a book when Michelle came out of the pharmacy. Michelle thought her older sister looked gorgeous in her peach tank top, sunlight splashing off her bare shoulders. Darcy knew some of the details about what had happened at the cabin, but not everything. Michelle didn't want to alienate her—Darcy was open-minded, but Michelle's story would stretch even her boundaries.

"Want to come to the store?" Darcy asked. "I've got a shipment of supplements coming in. I could really use the help stocking them."

Michelle had been helping Darcy cut boxes, stock shelves, and work the register all afternoon when she suddenly realized she hadn't thought about Cliff or the cabin for several hours. Working at Darcy's store had focused her attention elsewhere, made her feel normal, as if nothing were wrong, as if Cassie were at school.

When Michelle finished bagging a customer's groceries, she squatted down and rummaged through the boxes underneath the counter. Darcy was in the stockroom. It took less than a minute for Michelle to find Darcy's revolver. A gun for protection at a health food store. It seemed ironic to Michelle. The pistol was smaller than she had remembered. She looked at the cylinder and thought she saw bullets. Of course it was loaded. It had to be. What would be the point in keeping an unloaded gun behind the counter?

"Michelle?" Darcy called

"Yeah, what is it?" Michelle bolted up, wondering if Darcy had seen her with the gun.

"Can you give me a hand here?" Darcy said.

Darcy had cut the lid off a box and was arranging plastic containers on the shelf.

"Maybe I should start taking some of these," Michelle said, twirling one of the bottles in her hand.

"You don't need supplements, Michelle," Darcy said. "You need real food. You've turned into a stick figure."

Michelle knew she'd lost weight since returning from the cabin, but she had no appetite.

When Anna, Darcy's assistant, came in, Darcy showed her the stock that still needed to be put away. Michelle grabbed her shoulder bag from behind the front counter and walked to the back to wash her hands and brush her hair. The phone on Darcy's desk rang as Michelle was coming out of the bathroom.

"Nature's Plan," Michelle said, answering the phone.

"Is Michelle there?" the voice said.

"Cliff?"

He let out a breath. "I've been calling you all morning. Are you okay?"

"Fine. I've been helping Darcy at the store. I told you that. What's wrong?"

The long silence on the other end of the phone bothered Michelle.

"Cliff?" she said. She sat down in Darcy's desk chair, sliding her purse closer, feeling the hardness of the gun through the soft leather. Her eyes darted around Darcy's desk in search of extra cartridges, quickly realizing how irrational her thinking was. After all, how many times could she shoot herself?

"Are you okay," Cliff said. "Did you get your prescription refilled?"

"Yes, Darcy took me. But I need a car, Cliff." She still wasn't sure why they only had one.

"Michelle, I told you, you haven't driven in months. You said you couldn't focus behind the wheel. I wish you would remember."

She'd been trying, but it made no sense. She heard Cliff sniffle. Why was he crying?

"Michelle? Say something."

"I don't know what you want me to say. Okay, so maybe I couldn't focus before, but now I can, and I need a car."

"When is Darcy bringing you home?" he asked.

"I don't know. We're going shopping at the mall later. And dinner. Probably around ten."

"Don't be real late, okay?" Cliff said.

"Cliff, you're hovering. Don't treat me like a child. I don't have a fucking curfew. I'll get home when I get home."

Michelle sat at the desk after they hung up, thinking about Cliff crying, picturing the bullets in the gun. Michelle opened the drawer with Darcy's purse and rummaged through the bag for the keys to her Explorer. Darcy came into the storeroom just as Michelle was sliding the drawer shut.

"Anna can handle the store. When do you want to leave for the mall?"

"That was Cliff on the phone," Michelle said. "He wants to take me out to dinner tonight. Can we go shopping another time?"

"Sure. How are you getting home? I'll just drive you."

"No . . . actually, Cliff should be here in about fifteen minutes. He's a fucking mess, Darcy. He's smothering me."

"I think he's just trying to help, Chelle. Cliff has really changed over the past few months and . . ."

"Okay," Michelle said, putting her hand out to her sister. "I don't want to hear about the Cliff Stage Fan Club."

Darcy sighed. "It's not like that, Michelle. We're both just trying to help. You've been through a lot. You both have."

"I want to ask you something," Michelle said. "What do you really think about all this?"

"What do you mean?"

"About . . . everything. Like, me believing Cassie isn't dead. Everything I've told you about the cabin."

Michelle saw Darcy's expression grow pained. After a moment, she said, "I can't possibly know what it's like to lose a daughter, because I've never had children. But I know what it would be like to lose you, Chelle, and that would be unbearable."

"Then you *do* believe Cassie's dead? That means you must believe I'm crazy."

Darcy sighed. "I went to her funeral, Chelle. I sat with you and cried my eyes raw. Just like you. I don't know how to believe anything else."

"Then you think I'm crazy, right?"

Darcy smiled and took her hand. "Not at all. I love you."

Michelle tried a smile over her anxiety. "I have to go."

"Cliff's not here yet."

"He asked if I would meet him out by the edge of the parking lot. He's probably out there waiting." She hugged Darcy. "You know how he gets. Can I call you later?"

Darcy kissed her. "Of course."

Michelle smiled and rushed out the door, hating that she'd lied to her sister.

CHAPTER 8

Deceit was a unique kind of magic, Mattie thought. Sometimes it worked perfectly, reaping the user untold fortunes. At other times it brought only disaster. One thing Mattie knew with certainty: dishonesty was a brand of magic that could never be predicted or controlled.

"Well, Mama," Pink said again. "Do you think you can conjure me up something?"

"How about more pudding?" Mattie said as she watched Pink scrape the edge of the spoon along the inside of the glass goblet. Pink gathered every trace of pudding on the spoon then put it between his lips and smacked it clean.

"Business's been off," he said, the spoon tinkling when he dropped it inside the glass. "Folks ain't listing, and they ain't buying. Not from me. I'm going broke while the rest of the damn agents are selling real estate faster than mice fuck."

"Pink, do you have to talk like that?"

He looked up at her. "Can't you throw a little spell together, get me out of the mud, so to speak, so I don't lose my house?"

"You're not going to lose your house, Pink," Mattie said, removing the goblet to the sink.

"Well, maybe not," Pink said. "But I may have to lay off Clarence and

Lulu till things pick up. You love Lulu, remember, Mama? I mean, where would she get another job at her age?"

"Have you set up an altar?" Mattie asked. "I'll give you everything you need to perform a ritual yourself—green candles, patchouli oil, Lo John. You know how to cast a circle. It's not that difficult." She wanted him to take an interest in rituals, knowing it would focus his energies in more positive directions, put him in touch with deities, connect him with something more important than himself.

Pink wrinkled up his face and scratched his neck. "Mama, you know how Isabelle feels about all that stuff. Besides, I ain't much good at not moving. Now for you on the other hand, it's natural as breathing, Mama, all that praying and sitting still and picturing the moon and planets and whatever it is you think about when you're working magic. Me, I start thinking about lasagna and reruns of *Baywatch*."

She wanted to say, *No, Pink, I won't help you. You're having problems because you've built your life on lies.* But she would never say that to him, she couldn't, not without feeling like a hypocrite. Everything about the way Pink came into her life was rooted in deception, even though it had seemed like the right thing to do at the time. Nothing unusual happened when Ida handed her the baby. There had been no beam of sunlight vanishing suddenly beneath a black cloud, no dreadful cawing of crows in a distant field. It was one moment like any other. Ida had looked up, her face bubbled with sweat, her eyes red from crying and pushing, and placed her new baby in Mattie's arms. Mattie had smiled at the child, amazed at how light he felt, no more weight than a rooster. His slender arms rustled like windblown branches, his fingers curling and uncurling, like breathing. His face was red, his head slightly lopsided and cute, his legs already kicking at the new space around him, making room for a new person in the world. His hair, like his mama's, was damp and stringy, stuck to his forehead. Mattie had smoothed the hairs from his brow. His eyes had been puckered like rosebuds and he could only open them to slits. Mattie had smiled over at Ida then handed the baby back, but Ida shook her head, trying to sit up.

"No, Mattie," she'd said, almost pleading. "You keep him. He's yours."

"What?"

"He's yours, Mattie. You and Buck."

"But, Ida, he's your son! You can't give up your own flesh and blood!"

"Don't judge me, Mattie." Ida pushed her gown down between her legs, trying to sit up. "Do you want him or not?"

"Folks will know," Mattie said. "They'll wonder where this child came from."

"Folks won't know a damn thing lessen you tell them," Ida said, wiping her face with the bottom of her dress. "Besides, you and Buck live so far out here in the sticks you could have ten little 'uns and nobody'd be the wiser."

"What about Ruther? He'll want to know where the baby is?"

"Ruther doesn't want that baby." She stumbled as she tried to steady herself on the floor. "He won't come home till it's gone."

"You're getting up too soon!" Mattie placed the baby in the bassinet and rushed back over to Ida, grabbing her arm and helping her back onto the bed. "You stay put." When Ida closed her eyes, it had looked to Mattie as if Ida was leaving the planet, going off to start a new life somewhere else. Mattie had taken the baby into the bedroom and placed the bassinet next to her bed. When Mattie woke the next morning, she found Ida gone without a note, all the birthing sheets and towels cleaned and folded neatly on the bed. Mattie had gone back to the bedroom and picked up the baby. "Pink is love," she said, kissing him on the nose. "That'll be your name."

One moment like any other, Mattie thought. She'd had no idea at the time how many lives would change because of that one moment, including hers and Buck's. Buck had been in Texas, handling legal work for the US Army Corps of Engineers on a dam project. He'd call almost every night, excited about the progress. "Should bring some new life to this depressed area." Mattie listened, wanting to tell him about the baby but thinking it best to wait until he came home. It would only be two weeks. Of course, by then there was no way she'd give up Pink, no matter what Buck said.

Mattie never told Pink who his real parents were, and as tangled as things had become over the years, she never could without hurting too many folks, especially Pink. It would destroy him.

"So can you help, Mama?" Pink asked again. "Just a little magic to get me through?"

Mattie went over to the chair and picked up the besom she was working on for her neighbor's daughter's wedding. She gathered birch twigs into a bunch, cutting them with her bolline so they were the same length then attached them to the ash staff with willow binding. She layered another bunch of twigs, securing them with more willow twine.

"Mama," Pink said, strolling over to her side. "Now don't start ignoring me. It wouldn't take you no time at all to throw something together."

"Pink, it's not about time!" she snapped, glaring up at him. At moments like this it was hard for her to believe he was a grown man. When he wanted something, his voice took on the carefree timbre of youth, his blue eyes sparkling in the same incorruptible way they had when the owner of the pet store accused him of stealing a turtle. Unlike most folks, Pink became more charming when he was desperate.

"I hope that's not for Isabelle," Pink said, sitting on the edge of the couch, nodding toward the besom in Mattie's hands. "She nearly killed me with that last one you made her."

"Did you put it above her door like I told you?" Mattie asked, saddened that Isabelle had become so resistant to magic; she had been one of Mattie's best students. Mattie couldn't help but blame herself for Isabelle's illness. She had a reasonably good idea why Isabelle was so sick and not getting better, but there was no way to tell her or Pink.

"Well, sure, of course I did," Pink said. "Just like you told me." He pulled a cigar out of his pocket and thumbed his lighter.

"Don't smoke that in here. You know better."

"You burn all sorts of stuff in here smells a whole lot worse than this White Owl."

"Did you put the besom on the outside of the bedroom so she couldn't see it?" Mattie said, growing agitated with him.

Pink sat up, hands on knees, the fat cigar wedged between his stumpy fingers. "Well, no. I put it on the inside. You make them so pretty-looking I thought I should hang it where she could see it. Boy, did it rile her up! 'Get that goddamn witchcraft shit out of my house!' she screamed. Then she flew out of that deathbed of hers like her butt was on fire and tossed a slipper like a damn baseball to knock the broom off the wall. Then she hit me with it. Hurt like hell."

Pink got up and ambled across the room, picking up a small ceramic gnome sitting on the table. "If you don't have time to conjure a spell," he said. "Maybe you could carve me some kind of rune that'll do the trick, something I can carry in my pocket or hang from my rearview mirror."

"Pink, it doesn't work like that." Mattie dropped the besom in the basket at her feet. "It's not about me doing anything. It's about you, your attitude, your entire approach to things."

"Mama, you know I tried to learn all that stuff. I ain't much for reading, and I couldn't remember all those chants and gods and goddesses. I gave it my best shot."

She wasn't sure he'd finished even one book she'd given him, even though he'd said he'd read them all. None of it made any sense to him, he'd told her, "I'm too simple for the spirit world," he'd said. She assured him he wasn't and urged him to try harder.

"Well, what about that love spell thing you did for Isabelle and me?" Pink said, sitting down across from her again. "I didn't have to change my 'approach to things' for that."

Magic held no power over love. Mattie knew that, but Pink didn't and he was suggestable. Her little deception had worked for a while, at least on Pink, though Isabelle seemed to have seen through it. "That was different. You were already married, and it was to help you both through the rough times after Isabelle's mother . . ." Mattie said, remembering Isabelle's father that day, his palms covered in blood.

"Well, I could use a little love spell for that damn sister of Isabelle's," Pink said, jumping to his feet, strolling to Mattie's refrigerator. "That girl is always giving me trouble."

"What is that supposed to mean?" Mattie said, following Pink into the kitchen.

"Is there anymore of that pudding, Mama?" Pink bent over, his hand shifting past the vegetables and bowls in the fridge.

"What's this talk about Claire?" Mattie asked.

"She's always cracking how fat I am. Do you think I'm fat, Mama?"

"I mean the part about the love spell? You and her aren't up to anything, are you?"

Pink found a fried chicken breast wrapped in tin foil. He threw the foil in the trash and bit a chunk from the side, leaving a glowing white patch of exposed meat.

"Pink, you answer me."

"Mama, now, don't get yourself all worked up." Pink poured himself a glass of milk. "There ain't nothing going on between me and Claire. Hell, that skinny little girl is just a child."

Mattie eased down into the kitchen chair, rolling her fingers into a ball on her lap. It made her feel unfit as a mother that she couldn't tell if Pink was lying. She often wondered if he had grown in her own belly, if they'd shared a contract of blood, maybe then she would be capable of knowing him completely the way she imagined a natural mother would know her own offspring. She had hoped that time alone would bond them in such a way that she could tell what he was thinking before he knew his own thoughts. She conjured numerous fantasies about a real mother's connection to her child, how a real mother could peer into his soul, protect him from himself. She had tried to protect Pink, but it was all falling apart again. She looked into his eyes and prayed he was telling the truth.

*****

On Friday, Pink stayed home from the office. Friday was when Claire came to clean Pink and Isabelle's house. Pink watched from the couch as Claire elbowed open the front door, her skinny white arms hugging a mop and broom. A scrub bucket full of supplies—Mr. Clean, 409, Windex, an assortment of brushes and other things Pink didn't recognize—dangled from her hand. Her nails were painted red and shiny as plastic. She wore a skintight exercise outfit with a white tank top pulled over it. She asked how he was doing then went back to the front porch for the sweeper. The attachments rattled as she dragged the vacuum inside by the hose and shut the front door.

Claire asked Pink if he'd been fishing lately, told him that her Kenny was out the other day catching walleye down where the Little Pigeon River flowed into Lake Burtran.

"Under the bridge, there," she said. "Where everybody fishes. He's there now. At least that's where he said he was going. Him and Curly."

Like a magician, Claire pulled all kinds of cleaning supplies out of the bucket, including a long wand with a rainbow-feathered head she used to knock cobwebs from the fan blades. Pink watched the cheeks of her ass work like pistons, up and down, as she moved around the living room. Her hair was a bundle of curls piled on top of her head, and Pink figured the only thing holding them in place was the yellow plastic flower tucked behind her ear. He couldn't understand the mechanics of it.

"How's Isabelle feeling today, Pink?" she asked, dusting the ceramic wizards and unicorns on the mantel. With her back to him, she dusted the pewter figurines on the top shelf of the curio cabinet, working her way down to the bottom, bending over to wipe the porcelain swans and pigs. Pink pulled himself off the couch and clamped his hands to her hips, pressing up against her from behind. Still bent over, she looked up at him past her shoulder then motioned her head toward the sweeper. He stretched his toe out and clicked it on. The vacuum drowned out the noise of the television as Claire turned toward him and unzipped his pants. She guided him backward toward the couch and pushed on his chest to make him sit. She knelt on the floor between his legs and stuck her hand into his trousers. With her other hand, she grabbed the handle on the sweeper and pushed it back and forth, making it sound as if she were vacuuming. The television mixed with the roar of the vacuum as Pink closed his eyes and buried his fingers in Claire's bouncy curls.

When Claire finished, she stood, turned off the vacuum, and went to the kitchen. Each time the refrigerator door opened and closed, Pink could hear the bottles and jars in the door clink together. He zipped up his pants and thought about taking a nap. But listening to Claire rummaging through the cabinets and refrigerator made him hungry. Claire came out of the kitchen carrying a glass of milk in one hand and a plate of sliced sandwich sections, vegetable strips, and potato chips in the other.

"Is that for me, cuddle cakes?" Pink said.

Claire smirked and rolled her eyes, walking past him toward the back bedroom.

"Good," he said. "Because I hate them little carrot and celery sticks. It's like eating bamboo." Pink went over to the coffee table and grabbed the remote off the stack of *Glamour* magazines. He pushed the button, grimacing each time another program popped onto the screen. Men in suits, a woman wearing a necklace, a girl reading a diary, a preacher behind the pulpit, police cars racing down a country road after a blue car, a woman crying, a boy laughing at a frog, everybody talking, everybody caught inside that little box. He hoped to find a program on antelope hunting in Wyoming or peacock bass fishing in Mexico.

He thought maybe he should go fishing, call Clarence and head down to that bridge and sit with Kenny and jerk walleye out of the river and drink all of Kenny's beer and tell him what fine blowjobs Claire gave. No woman did it like Claire, Pink thought, especially not Isabelle. Isabelle gave him neurotic little blowjobs, gagging and choking the entire time, like she was being forced to swallow a lamp. That was before she got sick. Pink half-figured that's why she wasn't getting well, so she wouldn't have to perform orally anymore, or any other way.

Claire came out of the bedroom empty-handed and went to the kitchen. Pink walked out to see what she was doing.

"What are you going to do all day, Pink?" Claire asked, wiping down the countertops. "Sit around getting fatter?"

Pink sidled up beside her, wrapping his hands around her waist. "I thought I might go down there walleye fishing under the bridge with Kenny," Pink said, a grin pushing his plump cheeks apart.

"Kenny would like that, Pink. You should go." She pried his fingers from her waist. "Just don't forget about that .357 Magnum he's got stashed in the bottom of his tackle box."

Pink spun away from her and went to the fridge. He pulled the door open, scratching his head as he surveyed the shelves. After finding a couple of leftover pork chops from Fat Jack's Barbecue, he went out on the back porch and sat in the rocker. Before too long, Claire came out and draped a rug over the rail and proceeded to beat it with a broom. Lint, dust balls, and hair floated across the porch and stuck to Pink's pork chop.

"Goddamn it, Claire!" he said. "You're ruining my damn lunch."

"How many is that for you today, Pink?"

"Pork chops?"

"No, lunches," she said, folding the rug and taking it back inside.

"Why do you always have to make fun of how fat I am?" he shouted at the screen door behind her then looked down at his belly bulging over his pants. "Goddamn women," he said, throwing the pork chop bone at a sycamore tree in the backyard like he was throwing a hatchet, half expecting it to stick.

Pink was napping in the rocker when Claire stepped out and told him she was leaving. "Isabelle wants to see you," she said.

Pink rubbed his eyes and tried to focus. The afternoon was turning cool, the sky an empty, gray slate. "What's your sister want now?"

"She's sick, Pink. Can't you find any compassion?"

"I used it all up over the past few years. I'm plumb wore down to the rim."

"Don't make her wait," Claire said. "I've got to go."

Pink heard Claire start her Pacer as he walked to the back bedroom. He dreaded going in, hated the smell of sweat-soaked linen and vomit, the stench of disease. He grabbed a few cigars off the dresser in the spare bedroom—the bedroom he'd occupied since Isabelle had taken sick—then walked down the hall. He opened the door slowly, as if stealth could fool the germs, keep them from leaping into his lungs. He wasn't certain if she was contagious, no one was. Even the doctors couldn't accurately diagnose the ailment, her condition changing with the frequency of a storm front. Everything from fibromyalgia to Crohn's disease, they'd said, but Pink knew they were guessing. Pink believed that doctors were like weathermen; they got paid whether they were right or wrong, so it didn't matter what they said.

"Hey, Sweet Potato, how are we feeling today?" Pink asked, poking his head through the door.

"I don't have the energy, Pink. So don't bring that sweet-talk crap in here." Isabelle pushed herself up under the blankets, coughing.

"You always loved it when I called you Sweet Potato, Sweet Potato," he said, stepping into the room, still holding the doorknob behind his back.

"That's when I was seventeen, Pink. I didn't have a brain yet."

"But don't you remember? I'd say, 'Are you my little sweet potato?' and you'd say, 'I yam, I yam!'" Pink could hardly believe how terrible she looked, her eye sockets and parched mouth like deep craters on the surface of some forsaken planet. She seemed paler than putty and painfully swollen. Pink smiled and tried to look past her, envisioning the nest of curls on the top of Claire's head, the vanilla and citrus freshness of Claire's skin. "Claire said you wanted to see me."

"Could you get my book of crossword puzzles?" Isabelle said. "And a cup of hot tea with lemon and honey?"

"Sure, Sweet Potato," Pink said, about to leave.

"And, Pink," Isabelle said.

"Yes?"

"You can wipe that stupid grin off your face now," she said, adjusting the blankets.

"What?"

"Don't you think I know Claire gives you blowjobs when she comes over to clean? God only knows what twisted thrill she gets from sucking that fat little peter of yours." Isabelle collapsed back on the pillow, her mouth a square hole in her face. "You can get me that tea now, Sweet Potato. And don't break the bag."

CHAPTER 9

Isabelle ran her hand across the magazine page, over the photo of the white dress, tracing her finger along the lace sleeve. Her own wedding dress hadn't been that pretty. She and Pink had been married in the church, even though her parents had ordered the minister not to do it. The day before the wedding, Isabelle had been going over the last of the details with the minister—where the photographer would stand, how the bridesmaids would approach the altar—when her parents came into the church. Her father had stayed in the vestibule, his body looking like a shadow caught in the light of the opened doors. Her mother marched down the aisle and demanded that "this nonsense" be stopped immediately.

"Why, Ida?" the minister had said. "Pink and Isabelle love each other."

Isabelle's mother had protested to the minister, explaining that Pink and Isabelle were second cousins. "It isn't right," she'd told the minister. "They have the same blood flowing through their veins."

"Second cousins are hardly blood relatives at all," the minister had told her. "Don't worry. The Lord will bless this union."

Isabelle could still see the fire in her mother's eyes, glaring up at the minister, her hands balled to fists. "You'll burn in hell eternal if you go through with this," she said to the minister, then stormed out of the church. Isabelle shrugged at the minister, savoring every second of her mother's anguish. Her father stood a moment in the doorway. Isabelle could see his head bowed, shaking back and forth, his hat in his hands like an out-of-work salesman. The day Isabelle told her parents she was marrying Pink, her mother had put down her needlepoint and folded her hands in her lap, her eyes flat as mud. "You will not," she said, and then got up to leave.

"Yes I will," Isabelle said. "Next month. You're both invited."

Her mother walked across the room and slapped Isabelle across the face. Before Isabelle could say anything, she slapped her again and left the room.

"I won't pay for it," Isabelle's father said. "You'll get nothing from us."

"Oh, you'll pay for it, all right," Isabelle said, rubbing her cheek, smiling. "You'll pay for everything, the wedding cake, the flowers, the music, and then you'll walk me down that fucking aisle, kiss me on the cheek, and smile like you're giving away your most favorite daughter in the whole world. And then you'll walk up to Pink afterward and congratulate him and say, 'Welcome to the family, Son.'"

Her father huffed and shook his head. "You're sick, Isabelle," he said, the flesh beneath his right eye jumping. "There is something very wrong with you."

As he walked away, she tossed the invitations onto the couch. "And the honeymoon!" she yelled after him. "You'll pay for that too. Pink wants to go to Niagara-fucking-Falls! Can you believe it? Nobody goes there anymore, for shit's sake!"

Pink had shown up at the wedding looking like a funeral director. He'd gotten his tux from Clarence—whose uncle owned a mortuary in the next county. "What are you doing?" Isabelle had said, dragging Pink into the ladies' restroom. "You look like somebody from the Addams Family!" Pink had explained how he'd gotten the tux for free, that Clarence's uncle had even thrown in the alterations at no cost.

"Where did his uncle get the tux?"

"He's got lots of them . . . well, most of them are suits. All different colors," Pink had said. "I think they're for emergencies."

"Emergencies?" Isabelle said, shaking her head. "What kind of emergencies do they have at a funeral home?"

"I don't know, maybe—"

"Shut up, Pink. Sometimes you are so stupid. Clarence's uncle is steal-ing those suits off the dead bodies before he buries them! Christ, Pink, why didn't you go down to Connor's Department Store like I told you and rent something with nice lapels and a cummerbund!"

"A cummerbund?"

Isabelle pulled Pink out of the bathroom by the sleeve. Claire, her maid of honor, was standing in the back of the church, chewing gum. "Get rid of that, Claire, dammit." Isabelle looked around, not really surprised that her father hadn't shown, but disappointed nonetheless. She had known all along her mama wouldn't come.

"Go get your daddy," Isabelle had told Pink. When Pink came back with Buck, Isabelle asked Buck if he would walk her down the aisle.

Buck adjusted his glasses and shook his head. "I can't do that, Isabelle. I didn't even want to come. Mattie made me." As Buck turned to leave, he gave Pink a look so hard it forced Pink back a step, like he was about to be hit. But Buck spun away, then went and took his seat next to Mattie. Mattie looked as though she were crying.

"You still want to do this, don't you, Sweet Potato?" Pink had asked.

"Yes," Isabelle said, wiping her eyes. "And don't call me that anymore. I hate it." Almost as much as she hated her next thought. "Pink, go get Clarence and tell him to get his ass back here. You go back up and wait with the groomsmen."

"But Clarence is my best man."

"Shut up, Pink, and do what I told you, okay?"

Pink walked away down the side aisle. Claire was giggling with the other girls, pulling her dress up to expose her new nylons, then squeezing her breasts upward in her dress until they shined like domes.

When the music started, Isabelle flew into a rage, calling the organist an idiot, throwing her hands in the air. People in the last few pews turned around at the commotion.

"He's not supposed to start yet!" she'd said to Claire. "That's not even the right song!" She sent the flower girl down the aisle, then the ring bearer, then herded the bridesmaids into a line and forced them down the aisle.

Everyone was in place at the altar, and Isabelle could see Pink whispering something to Clarence. Clarence looked toward the rear of the church, craning his neck like he'd heard a wild turkey in the bush, then strolled down off the altar with a confused look on his face. He said *hello* to everyone he recognized with his customary thumbs-up greeting as he walked by. "Pink said you wanted to see me," Clarence said. Isabelle proceeded to push his hair off his forehead and straighten his tie. "Tuck in that shirt, Clarence," she said. "You look like a damn hobo." Clarence raised one shoulder then the other, shoving his hand down his pants, working the tail of his shirt into the waistband of his trousers. Isabelle shook her head when she noticed the sandals on Clarence's feet.

"What the hell are you wearing?"

"Found them at Sadie's Thrift Store," he said. "They keep the fungus from growing between my toes."

"Come on," she said, hooking his arm through hers. "Don't look anywhere but at the altar, and don't say nothing to nobody."

Isabelle and Clarence were halfway down the aisle when eyes shifted from them to the back of the church. Women put hands over their mouths or looked away. Men stood up as if there was going to be a fight, others peeked around the ones standing. A few people gasped, and Isabelle turned to see her father standing at the back of the church, his shirt and pants covered in blood. He shuffled toward her down the aisle. Clarence untangled his arm from Isabelle's and took a few steps back. People near the ends of the pews moved away, but her father's eyes were only for Isabelle. He stood in front of her, his eyes burnished and raw, his hands dangling at his sides big as shovels, dripping blood. "You're wicked, child," he said, drawing a deep breath, then backhanding her across the face. "You're Satan."

The memory made Isabelle close the magazine and drop it on the floor. She felt tired, ready to nap. After scooting down in the bed, she pulled the blankets up over her breasts, pausing a moment to touch them. Pink hadn't touched her breasts in over five years, even when they made love, which they hadn't done in a long time. She couldn't blame him though; she was death itself lying there. She wouldn't look in the mirror, afraid of what she might see staring back.

"Want your hair brushed?" Claire asked, poking her head through the doorway. Isabelle wiped her eyes.

"I didn't hear you come in," Isabelle said.

"Thought I'd drop by on the way to the store. See if you needed anything."

Claire came over to the bed, taking the brush off the dresser, and sitting next to Isabelle. She pulled up a thick sheaf of Isabelle's hair and combed it out, then gathered up another. Isabelle cried harder with each stroke of the brush.

"I'm thirty-eight years old and I look like a hundred," Isabelle said. "Why can't I get better, Claire? Why won't I get well?"

Claire laid the brush on the quilt and eased Isabelle's head to her chest.

"It's gonna be okay, baby," Claire said softly, running her fingertips along Isabelle's scalp. "It's gonna be okay."

CHAPTER 10

"I called the police, Michelle! I thought somebody stole my fucking car! Christ, what did you think I would do? What were you thinking?"

Michelle absently put away the groceries she'd purchased, the phone wedged between her cheek and shoulder, listening to her sister. She bought the food with cash in case Cliff checked their credit card account online.

"I'm sorry, Darce," Michelle said into the phone. "I need answers. I was going to ask you to bring me up here but . . . I panicked when Cliff called. I'm sorry."

"What am I supposed to do now, Michelle? How am I supposed to get to the store in the mornings to open up?" Darcy's voice trembled, breaking. "Had you thought about that?" Darcy burst into tears. Before Michelle could say anything, Darcy screamed into the receiver, "Goddamn you, Michelle! Why did you take my fucking gun? What are you planning to do with that?"

Michelle waited for Darcy to calm down, trying to harness her own thoughts into a cohesive response.

"I was just scared, is all, coming alone. You remember how dark it is up here. I'd never use it." Michelle was almost able to believe some of that was true. Yet there was no way to explain the other reason for taking it. There was no way to tell her sister that if she couldn't figure out what had happened the night she went looking for Cliff, if there was no explanation, rational or otherwise, for Cassie being alive when she'd left the cabin and dead in this new version of reality, she was prepared to end her own life.

"You know Cliff will come up there as soon as he finds out what you've done," Darcy said, a bit of residual anger in her words.

"I know," Michelle said. "That's where I need your help."

"What am I supposed to do, Michelle? Lie to him?"

"Why wouldn't you? You're my sister. Just tell him I'm spending the night with you." Michelle was a bit miffed she had to remind Darcy of where her allegiance should be. Why was she now Cliff's biggest devotee? After Cliff's affair became known, Darcy had led the crusade against him. "Dump that loser," she'd told Michelle. "He doesn't deserve you."

"Then, in the morning when he comes to pick me up from your condo," Michelle continued, "tell him I was gone when you woke up and you have no idea where I went. Whatever you do, don't tell him I have your Explorer. I need some time before he figures out where I am."

It felt like a full minute before Darcy spoke. "What are you going to do when he figures it out?"

"I don't know. Maybe by then I'll have some answers."

"Answers? To what, Michelle? Some mysterious cabin in the woods that disappears when you shine a light on it? To some inexplicable riddle that brings Cassie back from the grave? What answers, Michelle? What answers other than the most obvious ones? Grieving and anger are real and valid human reactions to tragedy, Michelle—not vanishing cabins and mysterious lights. You need help. Do you understand, Michelle? You need help and rest and time, not this bullshit . . . not guns and wild goose chases after real estate agents. Come home, Michelle. Please."

Michelle had hoped Darcy believed her story, or at least made room for the possibility. It was obvious now she hadn't.

"I've got to go," Michelle said. "I'll get your car back soon. Oh, and . . . I took some money from your register. I'll pay you back. Promise."

Darcy sighed. "I don't care about the money. Just come home tomorrow, okay?" Darcy's voice sounded calm, but strained. "I'll stall Cliff, tell him you drove to the grocery store to get donuts for breakfast. I'll make up some excuse." She paused. "Chelle, move in with me, take some time away from Cliff. You could work at the store. It'll be fun. We'll shop for clothes, get you a makeover at Apollo's Spa, throw together some of those pizzas the way we used to when Mom and Dad went out to the movies. You remember? Anchovies and pineapple and . . . something else . . ."

"Artichokes," Michelle said, relieved by her sister's new attitude. Darcy sounded more like an ally again.

"That's right, Michelle. Artichokes. God, I had forgotten that."

"I love you," Michelle said.

"Me too!" said Darcy.

Michelle drew the phone away from her cheek and pressed it into the cradle. She was glad they hung up on a high note. Being sisters had always been more important than being right.

Michelle rummaged in the dresser for her sweatpants. It had been Cliff's idea to leave clothes at the cabin so they didn't have to pack everything each time they went up.

She pulled a sweatshirt over her blouse, took a beer from the fridge, and walked out onto the deck. The night was clear, the sky splashed with stars. She looked down over the rail, half-expecting to see the dusk-to-dawn light so she could get this over with. When it wasn't there, she looked up and saw the silhouette of a bat dart across the blue-black sky. She took a sip of the beer, then went over and unfolded a deck chair, placing it near the railing. She sat, her feet propped up, watching the tiny lights of an airplane in the distance. The mountains to the east looked like the backs of elephants. The moon had not yet come up, but the glow of its approach was a bright smudge along the horizon.

Michelle tilted the bottle back, wondering how much time she'd have before Cliff arrived at the cabin. Would he go crazy, make a big scene, or just cry and act like she was torturing him? This was a new Cliff, one she didn't know.

CHAPTER 11

Pink turned from the window where he'd been watching a woman across the street trying to corral her three children into the back seat of her Lexus. Pink kept hoping that when she bent over to lash the baby into the toddler seat, her dress would blow up and he'd get a peek at her ass.

"Did that woman ever call back about the Taylor place?" Pink shouted toward the back office. Clarence didn't answer. "Clarence! Did that woman, that Mrs. Kaminsky, ever call back about the damn Taylor place?"

"I don't think so," Clarence said from the other room, his voice sounding muffled, as if he were wrapped in a blanket or something.

"What are you doing in there?" Pink shouted.

"Spraying my feet."

"What color?" Pink laughed.

Clarence walked into Pink's office carrying an aerosol can, his feet flour-white against his red sandals.

"What in God's name did you do to your damn feet, Clarence?"

"The fungus is back," Clarence said, staring down at his toes. "It's really bad this time. Doc told me to use this." Clarence held up a yellow can with a green lid. "It's some kind of antifungal agent or something."

Pink strolled over to Clarence and took the can from his hand. "This is for jock itch, Clarence. Did you know that?"

"Doc said it would work on my feet just the same. 'Fungus is fungus,' he told me."

Pink handed the can back. "Ever think maybe wearing shoes once in a while might help?"

"No, Doc said I was doing the right thing." Clarence bent over to spray a spot he'd missed. "Fungus don't like all that light and air. Told me not to wear socks either, at least for a while."

"You don't even own socks," Pink said. "Did Lulu call in sick again?" Over the past four weeks, Lulu had called in for messages and to tell Pink she wasn't feeling "up to par." Pink always thought it strange she used that expression because the closest she'd ever been to a golf course was when she went to the Marigold Cemetery to visit her dead husband. The Ardenwood Country Club people bought up the land adjacent to the cemetery and built their course. It caused quite a ripple with the folks of Ardenwood, especially the ones who had family resting up at Marigold. It was disconcerting for folks to visit a loved one and find a Titleist sitting on the grave.

"Haven't talked to her in two days," Clarence said.

"Maybe I better go check on her," Pink said, grabbing his truck keys off the desk.

"You bringing back lunch?" Clarence asked.

Pink glanced at his watch. "It's only ten-thirty in the damn morning. Hell, Clarence, I ain't even made a turd from breakfast yet."

"I think this fungus condition's what's got me so hungry," Clarence said. "Just bring me something from the bakery. You pass right by it on the way out to Lulu's. One of them bear claws if they have it."

Pink pulled the door closed and headed for his Suburban. The sun was already bearing down and Pink was sure it would hit seventy-five today.

"Excuse me," a woman said, stepping from an Explorer. "Are you Pink Souder?"

"You recognize me from my billboard, don't you?" Pink said, studying the attractive woman. Her hair was long and dark brown, except where the sun hit it, shifting it a shade toward orange. She wore it clipped up into a mop at the back of her head, the way Claire wore hers when she cleaned.

A bit on the scrawny side, Pink thought, but a nice set of face-warmers up top. "What can I help you with?"

"My name is Michelle Stage," she said, extending her hand. "I have a piece of property I want to sell. I was wondering if you could take a look at it."

"Well," Pink said, scratching behind his ear, then checking his watch. "I'm pretty busy today. Think you could come back tomorrow?" The woman seemed disappointed or frustrated, Pink wasn't sure. He didn't want to seem too eager. Prospective clients could sense desperation.

"I need you to come today," she said. "This morning."

"I was headed to check on a piece of property right now," he said. "But it can wait." Pink turned away and stuck his head through the front doorway. "Clarence, I ain't coming back till after lunch, so order a damn pizza if you're hungry. You can reach me on the cell."

Pink slid in under the steering wheel of his Suburban. Mrs. Stage climbed in the other side. He glanced at her legs while she buckled her seat belt. She smelled nice, not saturated in perfume like a lot of his wealthy clients. And she seemed to have a pretty smile, when she used it.

"Heard about the winter storm headed this way?" Pink asked.

"I did," Michelle said. "I didn't really listen to it, though."

"Hell, it's gonna hit eighty degrees out there today the way it's going," Pink said. "I don't much believe in doctors or weathermen. How many people you know got a job they can do wrong fifty percent of the time and still get paid?" Pink laughed and turned the knob on the air conditioner to make it colder.

"How do you know they're wrong fifty percent of the time?" she asked.

"Law of averages, little lady. Plain ol' math," Pink said confidently, even though he wasn't sure it was true. He'd done poorly in algebra and geometry, but always thought the "law of averages" was an interesting concept.

Pink was about to pull from the parking lot when he noticed Clarence in his side mirror hobbling from the office and waving. Pink rolled down the window of the Suburban. "What is it, Clarence?"

"Loudon just called, Pink, and . . ." Clarence said, letting his eyes fall to the pavement.

Pink waited a few seconds for Clarence to speak then said, "Come on, Clarence, I got a client sitting here."

"Lulu's dead. Loudon just found her."

Pink could only nod. "Does my mama know yet?"

Clarence shrugged. "Loudon didn't say. Just said Lulu was dead."

Clarence went back in and Pink sat a moment then looked over at Michelle. "I'm sorry, ma'am. I need to go attend to this. Can we . . ."

"I don't mind riding along—if you don't mind," she said.

Pink didn't mind. It just seemed strange. Why would anyone want to go see a dead body? Pink didn't even want to go.

"What did you say your first name was, Mrs. Stage?"

"Michelle."

"Pretty name," Pink said. "Like the song. Them Beatle fellas made you immortal."

Michelle nodded and smiled.

They drove toward Lulu's, Mrs. Stage sitting across from him quiet as a leaf. When he drove past the bakery, he thought about Clarence's bear claw. Pink couldn't figure out how Clarence could eat so much junk and stay thin as a cane pole. Pink's body fell in love with every calorie that passed through his stomach and saved them like old love letters. It wasn't fair, he thought, a man who loved to eat as much as he did. He looked over at Michelle, wondering what her breasts were like. They seemed to be holding up pretty well for a woman in her early forties. Maybe even younger, he guessed.

They pulled into Lulu's driveway. Loudon's police car was parked behind Lulu's Ford. "You can wait here," Pink said. "I'll just be a minute."

Pink walked toward the porch, and Lulu's Chihuahua met him half-way across the yard. "Come here, Burrito," he said to the dog, picking it up. It was odd to Pink that Lulu owned a dog. He always figured witches for cat lovers.

Sheets and towels waved from Lulu's clothesline. Loudon stood on the back porch.

"Hey, Pink," Loudon said.

"Loudon," Pink said. "What happened?"

"Neighbors called when they didn't see Lulu bring Burrito outside this morning. They said Lulu's been feeling poorly, so when they didn't hear the dog—"

"Busybodies," Pink said, and walked past Loudon to the back door. Lulu was stretched out on the kitchen floor. Pink squatted down and brushed the stringy, gray hair from her brow, her flesh cool and firm, like freshly kneaded dough. But her color made his stomach tighten, every purple and sapphire vein right there beneath her skin, like he was looking through ice.

"Sorry about Lulu," Loudon said. "Coroner should be here in a few minutes. I didn't call your mama yet. Thought you might want to do that."

Pink held Burrito in his left arm and flipped open his cell phone to call his mama.

"Stay till I get there," his mother said.

"Mama, I can't. I got a client sitting in my truck."

"Pink Souder, you wait for me or you'll be sorrier than you've ever been." She hung up.

Pink slipped the phone back in his pocket and strolled to the truck. He'd send Clarence up over the weekend to cut Lulu's lawn. Hide a damn rhino in there, the grass was so high, he thought. He walked to the passenger side of his Suburban and pulled the door open.

"Well, I'm gonna have to wait here for my mama," Pink said to Mrs. Stage. "Seems like Lulu had a stroke. You might as well get out for a spell."

"Is there anything I can do?"

"Not unless you're one of them preachers who can lay hands on a blind man and make him see."

"I don't mind waiting in the car."

Pink put Burrito down and walked to the backyard. He grabbed the clothes basket from the grass and started taking down the sheets, making sure they were dry. He shoved the clothespins in his pants pocket before dropping the laundry in the basket.

A maroon van pulled into the driveway, followed by a car Pink guessed to be the coroner. Neighbors appeared on front porches.

"Damn circus," Pink said under his breath.

Emerson, with his gray sideburns and yellow polo shirt emblazoned with the funeral home logo, got out of the van and ambled over to Pink.

"Hey there, Pink," said Emerson. Emerson introduced the coroner to Pink. Pink shook his hand and pointed him toward Lulu's back porch.

About then Pink's mother pulled up the driveway and rushed to the back of the house. Pink looked toward the Suburban and wondered where Michelle had gone. She wasn't in the front seat.

Emerson's assistant, a young man in jeans, rattled a gurney across the yard to where Emerson and Pink were standing. The coroner was bent over the body. Pink's mother knelt on the floor beside Lulu, rubbing her palm across her forehead. "Take her to the funeral home, Emerson," Mattie said. "And I'll be down later to tell you what needs to be done."

Emerson looked over at the sheriff. The sheriff shrugged.

"I don't want any of her things touched," Mattie said. "I'll take care of her belongings."

"Lulu didn't have any people, did she, Mattie?" Emerson said, removing a comb from his pocket, dragging it through his thick hair.

"Don't worry, Emerson," Mattie said. "I'll pay for everything."

Emerson's shoulders drooped. The coroner stood up and whispered something to the sheriff, then turned back toward the body.

"Does anyone know what name I should put on the death certificate?" the coroner asked.

"Lulu Martin," Pink said. "That's the only name I know."

"Lucretia Alessandra Genovese," Mattie said. Pink had never heard that name before, but his mother said it with such dead chilling conviction it sounded more like an invocation than a name. The coroner asked for the spelling and Mattie spoke each letter clearly, never taking her eyes from Lulu, leaning down to kiss her on the forehead when she finished. "Come take her, Emerson. And be careful."

Burrito squirmed in Pink's arms as Emerson and the young assistant transported the body to the van.

"Sorry about Lulu," Emerson said to Pink. "I know you two were real close."

"Yeah," Pink said, knowing it wasn't true. Lulu was his mother's dearest and oldest friend, and she worked in Pink's office where they tolerated each other on a daily basis, but they'd never been close.

"Isabelle feeling any better these days?" Emerson asked.

Pink shook his head. Emerson gave Pink a low wave as he shuffled back to the van. Burrito wiggled in Pink's arms, barking at the vehicle.

"I can't put you down," Pink said to the dog. "You're so stupid, you'll chase that van till you drop dead of exhaustion." Pink headed for the backyard, looking for Michelle. The sheriff paused a moment to talk with Pink. "Coroner figures Lulu died of a stroke sometime yesterday afternoon," the sheriff said.

"I know," Pink said.

"How could you know? Coroner himself isn't completely sure about the time."

"Her sheets were dry," Pink said. "If she'd hung them out this morning, they'd still be wet. And if she'd been alive yesterday evening, she'd have taken them down before dark."

The sheriff stared, apparently studying Pink's theory. Pink walked the sheriff back to his car. He searched the yard for Michelle until he saw her in the front seat of his Suburban. When the sheriff approached, Pink watched Michelle slink down in the seat, as if she didn't want to be noticed.

"Who's the woman?" the sheriff asked, looking in Michelle's direction as he opened the front door of his cruiser.

"Prospective client," Pink said. "Kind of pretty, don't you think?"

"Can't rightly say the way she's all slumped down in the seat. Will you lock up when your mama's done in there?" the sheriff asked, starting his engine.

Pink nodded.

"How's Isabelle?" the sheriff asked.

"Same."

"Hear about the storm?"

"It's seventy degrees out here, Loudon. I don't think it's gonna snow."

"That's what they thought in '93," the sheriff said, backing from the driveway. "I'll check on Lulu's place later. Give Isabelle my best."

After the sheriff drove off, Pink went over to his Suburban, holding Burrito like a baby. "Where did you disappear to?" he asked Michelle.

"A little walk, while you were taking care of things."

"It'll just be another few minutes." Pink went back across the yard, setting Burrito down in the grass.

Burrito ran to Mattie's side, sniffing her shoes. She leaned down and picked him up. "You'll come home with me," she said, kissing his head as he licked her face. She handed the dog to Pink. "Take Burrito to my place,

Pink. I have to take care of some things. And don't forget Burrito's dog food on Lulu's kitchen table. I set it out so you'd remember."

"Mama, can't you take the dog with you? I've got a client waiting on me."

Mattie swiveled toward Pink's Suburban, her eyes fixed on Michelle in the front seat. "Is that what she is?" Mattie glared at Pink, her mouth a hard line.

"Of course. What the hell you think she is?" Pink said.

"Don't talk to me that way, Pink. You should be ashamed, Isabelle lying home sick in bed while you hound around like some wild stud dog."

Pink spun from her and carried the dog to the car. "Mind watching him a second?" Pink asked Mrs. Stage. He reached the dog through the opened window, dropping him on the front seat. In a second the dog was in Michelle's lap, shaking. Pink was strolling back to the house when Mattie came out carrying a shopping bag and a small purple velvet sack with a crimson drawstring.

"Come help me a second, Pink."

Mattie set the grocery sack down on the porch, then turned and went back into the house. Pink followed, still perturbed by her accusation. Mattie was kneeling at the fireplace wiggling a stone from the hearth when Pink entered the room.

"Don't just stand there, Pink. Help me."

He came over and squatted down next to her.

"Pull that stone out," she said.

Pink gripped his fingertips around the rock and toggled it by the edges until it pulled free. Mattie reached inside the vacated hole and withdrew a small ornate silver container that looked to Pink like a ring box.

Mattie looked over at Pink then pushed off the hearth to get to her feet. "What's that?" Pink asked.

"Lulu's umbilical cord. Now lock up, Pink, and don't forget Burrito's food."

His mother grabbed the bags off the back porch on her way out, glancing over at Michelle before driving off.

"Was that your mother?" Michelle asked.

Pink climbed in behind the wheel. "Yeah. Sorry for the drama," he said, turning the key. "Let's go have a look at that property of yours."

CHAPTER 12

Michelle tried to remember what Sheriff Fisk had said about Lulu when he'd shared the Pink Souder story. Pink adjusted the air conditioner and sat a few minutes with the engine running, as if deep in thought. Michelle felt strangely calm, the most at ease she'd been since taking Darcy's car. Maybe it was the dog, she thought, giving him a kiss on top of his head. Pink backed out of Lulu's driveway, talking on his cell phone, telling someone about Lulu's death.

"Yes. Burrito's right here," he said, the phone pressed to his cheek. "He's going to Mama's house. Yes, I'll open a window if I stop for lunch. Yes. Yes, I said I would. Yes, I'll bring you soup. Tomato. I thought you liked tomato? Okay, no tomato. Chicken noodle if they have it. Okay."

When Pink clapped his phone shut, he sighed and threw it onto the seat. Before he could pull away, a neighbor came up to the window and rapped on the glass.

"Oh, hell's bells, what have we got now?" Pink said, rolling down the window. "Hi, Helen."

"Sorry about Lulu," Helen said. "She looked out of sorts these past few weeks. I thought maybe she'd fix herself a little something to pull out of it."

"No magic stronger than death, Helen," Pink said.

"When's the funeral?" Helen asked.

"Christ, Helen, I ain't sure Emerson's got her to the damn morgue, yet."

Helen glared at Pink, and then turned from the car. Pink hit the button for the electric window. "Damn busybody," Pink said. "People who don't know about Wiccans think magic can stop a damn runaway freight train. Lulu was a witch, like my mama. But ain't no besoms or candles gonna stop death."

"A witch?" Michelle said. "Your mother's a witch?" She remembered now that Sheriff Fisk had mentioned that to her at the cabin. Even so, it felt strange Pink offering the information so casually. And his mother hadn't appeared . . . otherworldly.

Pink looked over at her. "Wiccans aren't like Halloween goblins or anything. It's like a religion or something, you know."

"What's a besom?" she asked.

"A small broom," Pink said, spraying dirt and rock as he pulled from the driveway. "Supposed to ward off evil spirits and whatnot," Pink said, scratching under his chin as if he needed a shave.

Michelle checked Pink's finger for a wedding ring and saw a gold band cutting into his chubby knuckle.

"You married?" Michelle asked.

Pink turned toward her, smiling. "Why do you ask?"

"The ring." She held her own hand up and spun her diamond ring with her thumb.

"Yeah, I'm married," Pink said. "Isabelle."

Isabelle? Michelle was certain Isabelle was the woman the sheriff had spoken of, but now doubted her own memory. Wasn't she dead? "Are you still married to her?"

"You seem surprised," Pink said. "That's who I was talking to on the phone. She's real sickly. Never gets out of the damn bed anymore." Pink took his eyes back out the window, clearly not wanting to talk about her.

"So was Lulu your aunt or something?" Michelle asked.

"She was my mama's midwife, and her best friend. That's where my mama learned all her magic, from Lulu."

Michelle pictured Lulu's sheets swaying in the breeze. Having grown up in the city, Michelle had never hung wash out, always relying on a dryer. Lulu seemed to live simple and die simple, Michelle thought, but nothing was ever as simple as it seemed. Michelle's mind went back to Pink's wife, Isabelle, the sheriff saying how she'd disappeared and that everyone believed Pink had killed her. Pink didn't seem capable of killing anyone, and it was obvious that Isabelle was very much alive. Those realizations perplexed Michelle, eroding her resolve over why she'd driven back to Ardenwood in the first place. She could hear Darcy's desperate plea for her to come back home.

She sat up straight in the seat, her breathing strained.

"You okay, Mrs. Stage?" Pink asked. "You look vexed."

"No, I'm fine."

Pink asked about her property. "Some kind of family estate or one of those vacation homes? Lots of folks from Atlanta own up here," Pink said. "What's that, a couple hours' drive? Worth it to get away from that damn humidity down there. I don't know how you stand it."

Michelle wasn't sure what to tell him; she hadn't thought it through. "Just a weekend getaway place," she said. "Up on Souder Hill."

When she looked over at Pink, he wore a queer expression. "Souder Hill?" he said, sounding surprised. "Well, ain't that something. When Isabelle and me were kids, our daddies owned that whole mountain up there." Pink held a proud but peculiar smile. "They was gonna mine sapphires. Never did though. Not that there wasn't gems to be had, but they was too lazy to take part in such an enterprise. It was their partner, Jim Beam, who talked them into it." Pink laughed, looking over at Michelle. She didn't get it.

"I owned a cabin up there a few years back. Built it myself. I used to be pretty handy with a hammer and saw. I'm not sure if I could stick two boards together with a nail gun now."

Michelle wondered if Cliff had spoken to Darcy. Would he drive up from Atlanta to get her? Did Darcy lie or just take her phone off the hook to avoid confrontation? Darcy did that all the time.

If Darcy had told him the truth, Cliff could already be on his way. Michelle couldn't chance getting out of Pink's Suburban at Lulu's house for fear Sheriff Fisk might recognize her as the crazy woman who'd been taken away in an ambulance a few days earlier.

"I know all that property up there," Pink said. "What road's your place on?"

"Hurst Road."

Pink seemed to be pondering the information, his eyes straight ahead. "Is your place near Pink Souder Road?" he finally said.

"Yes." She wanted to tell Pink they were headed to his cabin, wanted to see his expression when she told him where she lived, still unsure what she hoped to discover.

"I'm embarrassed to say that road was named after me," Pink said. "My mama's idea. Seems like every damn road around here's named after somebody, but I had nothing to do with it. Which place is yours?"

"204 Hurst Road."

For a few minutes Pink didn't say anything and Michelle wondered what was wrong, why he suddenly seemed distant. "That's my old place," Pink finally said, "the one I was telling you about."

Michelle was about to acknowledge that she already knew that but decided not to. "Really?" she said.

"Can I ask you something, Mrs. Stage?" Pink said, tugging at his ear lobe.

"Sure," she said, curious about his new somber tone.

Pink studied the rearview mirror a second then twisted toward her in the seat. "I know it's none of my business, but are you in trouble with the law?"

"No. Of course not." She wondered if Pink had heard about her being whisked away in an ambulance, if the story of the *crazy woman from Atlanta* had merited enough interest to make the local rumor mill. Could that account for the new reticence in his tone, the concern in his voice?

She shifted her gaze to the road. The pavement wound along a clear river strewn with large boulders and frothy riffles. A moment later, the road swept up a hill then curved down to the left away from the stream. She had never been on this road before.

Pink cleared his throat. She glanced over, lost in her own thoughts, not having noticed how quiet Pink had become. His eyes were fixed, his expression dull.

When they rounded the next turn, a waterfall white with cascades came into view.

"Wow," Michelle said. "That's beautiful."

"Ever been to Niagara Falls?" Pink asked.

"No."

"That's where I wanted to go on my honeymoon," Pink said. "And we would have if it hadn't been for Isabelle's mother."

Michelle turned to look at Pink.

"She killed herself. Blew her fool head off with a dang shotgun." Pink twisted up his mouth. "I don't know what was wrong with that woman. The day of our wedding, Isabelle's daddy came into the church, all covered in blood. He said Isabelle was Satan. Can you imagine that picture in the wedding album? He died a few years later in a tractor accident. Isabelle never even went to the funeral. I think that's why she's so sick, but she won't hear it. Screams at me, says I don't know what the hell I'm talking about."

"What's wrong with her?"

"Doctors aren't sure, but they ain't growed tired of taking my money for drugs and tests."

Michelle took her eyes back out the window, recognizing the Mountain View Cottages, Holman's Stone Sales, and Brenshaw Tool and Rental with the line of red tractors parked out front.

"Since we're going right past it anyway, do you mind if we drop the dog off at my mama's house on the way up to the cabin?"

"Sure, no problem." She pictured the dilapidated shack. Pink's mother had seemed full of vitality at Lulu's, and Michelle couldn't imagine her living in such a dump. Maybe she'd moved but still lived nearby.

When Pink pulled into the driveway, Michelle recognized the house immediately—the picket fence, the shutters, the wooden porch—but everything was cared for and fresh. She remembered the enormous tree in the front yard.

"That hemlock's over two hundred years old," Pink said, as if he'd read her thoughts. "Lots of old hemlocks up here, if the dang blight don't kill 'em all off." He reached across the seat and lifted Burrito from Michelle's arms. "I'll only be a minute. Do you need to use the facilities?"

"The what?" Michelle asked.

"The bathroom."

Michelle was about to say no but decided she wanted to see the inside of Mattie's house. "Sure."

Pink twisted the knob and walked in. "She always leaves the back door unlocked," Pink said. "I tell her it ain't like it used to be up here, with all the transients now, but she won't listen."

When Pink set Burrito down, the dog's nails slipped on the linoleum floor. "Bathroom's through there."

Remembering Pink's open admission that his mother was a witch, Michelle was surprised by the interior of the house. It was nothing like she expected. The very sound of the word *witch* brought to mind all sorts of queer objects—jars filled with strange roots and herbs, newts and lizards. She imagined cobwebs hanging from each rafter, a cauldron sitting off to one side. Instead there were framed prints on the walls with cosmic motifs—moon, planets, and stars—and a metal pentagram on the kitchen table, similar to the one she'd found at the cabin behind the toilet, along with four placemats and a bowl of fruit—bananas, apples, and pears. Nothing remarkable. In the bathroom she noticed some brightly colored stones then another that looked like a crystal and one the color of honey. Next to the soap dish was a plastic cup with a toothbrush and a tube of Crest.

Michelle quietly opened the medicine cabinet—Vicks, floss, lipstick, eyeliner, nail polish, hand cream, ointments and razors, deodorant. Attached to the glass was a dreamcatcher and next to it a stained-glass ornament of a dove, light from outside illuminating its wings. Above the toilet, a shelving unit filled with colorful towels—red, pink, and lavender. It could have been Darcy's condo.

Michelle bent over the sink and doused her face with cold water. *How could you know if you were crazy?* she thought. The answer that came back was more disturbing than the question: you couldn't. She studied her face in the mirror. It was gaunt and drawn and nothing like she remembered. Michelle undid her jeans and pushed them down past her knees, checking for the scar where she'd cut herself. She ran her finger over the raised skin, barely red, nearly healed. She felt reassured, until she realized that the only thing the fresh scar proved was that she'd been tromping around in the woods that night. Nobody had disputed that.

Burrito was waiting at the door when she opened it. "Come here, you," she said, picking him up. "Why don't I take you home with me?" She walked past a room, the door partially open, then looked toward the kitchen. When she heard Pink rustling through the kitchen drawers, she shouldered the door open and was peeking inside when Pink rushed down the hallway. "Shit! Don't go in there!" he shouted, pushing past her, slamming the door shut.

Michelle bristled with embarrassment.

"My mama's altar and stuff is in there," he said. "That's her sacred room. Nobody's allowed. Not even me."

"I'm sorry. The dog ran in there and . . . I was just . . ."

"Hell, I don't care. Throw a damn stag party in there for all I care. But if my mama came in and saw you, hell, she'd blow a vein in her head, end up like Lulu."

Pink didn't seem upset as he strolled back toward the kitchen.

Michelle set Burrito on the floor and shoved her hands in the back pockets of her jeans. "Hey, Pink. I was thinking that maybe—"

"Let's get up to that cabin of yours," he said. "I haven't seen that thing in years."

CHAPTER 13

When Emerson flipped the switch at the top of the steps, the lights flickered and flashed in the preparation room below, reminding Mattie of a mad scientist's laboratory from an old movie. Mattie followed Emerson down the stairs, her eyes pulling around the room, the cabinets along two walls, the slender drawers, the small silver table filled with shiny instruments. Machines and tubes occupied the countertops, while brown glass bottles lined the metal shelf above the sink. The stainless steel precision of it made her stiffen. In front of Mattie was a massive steel table, a fluorescent fixture buzzing above it. On the table was a body covered in a white sheet. She assumed it was Lulu.

She set the paper grocery sack on the marble tile floor next to the table and proceeded to roll back the sheet.

"Hold on there," Emerson said, grabbing Mattie's wrist. "What are you doing?"

"I want to look at her."

"She's been disrobed. She's not ready for viewing."

Mattie pushed his hand from her wrist and drew back the cover. "Where's her amulet? The one that was around her neck?" Mattie glared at Emerson.

"It's upstairs with everything else we removed."

Mattie rolled up her sleeves, pulled a brush from her grocery sack, and began stroking Lulu's hair. Emerson reached out again, this time with more urgency, jerking Mattie's hand from the body. The brush flew from her grip and spun across the floor like a propeller, coming to a stop along the far wall at the base of the cabinets. Mattie went over and picked it up. "Why did you do that?" she said.

"I'm sorry, Mattie, but I can't have you coming in here and combing out Lulu's hair." His features creased with annoyance. "There's laws and rules, and you can't just do whatever you want. Now, why don't we go back upstairs and fill out the paperwork so I can get Lulu's body somewhere cool so it doesn't decompose before we're done."

"There's no need of that, Emerson. I've brought her dress, her makeup, and when I'm done, you can cremate her, and I'll get her ashes in the morning."

Emerson scratched his head, then peered over at Mattie. "That's about the craziest damn thing I ever heard, Mattie Souder. Even if I could let you put that dress on her and make her up and all that, I couldn't have her ashes for you in the morning. I have to wait twenty-four hours to cremate the body, *any* body! That's the law!"

The buzzer went off, announcing that someone had entered the funeral parlor. "Wait here," Emerson told her, clearly upset by the diversion. "And don't touch anything." He hurried up the steps.

Mattie looked down at Lulu's face, her wrinkled neck, the mole near her mouth, what Lulu called her Marilyn Monroe mark. Lulu loved Marilyn Monroe, thought she would have made a good witch the way she had cast a spell over an entire nation—not to mention a president and a famous baseball player. Mattie recalled the day Lulu told her she was going to die. "It will be soon," Lulu had said.

"No, Lulu. You're still young."

Even as Mattie had spoken those words, she had never forgotten how old Lulu really was. Even though she looked to be in her sixties, Lulu had been born in 1877. Lulu had been the seventh of nine children. Her mother had been married only once for a period of less than five years. Most of her brothers and sisters, like Lulu, had been born out of wedlock.

A man that Lulu's mother introduced as her great uncle Johann Krieg had helped raise Lulu—taught her about alchemy, about the Ladder of the

Planets, First Matter, the Emerald Tablet, explaining the subtle levels of reality. He'd shown her how to mix elixirs, cure ailments, manipulate the normal processes of time. "It's not so much magic as using the hidden forces of the universe—forces that exist for anyone willing to look," Johann had told Lulu.

When Lulu was thirteen, her mother had shown her a handwritten book, *The Philosophia Visita,* with entries dated from the late sixteen-hundreds. Inside the book was an etched portrait of her uncle, along with documentation of his successes in transmuting mercury and sulfur into gold. Johann claimed to have been born in Vienna in 1605 and was an ancestor of Lulu's mother. Despite Johann's vibrant and youthful appearance, neither Lulu nor her mother ever doubted his claim, even though he should have been dead for at least two centuries.

Johann had warned Lulu about "puffers," chemists who were driven by greed and took a strictly materialistic approach to alchemy, eschewing the three levels of transformation—spirit, soul, and body—concentrating their efforts only on gross matter. "They are charlatans, operating purely from trickery."

"Why are they called puffers?" Lulu had asked.

"They are only interested in fanning their bellows, blowing air at their fires. They care not for the essential nuance of alchemy—the emotional and mental state of the alchemist himself—so they are always doomed to fail."

Mattie was certain that if Pink ever took an interest in magic, he would have become a puffer, interested only in the outcome, what was to be gained. Mattie often wondered if she herself was a puffer and worried that her own intentions were not pure, her mind and soul muddled. Lulu had assured her not to worry, that to even question her motives was a move toward clarity, toward transformation.

Johann had opened astonishing worlds to Lulu, things she could never have imagined.

"I'm ready to die" is what Lulu had told Mattie a month before she passed. Lulu had cheated death for years using the techniques Johann had taught her, techniques Lulu tried to pass on to Mattie. But Mattie lacked the strength to withstand the rapture, growing frightened, short of breath, and collapsing each time they tried.

"But you can live as long as you want," Mattie had told her, not attempting to hide the desperation in her voice. Lulu hugged her close and whispered, "It's not natural. It's destroying me in other ways." Johann had managed to live for over three hundred years, but Lulu knew the price for stealing life.

"I don't want to end up like them," Lulu had told her. "They live, but their eyes are dead."

Mattie was jogged from the memory when Emerson clopped down the steps, his thick soles echoing in the metallic space of the prep room.

"How soon can I get her ashes?" Mattie asked, thinking about the full moon two nights away.

"I don't know," Emerson said, shoving his hands deep in his pockets. "How about early next week?"

"Too late," Mattie said. "I need them day after tomorrow."

"Now, Mattie, I know you're grieving and all, and I know how much you loved Lulu, but I can't just—"

"Yes, you can, Emerson. You own the place. You can do whatever needs to be done. And this needs to be done."

Emerson twisted his mouth and stared over at Mattie. "Oh, all right. But that's it! You're not dressing her up or putting on any of that makeup or anything else." Emerson stood unmoving, fists on hips. "Besides, why would you want to do all that if she's going to be cremated? It makes no sense."

"What difference does it make to you, Emerson? You don't have to pay for the dress, or the makeup, and I'm doing all the work. So why don't you go back up to your office while I take care of things down here."

Emerson turned red. "You can't do that, Mattie!"

"Nobody but you and me will ever know."

"Well, hell, Mattie. You're 'bout as stubborn as a dang possum." Emerson glared toward the closed door at the other end of the preparation room. "Let's at least get her over there into the dressing room." He scratched his head, shaking it from side to side. "Where the hell are all the dad-blame gurneys!"

CHAPTER 14

Pink took a right turn at the end of Pink Souder Road and headed up the mountain in the direction of the cabin. He told Michelle how he'd built it for Isabelle, how Isabelle had fallen sick a few months after they moved in, and how he'd sold it a year later.

"That cabin's probably sold five times since I built it. Loudon told me some folks from Atlanta . . ." Pink started to say then stopped, looking in her direction before taking his eyes back to the road.

"So you heard," Michelle said. "I'm the crazy woman from Atlanta."

"I don't judge," Pink said.

"Everybody judges, Pink." When they rounded the turn, Michelle shook her head. "Damn." A Range Rover sat in the driveway. Cliff stood at the railing of the deck, looking out over the mountains. She knew he'd come; she just hadn't expected him to get here so soon. She'd been careful to not use credit cards or an ATM. Darcy must have told him after all. She needed more time, time without Cliff hounding her.

"Just keep driving, please," Michelle said, slinking down in the seat.

"Are you okay? You look kind of—"

"I'm fine. Just go."

Pink accelerated up the hill and made a left onto a dirt road then drove about a mile or so before he pulled over and stopped. When he rolled the electric windows down, fresh air swept across Michelle's face. She felt defeated. How could she learn anything with Cliff trying to get her back home? "Maybe you should take me back to my car."

"Are you sure?" Pink said.

"I haven't been honest with you," she said. "And I'm sorry. Please take me back."

"Hell, it don't matter. I've been known to spin a tale or two myself." Pink's eyes met hers for only a moment before he opened the door and stepped out onto the gravel road. "Come with me," he said. "I want to show you something."

Michelle caught up to Pink and walked alongside him. Winding up a steep hill, they followed the path along a ridge that gave way to a view of the entire valley, mountains repeating themselves infinitely against a flawless blue sky.

Michelle wondered where she would stay tonight. An uneasiness began to unravel in her, and for a moment she had no idea what she was doing or where she was, and everything in her life seemed wrong, as though the details of her existence belonged to someone else.

She stopped in the middle of the path, her head pounding. In less than twenty-four hours she'd become a stranger in her own life. Just yesterday, she'd helped Darcy stock supplements and soymilk—then had stolen Darcy's car and her gun. The gun. Had she left it on the kitchen table next to the apples she'd bought at the grocery store? Cliff would go crazy finding the gun. And Darcy, what would she say to Cliff? Would Darcy be in trouble with the police? Was the gun even registered? Michelle felt something tighten inside. She bent over and threw up in the weeds.

Pink came to her side. "You look like hell. Maybe I better get you to the hospital."

"No, I'll be all right. Give me a second." She squatted down and sat back on her heels then wiped her mouth. When she tried to stand, Pink took her arm to steady her. "Let's keep walking," she said. "I feel better now."

"You don't look better. You're white as soap."

"I'm okay. Really."

Pink led the way through the woods. She stayed close to Pink as they traversed a wide log that crossed the creek. On the other side they climbed a hill of car-size boulders to a waterfall over seventy-five feet high. Michelle couldn't believe she'd never known about this amazing place so close to the cabin.

Michelle spied something in the treetops about thirty yards away, some kind of structure. "What's that?" she asked, pointing.

He nodded and motioned for her to follow. When they got closer, she could see boards attached between the trees, like a walkway of some kind, high up among the branches. Pink stopped beneath the rickety framework. Michelle's eyes followed the boards through the limbs until they disappeared over the ridge.

"What is it?" she asked.

"A path," Pink said.

He walked several yards and studied the trees, pulling at a ladder of boards nailed to one of the trunks. He put one foot on the bottom rung then pulled himself up by the next until he'd climbed to the top. Soon he was standing on the platform twenty feet above her.

"Come on up," Pink said. "If it'll hold me, it'll surely hold you."

Michelle climbed the wooden rungs and stood next to Pink on the narrow boards. The wood was weathered and seemed a bit rotten. "Is this safe?" she asked.

"I don't know," he said, leaning against the tree, his eyes drifting out over the valley.

"This is amazing," she said. "If you keep showing me these marvels, I'm going to run out of adjectives."

Pink laughed a little, then smiled. "I'm clean out of marvels, Mrs. Stage. I done showed you everything I got." Pink turned from her and picked his way along the boards, stepping carefully as he walked from tree to tree, holding onto branches and limbs. She followed. Pink was at least ten yards away from her now, walking the boards like a tightrope. Farther ahead, Michelle could see that someone had fashioned a rope railing along both sides of the wooden path. Pink waited for her, holding both ropes.

She looked down and saw a squirrel hopping along the branch beneath her.

"I should have put up more ropes," said Pink.

"You built this?" she asked.

"When Isabelle was twelve, she told me that when she died she wanted to come back as a squirrel because they could run through the treetops and never had to touch the ground. I built this path so she wouldn't be in such a hurry to die. It's held up better than Isabelle or me."

"She must have loved it," Michelle said.

"We had fun up here," Pink said. "You wouldn't have believed how beautiful she was then. She made me want to live forever, halfway made me believe I could." Pink looked over at Michelle, surprised, as if he'd forgotten she was there.

"Aw, hell. Listen to me going on," he said. "You got your own problems."

"Isabelle must be crazy about you," she said.

Pink scratched his cheek. "I don't think she's crazy about anything anymore," he said. "We should get going."

When they got back to the Suburban, Pink started looking under the front seat then leaned over the back and searched under some newspapers, visibly perplexed. Michelle slid in across from him.

"Can't find my camera," Pink said. "Clarence probably has it. He takes pictures of his dang feet to check the progress of his fungus."

"Fungus?" Michelle turned in the seat to see what Pink was doing.

"I'm sorry. I've got to go back and get the camera. I can't list your property without a picture."

"It's okay. I'm in no hurry." That wasn't true. With Cliff here now, time had become a precious commodity. She needed to ask Pink about the cabin, about Isabelle, about everything Sheriff Fisk had told her, but couldn't figure out how to broach the subject without sounding like a mental case. She wasn't even sure there was anything to know. After all, she was running on memories and speculations. All she really knew was this wasn't the life she'd been living before she'd gone down the mountainside.

Pink slowed as he passed the cabin. "Looks like that feller is gone," he said. "Want to stop?"

"No, let's go back to your office." Pink had to know she'd lied about wanting him to see the property, and that embarrassed her. "The path in the trees was magical," she said.

Pink glanced across the seat. "Magic might be the only thing holding it up."

*****

The drive back to town went by quickly.

"What the hell is going on?" Pink said.

Michelle looked up, amazed they were already at Pink's office. Three police cars sat angled in front, lights flashing, partially blocking one of the lanes. In the middle of the fray sat a green Range Rover and Darcy's Explorer, the police cars blocking them in. Cliff was talking to the police.

"Please don't stop," Michelle said.

Pink switched off the blinker and accelerated. After they drove through an intersection, Pink made a right turn toward the highway and told Michelle the coast was clear.

"Shit." Michelle sat up and looked back at the police surrounding her car.

"Husband or something? Not that it's any of my business."

"Yeah." Michelle said. If Cliff had called the police, Darcy must have told him about the gun. Why wouldn't he at least give her a chance to explain? Cliff was a stranger to her now. The old Cliff would never have called the police. Did he tell them the Explorer was stolen?

A sign above the highway read *Dedmonson, 49 miles.* "Why are we going there?" Michelle glanced over her shoulder, then back at Pink. "What's in Dedmonson?"

"Nothing," Pink said. "I'm just driving till you had a chance to gather yourself."

"Pull over," Michelle said, suddenly antsy. "I'm sorry, pull over. Please."

Pink veered the Suburban to the shoulder. Michelle popped the door open and got out. Maybe she could hitchhike to Dedmonson, but what would be the point of that? What would she do in Dedmonson? She'd have to rent a car. But where did she have to go? The only man who could possibly have any answers for her was sitting in the seat of the Suburban like a rosy-cheeked Buddha. She got back in the vehicle and closed the door.

"Pink?"

He swiveled his head toward her. "Yes, ma'am?"

"Would you take me to a motel?"

*****

The Ruby Motel was constructed in the shape of an L, two levels, thirty units, and a clean-looking pool with no water. Folded lawn chairs leaned against the fence.

"Is this okay?" Pink said. The man inside waved. Pink raised a hand, bringing his eyes back to Michelle. "I could take you up to the highway to one of them chains, Comfort Inn, Days Inn, Hampton Inn. My buddy Ed owns this, keeps it real clean, and he'll treat you right. I bring folks here who want to spend a few days looking at real estate. Affordable rates and all the amenities . . . except hi-speed internet. If you need a computer, I have a few at my office you can use."

Michelle was leery of Pink's kindness, even though it seemed genuine. Why wasn't he asking questions? He'd not said a word about the cabin, Cliff, or the police, just drove to the Ruby Motel and now sat patiently waiting, the engine running, for her to decide if this would work. Was he expecting sex? Did he think that she had troubles and would be an easy mark?

"I didn't mean anything when I said Ed had affordable rates," Pink said, "just that some of these chains charge more than they should for the use of four walls, a bed, and toilet. I'm sure you . . ."

"This is fine, Mr. Souder." She called him by his last name to reinstate a more formal relationship in case he had other ideas. "Thank you."

She got out and held the door. She didn't want him to leave but was afraid if she asked him to stay it would send the wrong message. But finding him was the reason she'd returned to Ardenwood. That, and hopes of seeing the dusk-to-dawn light again, which would be impossible now that Cliff was at the cabin.

"Would you mind waiting until I see if he has any rooms?"

"Ed always has rooms. But I can wait. I'll pull over there."

Michelle went in the office. The man smiled and pulled a clipboard and pen from under the counter. "Just your name. Don't worry about the rest of that stuff. Cash or credit card?"

Michelle opened her purse and saw the gun. She was relieved she hadn't left it on the table for Cliff to find. She tilted the bag away from the man and pulled her wallet out, sliding some cash across the counter.

He slid the money into a cash drawer. "I hear there's a big snowstorm coming," he said. "Almost May and they're talking about snow. Can you believe it? If you get caught here, I'll discount the room."

"Thank you."

"Here you go, ma'am."

Michelle looked up at the clerk and took the remote from his hand. "What's this for?"

"Television. Needed a new battery." He handed her the room key attached to an old-fashioned green plastic diamond with the numeral 7 incised in white. "Ice machine is in that back breezeway down from your room. Let me know if you need anything."

It felt strange not having a suitcase or two to throw on the bed and unpack. All her clothes were at the cabin.

Pink appeared in the doorway of her motel room, hands in pockets. "This going to work?"

"Yes, fine. Can you come in a second?"

"Just for a bit. Clarence'll forget to lock the dang office when he leaves if I'm not there."

Michelle closed the door and motioned for Pink to sit at the small round table.

"I feel I owe you some explanation," she said.

"None of my business, ma'am. I'm just a real estate salesman with a funny name and a weight problem. Folks is dealt all kinds of hands, none of them easy."

She wanted to leave it at that, but there wasn't time.

"My husband's up here to take me back to Atlanta," Michelle said.

Pink nodded as if he understood, leaving his arms lashed over his belly. "But you have your own car, don't you?"

"It's my sister's. She . . . lent it to me." Michelle hated to keep lying, but she needed Pink to listen, and if he thought she was crazy, he might just leave. He nodded again, this time leaning forward, his elbows on the table as if waiting for a supper plate to be set between his thick wrists.

"I need to tell you the story and would like for you to listen until I finish, okay?" Michelle said.

He nodded again.

Michelle took a deep breath before she started.

"Last week, my husband and I drove up from Atlanta to spend some time at the cabin, your cabin, the one you built. We got there late and I was tired, so I went to bed. Cliff is restless and has a hard time getting to sleep and decided to go out on the deck for fresh air. I guess I dozed off, because a short while later I woke up and heard him rustling through the drawers in the kitchen. I asked him what he was doing. He said he was looking for a flashlight. Then he told me to get up, that he wanted to show me something.

"A few minutes later I'm standing on the deck in my nightgown looking down the dark mountainside. I could barely focus my eyes. He directed my attention to a light down through the tangle of trees and limbs. I shrugged and said so what. He became very agitated, saying that there wasn't supposed to be light down there. Cliff was convinced there was a house below us, that the light was one of those driveway lights, you know . . . ?"

"One them dusk-to-dawn lights," Pink said. "That would have been my mama's place. You remember. Why did that bother him?"

Michelle had to think a moment before she spoke. "Um, it wasn't over toward her place. It was more toward the south, I guess. In that direction."

"There's nobody lives below you in that direction," Pink said. "That's all my mama's property almost to the highway."

"Okay, well anyway, Cliff was really angry saying that the real estate agent who sold us the property had lied to him, that she had told him that there was nobody living within miles of the cabin, that it was very secluded—"

"Sherri Franklin," Pink said.

"What?" Michelle said.

"Sherri Franklin," Pink repeated. "She'd shave her head and dress up like one of them Hare Krishnas if she thought she could sell you prayer beads and a stick of incense."

"Oh."

"That's who sold you the house. Sherri had the listing."

Michelle couldn't recall the woman's name and didn't care.

"Okay." Michelle cleared her throat before she continued. "Well, Cliff was so upset, he got in our car and drove down there to check on it. I went back to bed. A while later he came back and stood out on the deck, staring down the mountain. I found my robe and went out. He looked like he'd seen a ghost. I asked him what was wrong, and he pointed down the hill. He said, 'It's not there.' I asked him what wasn't there? He told me he drove all over down there and saw nothing. He couldn't find anything. 'But there it is,' he said, pointing at the light through the trees. I could see it too. We heard noises, like people talking and closing doors and such."

"Your husband must be a bit persnickety," Pink said, his brow squeezed to ridges.

"Yes, he can be intense at times. Anyway, Cliff decided to go down the mountainside toward the light—"

"On foot? In the dark? He a hunter or something?"

"No, not really."

"Well, that's insane. Folks not used to this area get lost in broad daylight. At night . . . well, hell . . ." Pink laughed a little, shaking his head.

"Anyway, I went back to bed, and the next morning when I woke, I saw Cliff wasn't there. I thought maybe he went for a walk, but when he wasn't back by noon, I called the police."

"He got himself lost," Pink said. "I'm telling you, not hard to do around here."

"Sheriff Fisk showed up with his deputy—"

"Elmer? Elmer Bogan."

"I believe so. Anyway, they searched for him, even had some men come out with dogs—"

"Yeah, them dogs could find Sasquatch in a snowstorm. That how they found your husband?"

"No, actually the dogs had the trail for a while, but lost it. Sheriff Fisk even had a helicopter come out and search the area." Michelle left out the part about the disappearing house. It was too strange, and she was never sure if the sheriff had really understood what the pilot was saying. After all, it had been very noisy with the craft right above them.

"So that night I went down the hill to find Cliff."

"By yourself?" Pink said. "That's gutsy, ma'am. Though probably a might early for rattlesnakes. But still, gutsy."

Rattlesnakes. Michelle had no idea there were rattlesnakes up there. "So I worked my way down the mountainside until I came to a cabin that looked exactly like the one we own . . . the one you built . . ."

"Yeah, that don't surprise me none," Pink said. "You can get turned ass-side-up in these woods even in the daylight. You just came round on yourself and ended up where you started. It happens when you're lost . . . or in the dark."

Michelle paused a moment. "I don't think that's what happened."

Pink's expression soured, but he listened quietly as Michelle continued.

"Anyway, the queerest thing is that Sheriff Fisk's car was there, and when Cliff opened the door, he was relieved to see me . . ."

"So Fisk found him and brought him back?" Pink said. "Where'd your husband end up? Down by the highway? Keep heading down the mountain and eventually you come to the—"

"No . . . Sheriff Fisk didn't find him. At that point it seems Cliff was never lost. But everything had changed. He had a scar on his forehead that had never been there before, and one of his fingers was missing from an apparent car accident that happened a year earlier. And even though Sheriff Fisk was inside with Cliff, he didn't recognize me from only a few hours earlier . . ." She paused her story to study Pink's eyes for signs of skepticism. Pink sat stone-faced as a professional gambler with a royal flush.

"They said I was the one who had gone missing," Michelle said. "That they had been looking for me all that time, and that Cliff had never gone down the mountainside or searched for any light."

Michelle didn't tell Pink what the sheriff had said about him killing his wife, about the authorities digging up the yard searching for the body, about Pink and his mother disappearing. She also didn't tell him about Cassie. It was too painful, too dangerous to acknowledge that aspect to another person, as if talking about her death could make it real.

Pink stared at the wall behind her head. "Why doesn't your husband remember hiking down the mountain?" Pink finally asked after a long silence.

Was Pink trying to punch holes in her story, make her see how ridiculous it all was? Yet he seemed genuinely perplexed by the riddle, as was she.

"I don't know," she said. "He claims to remember nothing about any light either."

"Well, I know there's nobody below your cabin on my mama's road because like I told you before, she owns all that land," Pink said. "There may be somebody below her land, but it would be a long way off."

The way Pink was talking—as if he believed her—put her at ease, but there was more to tell him and she wanted to get it over with. "When I rode down there with the sheriff and deputy—"

"You're talking about Loudon and Elmer again, right?"

She nodded.

"Well, hell, I'll talk to Fisk and see what he remembers . . ."

"No. You can't. I mean . . . that won't work," Michelle said, trying to smother the urgency from her voice. "They don't remember any of it either. Cliff talked to them at the hospital. They said they'd never seen me before."

Pink's expression changed from hopeful to strained, as if he'd bitten into something sour. When he toggled his head back and forth, she knew she'd lost him. She'd been hoping for validation, a knowing smirk, a shrewd glint to his eye, something to betray his complicity. But it was obvious none of this made any sense to him.

Michelle felt something give way inside her, like a faulty wall collapsing.

"So, what you're saying is, Loudon and Elmer remember looking for you but don't remember looking for your husband. That about right?"

Michelle didn't like the severe look Pink had attached to his question, or the tone with which he'd asked it. She got up and walked to the door.

"Never mind," she said, opening the door. "Thanks for everything."

"Look," he said, twisting in his chair. "These woods around here can be vexing. Easy for folks to get turned around and confused, think they see things that ain't there. Me and Clarence been out coon hunting on nights so dark and disorienting I could get myself lost in my own backyard. I don't know what happened to you that night, but I'm sure there's a reasonable explanation."

Michelle held the door and looked at the parking lot. A woman crossed the pavement with her young daughter, holding the child's hand. The little girl dangled a tiny yellow purse from her free hand, and Michelle missed Cassie more than ever. "Please, just go."

Pink stood and hitched up his trousers. "I'm sorry, ma'am. You seem disappointed in me, like I was supposed to have something for you and didn't. And I can't think what it would be." He stepped past Michelle and ambled across the parking lot.

Michelle closed the door and sat on the edge of the bed, her open purse next to her, the gun barrel aimed at the ceiling.

CHAPTER 15

Pink had never been lost in the woods, day or night, sober or drunk. He'd lied about the coon hunting hoping it would make her feel better. Truth was never as comforting as lies. Obviously, his lies hadn't helped her though. He couldn't deny he was attracted to her, and he wished he'd been able to provide her with whatever it was she was so desperately seeking. A gift like that might be rewarded with unbridled gratitude. He'd gotten a little aroused when she'd asked him to stay a few minutes, even though he was fairly certain sex wasn't part of the offer. Her story was strange, but no stranger than most stories he'd heard from the lips of women. And he knew she was in some kind of trouble and that maybe she was dangerous by the gun she was trying to hide in her purse—although she hadn't done a very good job of concealing it with her bag hanging open like the jaws of an old catfish.

The police cars were gone when Pink got to the office. Mrs. Stage's Explorer was still there. If she was telling the truth—that her husband planned to take her back to Atlanta—then why hadn't Loudon towed her vehicle? Was Fisk planning some kind of trap, leaving the Explorer as bait? Pink laughed to himself and looked over toward the strip of stores, the Subway sandwich shop, Tom and Lois's Family Restaurant, the office supply store. Pink pictured Loudon and Elmer parked by the dumpster behind the stores, engine running, lights off, waiting for the signal to race out and nab Mrs.

Stage. But Loudon and Elmer weren't idiots or small-town hick cops who weren't allowed to carry bullets. Loudon and Elmer had serious jobs, breaking up theft rings, dragging dead bodies from the bottom of Burtran Lake, raiding meth labs, dangerous work that meant putting their lives on the line. But Pink still couldn't help chuckling to himself imagining the headline, "Sheriff Fisk and Deputy Bogan of Ardenwood apprehend the notorious Mrs. Stage during a dramatic bust in front of the Pink Souder Real Estate office."

It would be good advertising, Pink thought. He checked his desk for messages then walked back to Clarence's office to find his digital camera on a stack of papers next to Clarence's antifungal spray. Pink switched it on and perused the photos, clicking through shot after shot of Clarence's toes.

He stuck the camera in his pocket, realizing he didn't need to take pictures of Michelle's cabin. He wasn't going to list it. That wasn't why she was here.

Pink turned out the office lights and locked the front door. He thought about driving around behind Subway and seeing if Loudon and Elmer were back there. He slipped the key in the ignition and an odd notion hit him: if Mrs. Stage was a lunatic being hounded by her husband and the police, why had she come to his office in the first place? It made no sense. Did insane women on the lam suddenly feel the urge to sell property? Besides, he was fairly sure she had known the cabin had been his even before he told her. There were things she'd left out, like her reason for wanting to know so much about him.

He thought about stopping at the Ruby Motel, telling Michelle that the Explorer was at the office. He imagined her shock when he'd show up at the door. Maybe she wouldn't even recognize him and start screaming or crying and Ed would have to call Loudon to calm her down. Pink wasn't sure what a crazy woman would do, even though he'd lived with Isabelle all these years. He should be an expert by now. But he had difficulty believing Michelle Stage was crazy. Scared maybe, even angry and distrustful. But not crazy.

The evening was starting to cool as Pink pulled into his driveway. Isabelle had the windows open, the curtains sucking in and blowing out like the whole house was straining for breath. It was eerie. He wondered if she was asleep and had forgotten to close them. She didn't like the cold and certainly wouldn't have welcomed the crisp evening breeze.

Isabelle was seated at the kitchen table eating a bowl of soup when he walked in.

"Feeling better today, Turtledove?"

"No. And stop calling me those idiotic names. You haven't called me Isabelle in over ten years. Do you know that?"

Pink didn't know and didn't care. He couldn't stand the sickly sight of her, especially now, dragging her mysterious germs through the house, infecting the table and chairs, the couch cushions, the canned goods. He'd have to call Claire to come over and disinfect everything.

"Where have you been all day?" she asked.

"Working to pay for this palace, Honey Pie."

"Bullshit. Clarence said you left with some woman before lunch and never came back."

"Clarence. What does he know? He's got fungus on the brain."

"Were you with Claire? Was Clarence covering for you?"

How dumb would that be, Pink thought, covering up one affair with another? But then that would be like Clarence to cover a bad situation with a worse one.

"I was showing property. Some rich woman with deep Atlanta pockets wanted a mountain retreat for her and hubby."

Isabelle grimaced, shaking her head. "Stop it, Pink. My illness has got me weak, not stupid. I know you can't keep that tiny peter of yours in your pants, but you best not be poking it in Claire. I mean it. Kenny won't put up with it. He'll shoot you dead and go for beer to celebrate."

"I'm glad you care so much about me, Sweet Potato."

"Fuck you, Pink!" The bowl flew across the kitchen, crashing against the refrigerator. Some kind of red soup trickled down the olive-colored door.

"That's why we don't have nice things, Doe Eyes," Pink said, walking to the sink, grabbing a dishcloth to wipe up the mess. He cupped the ceramic shards in his palm and dumped them in the trash can. The red soup reminded him of blood, and he couldn't stand the sight of it. The most blood he'd ever seen was on Isabelle's father's hands at the wedding. From the altar it looked as if Ruther had been wearing red gloves. Pink could still see the smeared blood on the floor where people had tracked through it exiting the church. From that moment, Pink felt his marriage to Isabelle had been cursed. Maybe they shouldn't have married. Maybe Isabelle's mother had been right, that God would condemn a marriage between kin, even if they were only second cousins.

Pink wasn't sure he believed in God and didn't like thinking about any being having that much power hitched to that much attitude. It was too intimidating, especially for someone who took such great delight in sin as Pink did.

"Your new girlfriend called," Isabelle said.

Pink turned from the towel rack. Isabelle was hoisting herself from the chair, pushing at the edge of the table to steady herself. The hem of her nightgown was loose, dragging along the linoleum floor. He had bought her a new one, but she refused to wear it, said the color was wrong, that he should give it to his mother. "It's Mattie that likes purple, not me," she'd told him.

"Who called?" Pink asked, following behind Isabelle.

"I didn't ask her fucking name, Pink. She said she wanted to talk to you. When I asked her for a phone number, she gave me the Ruby Motel. It took her a few minutes to figure out what goddamn room she was in. What is it that attracts you to bimbos, Pink? Are they better in bed, or just easier to fool?"

CHAPTER 16

Michelle had been trying Darcy's phone number for the past hour, getting the machine. She'd ordered pizza and managed to eat one slice before closing the box. She dialed Darcy again.

Darcy answered on the third ring.

"Hey, Darcy, it's me. Michelle."

"Michelle, I was hoping you would call. Where are you?"

"Uh . . . The Ruby Motel. In Ardenwood."

"Are you okay?"

"Yeah, I'm fine. I'm just a little dizzy. Hey, I'm sorry about your car," Michelle said.

"Don't worry about the car. I'm worried about you. Come home and forget all this nonsense."

Nonsense? Darcy hadn't called it nonsense before. Mostly she'd said nothing, just listened attentively, but never lashed out. *Nonsense.* It hurt Michelle more than she wanted to admit. Who would believe her? Did she even believe herself anymore? Here she was in the Ruby Motel, no clothes, no car, unable to eat, and for what? How could she be right and everyone else wrong? Was everyone lying? Her own sister, Sheriff Fisk, Deputy Bogan. Even Pink Souder? Had Cliff put them all up to this? The most passionate conspiracy theorists wouldn't touch that one. It was insane, and the realization dropped Michelle to the floor. She let go of the phone and thought she saw it roll under the bed, but how was that possible? Cell phones didn't roll. The television came on, blaring into her ears, filling the room with laughter. She called out to Darcy but it was too late; Michelle was in a free fall now, grabbing at thin air . . .

"Michelle," a man's voice said. "Michelle!"

The hallucination evaporated. Michelle focused on Pink first, then Ed, then rolled over and puked off the side of the bed. "Get the trashcan, Ed," Pink said. "And a wet washcloth." She felt Pink's hand on her back, a gentle touch below her bra strap. He rubbed his hand in circles the way she used to rub Cassie's back at nap time when Cassie was a baby. The washcloth was cool on Michelle's neck and the urge to vomit passed. She didn't remember passing out.

"I'll get a mop to clean this up," Ed told Pink. "Why don't you move her over to room nine. It's clean."

Michelle looked around the room for her handbag. Pink had it tucked under his arm. "Can you get to your feet?" Pink asked. She nodded, wondering if Pink had seen her gun.

The room continued spinning as Pink helped her to a sitting position. She saw Ed come in with a mop.

"I'm really sorry," Michelle said, wiping her mouth with the washcloth.

"You should see these rooms after prom night," Ed said, chuckling. "No problem, Mrs. Stage. Let Pink there help you into nine. It has a good battery in the remote."

Pink switched on the light then escorted her to the bed. "Best to stay upright when you got the spins." He removed her shoes, setting them on the floor.

"What are you doing here?" Michelle had no idea what time it was.

"Isabelle said you called."

Michelle remembered now. She'd lied to Ed, said she needed to talk to Pink before morning. Ed probably would have given her the home number without the lie, but she didn't want to chance it; a lie that came after the truth always sounded like a lie.

"I don't know what happened. I was talking to my sister in Atlanta and I blacked out."

"I heard you moaning and had Ed open the door," Pink said. "I knocked first and was afraid . . . just wanted to make sure you were okay."

Michelle felt the room slowing down and looked over at Pink. "Did you believe anything I told you before?"

Pink pulled at the bedspread with his thumb and forefinger, releasing the material, then grasping it again until he'd made a formidable wrinkle along the surface, which he then tried to smooth out. "Why does that matter? I'm nobody. Who cares if I believe you or not? I know you got troubles. And if I can help, I'd like to."

Michelle got up to go to the bathroom. "Do you have a few minutes, or is Isabelle waiting for you? I hope I didn't cause trouble for you at home."

"Have you eaten today?" Pink asked.

"A piece of pizza."

"Let's go," Pink said. "We can talk over dinner."

*****

Michelle expected a Sizzler steak house or a Denny's, not a deserted mansion in the middle of nowhere. The building sat alone at the top of a steep hill. On the drive up, they passed an apartment complex and a few houses, but for the last mile or so there had been nothing but trees and pavement, and at the end, even the pavement ran out, leaving a rutted gravel road.

The structure was a dark monolith in the center of an even darker parking lot with several SUVs and pickup trucks parked near the entrance. Pink pulled a plastic Coke bottle filled with clear liquid from the back seat.

"What is this place?" she asked.

"The Hilltop. Private club. When George finishes, it'll be the finest B & B around. Right now, he's just got the Hilltop Club opened. George has vision."

They walked to a side entrance. Music rolled up the stairwell to meet them as they descended beneath ground level. Pink held the door for Michelle, then guided her through the crowd with his hand on her back. They took a table near the stage. The Hilltop Club had the ambience of a hotel lounge—colored lights, bar signs, live music—but without that transient feel of misplaced travelers trying to drink away loneliness. The Hilltop felt like a celebration. People danced and laughed, and Michelle would never have imagined a place like this anywhere near Ardenwood.

A man walked up to the table, and Pink introduced him as George. George smiled and placed two empty glasses in front of them, along with two menus, then disappeared back into the crowd.

When George came back, he picked up the Coke bottle Pink had brought. He held it up to a light then shook it and inspected it. "Lyman's?" he asked Pink. "Looks to be over a hundred proof. Have you tried it?"

"Help yourself," Pink said, his eyes darting around the crowd.

George unscrewed the cap, hoisted the bottle, and swigged it back. "Smooth."

"Let Michelle have a taste," Pink said.

George handed the bottle to her, but she didn't want to try it. "Maybe later."

"Finest corn liquor around," George said. "Nobody makes it like Lyman."

Michelle asked how he could tell it was over a hundred proof by looking at it.

George took the bottle and screwed the cap back on, then shook it. He squatted down next to Michelle's chair and held the bottle still, the liquid-line level with her eyes, and told her to watch. In seconds, bubbles formed along the top edge of the liquid. Michelle kept watching, unsure what she was looking for.

"See how the bubbles are big and ride the top of that line? That means it's over a hundred proof. If they stay small and hang from the bottom of the line, it's less than a hundred."

Pink took the bottle from George, undid the cap, and poured both glasses full. "I don't need proof of proof," Pink said. "Just keep pouring."

George took their order. Pink brought the glass to his lips and downed it then poured another.

"I didn't know you could bring your own liquor into a bar," Michelle said.

"That's the only way you're gonna drink liquor around here. Dry county.

George charges for the table, the food, and the glasses. He does all right." Pink tilted back the glass and seemed to be more patient with his second drink.

A man walked over to the table. "Who's this pretty lady with you tonight, Pink?" He stood over them with the longest legs Michelle had ever seen, his enormous belt buckle level with the top of her head. Pink introduced the man as Lyman. "Howdy, ma'am." He took her outstretched hand and gave it one down and up tug, as if he were opening the latch on a gate. "Nice to make your acquaintance."

Pink finished what little was left in his glass and poured another. Lyman eyed Michelle's glass suspiciously then asked why she hadn't touched it yet. She assured him she would, but she wanted to eat something first.

"Well, let's have us a dance while you're waiting on George to burn your dinner."

"No, thank you. I think I—"

"Go on, Michelle," Pink said. "The only thing Lyman does better than make corn liquor is the two-step."

Michelle hadn't danced in years and had never done the two-step, but before she could protest again, Lyman had her on the dance floor. He showed her the steps, how to move. Michelle was amazed how fluid the large man was.

"So how is it one gets so good at dancing and making corn liquor?" Michelle asked. "Or is that a secret?"

"Yes, ma'am, that is a bit of a secret. But I can tell you how to make corn liquor." Lyman laughed and spun her around.

Michelle had almost forgotten how morose she'd been at the motel earlier that evening, how much she'd wanted to die. Anytime she thought Cliff's reality might be the only one, the right one, she lost all energy for life. The only one? The right one? How many realities are there? she thought, feeling stupid for having asked the question of herself. *There's one, Michelle,* a voice came back inside her head. *One reality per person, that's all you get.* It was only during these brief moments of normalcy, like dancing or swimming laps or driving with the windows down, that Michelle even questioned the night Cliff disappeared. She wondered if it actually *had* happened, if she had scrambled down the hill in the dark following some mysterious light. Then there was Darcy's voice on the phone earlier, asking Michelle to come home. What would Darcy think if she saw Michelle two-stepping at the Hilltop with a moonshiner named Lyman? How real was this?

When the song ended, Lyman escorted Michelle back to the table and thanked her for the dance. Pink smiled and pushed the plate toward her. "The finest ostrich burger in all of Ardenwood. How was your dance?"

"Good," Michelle said, sipping the liquor Pink had put in front of her. She couldn't believe how jumpy she was over what she had to say to Pink. She felt like a smashed watch—the cogs, gears, and springs exposed. She drained the glass, and the sting of the liquid spread through her sinuses. Pink handed her a glass of water. "Whew, it's really strong," she said, downing the water.

"Pink," Michelle began. "There are things I didn't tell you earlier, things I need you to hear. But they'll sound even crazier than the other stuff. And if you couldn't believe that, then . . ."

"Hell, Mrs. Stage, if you got something you need me to hear . . . well, I'll listen. Maybe it ain't about me believing anything. Maybe it's about you needing to say some things, get 'em off your chest."

"This isn't easy to say, Mr. Souder. It's about the night my husband, Cliff, disappeared. Remember how I told you about Cliff going down the mountain looking for the light—"

"I thought you said you were the one that went down the mountain in the dark," Pink said. "Isn't that what you told me?"

Michelle stuttered a bit. "Well, that's how it ended up, I guess. But originally Cliff was missing—"

"This here is a dad-blamed difficult yarn to follow," Pink said, taking a drink of corn liquor.

"I know it is," she said. "But remember how I said I called the police and Sheriff Fisk arrived with—"

"Elmer. Yep."

"Yes, Elmer," Michelle said. She glanced down at her hands, then back to Pink. She tried to settle herself before speaking. "Well, Sheriff Fisk told me a story about how the state police had dug up the entire yard at the cabin, at your cabin . . ."

Pink jerked backward, his expression dark. "Why would he tell you such a thing? That never happened . . . Why would they dig up the yard at my cabin?"

"They were looking for a body—"

"A body!" Pink shouted. Heads turned toward their table. "Whose body?"

"Isabelle's."

Pink's eyes pressed to slits, cutting fat creases across his cheeks. "Why the hell would Loudon go and say a fool thing like that? He's lost his cotton-pickin' mind. I'm gonna have a talk with—"

"He won't remember saying it," Michelle told Pink. "He didn't say it here . . . in this . . . oh, never mind. He wouldn't remember, that's all, so there's no use talking to him."

Pink sat a moment, glaring at the floor. "Let me get this straight. You said your husband doesn't remember any of this, and Loudon and Elmer don't remember any of this, but you do."

The statement was more accusation than question. It made Michelle uncomfortable.

"How was she supposed to have died?" Pink asked. "Who buried her there?"

Michelle gulped down the last of her corn liquor, thinking about the bubbles, hundred proof. Proof. That's what she lacked. "Everyone thought you did, Pink. They believed you killed Isabelle and buried her at the cabin." The words sounded harsh and she couldn't believe she'd said them out loud.

At first Pink just stared at her, the way one might regard a door-to-door salesman. Then he burst out laughing. "I'm sorry, Mrs. Stage, but you're nuttier than a PayDay candy bar! But you are entertaining!"

Pink stood up and placed a twenty on the table near Michelle's plate. "The least I can do is buy you dinner," he said. "Thanks for the memorable evening!" Pink shuffled through the club, tucking his wallet into the back pocket of his trousers, laughing all the way to the stairs.

*****

Lyman walked in silence beside Michelle, opening the door for her when they got to his truck. The sky was quilted with dark clouds, the faint smell of winter riding the crisp night air. Michelle wished she'd brought a jacket with her. She pulled the door closed as Lyman climbed in behind the steering wheel.

"I appreciate the ride," Michelle said.

"Where you staying?" he asked.

Michelle was about to say the Ruby Motel. "Do you know where Mr. Souder lives?"

"Pink?"

"Yes. Can you take me there? To his house?"

Lyman turned the key in the ignition. "That's not a good idea. Pink'll have my ass if I take you over there. What you want to go there for anyway?"

"I have to. I'm running out of time." The cab of Lyman's truck was dark, the dash lights a faint yellow, making everything look nicotine-stained, even though the truck smelled of fresh pine. "I want to apologize to him," Michelle finally added.

Apologizing was part of her reason for wanting to go, but mostly she had to meet Isabelle, look into her eyes. Michelle didn't know what she expected to find, but time was compressing, squeezing out options and hope. How long would it be before Cliff found her? And now that she'd made a fool of herself with Pink, would he call Sheriff Fisk and tell him he'd found the crazy woman from Atlanta?

Lyman switched the headlights on and backed out. They wound down past the apartments onto the main road. All the shops were closed, except for Anthony's Restaurant, the plastic sign boasting big screen television and some upcoming fight on HBO.

Light from an oncoming vehicle filled Lyman's cab, then quickly passed, leaving them in darkness again. Michelle had paid no attention to the route Lyman was taking to Pink's house; she'd never have been able to find her way back. It worried her that she'd cast her faith with the stranger sitting across the seat. She knew nothing about Lyman except that he was great on the dance floor and had a knack for making mountain whiskey.

Lyman drove past some tall shrubs and made a right turn into a driveway. The house in front of them was pale and small, the windows dark. Lyman's headlights revealed a boat and trailer sitting next to the house. A tan metal shed sat behind the boat. When Lyman cut the headlights, everything went black.

"Is this Pink's house?" Michelle asked.

"No. It's mine."

Lyman got out of the truck and walked around to Michelle's door. She quickly pushed the lock down, then leaned over the seat and pushed his down. Lyman stared through the window. She pulled out the gun and pointed it at him. "Whatever you have in mind, Lyman, it's not happening," Michelle said.

"I mean no harm, ma'am. I promise," Lyman said, raising his hands as if he were under arrest. "It's just that I want to phone Pink first, see if he and Isabelle are up to company this late. It's after eleven o'clock, and Isabelle's a sickly woman."

Michelle lowered the gun, shocked, as if she'd been watching someone else threatening Lyman. If Lyman hadn't thought she was crazy before, he certainly would now. "I'm sorry," she said through the glass, not yet ready to unlock the door.

"I just thought you might like to come in. But you can wait in the truck if you feel more comfortable." Lyman turned and headed for the house.

"Wait," she said, unlocking the door, throwing it open. "Wait, Lyman. I'm really sorry. You must think I'm a nutcase. I'm just . . . frazzled is all."

"Frazzled?"

"Going to Mr. Souder's house was probably a bad idea. I'm staying at the Ruby Motel. Do you know where that is?"

They got back in the truck and Lyman drove out to the highway. In less than fifteen minutes they were turning under the Ruby Motel sign. Lyman eased the truck into a parking space and left the engine running. They had not said a word since they'd left Lyman's house.

"Thanks for the dance, and everything," she said. "Sorry about the gun."

"It's none of my business, ma'am, but if you're one of Pink's . . . lady friends, you might want to steer clear of Isabelle. She may be sick, but she's nobody to cross."

Michelle nodded and stepped down from the cab. Lyman backed out of the space and vanished down the empty road. Michelle felt like a fool. She pushed her hand past the gun in the purse until she felt the plastic diamond room key. After letting herself in, she bolted the door. She dropped her purse on the floor and sat on the edge of the bed, letting the events of the evening wash over her. This is ridiculous, she thought, starting to see things from Darcy and Cliff's perspective. It scared her though, as if she were giving up on Cassie. She undressed and went into the bathroom. Everything was surreal. She was about to step into the shower when she heard a knock at the door.

CHAPTER 17

Pink often thought about killing Isabelle, the same way he thought about hang gliding, or running for President of the United States—fleeting notions with no foothold in reality. Fantasies. Yet hearing Mrs. Stage accuse him of murdering Isabelle and burying her in the yard set off an avalanche of emotions, something Pink wasn't used to. He knew Mrs. Stage was troubled and probably a bit eccentric, but he wished he hadn't just walked out on her. He thought about driving back to get her then decided to see if Claire was home instead.

Kenny worked second shift at Ardenwood Power and didn't get off until one in the morning. Pink wasn't sure what Kenny did at the power company, but Claire had told him once that Kenny was a stationary engineer. "Does that mean he stands there and does nothing?" Pink had said. Claire explained that Kenny kept the machinery running, fixing motors that broke down or needed maintenance.

Claire and Kenny's house was dark when Pink pulled in the driveway. He tried the front door, then the back. The back was unlocked. He could hear the television in the bedroom and crept toward the doorway, following the blue glow.

"Claire?" he called. "You up?"

"Who is that? Kenny?" she called back, appearing in the doorway a moment later wearing a nightgown and big puffy slippers. "Pink. What the hell you doing here? Kenny'll be home in less than an hour. Are you crazy?"

"No, Cuddle Cakes, I'm horny."

"You know I hate when you call me that, don't you?" Claire turned and nodded for him to follow. "I have to finish this first." She climbed on the bed and sat cross-legged, showing Pink a jigsaw puzzle box, hundreds of colorful puzzle pieces scattered across a square of plywood sitting on the spread. The photo was of some kind of horse. Pink was never good with horses, and horses never liked him much either.

"How much longer is that going to take?"

"I don't know. I've been working on it all week."

"Well, Jesus Christ, Claire! Kenny'll be home in less than an hour!"

"I already told you that, Pink. You got some kind of bur in your shorts. What's bothering you? Isabelle? She bitchy tonight?"

"She's bitchy every night. Hell, do your damn puzzle. I'm not in the mood anymore anyway." He sat in the chair opposite the bed and found himself staring at Claire's bare thighs where her nightgown had hitched up, unable to get his mind off Mrs. Stage. He felt worse than ever he'd made fun of her. He liked her, liked talking with her, liked the quality of their silence when they weren't talking. He and Isabelle never really talked anymore. Bickering and fighting consumed every waking moment, leaving no time for conversation. Then again, they never had been big talkers, needing a more physical expression to communicate feelings.

"You wanna help?" Claire asked, handing Pink the box lid. Pink stared at the picture.

"Come on. It'll be fun," she said.

"I'm not good at puzzles."

"There's no skill involved, Pink. It's just a puzzle."

He wanted to tell her about Michelle, what Michelle had said about the cabin, about Isabelle. "You think Isabelle'll ever get well?" Pink said. He got up and stood at the window.

"Come away from the window, Pink. Neighbors might see."

Pink leaned his forehead against the glass and swiveled his head from side to side. Claire and Kenny had no neighbors for a hundred yards in either direction. Pink came over and sat on the edge of the bed.

"I didn't know better, I'd say you're having some kind of woman problem," Claire said, pressing the horse's eye into place.

"Aw, what do you know about it?" Pink leaned over and wrapped his fingers around her ankle, sliding them up over her calf, her thigh. "I'm getting back in the mood."

Claire straightened and pushed his hand away. "Did you hear that? It's Kenny." Claire jumped up and grabbed her robe off the door. "Shit, Pink. Go out the back."

"Well, hell, Claire. Don't you think he's seen my Suburban in the driveway?"

"Don't just stand there—"

"We'll tell him Isabelle's doing real bad tonight and I came over to get something."

"Like what?"

"Christ, Claire, I don't know. She's your sister. What would she want?"

A moment later Kenny appeared in the doorway, his metal Thermos clutched in his hand. "Pink helping you with the horse's ass?" Kenny said to Claire.

"Pink came over to get something for Isabelle . . ."

"Soup," Pink said. "She can't keep anything down and the stores are all closed. I thought you and Claire might have some . . ."

Kenny smiled. "Well, sure, Pink. We got lots of soup. Come on out to the kitchen and see what hits you." Kenny turned in the doorway and disappeared down the hall. Pink shrugged at Claire. Claire pushed Pink away and glared at him.

"Lots of soup," Kenny said, pulling cans down from the cupboard. Claire followed Pink into the kitchen. "Tomato, cream of broccoli, chicken noodle . . . that's supposed to be good when you're sick, right?"

"I'll take the chicken noodle," Pink said. "And the tomato, if you don't mind." He thought he might eat them both when he got home.

"That's what family's for, Pink." Kenny shoved the cans into Pink's opened palms. "Hope Isabelle's feeling better soon."

Pink thanked him again, said goodnight to Claire, and hurried out to his Suburban, thinking the lie had gone pretty well. When he reached the driveway he stopped and scratched his ear. Kenny had parked his pickup truck directly behind Pink's Suburban, the bumpers practically touching. Pink didn't want to go back in and confront Kenny and ask him to move his truck; it might tax Kenny's charitable mood. He opened Kenny's door and tried to pull the shifter into neutral. That was the problem with automatics; nothing worked without the key. He pushed on the front fender, trying to roll the truck back enough to pull his Suburban forward and back out around it. The truck barely rocked, the tires unmoving.

Pink started his Suburban and pulled forward until the front bumper nudged the siding on the house. It made a crinkling sound. "Damn. I hope he didn't hear that." He backed up, cutting the front wheels hard to the left until his back bumper kissed the front bumper of Kenny's truck. For several more minutes, Pink pulled forward and backward, unable to move his vehicle much more than a foot in either direction. "This'll take all year. I'll run out of gas before I get out of the damn driveway."

With the motor running, Pink got out of the Suburban, hitched up his trousers, and shuffled toward the front porch steps. He cleared his throat before knocking.

"Door's open, Pink." It was Kenny's voice. The sound of it bothered Pink, as if Kenny had been expecting him to come back. Pink went in. Light from the kitchen bled into the dark living room. In the dim setting, Pink could make out the outline of Kenny sitting in the lounger, Claire sitting on the couch dressed in jeans and a white blouse. Kenny smoked a cigarette with one hand and pointed a chrome-plated .357 Magnum pistol at Pink with the other.

"Trouble getting out?" Kenny said.

CHAPTER 18

Michelle turned off the shower and waited for another knock. It came like the last sound in the world. At first she thought it might be Lyman, or maybe Pink, but mostly she figured it was the police. Pink probably called Sheriff Fisk, related the crazy things she'd said at the Hilltop and how he'd found her earlier that evening curled on the floor like an overdose victim. Pink may even have told Fisk the story about the cabin and Cliff disappearing. Fisk would surely remember her then, the woman they'd taken away in an ambulance, the drugs they'd shot her full of to end her ranting.

The knock came louder this time, and Michelle wished she had undressed and showered in the dark and just gone to bed. Weariness overtook her, anxiety propping her back up. She couldn't have Sheriff Fisk take her to the station for threatening Lyman with a gun.

"Shit!" She grabbed her blouse and jeans off the bed and struggled to put everything on at once, pushing her feet into her shoes. Still buttoning her blouse, she hurried back to the bathroom, to the small window above the toilet. She snapped her jeans then ran back for her purse, the gun. The window looked too small. The pounding continued at the door, growing louder, impatient. She thought she heard someone shouting her name.

Michelle climbed up on the toilet and jerked the window open, the top of it pulling down slightly. She tried to wrestle it free from the aluminum frame so she could fit through the small space.

"Michelle, open up!" someone called from outside.

She pounded the metal on the side with her palm, trying to free it then grabbed the top edge of the glass and pulled down with all her weight until it shattered, showering her head and arms. Glass scattered across the toilet and floor like hail.

"Michelle! Open up. Are you okay?"

Using the barrel of the gun, she broke the remaining glass from the window frame, sliding the barrel back and forth along the aluminum until all the pieces were gone. She stared at the opening for a long moment before the tears started. If she pulled the entire window frame out of the wall, the hole would still not be large enough for her to crawl out.

She wiped her eyes as she walked toward the front door, the knob rattling as someone tried to open it from the outside. The door had no peephole, and she didn't want to pull the curtain back. But what difference would it make now? Whoever it was knew she was in the room, and she had no way out.

She unlocked the latch and slid off the chain. Cliff rushed in "Are you okay? Jesus, I thought I heard glass breaking." Michelle turned away from Cliff and sat on the bed next to her purse. She wondered if Darcy had told him about the gun.

Ed arrived. "Everyone okay here?" he said. "Ma'am, you okay? Looks like you cut yourself."

Cliff grabbed her hand to see how bad it was.

"I got a first aid kit in the office," Ed told them. "Be right back."

In a few minutes Ed was cleaning her wound, wrapping it with a Band-Aid. "Ah, you'll be fine. Just a little cut but one heck of a bleeder. Must be a full moon coming, though you can't see it for all the clouds.

"Thank you," Cliff said. "We'll pay for the window."

Ed glanced back toward the bathroom, the broken glass on the floor. "Those windows are old. Needed replacing anyway. I'm just glad you're okay, ma'am."

"Come on, Michelle. Let's go home." Cliff reached his hand out to her.

"If you're checking out, here," Ed told them. "Let me refund your money. I'll be right back."

"No," Michelle said. "Please, I've caused you enough problems tonight. Keep the money and send me a bill for the window. You have my address."

Ed stayed behind when they walked from the room.

Michelle headed into the parking lot. The night was brisk. Michelle had nothing but her lightweight cotton blouse. Snowflakes floated down onto the hood of a parked car. Cupping the bottom of her purse, she felt the pistol. She ran her fingers along the barrel. What was she doing with a gun? What was she doing here? She bent her head back and looked up at the night sky, milky black and bloated with snow. It had been nearly seventy degrees at noon, Michelle thought, wondering how the day could have changed so completely. Maybe she hadn't been paying attention.

"Here, put this on." Cliff slipped his jacket over her shoulders.

Cliff unlocked the passenger-side door. Michelle climbed in and started shivering. The windows fogged. Cliff turned the key, his profile a dark silhouette against the lights of the motel. She watched Ed walk toward her room carrying a piece of cardboard and a roll of duct tape.

When Cliff turned from the motel parking lot onto Main Street, a string of yellow traffic lights flashed above the street, blinking haphazardly, like a swarm of frenzied fireflies. The street was abandoned, the dark windows of businesses reflecting other businesses, most of the signs unlit. They passed Pink's real estate office. Darcy's Explorer still sat where Michelle had left it that morning.

"Cliff, stop. I'm gonna drive Darcy's car up to the cabin."

"We'll get it tomorrow. On the way home."

He hadn't even bothered looking over, as if he'd already made up his mind to leave it, had already decided their future. She felt a heat rising up in her chest against Cliff's assumption she was flawed in some way, weak, feeble, incapable of directing her own life.

"Stop the fucking car!" Michelle grabbed the wheel.

"Christ, Michelle, you trying to kill us . . . !"

"Pull over, Cliff. Pull over now!"

Cliff glanced over briefly before shifting his eyes back to the road. Snow blew past the headlights. He eased the car to the shoulder.

"I've had it, Cliff," she said. "You're not making all the decisions. You're not telling me what to do! I'm driving Darcy's car back to the cabin."

She was almost out the door when Cliff grabbed her arm. She glared back at him, at his hand squeezing her bicep. "Be careful, okay?" he said.

"Jesus, Cliff, I'm not fucking helpless." She was almost out the door then stopped.

"You called the police on me, Cliff?" she said. "Why would you do that?"

"I don't know what you're—"

"Christ, Cliff, I saw them in front of the real estate office. How could you?"

"I don't know what you're talking about, Michelle. I didn't call the police. I came into town for groceries and saw Darcy's Explorer, so I made a quick left and cut some guy off and he ran into a parked car. Luckily no one was hurt. That's why the police were there."

She stared at him a second. "Fuck." She jumped out and slammed the door.

Cliff's car sat motionless, the brake lights burning bright red across the snow-dusted pavement, as Michelle walked back to Darcy's Explorer. The cold felt good on her face, the snowflakes refreshing. She looked back. Cliff's vehicle hadn't moved. Why did he have to come? For once, why couldn't he just let it be, leave her to figure this out on her own? She didn't want his help. He couldn't help anyway. They might as well have been strangers who'd never met before and having him here was frustrating.

CHAPTER 19

Pink drove his Suburban. Claire sat in the back seat, Kenny in the front, his back against the door, gun pointed at Pink. Occasionally Kenny glanced back at Claire, smiled and then brought his eyes back to Pink. Pink wasn't sure if Kenny was crazy enough to shoot them or not, but when they were younger, he'd seen Kenny wound rats with a pellet rifle down by the water treatment plant. Kenny loved to watch them spin in circles trying to get up. Eventually he'd walk over and crunch their skulls with his boot—but not until he'd heard a good bit of squealing.

"What's that on the seat, Claire?" Kenny pointed the gun at something shiny next to her. She picked it up.

"A camera."

"Hand it here."

Claire reached it over the seat.

"This is one of them digital cameras, like you got—isn't it, Claire?" Kenny said. "Looks like the same brand." Kenny poked Pink in the shoulder with the tip of the pistol. "You get a two for one special on cameras or something?"

"I bought my camera with my own damn money!" Claire said.

It was true, she had paid for it with her own money, but Pink had gotten both cameras from a man who dealt in stolen goods. Claire had wanted a digital so she wouldn't have to wait for her pictures. She'd shown Pink how to take the memory card to Val-U-Mart and print out the photos. "See how easy it is?" she'd told him. Pink thought it was a lot of unnecessary trouble, but it did save time with newspaper listings. For those, he only had to take the card to the Ardenwood Press and Ramsey took care of copying the images.

Kenny turned the camera on and perused the pictures in memory. "Why in hell did Clarence take pictures of his nasty toes? Did you see these, Claire?" Laughing, Kenny turned the camera display so Claire could see.

"Oh, stop it, Kenny. Let's go back home. This is silly."

"What's silly is you and Pink, Claire." Kenny laughed again, studying the photos of Clarence's feet. "You're cousins, for Christ's sake. That's disgusting."

"Second cousins," Claire said. "And I don't know where you got the idea Pink and me is having an affair. That's just stupid."

Kenny turned in the seat, held up the camera and snapped a flash picture of Claire. Claire was shouting, slapping her hands on the seat for Kenny to stop when he snapped one of Pink.

"Are you having fun, Kenny?" Pink switched on the wipers. The snow was getting thicker but still melted when it hit the windshield. "Where we going, Kenny? Storm's getting worse. Weatherman said a hell of a blow is headed this way. We don't want to get caught out here."

"You got four-wheel drive," Kenny said, snapping another picture of him. "Besides, if I were you, I'd be more concerned about what's going to happen to *you* instead worrying about the damn weather." Kenny held the camera out toward the windshield and took a picture of Pink's face from the front.

"Goddamn it, Kenny! Let's go back home and stop this nonsense," Claire said, leaning forward in the seat to grab Kenny's arm. He shoved her away.

"Now there's no need . . ." Pink said—but then fell mute when Kenny pushed the cold ring of the barrel against his temple and clicked the hammer back.

"When you come to Highway 29, turn toward Curly's Marina," Kenny said, easing the gun away from Pink's head.

Pink had no idea why Kenny was taking them toward Burtran Lake, or Curly's Marina. Kenny and Curly were old friends, and Curly was about as corrupt as they come. Every few years or so, after a storm, Curly would go out and sink a few of his small fishing boats, tell the insurance company they broke free and sunk out in deep water. But when Hurricane Ivan came inland and tore the roof off Curly's Marina, Curly went out and sunk two of his houseboats. The insurance adjuster finally arrived in early March needing proof, so Curly took him for a boat ride in thirty-degree temperatures, running his sonar, drinking beer, until the agent was too cold to think and told Curly to take him in. By spring, Curly's fleet was back at full strength with two brand new houseboats for the summer tourists.

"You hear about that feller down in Georgia who broke free from that sheriff woman and shot her with her own gun, then shot the courtroom clerk and the judge?" Kenny was talking to Pink. Pink kept his eyes on the road, trying to figure out how to get out of this mess before they got to Curly's.

"They got some kind of law down in Georgia that if a man commits a felony crime, the state pays for his defense. Ain't that a hell of a deal?" Kenny said, scratching the barrel of his pistol across his whiskers. "I read that it's gonna cost them government folks a million dollars to try that feller. A million dollars, Pink. I don't have a college education or nothing, but I think if they'd a just given that sorry bastard the damn million dollars to begin with, he wouldn't had no call to shoot anybody. He'd a probably said, 'Thank you,' and gone about his business."

They passed a blue sign with yellow letters: Curly's Marina, 5 Miles Ahead. To one side of Curly's name was a drawing of a houseboat and on the other, a woman in a bikini.

"Hell, if some state feller was to come and offer me a million dollars to let you and Claire go, I wouldn't have to think about it twice. You and Claire could get back to whatever it was you were doing when I pulled in the driveway, and I'd go spend the rest of my days on a beach in Costa Rica."

"There was nothing going on, Kenny," Pink said. "I'm telling you—"

"Shut the fuck up, Pink. And don't you even start, Claire. Christ, who haven't you fucked in Ardenwood, Claire? Is there anybody?"

"Only you, Kenny!" she said.

Kenny swung his gun toward the back seat and pulled the trigger. The blast from the .357 Magnum lit up the interior of the Suburban. Smoke filled the vehicle, the piercing whine ringing Pink's eardrums. Pink nearly drove off the road. The reverberation of the gunshot caused Pink's jaw and teeth to throb. He checked the rearview mirror expecting to see Claire slumped over, her chest opened, blood covering the seat. What he saw was Claire holding her ears, her face scrunched. She screamed, kicking the back of the seat. "You cocksucker! You dirty motherfucker!"

Pink stole another quick glance at the smoking hole in the fabric. Kenny laughed and pounded the dashboard with his free hand. "She's one crazy bitch," Kenny said. "Her and her damn sister, right, Pink? That's why we married 'em."

Claire had always seemed a bit foolish, but not Isabelle, Pink thought. Isabelle had never seemed ridiculous or silly. In fact, she had been the most stable and real thing in Pink's life. That's why he married her. Pink's father had hardly ever spoken to him, not even when Pink was young, and his mother always practiced witchcraft, saying, doing, and wearing bizarre things. Pink and Isabelle would run off to the woods and make fun of his mom, making up chants and casting spells on unsuspecting possums, then laugh and go skinny-dipping in the waterfall. Isabelle had only turned a little crazy when she learned she couldn't have children, even though she said she never wanted any. When the illness overtook her, Isabelle became irritable and impossible to talk to, but she was nothing like Claire, who never had any sense at all, good or otherwise.

"Don't miss the damn turn, Pink." Kenny pointed the revolver at one of Curly's signs boasting a girl in a bikini driving a jet ski, waving. Vandals had painted nipples on the bikini top, making the woman into a modern-day Lady Godiva.

"You wouldn't catch me riding one of those," Kenny said, as he clicked through Pink's camera erasing all the photographs. Pink looked over.

"Keep your eyes on the road, Pink. Snow's getting bad."

When they approached a bridge that crossed the lake, Kenny told Pink to pull over and leave the engine running. "Leave the lights on. We don't want to get killed by some crazy drunk," Kenny said.

"We're in the middle of the damn bridge, Kenny," Pink said. The bridge was more like a highway overpass, with no steel structure above, just a short concrete wall on either side to keep cars from driving off.

"Get out, both of you," Kenny said.

Pink got out first, the sharp wind invigorating him. Claire protested, telling Kenny she wasn't getting out of the car without a coat. Kenny walked around to her door. When he reached for the handle, she locked it. He shot out the driver's side glass, reached his arm through and unlocked the doors. "Now get out of the fucking car!"

Reluctantly, she popped open the back door and stood on the pavement next to Pink.

"Get undressed." Kenny waved the gun like a pointer at Pink then nodded at Claire. "Come on, now. Both of you get undressed. Hell, I thought you'd like this part as much as you two seem to like getting naked with each other."

"Nothing's going on between us, Kenny!" Claire screamed. "Now let's go back home, go to bed, and have breakfast at Shoney's in the morning."

Pink knew why she added the part about Shoney's—it was Kenny's favorite place to eat—yet in the context of the situation, it seemed not only inappropriate but stupid.

"That's a great idea," Kenny said. "I'll go there for breakfast and celebrate our divorce, if it takes. Now get your damn clothes off, Claire."

Pink stripped first, nodding toward Claire. Tears rolled off her cheeks as she undid her blouse, then her jeans, stepping out of her sandals.

"You can leave your damn underwear on. Both of you."

A pile of clothes sat on the shoulder of the highway. Pink hoped maybe someone would come along, even though he knew it would be a miracle if they did. It was too early in the season for kayakers, bicyclists, and hikers, and too cold and late at night for fishermen.

"All right, now. Pink, you help the little lady up onto the concrete ledge." When Pink hesitated, Kenny jerked the gun toward Pink. "Come on, now. Help her up."

Claire's skin felt warm against Pink's hands as he made a stirrup of his fingers for her to step into. She put a hand on his shoulder and balanced herself on top of the cement railing. It was over two feet wide, with plenty of space to stand, but Claire was wobbly between the shivering and sobbing. Pink tried to steady her legs by holding her ankles.

"Don't grab my damn ankles, Pink! You trying to knock me in the goddamn lake?"

Pink let go, the beam from the Suburban's headlights causing Claire's legs to glow a pale, beautiful white.

"Now you, Pink," Kenny said. "Climb up next to your girlfriend, there."

Pink tried to find a foothold in the concrete wall.

"Get your fat ass up there, Pink!"

Pink scraped his knee on the rough edge of the cement, wriggling to get up. There was nothing to hold onto. When he finally managed to land both knees on the top, he stood up slowly, balancing himself by holding gently to Claire's knee. He looked into Claire's eyes and thought he saw anger at first then a sort of sad love. Or was it terror? He wasn't sure. He slid his palms onto her arms and pulled her close. She melted into him, and Pink didn't care if Kenny shot them both for the transgression. Pink closed his eyes, felt the warmth of Claire's breasts against his chest and squeezed her tighter. It was then Pink saw a flash of light through his closed eyelids, then another. He had heard no explosion, felt no sting of steel. When he opened his eyes, Kenny was steadying the camera to take another snapshot.

"Aw, now that's sweet," Kenny said, the flash causing spots before Pink's eyes. "You two look so damn cute together."

"Stop it, Kenny," Pink said. "You've humiliated us enough. If you're going to shoot us, then get it over with. Stop being an asshole about it." Claire whimpered into Pink's chest.

"Hell, Pink. You think I brought you all the way out here to shoot you? I could've done that at the house, buried you in the damn yard, and been asleep by now." Kenny started laughing and took another picture. "Now turn toward the lake so I can get your backsides."

Pink held Claire tightly and eased her in a small arc away from Kenny. From his peripheral vision he saw the flash of the camera. Kenny took two more shots before he told them to jump.

"On the count of three."

"Christ, Kenny. It's over thirty damn feet to the water," Pink said.

"Yeah, I know. You're lucky. If the lake was still at winter pool, you'd be looking at a seventy-foot drop. That would surely kill your fat ass. Thirty feet, you might actually survive if you don't go and drown yourself."

Claire let out a long wail, stomped her feet, and shook in Pink's arms. She said something into his chest that he couldn't understand at first.

"I can't swim!" she said again, "and that bastard knows it!"

Claire started convulsing. Pink whispered for Claire not to let go of him, then looked over at Kenny who was one big smile.

"Now, Claire," Kenny said. "I want you to think of this as a trial separation. If you die, then we are officially finished. But if you live, you can come back home, and all's forgiven. Okay?"

Wrapped in Pink's arms, Claire stomped her bare feet and screamed muffled obscenities into Pink's flabby chest.

"Did she agree, Pink?" Kenny asked. "It sounded to me like she did."

Pink shook his head, disgusted, the cold burrowing into his skin. If he and Claire didn't get crushed when they hit the water or freeze to death from hypothermia and didn't break a leg or an arm making it impossible to swim—

"One . . ." Kenny started the count, interrupting Pink's inventory of possible scenarios.

"Two . . ."

There were so many ways to die, why did it have to be so . . .

"Three."

Undignified?

CHAPTER 20

Cliff was still turning on the lights at the cabin when he heard Michelle pull in the driveway. He fought the urge to go out onto the deck to meet her. He hadn't even been sure she would follow him to the cabin. On the drive back, he had constantly checked his rearview mirror for the Explorer. Several times her headlights had gotten lost in the snow blowing across the highway. He was still playing the scene at the motel over in his head when she came through the door.

Michelle said nothing, just dropped her purse by the bed the way she always did and went into the bathroom. Cliff gave her a moment after she came out. She was changing clothes when he asked if they could talk.

"What do you want to talk about, Cliff?" she said, pulling her blouse off over her head.

"Why were you at the Ruby Motel?" he asked. "Why didn't you just stay up here at the cabin?"

"I don't know," she said. She slid her jeans off and left them on the floor. "I guess because I knew you were here."

How could she have known he was here? She was at the motel and didn't have a car. How did she even get to the motel? She wasn't making sense. "I want to help you," Cliff said.

She spun toward him. "Do you, Cliff? Really? I don't think so. No, you want me to step in line, accept your reality," she said. "You haven't *heard* one thing I've said to you over the past week. You just look at me like I'm a piece of meat going bad in the fridge. Like there's something wrong with *me.*"

"Accept *my* reality?" Cliff said. "How many realities are there, Chelle? Our daughter is dead. That's my reality. My finger is gone! That's my reality!" Cliff could feel his resolve melting, could feel his strength leaving him. "I killed our daughter—that's my reality."

Michelle looked at him. Cliff saw the disgust in her eyes. He deserved that. He deserved worse than that. He could hardly live with himself. But he wanted, needed, to move beyond the blame, the guilt, the revulsion he saw on her face.

"Just stop, Cliff," Michelle said, walking toward the bathroom.

"Please talk to me, Michelle. Don't walk away."

"What, Cliff? I tell you what happened to me, and you hand me a fucking pill! I don't need a pill—I need answers!"

"Answers to what, Michelle? This is maddening! I want . . . I want . . ."

"You want? I don't care what you want, Cliff. It's always about what you want."

"I want our life back," Cliff said. "I want *us* back." Cliff couldn't take any more of the mental push and pull. He waited for her to come back in the room. He hadn't noticed till just now that he was shaking. He tried a deep breath, but it came up short.

"Michelle," Cliff said. She ignored him. "Michelle, how did you get to the Ruby Motel? You didn't have Darcy's—"

"What does that matter, Cliff?"

"I don't know. I just want to talk."

"Okay, let's talk," she said. "I came back to Ardenwood to talk to Pink Souder. He's a real estate agent, but more than that, he's the man who actually built this cabin and lived here for a while."

"That the guy with the big pink billboard on the highway?" Cliff asked.

"Yes, that's the one."

"Why? I'm very confused, Michelle. Do you want to sell the cabin? I get that, but can't we talk about it—"

"It's not about selling the fucking cabin. It's about Pink Souder . . . some stories Sheriff Fisk told me when I met him the first time . . ."

Now Cliff was really baffled. "You only met him once . . . when you got lost that night, but . . . you never really talked with him. You were really out of it that—"

"Cliff! You have to let me finish. Jesus."

Cliff sat back, hurt by her admonishment, exhausted from this unrelenting onslaught of lunacy.

"I met up with Pink today and told him I had a property to list, which was a lie, but I needed to talk to him. It was a crazy day. Some friend of his mother's died and we took care of that, then when we came up here to the cabin . . . but, you were here and I didn't want to stop . . ."

"So that's how you knew I was here . . ." Cliff said.

"Yeah, so we drove on and later, when we got into town, there were all those police cars in front of Pink's office, where you had the accident, but of course I didn't know it at the time. I figured you called the police on me and—"

"But I didn't. I told you what happened."

"Yes, I know that now." Michelle took a deep breath. "Anyway, I needed time to figure things out, so I had Pink drive me to a motel. The Ruby. Where you found me. I wasn't doing so well, I hadn't eaten all day, so Pink offered to take me to dinner. And at this place called the Hilltop or something, one of Pink's friends asked me to dance and for a few minutes I felt like a human being again. I ate dinner and even tried moonshine whiskey. And then . . ."

Cliff was perplexed, trying to make sense of what she was saying. "Are you having an affair with this Pink character?" he said. "Is that what this is all about? Is that where you were the night you went missing? With him? Jesus, Michelle. What the fuck?"

"Hold your horses, pal! You're not turning this around on me. Just fucking listen to what I'm saying. You said you wanted to have a talk . . . Well, we're having it."

"What do you want with this guy? I don't get it, Michelle. This is fucking bizarre. Is this some kind of fucked-up payback for Glenda? Jesus, how long do I have to pay for that?"

"You son of a bitch!" Michelle screamed, then broke down crying.

Cliff sighed and touched her arm. He wasn't sure how much more of this he could take, the manic swings, the outbursts, the delusions. She needed help, he knew that, but she refused to get it. And on some level, he knew it was all his fault. He was losing her. "What's wrong?" he said, trying to soften his tone. "What's this really all about?"

"Cassie, Cliff! It's about Cassie! Why won't you believe I spoke with her just last week? Why can't you make room for that possibility, Cliff? Why can't you believe she's alive? Are you glad she's dead or something? Is that why you never wanted more children? Don't you have room in your heart even for Cassie anymore?"

The anger surged like a volcano, volatile and explosive. "Christ, Michelle! Just shut up about all this nonsense! This is just fucking crazy! I wish you could hear yourself? You sound insane!"

His statement ricocheted back in his head. He felt horrible he'd told her to shut up. That he told her she sounded insane. Michelle sat upright, then stood and was walking away when she turned back.

"You, Cliff . . . you killed everything in our life that mattered—our love, my trust . . . and I guess our daughter, the way you tell it. What's left, Cliff? What's left to kill?"

Cliff had to leave the room. He walked outside, tried to focus on the snow, the trees, attempting to wash away his grief. It was all falling apart. It would never fit back together again. It would never be how it was. All because of him. Why did he ever get involved with Glenda? Remembering Cassie pushed so hard into his chest he couldn't breathe. He sat on the deck boards, slumped over and started crying.

After a while, Cliff felt chilled and went back in to find Michelle asleep on the couch, half-sitting, slumped to the side. The bottle of Xanax sat on the coffee table. For a quick moment he thought she might have taken the whole bottle. But that wasn't Michelle. She'd never do that. He inspected the container just in case.

He carried her to bed, undressed her, and then pulled the comforter over her shoulders. She slept better with her shoulders covered. She hadn't moved since. Cliff felt it was too late for phone calls, even though Darcy had told him to contact her as soon as he had news about Michelle.

Out of habit, Cliff tried to use his cell phone first, but there was no signal, so he dialed on the landline phone. Darcy picked up. She sounded groggy.

"I'm sorry I woke you. It's Cliff."

"Did you find her?"

"Yes." The realization flooded him with mixed emotions—the relief that she was safe against the grief of knowing she was sinking deeper into delusion. The combativeness, the rage. It was exhausting.

"Is she okay?" Darcy asked.

He sniffled. "Yes."

"Where was she?"

"At the Ruby Motel, like you told me," Cliff said. "She wasn't in her room when I got there, so I waited. Some guy in a pickup truck brought her back. It was after midnight, Darcy. She had been at some bar, dancing, drinking moonshine whiskey. It's crazy shit, Darcy. She smelled like an ashtray. Michelle never drinks. And she doesn't go off with guys in fucking pickup trucks . . ."

"Cliff. Don't worry. She's back with you now. She's safe. You're safe. That's all that matters."

"She broke the bathroom window in the motel room trying to get away, Darcy," Cliff said. "I don't know what to do with her. She wanted to drive your Explorer—"

"You didn't let her, did you?"

"I didn't have a choice, Darce. She threw a fit. Practically ran us off the road.

"When are you coming back to Atlanta?"

Cliff rubbed his forehead. "I don't know. I guess . . . tomorrow. It's snowing here . . . I think we'll be able to get out. I don't know." He wasn't sure he had the strength to fight another battle with Michelle. If she wouldn't go back, what would he do? His business was starting to falter from him being gone so much and his loss of focus. He wasn't sure what mattered anymore.

"Cliff, are you still . . . ?"

"I can't take much more, Darcy," Cliff said. "I don't think I . . ."

Cliff hadn't wanted to cry on the phone, but something swirled inside him in such a way he couldn't stop it. The world had always been a solid, predictable thing with Michelle in his life, his daughter, the business, their home. It followed a logical trajectory that had always made sense. But when Cassie was killed, the gyro slipped off center, wobbling uncontrollably ever since.

"Cliff," Darcy said. "Do you want me to come up there? I could drive Michelle back? The store's closed tomorrow. Anna won't mind driving me up."

Cliff wiped his eyes. "The roads might be bad by tomorrow. It's snowing like crazy. We'll be all right."

"I'm so sorry, Cliff. You've both been through so much this past year. I wish there was something I could do."

"I better hang up now. I want to get an early start in the morning."

"Call me when you get home. I'll come over and help with Michelle."

Cliff placed the phone in the cradle then sat a moment rubbing the knot in his neck. He rolled his shoulders and pressed his fingertips into the base of his skull.

He switched off the living room light on his way out and stood on the deck, the snowflakes cold pinpoints on his face. In the distance the mountains drew jagged black shapes across the milky night sky. Clouds drifting past created the illusion that the mountains were moving, lumbering through the valley like a herd of enormous buffalo. Cliff found solace in the illusion, the silent sanctity of it.

In a few moments he found himself standing at the railing, unaware of the cold, his palms resting in a quarter inch of snow. Looking down through the lattice of branches and leaves, his eyes searched for the possibility of a light, a light he was certain didn't exist even though Michelle insisted it did. Nothing but darkness, solid and impenetrable. He brushed the snow from his palms then placed his hands to his neck, wondering what to do with Michelle. The muffled sound of the phone ringing inside the house wrenched him from his deliberation. He hurried toward the door, wanting to get to it before it woke Michelle.

"Hello?"

"It's Darcy. Sorry to call, but I had to tell you something I should have told you before."

Cliff waited, glancing toward the bed at the dark shape of Michelle's body mounded beneath the blankets.

"Michelle has my gun, Cliff."

"Gun?"

"She took it from the store. I should have gotten rid of that damn thing years ago. I'm sorry. I don't know why she took it. Maybe she was scared to go up there by herself. Maybe she . . . I don't know, Cliff. Try to find it, okay?"

"I will, Darcy. Thanks."

Cliff wondered what Michelle had planned to do with a gun. If she had it, it would be in her shoulder bag; she put everything in there. Cliff went to the foot of the bed, lifting it by the strap. He carried it to the kitchen and placed it on the table. As soon as he opened it, he spotted the gun sticking out from beneath her wallet. Cliff slipped it from the bag and studied the shape of it, the power of it, turning it over in his hands, then placing it on the kitchen table.

He went to the fridge and got a can of beer from the shelf. After switching off the kitchen light, he picked up the gun and carried it out onto the deck. He dragged one of the folding chairs over next to the railing and eased back into it. He tilted the beer back, the carbonation rough on the back of his throat. He set the can down and raised the gun in both hands, revolving it like a Rubik's Cube a foot from his face, inspecting it. After Cassie's death, Cliff couldn't count the times he'd taken his .38 from the drawer of his desk and pushed the snubbed barrel into his temple, hoping it would go off. He could never pull the trigger. Michelle's face would always snap into his head as he eased his fingertip over the curved steel, her eyes and nose were so much like Cassie's that he'd start to cry. Shaking, he would lower the gun back into the drawer, wishing just once her image wouldn't stop him.

Cliff pulled the beer to his lips and finished it. He dropped the can into the snow at the side of the chair, then placed the gun barrel to the soft underside of his chin and closed his eyes, waiting for Michelle to come, tell him no, smile and touch his hand, reassure him, tell him she forgave him. He had placed his faith in the normal process of time. But time had become a dark edge—an unreliable partner. Cliff knew now that no matter what changed or how much time passed, he would always feel the Cherokee buckling around him as it rolled over and over, would always hear Cassie screaming, would always remember the numbing silence that froze the vehicle when it finally came to rest on its side, Cassie hanging limp from her shoulder harness, hair drenched in blood.

Cliff opened his eyes to make the image disappear, then he squeezed the trigger.

CHAPTER 21

Pink had expected the fall to last a lot longer, the impact to be more jarring, the water to be like ice. Oddly, the lake felt warm. At some point during the drop, Claire had let go of him, pushing him away, screaming.

When Pink came to the surface, frigid air cut across his shoulders and face. He searched the inky blackness for Claire, calling her name, splashing his arms back and forth to stay afloat. It had been years since he'd been swimming. He kicked his feet to keep his chin above the surface, buoyancy losing out to gravity.

A moment later Claire popped up, coughing and choking. Pink saw the terrified whites of her eyes, scanning the dark like searchlights. When her gaze finally locked onto him, she started thrashing toward him, windmilling her arms in a futile attempt to swim. He told her to go the other way, toward the bank. She spun to look in the direction he pointed, then turned back and lunged for his head.

"Jesus Christ, Cla—!" With her hands wrapped over his ears, Claire's weight pushed him under. Water rushed up his nose. Pink kicked, trying to free himself from her grip. When he sank too deep for her to hold on any longer without going under herself, he felt her feet on his shoulders. She danced frantically, plunging him deeper. He swatted at her ankles, twisting away, swimming for the surface.

He came up choking, hardly catching a breath before she was on him again. He pushed her away, then kicked at her, catching her in the stomach. She went under.

"Oh, for Christ's sake!" Pink paddled over to where she went down. He was about to call Claire's name again when he felt her grab his legs underwater, then his BVDs; she was climbing him like a ladder, dragging him down. When her head popped up, he tried to spin her, catch her from behind under the arms so he could subdue her, talk some sense into her. She flailed, kicking and chopping her arms on the water, clocking him under the chin with her head.

"Goddamn it, Claire, stop fighting!"

She was choking again, coughing and spitting, then screaming and struggling. The cold was beginning to penetrate, the water no longer warm to his flesh. He slapped her across the face then wrenched her shoulders around until she faced away. Claire continued flailing. He hauled her backward, frog-kicking his legs beneath the water, using his free arm to haul them forward. In a matter of seconds his calves were like lead, drawing them both down, the cold stiffening his thigh muscles. Claire beat the water with her open palms, gurgling and babbling. Pink thought about releasing her, shoving her away, suddenly unsure if he could make it to shore alone, much less towing her. Maybe if he left her, he could rest a second, gather his strength, go back and save her. The bank looked to be only forty feet away. Even so, he knew she would drown before he had a chance to swim back for her.

He kicked his legs again, hoping for an adrenaline surge, the kind of crazed, instantaneous strength that allows a man to lift an automobile off a trapped child. Just then, Claire's struggled ended. She went limp in his arms. He knew she wasn't dead—she had screamed too much to have any water in her lungs. The absence of her fight buoyed him.

In minutes he was sliding her up the mud bank, her body pale and lifeless against the dark weeds. He couldn't stop shivering.

"Wake up, Claire." He slapped her lightly on the cheek at first, then harder when she didn't respond. "Come on, Claire."

Pink grabbed her wrists and tried dragging her up the hill, moving her only a few inches before exhaustion set in. Out of breath and perspiring, he felt the cold overtaking him, sweat freezing in his hair.

Claire's breasts bobbed in her wet bra as he seized her wrists and leaned back to get her moving again. Catching on branches and undergrowth, her panties began to roll down her hips until Pink could see the top edge of her pubic hair. Her backside must have come against something sharp because her eyes shot open and she yelped. She yanked her arms away from him and knotted them across her chest, shivering, then shaking. "I'm freezing to death, Pink."

He touched her hair. It was cold and brittle. "Come on," he said, reaching out his hand to her. "Let's get to the road."

"Then what?" she said, staring up at him, her body wound into a tight ball. "Freeze to death up there? Let's make a fire. Can't you make a fire or something?"

"With what, Claire?" Pink tugged at his underwear. "You think I'm hiding matches in here? I ain't no damn Boy Scout. Now get up off your ass."

He climbed the hill without her, thinking about Kenny, about how he would kill him. Pink heard Claire rustle to her feet and scrabble up behind him, grabbing his ankle. "Wait for me."

Pink had no idea what they would do when they reached the road. There would be no one to drive by and give them a ride, not out here. Snow came down heavier now, making it difficult to see more than a few feet.

Within several yards of cresting the hill, Pink thought he spotted a light up on the bridge. "Come on, Claire. There's a car stopped up here."

He clawed at the steep bank, scraping his bare knees on rocks and sticks. Limbs swept past his crotch, poking him. With every jab to his testicles, Pink planned his revenge. "That bastard."

"What'd you say, Pink?" Claire tried to keep up, grabbing at his legs.

"Nothing." Pink glanced up at the bridge again, the presence of a car obvious now, the amber flashing lights.

"Hurry up, Claire, before they leave." Pink fought through a bramble at the edge of the scrub, the stickers ripping at his arms and legs, picking at the fabric of his shorts. He broke free and jogged toward the red glow of the taillights, then stopped dead. Claire ran up next to him, hugging her arms across her chest.

"Come on, Pink. What are you stopping for?"

He grabbed her wrist as she started toward the vehicle, exhaust pouring from the tailpipe.

"That's my Suburban, Claire."

Shifting her gaze between the vehicle and Pink, she tried to twist free from his grasp. "So what? I'm freezing my ass off. Come on."

"Kenny could be waiting for us," Pink said quietly. "Do you see him anywhere? If he didn't take the car, where is he?"

Claire stopped struggling, and Pink let her hand fall. He told her to wait, and then approached the vehicle, the gravel pricking his bare feet. Snow dusting the windows made it impossible to see if someone was inside. He looked past the passenger side of the car, at the ground where he and Claire had disrobed, hoping to see their clothes. Nothing. Stealing up on the back bumper, Pink felt his heart clunking in his chest. How cruel a bastard could Kenny be, Pink thought, making them strip on the side of the highway, jump into freezing water, then struggle up the fucking hill only to be shot next to his own Suburban while Kenny laughed, his big, fat teeth shining in the dash lights?

Pink peeked in the back window, then the front, then he hurried past the hood. "Come on, Claire. He's not here."

Pink jerked the door open and threw himself into the warmth of the interior, the heater turned to high. Claire shot in the other side and slammed the door.

"That crazy fucking husband of yours left the heater on for us. Can you beat that?" Pink rubbed heat back into his knees, then shoved his hands at the vent, leaning his face into the warm stream of air.

"Yeah, but he didn't leave our clothes. Let's get out of here," Claire said, sniffling.

"Where we gonna go without clothes, Claire."

"Your house."

"Sure, we'll walk in naked and ask Isabelle to round us up some hot chocolate."

"Hot chocolate sounds good," Claire said, teeth chattering, looking past Pink at the jagged hole where the driver's side window used to be. "I feel a draught."

"Jesus Christ, Claire, scoot closer to the damn vent. And get out of those wet underwear."

"What will I put on?"

"How do I know?"

"Let's drive to your office."

"Why? I don't have clothes there."

Claire rubbed her thighs and knees, rocking back and forth in the seat. "Where do you think Kenny went?" she finally said.

"I don't know. Probably called that lunatic Curly to come get him." Pink twisted in the seat and leaned over the back between the headrests searching for something Claire could cover herself with so she'd shut up. On the seat, next to the ragged hole Kenny had blasted through the upholstery, Pink spied their mound of clothes. He spun around to tell Claire when he noticed she was naked, huddled near the vent, her underwear in a wet lump on the floor mat. Each time she rubbed her upper arms, her breasts jiggled. The sight was wildly erotic.

"Find anything?" she asked, turning toward him. "Oh, for Pete's sake, Pink! What are you doing with a boner? We nearly drowned, now we're freezing to death, and you have a boner?"

He slipped his soaked underpants off. "I can't control this anymore than you can keep your nipples from getting hard."

"Why did you take your shorts off?"

"Come on, Claire. We might as well make the most of this. It'll warm us up . . ."

"You're crazier then Kenny!"

"It'll do us both some good. Besides, it's kind of romantic."

"Romantic my ass. It's creepy is what it is." Claire looked out the window, then over at Pink. "Why didn't you protect me?"

"You're here, aren't you? You're alive."

Unfolding her arms, she eased her hand across his lap and took him in her palm. "I guess it would warm me up, that big ol' body of yours on top of me." She scrunched down in the seat, wrestling her right leg under the steering wheel, guiding him between her knees.

CHAPTER 22

Snow had drifted up against the sliding glass doors of Michelle and Cliff's bedroom. Glare off the frozen white surface washed the room in light, making it difficult to see. Michelle pushed up on one elbow, squinted, then rolled away from the windows and wrapped the blankets around her shoulders. For just a moment she'd thought she was still at the Ruby Motel. The previous evening flooded back—breaking the bathroom window, Cliff's flattened expression as she walked past him from the motel room. She recalled the ride up to the cabin, the horrible accusations she'd made, blaming Cliff for ruining everything. She felt terrible and wanted to apologize but wasn't sure she could.

Sitting up, Michelle noticed she was wearing her nightgown but couldn't remember changing out of her clothes. She smelled coffee brewing and swept her feet along the floor, searching for her slippers. The cabin was cold. She went to the bathroom and pulled her robe from the door. Not wanting to confront Cliff yet, she considered heading back to bed. He would want to get an early start back to Atlanta, get on the road by nine. She wondered if the highways were bad, if they could even get off the mountain. But that wouldn't stop Cliff. That's why they had four-wheel drive, he would remind her. The Rover would get through the snow without a problem. She had always wondered why they needed four-wheel drive living in Atlanta, and he would always reply, "You never know. Better to be prepared."

Better to be prepared? she thought. How could you prepare for every possibility? Shuffling toward the kitchen, Michelle smelled the fresh coffee; brewing coffee was the first thing Cliff did every morning.

Her head throbbed, and she wondered if it was from the corn liquor. Corn liquor. What a strange night it had been, drinking homemade moonshine—was it moonshine?—dancing with Pink's friend at the Hilltop, Pink walking out on her. It seemed as if it had all happened to someone else, or hadn't happened at all.

Michelle slid the carafe from the coffeemaker and poured herself a cup. She went to the thermostat and turned it up to seventy then sat on the couch and tucked her legs under her robe. She looked out and thought how beautiful the snow was, billowy and perfect, as though overnight the world had been made new again. Branches thick with snow hung low and heavy and still, and she was suddenly relieved Cliff wasn't around. He'd often go for morning walks along the gravel roads before she woke, yet she saw no footprints in the snow leading to the steps. He would probably come back with damp clothes imploring her to come for a hike with him and see how glorious the morning was.

Sunlight glistened across the crust of snow on the deck. Michelle got up, wiggled her feet into her slippers and went outside, her feet sinking in the thick powder. It was not nearly as cold as she had expected. The snow was deeper near the edge of the deck, nearly a foot or more. She didn't care her feet were getting wet. The landscape brought to mind pictures she'd seen of the moon, everything rounded and formless and puffy. Even the deck chairs and table looked like some sort of alien topography or contemporary art, smooth and elegant as a Henry Moore sculpture.

One of the chairs looked oddly formed, as if she or Cliff had left something sitting in it the last time they were at the cabin. She walked over to it, curious about the queer mound. As she scraped her hand across it, the snow turned from white to pink, then more reddish the deeper she dug. At first her mind refused to register what she was looking at. The eyes looked like Cliff's, only waxy and hard, like a statue. Using both hands, she cut and carved the snow from his nose and chin, the flesh unnaturally frozen and firm. She brushed snow from his lips, his hair and ears, as if digging a man out of an avalanche. His skin was almost a translucent blue. She refused to see the matted and frozen hair around the wound on the top of his head, and the torn flesh of the red, gnarled hole beneath his chin.

She thought she screamed, but with no one around to hear, the scream seemed to catch in the brittle air, soundless as the cold itself. She scooped more powder from his arms and legs. She knelt next to the chair and cleared his pants, his shoes, his hands. His right hand sat on his stomach, Darcy's gun resting against the belt of his jeans. She tried prying the gun from his fingers, the digits solid, inflexible.

"Wake up, Cliff. Come inside," she said with urgency." You'll freeze out here."

She leaned over his body and tried patting life back into his cheeks then his hands. After struggling to her feet, she tugged at his hand, the flesh rigid and unyielding, his skin the texture of a rubber glove. She leaned in close, pulled his head to her chest. "No, Cliff!"

Grabbing the back of his chair, she tried pulling it toward the house until Cliff's body shifted, the weight of it taking the chair over, dumping him in the snow.

"No, no, no, no."

Michelle grabbed Cliff's jacket by the shoulders to move him toward the cabin, get him inside, into the warmth, unable to look at him still bent into a queer sitting position. She thought of a hot bath, soaking his body to thaw it, denying the injury to his head, as if heat alone could restore him to life. She threw open the door, then ran to the bathroom and turned on the faucet in the tub, then hurried back to Cliff. She tried prying his arms away from his body, but his limbs were stiff, and she had to lean back trying to find traction on the slippery deck.

"We'll get you in a hot bath, then wrap you in blankets until the ambulance comes."

The ambulance. Michelle hadn't called yet. She ran back inside and grabbed for the phone, knocking it from the table. It lay silent on the floor and for a moment Michelle thought maybe it was dead, until the dial tone began its low and steady drone, a sound Michelle had always found annoying. 911. She'd never had to dial those three numbers before. How many people had occasion in their life to dial 911? Was this an emergency? Or had the emergency already passed? She wasn't sure if those three numbers would even work in a small town. Maybe it only worked in large cities. A man answered.

She would not allow herself to mention the wound in Cliff's head or the glassy sheen to his eyes, the unbending limbs. "Send an ambulance. Please."

The man asked questions, wanted to know what was wrong, if she was in danger, her name, the address. Michelle rattled off answers, could hear herself speaking, uncertain of the words. Her attention went to Cliff's body outside the glass doors, the side of his face lying in snow, his knees bent oddly, his hand still clutching the pistol to his lap. She had to put her eyes somewhere and looked down at her own feet. Her slippers were gone, probably buried under the snow outside, even though she didn't remember losing them. Her toes were bright red, the tingle of numbness slowly burning away. The bottom of her nightgown was wet and caked with snow, beginning to melt and drip onto the floor.

Then there was the smell of freshly brewed coffee. That was the worst trick of all. Cliff always measured the grounds the night before, filled the reservoir with water, then set the timer so he could wake up to the sweet aroma of Irish cream. The fragrance had given her no reason to believe anything was wrong, that Cliff was gone, or worse. And the gunshot. Why had she not heard the gunshot? But she had. She remembered now, the loud bang in the night that shook her from sleep. She had opened her eyes and waited to hear it again, as she had on other nights when awakened by what seemed a loud noise or someone speaking her name in a dream. But there had been no other sound, and she'd fallen back asleep.

"Is your husband dead?"

Michelle looked out toward Cliff's body, the unmoving reality of it. If that wasn't him lying there in the snow, then where was he? Out walking in the woods? Sitting in his office back in Atlanta? Buying cars at auction?

"Ma'am? Are you there?"

They will want to know whose gun it is, Michelle thought. How did

Cliff find it? Had he gone through her purse or had she left it out for him to find? If she hadn't taken it from the store, this would never have happened.

"I've dispatched the police, ma'am. And an ambulance. They should be there soon if the road is passable."

Michelle did not recall saying goodbye or hanging up the phone. She heard water spilling onto the bathroom floor and figured the toilet was overflowing again. But it was the bathtub. She sat on the edge of the tub and twisted the nozzles off, water welling up over the edge, soaking her gown. No amount of warmth would help Cliff now, she realized. She reached down and pulled up the stopper to release the water, then sat until the last of it swept down the drain.

On her way back to the deck, she pulled the comforter from the couch to cover Cliff's body, the one she always wrapped herself in to watch a DVD or read a book. She brushed the hair from Cliff's forehead and tried to ease his eyelids shut. They would not close. She pulled the blanket up over his face and held the fringed edge between her fingers. Icicles hung from the railing like Christmas decorations. She sat down in the snow next to Cliff's body and watched them drip, the sun burning high above the mountains.

CHAPTER 23

Claire looked awfully good sleeping on the couch when Pink got up to use the bathroom. He had half a mind to wake her for sex, until the phone rang.

"I can't get off the mountain because of the snow," his mother said. "I need Lulu's ashes."

"Can't it wait, Mama? Snow looks awful deep here too."

"You have four-wheel drive, Pink. And I need them for tonight. Now, please go, and don't give me a hard time, okay?"

Even though Pink didn't feel like driving into Emerson's, he was glad to get out of the house before Isabelle woke. He knew she would still be angry from the night before when he and Claire came back so late.

He pulled on his pants and shirt then paused at the couch a moment to peak under the blanket at Claire's breasts then her hips and pubic hair. Claire always slept in the nude, and even though it was too early to run the sweeper, Pink knew Isabelle had taken her sleeping pills and would certainly remain comatose through a quickie. Claire barely stirred when he tweaked her nipple, except to grimace and push his hand away.

He sat on the chair and tied his shoes. He wasn't really in the mood anyway. Besides, he was still a little upset with her from the night before. They had agreed on a story, but as soon as Isabelle questioned Claire about Pink being at her house, Claire said he came over to get something.

"Soup," Claire had told Isabelle. "Pink said you couldn't keep anything down, and the stores were all closed. Anyway, Kenny didn't believe a word of it and told us both to get out."

Pink knew Isabelle would never believe a story as stupid as that because he hadn't even spoken to her the night before to know how she was feeling, and he could tell by the look on her face she was more upset than ever. After Isabelle went to bed, Pink had crept back into the living room and asked Claire why she hadn't stuck to the story they had agreed upon, the one where she called him because Kenny came home drunk and threw her out of the house.

"That was a dumb story, Pink," Claire had said. "Besides, you expected Kenny to believe that stupid soup story, why shouldn't Isabelle?"

"Because Kenny's dumber than cardboard, and Isabelle will never let me hear the end of it. Aw, hell, it doesn't matter anyway. She's always mad at me about something." When he'd reached out to touch Claire's breast in a gesture of reconciliation, she'd slapped his hand away. "What'd you do that for?" he'd said.

"For Christ's sakes, Pink, go back to bed." Claire had jerked the blanket up over her shoulders. "I gotta get some sleep so I can figure out what to tell Kenny."

Pink hadn't understood that last comment. He'd never figured out anything in his sleep, always waking with the same problems he'd gone to bed with.

He closed the front door behind him and shielded his eyes from the glare off the snow. The buds on the trees were blanketed with white, and Pink couldn't comprehend how Mother Nature could let a thing like this happen, all those brand-new buds frozen solid. *Maybe it did have to do with the Quickening*, Pink thought. Clarence had told Pink all about it after hearing something on late-night public radio. "The Quickening," Clarence had said, his eyes dark and serious as drilled holes, "I'm not fooling, Pink. Feller on the radio said all kind of strange things would happen closer we come to end-times." End of April snowfall would surely have to count as a strange thing, but it had happened before, not that long ago, and much worse than this.

Pink recalled the snowstorm of '93. Over thirty inches deep in some places on the mountains, with eight-foot drifts. Weekenders from Georgia, Alabama, and Florida were trapped in their vacation homes, no power, no phones, a two-day supply of food, and depleted end-of-winter woodpiles. Some folks burned expensive chairs and dressers, huddled next to the fireplace under blankets to stay warm, while others tested the drifts and howling winds on foot, only to be turned back by exhaustion and fear. Unsure how long the snowstorm had been predicted to last, Pink, Loudon, and a few of Loudon's deputies had tried to rescue some of those people stuck on the mountains. All they'd managed after eight hours effort was to burn up two Hummers and a Jeep when snow caked the drive trains and plugged the radiators, overheating the engines and seizing the pistons. *The Quickening*, Pink thought, snickering to himself. Coddled folks with too much time and imagination came up with some pretty crazy notions.

Pink opened the door of the Suburban and brushed snow off the seat where it had blown through the missing window. The truck fired after a few cranks. Pink dropped it into four-wheel drive, adjusted the heater—even though it didn't feel all that cold—then backed out of the driveway. He couldn't stop thinking about the night before: Kenny holding a gun on them, Claire standing on the bridge railing wearing less clothing than a Bible-belt stripper, jumping into the lake. It had been quite exhilarating, and the sex afterward in the front seat was right up there with the best he could remember. Even Claire had seemed to ride the rush of fear, having two orgasms before worry set in.

"What if Kenny comes back with Curly?" she'd said.

"Christ, Claire. Forget about Kenny and Curly. Their noses are probably packed full of coke by now. They're not going—"

"Let's get out of here," she'd said, pushing away.

No amount of pleading had swayed her from leaving, and Pink had only prayed it wouldn't take jumping off a bridge naked before he had great sex again. But he would jump every day if that's what it took, it was that good.

Pink was still mesmerized with the fragrance of Claire's lilac shampoo when he turned onto the road leading to his mama's house. Loudon, his badge sparkling like a gold brooch, stood in the road, his jacket puffed up around his neck and ears to block the wind. Pink stared at him through the jagged opening of the broken window. "Lose your car, Loudon?"

"Something like that," Loudon said. "How about that window?"

"Cold shattered it," Pink said. "Ain't that a hell of a thing?"

Loudon nodded, his eyes narrowed in disbelief. Before Loudon could ponder the lie much longer, Pink asked him why he was standing in the middle of the road without a car.

"Elmer was so damn sure he could make it up the mountain," Loudon said. "Even though I told him the snow was too deep."

"Where is he?"

"Around the first bend. Put it right into a damn drift three feet deep. He's calling for backup. Slider has the four-wheel drive up on Slocum Mountain trying to help some folks get down to the grocery store. Hell, if it's not just like the storm of '93, all the damn roads—"

"Hell, Loudon, this ain't nothing like '93. You need a ride up the road? Hop in."

"I don't think you can make it."

"Get in, Loudon. I'll get you up the dang hill."

"Pink, the drifts are a lot deeper than you think."

Pink leaned across the seat and popped the door open. "Come on, Loudon. We can even pick up Elmer. Where you needing to go?"

As Loudon pulled himself into the front seat, Elmer came stiff-legged down the road like a man trying to walk on ice skates. "Stay down here and wait for Slider," Loudon yelled at him before slamming the door. Elmer nodded, then slipped and fell on his butt. "Christ," Loudon said to Pink, shaking his head.

"You okay, Elmer?" Loudon asked.

Elmer held up his left hand, waving them off as if to say, "I'm fine," then steadied himself with his right hand as he rolled to his side and tried to stand.

"Go on, Pink. I can't watch this."

"You got snow caked on the back of your trousers, Elmer," Pink yelled as he rolled by. "Makes your ass look like a powdered donut." Elmer laughed and shook his head, his cheeks pink and round as Valentine cupcakes.

The snow grew deeper as they passed the squad car, its hood and fender nose-down in the embankment like the shiny flat side of a new shovel. As the incline increased, Pink fed more gas to his Suburban. He felt a tire or two slip and catch, then another, as if the wheels were playing a game of tag on the frozen pavement. The vehicle never stopped moving forward, even though the tires spun on one side, then the other.

Halfway up the mountain, the road and shoulders turned into a continuous ribbon of white, a scraggly row of white pines, poplars, and beech trees marking the edges, the branches fat and sagging with snow.

Loudon wore his grave expression, the same one he wore whether he was fly-fishing the Chattooga River for enormous rainbows and browns or sitting at the courthouse listening to a defendant lie about being innocent. Pink had urged Loudon to spend some time in the poker room in Tunica. "No one can read your mug," Pink had told him.

"I don't go in much for gambling, Pink," Loudon had said. "If I was sure I would win, I might give it a try."

"Then it wouldn't be gambling," Pink had said.

"I 'spect not."

Pink laughed to himself, remembering, then turned to Loudon. "You got folks up here stranded?" Pink asked.

Loudon shook his head and looked over at Pink. "Got a dead man."

"Die trying to get off the mountain?"

"Nope. Far as I can tell he shot himself. Dispatcher wasn't sure. Damn fool thing to do if you ask me. There's nothing bad enough to blow your brains out. I reckon I even know who he is. That man and his wife that was up here a week or so ago. Folks that own your old place, Pink. I never told you about them."

"Michelle Stage?"

"You know 'em?"

Pink didn't want to tell Loudon about running out on her at the Hilltop, that would take too much explaining. Yet he wanted to know what had happened after he'd left. He knew she'd be safe with Lyman, that he'd drive her back to the motel, a perfect gentleman. But how did the husband find her at the Ruby? Had she called him? "Michelle . . . Mrs. Stage, contacted me about selling the cabin. Tired of the long drives, I guess."

"Atlanta, if I remember right." Loudon looked over at Pink with enough squint in his eyes that Pink knew he was fixing to share a secret. "Between you and me, she's crazier than a one-winged bumblebee in a flower house." Loudon told him the story of how she ran off and got lost in the woods, then came back to the cabin and went insane, yelling and running around, talking gibberish, how she had to be restrained and spent a few days at Ardenwood Medical.

"Lost her daughter about a year ago, her husband told me," Loudon said. "In a car accident. Hasn't been right since. A thing like that can pervert a person's mind for life. She even has a restraining order against her. Attacked some woman or something in Atlanta."

"How do you know all that?"

"It's my business to know, Pink. Like it's your business to know a termite trail from a wasp's nest. I heard about that little incident, Pink. Man called my office pretty upset. You shouldn't go around trying to hoodwink college-educated, wealthy folks."

"He was window-shopping anyways," Pink said. "I can tell the ones that's ready to part with some digits from their bank account."

Loudon didn't seem smug with his admonishment of Pink nor did he seem upset about the incident, but Pink could tell he was concerned about Michelle. Pink thought about her, what she'd said about her husband, her daughter, and especially about him and Isabelle. Pink wanted to tell Loudon all of that, but it was too queer and troublesome to repeat. Besides, strange talk could lead to even stranger consequences.

When Pink turned into the driveway, Loudon leaned to the side and unsnapped the strap that secured his weapon. "Why don't you wait here, Pink. Let me see what we've got."

"I'll be fine." Pink shut off the engine. "Besides, I've got you and that cannon strapped to your hip to protect me," Pink said.

"This is no joke, Pink. You don't know people like I do. Folks do things you'd never imagine in a million years. A tiny circuit misfires in their brain and suddenly they've got a gun stuck to their head . . . or yours."

Pink strode behind Loudon, who had drawn his weapon and held it with both hands, the barrel pointed down and away. A breath caught in

Pink's lungs and wedged there, and for a moment he thought to wait in the car. What was he afraid of? Michelle seemed harmless. Crazy, yes, but what woman wasn't? Nobody was moodier than Isabelle, and as for Claire—

"Let me see your hands, ma'am," Loudon said, his voice firm and deep. Loudon had stopped bolt-still, holding his pistol two-hand-steady, leveled at someone on the porch. Pink almost walked into Loudon's back, unaware he'd stopped. He peered around Loudon to see who he was pointing his pistol at. Michelle was nested in the snow wearing her nightgown, staring at Loudon, the nightgown covered in blood. It brought to mind Clarence bending over that nine-point buck several years back near Caney Creek. They'd tracked it for seven hours, almost to dusk, the animal finally dying in a patch of blood-soaked snow. Pink glanced toward a lawn chair toppled over on the deck, blood cutting into the white the way red syrup ate into the shaved ice of a snow cone. Blood-streaked snow covered the deck, pink in some places, deep red near the chair.

Michelle sat motionless. Loudon repeated his order. "Please show me your hands, ma'am." Pink couldn't see Michelle's hands under the comforter. She raised her right arm, and Loudon cautioned her to do it real slow. She brought out the right palm and held it up to Loudon, then the left, both of them red as stop signs. It reminded Pink of his wedding to Isabelle, her father coming into the church dripping blood from his fingers.

"Thank you, ma'am. Now could you please pull back that blanket so I can see what's underneath."

Michelle looked dazed, lost, but certainly not dangerous, and Pink couldn't understand Loudon's intensity. Loudon was sober as a Shriner, his eyes wary and unflinching, as if he'd just caught Charles Manson stealing deck furniture. Loudon wasn't morose, exactly, but he wore gravity like a three-day beard. Once, driving home from the Little Pigeon River, he'd told Pink how mankind teetered at the edge of chaos, how every man, woman, and child was no more than a breath away from violent crime. "Folks wait in checkout lines at Val-U-Mart, pump fuel at the BP, eat dinner with their family down at Pizza Hut with absolute certainty no one will walk up and shoot them dead. But that security is only an illusion, Pink, and folks don't understand how fragile it is . . . thinner than spring ice." Loudon's gritty manner softened somewhat around women though. Pink had seen that a time or two and always figured women put the salty sheriff off-kilter somehow. It was kind of funny to watch, Loudon fumbling with a smile, his hands dipping in and out of his pockets like a couple of chipmunks playing hide-and-seek.

"Is this police procedure?" Pink asked, hoping that Loudon might lighten up a bit.

"You tell me, Pink. You're the one watches all the television." Without blinking, Loudon took a step toward Michelle and waited as she peeled the blanket back. Pink was struck by the severity of the dead man's gaze, his eyes staring, undead, the large rip in his head attesting otherwise.

"His eyes won't shut," Michelle uttered in a flat tone.

"I understand, ma'am. I would like you to gently scoot out from under your husband and move to that chair over there." Loudon pointed at the lounge chair with his gun as if to lead her across the deck. Michelle slowly set her husband's head down in the snow as she uncurled her legs, having trouble standing as though she'd sat too long. Wobbling to her feet, tears filled her eyes as she steadied herself against the railing. She shuffled through the bloody snow, righted the chair, and sat down.

Loudon moved precisely, apparently intent on retrieving the gun clutched in the dead man's hand. "Stand over there by Mrs. Stage, Pink."

Pink walked slowly toward Michelle, his eyes shifting between Loudon, Michelle, and the body. Pink was surprised the man was still holding the gun and couldn't figure out how that could have happened. Wouldn't a dead man have dropped it? Loudon knelt by the body and tried working the firearm from his fingers, having little success. "Take her inside, will you, Pink. And don't let her change clothes just yet."

Pink wasn't sure why Loudon was so concerned. It was obvious Michelle had no weapon since she was naked under her nightgown, and she didn't seem to possess the strength or inclination to use one. Michelle fell easily into Pink's step as he guided her by the shoulders toward the house. Once inside, he led her to the bedroom and sat her on the mattress, the blankets and sheets still balled and twisted from a restless sleep. He went to the bathroom for a hot washcloth then remembered what Loudon had said about not letting her change.

Loudon came in and used the phone.

"Can I get Mrs. Stage out of this wet gown?" Pink asked. "It's frozen hard as a damn ice cube."

Loudon nodded toward Pink then turned away and talked low to someone on the phone.

Pink pulled the blanket from the bed and wrapped Michelle in it. "I'm going to pull your gown off; then we can clean you up, okay? Hold the blanket over you."

He stepped closer and could smell the nicotine in her hair from the Hilltop the night before, along with a dying trace of perfume. He liked the smell, unlike the strong odor that strippers wore. Michelle raised her arms as Pink slipped the gown over her head. The blanket Pink had wrapped her in for privacy fell to her lap and Pink turned away, but not before glimpsing the roundness of her breasts. "Sorry, ma'am," he said. But she hadn't seen him look, didn't seem to care anyway, her gaze somewhere off in another county.

With his head turned, he groped for the blanket and eased it back up over her shoulders. Her fingers gently fastened the blanket across her chest.

"Slider's on his way," Loudon said, hanging up the phone. "Everything okay in there, Pink?"

"I'm going to help her into the shower so she can clean up."

"We don't have time for that, Pink. Get something on her. They'll clean her up down at the hospital."

Now that Loudon had the gun, he didn't seem all that concerned about Michelle anymore. Pink heard the sliding glass door open and shut and figured Loudon would wait on the deck for Slider.

"I'm sorry about what I said to you last night, Pink," Michelle said, looking up at him. "It was very wrong."

"It was wrong of me to run out on you the way I did," Pink said. "Hope Lyman treated you right. He's a good man, churchgoing, sings in the choir and all. I knew you'd be all right."

"It's my fault Cliff is dead," she said, looking out at the snow on the side deck. "I blamed him for everything. That's why he shot himself."

Pink remembered what Loudon had said on the drive up the mountain. "Ain't nothing bad enough for a man to kill himself," Pink told her, "and it sure ain't your fault."

"Some things are bad enough, Pink. Some things are. Cliff believed he killed our daughter on his way over to see his girlfriend. Hard to pull yourself up from that."

"Some folks are survivors, ma'am. Some folks aren't," Pink said, searching for something he could easily dress her in. When he would help Isabelle into something, it was usually her robe. He couldn't recall the last time he'd seen her in regular clothes—a dress, jeans, a pretty blouse. Pink slipped Michelle's robe off the hook on the door and guided her right arm into the sleeve, then the left. She stood and let the blanket fall away. He reached over to cinch the belt at her waist, but she eased his hands away and did it herself. "I don't know where my tennis shoes are, and I lost my slippers in the snow," Michelle said, her eyes brimming with tears.

"I saw your shoes under the coffee table in the living room," Pink said, and went to retrieve them. When he returned, Michelle was slumped on the floor at the foot of the bed, sobbing silently into her knees, her shoulders jerking. Pink heard the siren coming up the hill as he knelt next to Michelle and placed his arm around her shoulder. He'd never been much of a nurturer, felt awkward even pretending, so he tried to remember how he'd seen men do it in movies. They always did it without words. But it was hard not saying anything.

*****

Death grip. That's what Loudon called it. Told Pink he had to break the husband's fingers. "Had to snap 'em like twigs," Loudon explained to Pink. "That's why I had you take her inside. Couldn't have her seeing that."

Michelle had not struggled when Slider escorted her to the cruiser. She sat in the back seat staring out the window, like a damn puppy headed to the pound, Pink thought. There wasn't anything he could do for her. Even so, something purled in his chest at the sorry sight of her.

Loudon went back in the house and called Emerson to come fetch the body.

"Oh, shit, Loudon," Pink said, following behind. "Tell Emerson to bring Lulu's ashes with him. I plumb forgot 'em this morning."

After Loudon relayed the message, he grimaced and handed the phone to Pink. "What is it, Emerson?" Pink said, jerking the phone to his mouth. He didn't want to talk to Emerson or listen to whining about proper procedures.

"Well, Mattie didn't pick out an urn or anything. What should I bring them in?"

"Bring 'em in a dang baggie for all I care. They're ashes, for Christ's sake."

Loudon shook his head. "They're the remains of your mama's beloved friend, Pink."

"Shit, now I'm getting it from Loudon too," Pink said, turning his back to Loudon. "What do you put ashes in when folks ain't got much money?"

"A plastic container with their name on the outside," Emerson said. "Containers come in brown, tan, and green, although not many folks choose the green 'cause it kind of looks like mold and I guess folks don't want their loved ones remembered that way. Then I put a nice label on the end with the name of the loved one and the name of my funeral home in case—"

"Brown box'll be fine. Thanks. And hurry. This body up here is thawing and it doesn't look good." Pink hung up the phone without waiting for Emerson to answer.

"You have a hard way about you, Pink," Loudon said, gathering up Michelle's purse and personal items. "See if she has a trash bag in the pantry there, one of those white kitchen deals to put these clothes in."

A hard way? Pink thought, taking offense at Loudon's statement. Well, *if that ain't the grounds calling the coffee black,* he was about to say, but went to the pantry instead and found a yellow box full of Glad kitchen bags. Loudon was looking through Michelle's purse when Pink came back. "That ain't legal, is it?" Pink said.

Loudon shifted his eyes toward Pink then continued stirring the contents with his pen, setting a few items on the kitchen table. One of them caught Pink's eye. He picked it up and studied it.

"That's one of those pentagrams, isn't it?" Loudon asked.

Pink nodded. "Isabelle had one like it years ago. Used to wear it around her neck all the time. My mama gave it to her when she was thirteen." Pink palmed the pendant, the chain dangling from his closed fist as if his concentration alone might reveal the source of the jewelry. Getting nothing but blanks, Pink popped his fingers open suddenly to have another peek.

"Looks just like it," Pink said, shaking his head.

Loudon grabbed the pendant and dropped it in the purse. "Must be thousands like it, Pink. I see kids wearing them all the time."

"I never have," Pink said.

"*You* wouldn't, unless it happened to be draped across a girl's low-cut tank top, or swinging from her rear end over a tight pair of jeans."

"That's just mean, Loudon," Pink said. "But I like how you think."

Loudon shook his head, taking the gun he'd removed from the husband's hand and putting it in a clear plastic food bag. "I got to run a check on this. Wish to hell Emerson would get here so I could get back to the station. I gotta get the coroner on this to make sure it was a suicide before I let Mrs. Stage go back to Atlanta."

"Christ, Loudon, you think the woman shot her husband, then super-glued the damn gun in his hand?" Pink laughed, but Loudon didn't share the humor, intent on staring at the door like a housebroke dog. Pink dug in his pocket and brought out his keys. "Take the Suburban down and leave it at the bottom of the hill. Elmer must have gotten the squad car towed out by now. I'll help Emerson with the body then ride down with him."

Loudon squinted with concern. "Well, this probably isn't the best idea I've heard all year. But thank you, Pink," Loudon took the keys. "And don't touch anything. It's not your house anymore."

"Yeah, right, but I been thinking about buying it back since it's going on the market. Isabelle doesn't seem to want to sleep under the same roof with me anymore anyways, and I've always loved this place. Built it with my own two hands. Even did the wiring and plumbing."

"You're right handy, Pink. No one would argue that." Loudon jangled the keys and let himself out carrying Michelle's things.

When Pink was sure Loudon was gone, he rummaged through the dresser drawers and closets, the kitchen cabinets, the medicine cabinet in the bathroom, curious how Michelle and her husband lived. In the back of his mind he was certain she owned a vibrator, something Isabelle would never tolerate in the house. Pink had bought one at the Lion's Den years ago. Isabelle could barely stop laughing. "That's not going inside me! If you want me to cram that up *your* ass, I'll be glad to. I'll use a damn hammer if you want."

Pink searched the cabinet under the bathroom sink, making it okay in his mind by telling himself if he was going to list the house, it was best he knew as much about it as possible.

"What you doing there, Pink?" a voice said.

Pink shot up from the cabinet, hitting his head on the edge of the countertop. "Damn, Emerson! You wearing cotton shoes? Make a damn noise when you sneak up on somebody!"

"You gonna help me with the body. Curt didn't come in today."

"Who the hell is Curt?"

"That young kid I got working for me. Up from Valdosta, Georgia. Trying life with his pa for a while. Boy isn't much use, but I need the help."

"Well if he ain't much help . . . how can he be any help?"

"I don't even know what you're trying to ask me, Pink, and I don't have time to figure it out. Got to get this body loaded and skedaddle. Got a bereaved family coming up from Buncombe at two, and I haven't even suited the dearly departed yet."

Pink followed Emerson out to the deck. Emerson unzipped the black bag and spread it out next to the body. "Sure is a mess," Emerson said. "Closed casket for sure. Can't hardly patch a hole that big and make it look natural."

"Christ, Emerson. Save the shoptalk for Curt when he comes back to work. Let's get him in the bag."

They rolled the body into the sack, then wrestled the limbs in, and zipped it shut. "Let me get the gurney," Emerson said. "That way we won't have to carry him so far."

Pink watched as Emerson tried to force the gurney through the snow in the driveway. "Hell of a storm, hey, Pink? Bad as '93."

"You and Loudon," Pink said. "Can't nobody remember '93 was worse? Way worse. Twice as bad."

"This one's pretty bad too, Pink. Had a hard time getting up the hill."

"Let's get this thing on the damn gurney so I can get the hell out of here."

They lifted the bag onto the table, the metal zipper clattering when they flopped it down. Pink helped Emerson guide the gurney through the snow. They lifted it into the back of the camper shell.

"Whose pickup is this?" Pink asked.

"Kelsey's. My brother-in-law. I knew the van wouldn't get up the mountain, so I asked Kelsey if I could borrow his truck. He's giving me a hand down at the mortuary with Curt gone and all. Kelsey doesn't do much, but I need the help."

"Right. Good luck with . . . whatever," Pink said.

"Yeah, we'll see you later, Pink."

Emerson was pulling out of the driveway when Pink ran after him yelling, pounding his fist on the camper shell. When Emerson stopped, Pink jerked the door open and threw himself into the cab. "Loudon took my truck down the hill," Pink said, out of breath. "I need a ride." Pink looked down at the plain brown box on the seat next to him then pushed it closer to Emerson to make more room for himself.

"Oh yeah. Almost forgot. Them's Lulu's ashes," Emerson said. "I think the brown was a good choice, even though tan seems to be the most popular. I think folks like the tan because it looks like fine oak wood or something. You know. The brown, well, it just looks plastic."

CHAPTER 24

His mother handed Pink a shovel and broom and asked him to clear snow from the circle. When he set the plastic box with Lulu's ashes on the coffee table, her eyes grew bright for a moment. Burrito yapped at his ankles then darted over to Mattie and shook until she bent over and picked him up.

"You okay, Mama?" Pink said.

"Yes, yes. Please shovel the circle for me, Pink."

Pink strolled to the back door and tested his way down the hill through the snow, using the shovel and broom like walking sticks to keep his footing. The snow was deep, and Pink wasn't even sure he could find the ceremonial circle—the fresh powder was disorienting—until he tripped over the stones marking its edge.

His mama's rituals were a mystery, and Pink didn't really buy into this sacred circle business, but there was something about her, about what she did, that was powerful. He was certain of that. She'd prepared tinctures and elixirs for folks over the years, and sure enough, eventually they'd heal. Everything from asthma to worms. She had shown him how to prepare "Melissa" when Isabelle was down with stomach flu, but he'd grown impatient when she told him to grind the herbs between his palms. "Can't we just use the coffee grinder?" he'd asked. To release the most potential from the herbs, she'd told him, it was important to "connect" with them and meditate on what you were doing. The day they were to prepare the "Melissa," she'd had him arrive at five in the morning on a Thursday. "We have to start preparing it immediately after sunrise," she'd told him. The day of the week, as well as the hour, were crucial to the tincture's potency and success in treating ailments. When she'd explained about planetary influences and salt level charts, he'd felt his brain go numb, then headed for her refrigerator to find something to eat. That was the last time she'd asked him to help.

After Pink shoveled the perimeter of the circle, he swept the last of the snow out with the broom, down to grass. He removed the snow beneath the arched trellis that served as the entrance to the circle, then cleared a path back up to his mama's house. By the time he reached her back porch, sweat soaked his jacket. His shirt, undershirt, and undershorts were drenched. He hated working this hard. If he was going to sweat, he wanted it to be for a good reason. Pink suddenly pictured Claire's breasts tolling like bells as she rocked on top of him in the front seat of his Suburban. If Kenny had known how amenable and horny his little game of bridge-jumping had made Claire, he'd no doubt perfect hundreds of new death threats.

"Thank you, Pink," Mattie said, appearing at the back door. "Would you help me carry these things down?" She set a clay chimenea on the deck, along with a box filled with gold and red silk scarves.

"How about some breakfast first?" Pink said, leaning the shovel and broom against the railing.

"Isabelle called," Mattie said. "She sounded angry. What'd you do?"

"Nothing. You have any eggs and ham steak going to waste in that refrigerator of yours?"

"Come in and warm up. I'll fix you something."

Pink threw himself in a kitchen chair as Mattie bent over to fish a frying pan from the bottom cabinet. Pink could tell she was crying, even though she was trying to hide it. His stomach had been growling since seven that morning, and he didn't want to sidetrack her from cooking the ham and eggs by asking what was wrong, but he did anyway, hoping it wasn't about Isabelle or Claire.

"I miss her so much," his mama said, directing her gaze toward the living room, toward Lulu's ashes sitting on the coffee table. "She was like a grandmother to you and a mother to me. And a best friend."

Those were the last words Mattie spoke before turning away to cook his breakfast. Pink was thankful for the silent interlude; it gave him time to think about Claire. Over the past few years it had grown harder to remember how Isabelle had been before she took sick, how beautiful she'd been, how funny, how affectionate, how strong. He'd fantasized about coming home from the office and finding Isabelle dead, so he and Claire could take up together after she dumped Kenny. Then he and Claire could move somewhere new. A fresh start. Folks did it all the time, though not many from Ardenwood seemed to. The fantasy floated him, gave him prospects, even though being with Claire wouldn't be a swim in the punch bowl either. But Claire was simpler, not nearly as bright as Isabelle. He'd be able to sneak a lot past Claire.

Mattie rattled a plate from the cabinet and swept the ham and eggs onto it with her spatula. "Do you want coffee, sweetheart?" she asked, twisting toward him. He nodded, speechless at the sudden and unexpected kindness in her voice. She was like an ebbing tide, one second gruff, the next pleasant. She set the plate and coffee in front of him. After practically dropping the fork, knife, and ketchup bottle on the table next to Pink, Mattie dropped into the chair. She let out a sigh and deflated like a balloon with a fast leak. She wiped her eyes as she glanced across at him. "I'm sorry I was so cross with you this morning, Pink. Lulu's death is hitting me hard." She shifted her eyes toward the living room and shook her head. "And Emerson. How could he put Lulu in such an awful thing? I told him I'd pay for everything and he puts her ashes in a plastic box the color of rubber dog poop. I don't understand it." Pink speared a fat piece of ham and slid it past his lips, not about to confess that the box was his idea.

"Did you have trouble getting up the road," she asked, turning the bottom of her apron in her fingers.

"Not a bit," he said, chewing a mouthful of food.

"What took you so long? Isabelle said you left the house over two hours ago."

"Gave Loudon a lift up the hill. Some feller shot himself, and Loudon and Elmer—"

"Shot himself? Like a hunting accident? Is he all right?"

"Blew his own dang head off. Don't think it was no accident."

Mattie recoiled, covering her mouth, and Pink heard a feeble whimper squeeze from her throat, not much more than a squeak.

"It was them folks from Atlanta that bought my cabin," Pink told her.

"The man whose wife ran off and got lost in the woods a few weeks back?"

"How'd you know about that?" Pink asked.

"Loudon told me. Pink, that's awful. Was she there when it happened? Is she okay?"

"She found the body. She's a little loony herself, so I'm not sure it fully registered in that cobweb brain of hers."

"That's an awful thing to say, Pink. She was probably in shock."

Maybe she was, he thought. He'd never seen anyone in shock, didn't really know what that meant. He forked the scrambled eggs until the tines were covered. *Mattie's head was shaking of its own free will*, Pink thought, her eyes roaming the floor.

"Why do you think she's not right in the head?" Mattie finally said. "Do you know her?"

Pink referred to Michelle as Mrs. Stage when he told about her coming to his office, about how she'd lied about wanting to sell the cabin so she could talk with him, about her husband coming up from Atlanta to take her back. As soon as he finished, he could tell by his mama's vexed expression that he shouldn't have said a word.

"What business she have with you? And couldn't she just pick up the phone and call you?"

"Mama, it ain't nothing. Just something about the property, and—"

"Don't lie to me, Pink. Are you fooling around with that woman? What's going on?"

"Ain't nothing going on. Hellfire, Mama. Why's everything gotta be a dang scandal?"

Mattie eased back in her chair, freezing him in her gaze.

"You have any pie?" he asked, not enjoying the contest.

"Isabelle was very angry when she called this morning. There's something going on, Pink. Is it about this Mrs. Stage? How are you involved with Mrs. Stage?"

Pink sucked at the threads of ham caught in his teeth, trying to floss his bicuspid with the tip of his tongue. "It ain't nothing, just some crazy notion took up residence in that woman's confused head." He told his mother everything Michelle had told him, about Cliff disappearing, how she'd gone to look for him, how Loudon had searched and found nothing, about taking Michelle to the Hilltop, feeding her corn liquor. "Then she said Louden told her I killed Isabelle and disappeared, like a damn ghost or something," Pink said. "Can you beat that?"

While relating the story, Pink had been careful not to address his mother directly, letting his eyes dance around the fan blades above them as if he'd been talking to the ceiling. When he let his eyes fall back to her, he could tell she was disturbed. But more than that, she was scared, scared as if she'd swallowed some kind of slow-acting poison and knew it.

He studied her as she looked to the side then at the table, at his empty breakfast plate, mesmerized as if some movie played in her head, one she didn't care much for.

"Loudon said you killed Isabelle then disappeared?" she finally said.

"Loudon didn't tell her anything like that, Mama. Don't you get it? Mrs. Stage is delusional—schizophrenic or something. Maybe she has one of them multiplied personality disorders, like that Sybil picture with Sally Moore or whatever the hell her name was."

Mattie stared through him.

"Let's look at the facts, Mama," Pink said, screeching the chair legs along the floor as he pushed away from the table. "I'm here. You're here. And I'm pretty sure Isabelle is still at home. Ain't nobody disappeared, and I can guarantee you there ain't no damn dead bodies buried up at the cabin. She's abnormal, and that's all there is to it. Now, let's get this circle of yours decorated up so I can get on home before Isabelle starts calling here again."

Burrito barked as Pink stretched to his feet. Mattie didn't move, still seated and staring. The dog ran to her chair then to its empty water bowl and whimpered. Mattie stood slowly and walked over to the sink, absently picking up the dog's dish and filling it with water. Several pieces of dried dog food floated to the top and bobbed like flotsam. Burrito nosed the chunks for a second then jumped back and barked at them.

*****

Pink had not planned staying at his mother's as long as he had. Isabelle called again.

"Can't she set up her own damn circle?" Isabelle said.

"We're almost done, Sugar Plum. Probably another hour," Pink said, trying to paint a pleasant face on his side of the conversation in case his mama was listening.

"That'll give you time to come up with a better story than the one you told me last night, you bastard. You keep fucking Claire and you're gonna get your damn balls snapped off. I'm telling you. I swear, Pink, you get her pregnant, you'll be putting a down payment on hell. You'll regret it the rest of your miserable, fucking life."

"Save the sweet talk for when I get home, Gumdrop. Okay?"

Pink kept talking, even though Isabelle had already slammed the phone down. "Yes, not much longer. Need anything from the store?" He glanced toward the living room to see where his mama was. She was studying the plastic box of ashes, rotating it slowly as if trying to figure out how to get into it. Pink wasn't sure himself. It appeared to be sealed, but he wasn't about to call Emerson.

They carried more things down to the circle and worked in silence. Pink wrapped the red and gold scarves around the trellis, alternating them the way his mother had shown him. Standing on the ladder, he wrapped the top of the trellis, then stepped down to finish the sides. His mama was busy setting up candles, adjusting the cauldron stand so the metal pot would hang over the center of the firepit. Anytime Pink saw her cauldron, which was no bigger than half a watermelon, he always pictured those enormous iron vessels requiring two hands to stir, a wall of eerily-lit jars behind, the tiny eyes of dead critters staring bleakly at the fire. But this was nothing like that, and he often wondered if his mother's demure approach to witchcraft was a disservice to the occult. Maybe if she wore all black with a pointed hat and donned a ridiculously large wart on her nose and employed a scorching inferno beneath her caldron, maybe he could believe something supernatural could happen. As it was, her ceremonies were no more mysterious and frightening than a Tupperware party. In fact, they bordered on boring. Nobody's eyes rolled back in their heads, no one spoke in tongues, or burst into flames. And for the few he'd attended, his biggest obstacle had been staying awake.

When Pink tied off the last scarf, he adjusted them so the red and gold seemed evenly spaced. If they weren't, his mama might make him take them all down and start over. Even though the sun burned high in the sky, the air was still plenty cold, his fingers turning numb. "Maybe we should get us a fire going in that pit of yours," Pink said, blowing into his palms.

Mattie looked first at him, then at the scarves. She scratched the line of her jaw with her gloved fingers. He took this as approval. Pink recalled the afternoon he'd found Lulu's body, about the stone his mama had wiggled from the hearth.

"Remember that silver box you took from Lulu's house, the one with Lulu's belly button cord?" Pink asked. "What are you going to do with that?"

Mattie was bent over at the west side of the circle, fitting a blue cloth over one of the four small altars. The circle was laid out in the four directions, each with its own color, its own unique accouterments. Pink had no idea what any of it meant. Mattie straightened and stretched, arching her torso with her head laid back. Pink thought she looked weary.

"Why, Pink? You don't care about any of this."

"It's kind of freaky, don't you think? Somebody sticking their damn ripcord in a little jewelry box and stashing it in their fireplace. No wonder folks knock down your mailboxes and burn your tool sheds." Pink remembered his mother's friend Jesse's little wooden outbuilding in flames, a sign stuck in his yard saying witches weren't welcome in Ardenwood. "Sane folks don't do things like that."

Mattie turned away, then pulled a yellow cloth from the box and arranged it on the east altar.

"Is there anything else you need me to do, Mama? I told Isabelle I'd be home around two o'clock," he said, glancing down at his wrist even though his sleeve hid the face of his watch.

"You're coming tonight for Lulu, aren't you?" she said.

Pink didn't want anything to do with whatever corny shindig his mother had in mind for poor, dead Lulu's spirit. He told her Isabelle didn't like him gone at night, that he needed to be there for his wife.

"Lulu was like a grandmother to you," she said. "She loved you, watched after you . . . protected you." His mama's eyes grew so hard he thought they were going to crack under the stare. "Lulu—" She stopped as if to consider what she was about to say. "Lulu did things for you that you didn't even know about."

"Maybe if I knew all these wonderful things she did for me, I'd feel different," Pink said, his breath hanging in the frosty air, the sound of his own words repugnant to him. He tried to apologize, but she gave him her back and hurried toward the house. Before she'd turned away, her expression flashed anger first, then hurt. It was the hurt that bothered Pink the most.

*****

The look his mama had given Pink as she'd left the circle still burned in his head. He hated arguing with her and hadn't intended on saying mean things, but the truth was, he was embarrassed she carried on the way she did, lighting candles, chanting out in front of trees and God, cutting circles in the air with her sacred knife, talking about deities, names he'd never heard and couldn't pronounce. The knife had a special name too, but he couldn't remember what it was. It had a sharp, curved blade that looked like it might be handy for cleaning squirrels or trimming carpet. Once he'd suggested that very thing while rolling it over in his fingers. It was the closest he'd ever come to being slapped by his mama. "Don't ever touch that, Pink!" she'd yelled, snatching it from him and marching off to the spare bedroom she used as her sacred space. He'd peeked in there on occasion and was surprised by how unremarkable it was. The glass trinket case at the 74 Truck Stop was more interesting.

Pink turned onto Howdershoot Road and thought about stopping at the office. Not that there was anything to do there, but it beat going home and dealing with Isabelle. He glanced at the dash clock and figured Isabelle was probably worn out from anger and waiting and most likely had fallen asleep. Over the past twelve years *anger and waiting* seemed to be at the heart of her diet, the food that propelled her forward, like jet fuel to a 727. Now with her unidentifiable illness costing him hundreds of dollars a month in diagnosis technology (he figured he'd probably paid for one of those MRI machines over the past four years), Isabelle could only endure an hour or so of anger and waiting before it sapped her strength and put her flat on her back.

He wondered if Claire was still at the house, or if she'd crawled home, soggy-eyed and filled with remorse, to Kenny. What Claire saw in Kenny, Pink could never figure out.

Snow melted in the driveway, the rectangular bare spot where his Suburban had been parked overnight completely dry, with sprigs of green grass struggling up through the gravel. The argument he'd had with his mama rumbled through his brain. It was her hurt he couldn't cleanse from his mind.

Claire was painting her nails at the kitchen table when he walked in. He heard the sizzle of something cooking on the stove, the smell of fried chicken layered with the pungent stink of lacquer. Claire looked up. "Where have you been all day?"

"Don't start. And why do you have to do that in here?" He glanced at her spread fingers. "It ruins half the pleasure of having fried chicken."

She waved him off then screwed on the lid of the red bottle with her thumb and ring finger.

"Isabelle sleeping?" he asked.

Claire nodded, getting up to turn the chicken.

"Just you and me for dinner, huh?"

Claire smiled at him and, for a moment, he didn't trust her kindness, but it seemed sincere. She'd never smiled at him like that before.

"I rented a movie to watch with dinner," she said, pulling a tin of rolls from the oven. "It's that one with George Clooney, the one about the big storm. I've never seen it, have you?"

Pink sat at the table. "I don't know who George Clooney is, but if you like it, I'll watch it."

"How was your day?" she said, smiling over her shoulder at him.

"Fine. I helped Emerson load a dead guy in somebody's pickup today. The top of his head looked like a barbecue grill."

Claire spun from the stove, her face twisted painfully. Her smile returned slowly, the one Pink was uncomfortable with. "You're kidding, right?" she said.

"No. Fool shot his brains out. His wife found him out on the deck this morning, frozen. Loudon and Elmer couldn't get up the hill so I—"

"Stop, Pink! I don't want to hear anymore of this. Let's just eat and watch the damn movie."

CHAPTER 25

"Your sister's here," the nurse said, her vague shape moving away as the silhouette of someone else passed through the bright doorway. The dusty, blue light of evening had settled over the room like smoke, leaving everything bleary. Michelle tried to push herself up from the bed, her arms as heavy and useless as damp laundry. She wanted to snap on a light, flush the fatigue from her head and her bones, but she could hardly move.

"Don't get up, sweetie."

Michelle recognized the voice, still unable to focus. Darcy touched her hand.

"Where am I, Darcy?" Michelle knew she was in a hospital, but had no idea where, Ardenwood or Atlanta, or how long she'd been there. She remembered the police officer talking to her in the car, asking if she was warm enough, turning up the heat, the police radio bleating serious sounds and garbled sentences. She even recalled the sun reflecting off the metal letters of the hospital sign on the side of the building. That was her last memory. Everything had gone black at that point, and she'd been swimming in her pool at home, the water cool and too blue, the sun soothing and steady, dependable and shadow free. But all the other houses had disappeared. Even the stockade fence Cliff had built was gone, nothing but pool and sky, as if they were reflections of each other, the pool expanding as she pulled herself forward through the water, her body cutting a path toward the horizon.

"Ardenwood, Michelle. I left Atlanta as soon as the sheriff called."

"What day is it?"

"Sunday. Sunday night."

Michelle remembered Cliff, his body solid and unmoving, caked and powdered with snow. "My God, Darcy." Michelle couldn't stop the tears. Darcy placed her hand on Michelle's forehead, brushing back her hair.

"It's my fault, isn't it?" Michelle said. "What have I done?"

For a moment, Michelle blamed herself for not accepting Cassie's death or Cliff's pleas. Was she insane like Cliff had told her? That notion brought more tears, more remorse, followed by the memory of Cassie's voice on the phone at the cabin. Had that been a dream? Would she wake up to find Cliff alive? Was his suicide a dream? In the turbulence of conflicting truths, Michelle felt something curl in her stomach, then lurch. She tried for the bathroom, but was too late, losing her stomach on the floor near the bathroom door. Darcy jumped up, helping Michelle back into bed, trying to calm her.

"That's probably the meds, Chelle. It'll pass."

After the nurse placed a cold washcloth on the back of Michelle's neck, she cleaned up the room. Why had she come back to Ardenwood? She could've stayed in Atlanta, waited out the impulse to prove everyone wrong about Cassie, give herself time to catch up to Cliff's reality. If only she could have trusted Cliff . . . but she'd never been able to. *Is this what it's like to be mad?* she thought. Is this how it will always be, believing one thing is real and then believing its opposite, each notion as authentic as the other? She couldn't stand it, couldn't stand the thought that the rest of her life could be a jumble of truths, one no more real than the next.

"We'll head home in the morning if you're up to it," Darcy said.

Michelle closed her eyes, easing her hand from Darcy's, a throng of faces staring at her from the darkness deep inside her head. For a moment, she couldn't distinguish one from another, until they stepped forward— Cliff, Pink, Cassie, Sheriff Fisk, Cliff standing in his tux at the altar on their wedding day, Cliff sitting on the bed, his finger missing, then a beautiful young woman Michelle didn't recognize, her hair wet and stringy and dark—

CHAPTER 26

"Where are you going? I have another movie," Claire said, taking the disc out of the DVD player. Pink hated the stupid movie. Claire insisted *The Perfect Storm* was a true story, and Pink said it was *based* on a true story.

"What's the difference?" she said.

"Reality!" He tried to explain that no one could know the details depicted in the movie if everyone died in the storm.

"Well, I like true stories," Claire said. "They're more exciting because they really happened."

"The only thing that really happened was the damn boat sinking. The rest of it is horse shit."

"Well, how do you know it didn't happen that way? Maybe somebody recorded it from the radio?"

"The radio was dead."

"I guess you don't think shows like *Survivor* are real, either?"

"I've got to go. Mama's having a ceremony for Lulu tonight."

"Doesn't that witchcraft stuff make your skin crawl? It does mine. I don't know how you can think *Survivor* and *The Perfect Storm* is all horse-shit and then believe in witchcraft. That makes no sense."

"Who said I believe in witchcraft? Anyway, I gotta go. The roads are gonna turn bad when the temperature drops."

"What am I gonna do here alone? My puzzles are all at the house."

"Watch your movie. I'll be home by the time it's over. Then we can . . . you know . . ."

"Why don't I pull down my jeans and you can give me a good screwing before you leave," she said, unsnapping her pants.

Pink stopped putting on his coat, even though he was pretty sure Claire was being sarcastic. "We could . . ."

"For Pete's sake, Pink! What about some kissing and cuddling? What about a little foreplay?"

"Foreplay? I've been *thinking* about sex ever since last night. Doesn't that count?"

Claire hurled the DVD box across the room, clipping Pink in the forehead.

"Damn, Claire. You're ornery as your damn sister."

Pink was thankful for the slap of cold air when he walked outside to his Suburban, glad to be free of the house, of Isabelle—even though she had slept most of the evening—and especially to be away from Claire. How could he live with a woman no smarter than a leather belt? Then he thought about Claire's breasts, her plump round ass, the way she cooed and moaned when they screwed. He'd have to find a hobby that kept him out of the house most of the time. That's probably why Kenny took up walleye fishing and cocaine.

Pink turned the key in the ignition, squinting toward the house, half-expecting to see the curtains pulled back, Claire peeking out into the darkness.

Where was Kenny? *He hadn't bothered to call Claire at the house or drive by,* Pink thought, finally mustering a little anger over the stunt Kenny had pulled at Burtran Lake. Pink had felt some humiliation, but it was quickly drowned out by fear then a bit of amusement over the scenario: he and Claire practically naked standing on the railing of the bridge in the middle of the night. Picturing Claire's panties rolling down her hips as he'd dragged her up the hill aroused him again. It was hard to stay mad with a mind full of stimulating images.

Pink turned off the radio as he drove along the winding road to his mama's house, passing the road sign with his name on it. He hated that sign, almost as much as he hated these ceremonies.

Before he pulled into his mama's driveway, he saw the orange glow of fire flickering off the tree trunks. A serpent of smoke crawled up through the naked limbs. He half expected to walk around to her backyard and find an angry mob waving lit torches, his mother in the center tied to a huge pine stake, dry straw crackling in a tribe of flames. What he saw when he began the long trudge down the hill was far less dramatic but nearly as surprising. His mother stood in the center of her sacred circle completely alone. He couldn't believe no one had shown for Lulu's farewell.

"Mama?" Pink said, almost in a whisper, not wanting to startle her.

His mother looked over, her eyes shiny and orange with fire. Pink stepped back, frightened momentarily by his mother's queer appearance, until she wiped her hand across her cheeks. She stepped toward him and drew her athame from the pocket of her robe, using the black-handled knife to slice an imaginary circular door in the invisible barrier beneath the arbor. Pink knew not to step over the stones or enter the ceremonial circle through the arbor before his mother performed this ritual, even though he thought it was silly.

He entered quietly and took his place at the south altar, next to the chimenea. Maybe the heat would warm his legs and toes. He wished he'd worn long underwear.

"No, Pink. Come stand with me," his mother said, taking his hand, guiding him toward the altar covered in green cloth. A white candle burned next to the brown plastic container holding Lulu's ashes.

"Where is everyone?" Pink asked, feeling a draft of warm air from the fire beneath the cauldron.

"Don't speak, son." She pointed at the box of ashes, indicating that Pink should pick them up. When he did, she stepped back and nodded for him to stand beside her. After reaching her hand into Lulu's ashes, she faced east and extended her arm straight out from her body.

"Ye Lords of the Watchtowers of the East, ye Lords of Air, please witness these ashes and carry Lulu on sacred winds, that we may breathe her in with each and every breath. With these ashes I honor Lulu's descendants, offspring born not of her womb, but of her spirit, the blood which lived in her veins now lives in theirs, and theirs in hers." His mother closed her eyes and opened her fingers slowly, releasing the ashes into the night air. After a moment of silence, she faced south, evoking the Lords of Fire, honoring Lulu's descendants once again, releasing ashes into the air, then she turned to the west. Tears trailed down her face, "Ye Lords of Death and Initiation, please witness these ashes and embrace her warmly, that we may feel her presence in the rain that falls, in the tears that grace our flesh." She finished by facing north, repeating her incantations into the frigid air, steam billowing from her lips.

Even though Mattie released Lulu's ashes, the container seemed to be getting no lighter. Pink readjusted the brown container, supporting it against his belly, hoping his mama wouldn't notice his fatigue. Her unflinching resolve made him feel weak. She was dressed in nothing but a robe—no coat, hat, or gloves, frost forming on her eyebrows—and yet she seemed impervious to the chill, while Pink's feet were hard and cold as hammers. He wanted to ask how much longer this would go on, but fought the urge, knowing she would never acknowledge his plea anyway and reprimand him afterward.

She performed the ritual to each direction again, this time releasing the ashes below knee level, honoring Lulu's ancestors. With the final invocations to the four directions, she released Lulu's ashes at waist level while honoring her own relationship to Lulu. When she finished, the container was empty and Pink figured they were done. He was ready to warm up at the house and make a sandwich. He remembered the leftover blood sausage in his mama's fridge and could almost taste it. He waited, trying to bolster his patience, as she stood facing north, unmoving. Wind raced down the mountain, sending a shiver through Pink.

After a few moments, his mother picked up a silver spade with a plain wooden handle and used her athame to cut a door into the space beneath the arbor. "Pink, please bring that small silver box."

Pink didn't want to pick it up. He pictured Lulu's shriveled, brown umbilical cord inside. He knew he'd never eat beef jerky again. He was about to protest his mama's request when she turned away from him, knelt in the snow outside the north edge of the ceremonial circle, and started digging. Pink picked up the filigreed box and carried it like a dead mouse to his mother's side.

"Take it out, Pink," she said, still kneeling in the snow.

"Aw, Mama. I don't want to touch that thing."

The disappointment on her face nearly crushed him. "That *thing* was Lulu's lifeline, her connection between this life and the other. It is Lulu. I want you to place it in this hole, Pink."

Pink opened the box carefully, staring at the dried hunk as if it were a scorpion. Using his thumb and forefinger, he withdrew the shriveled flesh, squatted down, and placed it in the hole. When he stood up, his mother reached into the pocket of her robe and withdrew a small seed and placed it next to the umbilical. With her bare hands, she eased the piled dirt from the verge of the hole and carefully covered the items.

"What was that, Mama?"

"The seed of a rowan tree. It will grow here, and Lulu will be born again in its roots and limbs."

"We finished now?" Pink said, stepping from foot to foot to pump heat into his toes.

His mother glared up at him. "No, not yet, son. There's something we must do tonight."

CHAPTER 27

A woman stood at the window holding the curtains open, staring out, light from the hospital parking lot burning a bright line along the hard, angular profile of her face. Michelle knew it wasn't Darcy, thinking at first it might be a nurse. But the woman wore the same kind of flowered blue gown Michelle was wearing. Michelle pushed herself up, groggy from the medication she'd taken, wondering what time it was, where Darcy had gone.

"I'm sorry if I woke you," the woman said, glancing at Michelle.

"You didn't."

"I'm your roommate."

Michelle had heard someone speaking with the nurse earlier but had been unable to see who she was because the nurse had drawn the privacy curtain.

Cliff's suicide flashed across Michelle's mind in such a way that it felt at first like a distant memory, an event caught in a safe and comfortable orbit outside her life. Soon the image of Cliff spiraled closer, growing larger—his blank frozen eyes, the frost covering his face and hair, his snow-encrusted fingers clutching the gun.

"Are you okay?" the woman said, sitting down on the corner of Michelle's bed, taking her hand.

"Yes." She took a deep breath, grateful for the woman's warm touch, the softness in her voice. "I'm Michelle."

The woman looked toward the white message board on the wall where Michelle Stage was written in blue marker, alongside it the attending nurse's name. "Yes, I know. I'm the other name, Ms. Smith . . . at least that's what they're calling me. I'm glad they didn't put Jane Doe."

"I'm sorry," Michelle said. "I don't understand."

The woman looked toward the white message board. "I don't know who I am. They had to call me something."

The woman spoke slowly, deliberately, as if she were on a budget and words were costly. Michelle thought maybe the woman was speaking precisely for her benefit, until it occurred to her that maybe the woman was piecing the story together from what people had told her. Occasionally the woman glanced back toward the window, then at Michelle, as she explained that she had been found on the AT a few days earlier with no food or shoes, nothing but the clothes on her back. A young couple, hikers from Virginia, had found her and called the police with their cell phone.

"The nurse said I hadn't spoken to them, only stared." The woman smiled wryly. "I have no idea why I was up in the mountains."

"What's the AT?"

"The Appalachian Trail," the woman said. "That's what the psychiatrist told me. They thought maybe I was a through-hiker, so they searched the surrounding area where the couple had found me for some sign of a tent, or backpack, but found nothing." The woman laughed nervously, looking over at Michelle. "Sounds like one of those bad movies you see on cable television, doesn't it?"

"At least you remember cable television," Michelle said, instantly regretting the stupid remark. "I'm sorry, that was—"

"Don't apologize. You're absolutely right. I mean . . . I'm thankful I can remember how to talk, and walk, and feed myself with a spoon. I'd hate to start over at my age."

"So you remember your age?"

"No, dear. But I've looked in the mirror. I haven't forgotten what old looks like."

Michelle's mind spun with questions she wouldn't allow herself to ask—Can they cure it? Is it permanent? What will you do? Where will you go?

"Everyone's been very nice," the woman told Michelle, "especially since there's every chance I will not be able to pay. If this had happened in Chicago . . ."

The woman broke off suddenly, staring at the wall. "Why did I say Chicago?" Her face brightened for a moment, then faded. "The doctor mentioned Chicago the other day. He's from Chicago, and he thought my speech pattern sounded familiar. It's not my own memory."

How horrible, Michelle thought, to have your life handed back to you by strangers, as if you were expected to take what they'd given you and build your existence from the scraps. Is that what Cliff and Darcy had been trying to do, hand Michelle her life back, a life she had blocked out? Had Cassie's death been too crushing a blow? Cassie had become Michelle's entire life, especially when Cliff's presence faded from the marriage. Had Cassie's death made her life intolerable?

Michelle despaired, not only for this woman's situation, but her own as well. According to Cliff, everyone close to her had been trying to resurrect Michelle's own memories for over a year to no avail. What would this woman do? Live alone in hospitals until she recalled who she was? Would they even let her? And what if she never remembered who she was, or where she belonged? Disturbing images of homeless wanderers flooded Michelle's mind, shuffling nomads in search of themselves, living a life that wasn't theirs, in search of one that was.

"We always have slightly more strength than the adversity we face," the woman said, stepping back to the window.

"How do you know that?" Michelle said, contemplating the strange statement, imagining Cliff all alone on the deck, a cold gun barrel pressed under his jaw.

"I don't know how I know, dear. I just do."

"What about people who commit suicide?" Michelle asked, feeling a new impatience with the woman.

The woman looked over at Michelle, her eyes shining from her dull face like the last living things there. "I guess they forget. I guess for that one unfortunate, irretrievable moment, they forget."

Michelle was sorry she had spoken to her in the harsh tone. The woman said something Michelle didn't catch.

"What?" Michelle asked.

The woman had resumed her station at the window, the curtains pulled back, a stark parking lot light defining the edge of her forehead and nose.

"I know I'm out there somewhere," the woman said, her features doubled in the glass.

CHAPTER 28

Mattie didn't want to talk, but Pink wouldn't stop asking questions or voicing protests. She ignored his complaints and told him to keep his eyes on the road, unable to look at her son, her mind on Lulu. Even though Lulu and she had talked at great length about Lulu's impending death, preparing her, Mattie had never imagined how lost she'd feel, how alone, when Lulu was gone. She needed to ask Lulu things, needed to confide in her, ask her advice. Lulu would know what to do now and had warned Mattie that something like this could happen if they tricked the natural order of things. "Cheating one's fate can bring about an even worse fate," Lulu had warned Mattie. But Mattie had not wanted to lose Pink and pleaded with Lulu to help her. Lulu reluctantly agreed. Now, Mattie thought, she might lose Pink anyway, not to mention the damage done to Mrs. Stage and her family.

"They ain't gonna let you in the dang hospital, Mama," Pink said, interrupting her thoughts. "It's too late. It's after midnight!"

"Evelyn will. Lulu cured Hubie's erysipelas. She owes Lulu. She'll do it for Lulu."

"How do you know the Stage woman is even at the dang hospital anymore? Maybe they released her."

"Loudon told me they might release her tomorrow. She's in the psychiatric ward."

"Well, I don't know why you want to see her anyway. You don't even know her."

"I think I can help."

Pink huffed and fell quiet until they came within sight of the hospital. "Aw, this is crazy, Mama. Heck, I think Evelyn works in the cafeteria or something. How's she going to get you in the psychiatric ward?"

"She will. Drop me at the front doors."

"I better come in with you," Pink said.

"No. You wait here. I'll only be a minute."

"Well, shoot, Mama, you don't even know what Mrs. Stage looks like."

"I'll find her, Pink. Just wait here."

No matter how quietly Mattie tried to walk the hospital corridor, her shoes echoed rudely in the empty hall. Evelyn was seated behind the reception desk, her auburn hair pulled into a tight bun, her white scalp showing through her thinning hair. She appeared to be doing paperwork, when in fact she was reading a novel.

"Hello, Evelyn."

"Mattie. What are you doing here?" Evelyn spread her novel face down on the desk, the spine wrinkled and strained at the center.

"I need to see someone in the psychiatric ward."

Evelyn shook her head, her features glum and confused. "I can't let you on any of the floors, Mattie. It's after hours."

"Take me up the back way. Surely there must be a back entrance to all the floors."

"I would get in so much trouble, Mattie. Can't you come back tomorrow?"

"No. Tonight."

"But . . ."

"Did you know Lulu died?"

Evelyn looked down at her novel, running her finger along the spine "Yes, I heard. I'm sorry."

"How is Hubie?"

Evelyn looked up. "Hubie went back to work, took a job over at the recreation center. No more bouts with the fire. I've never seen him so content."

"I'm happy for him," Mattie said. "I'm happy for both of you."

Evelyn stood up, reading Mattie perfectly. She lifted the ring of keys from her desk and placed them in the pocket of her sweater. "Follow me, Mattie."

*****

Michelle heard a noise and thought it was Ms. Smith searching for something in the dark. "Connie, is that you? Turn the light on." Ms. Smith had told Michelle to call her Connie, a name she'd heard on television a few days earlier and liked. "Maybe that's my real name," Connie had said.

A woman appeared at the foot of Michelle's bed, a woman Michelle didn't recognize from the hospital staff, but who looked vaguely familiar nonetheless, with her gray-streaked black hair, round face, and deep, hooded eyes.

"I'm Mattie Souder," the woman said, scooting the chair closer to Michelle's bed. "I hope you don't mind if I sit a moment."

Pink's mother. Michelle remembered her from Lulu's house the day Lulu died.

"Please. Yes, have a seat." Michelle sat up, uncomfortable with the woman's presence, a bit dizzy from medication.

"I'm very sorry about your husband," said Mrs. Souder.

It was strange to Michelle how she could wake and, for a moment, be unaware of anything in her life, as if it had just begun upon opening her eyes. But Mattie's condolences brought the past back instantly—Cliff's death, Cassie's gravestone. Michelle had no idea how to start over. What would that even look like?

"Are you okay?" Mrs. Souder asked.

"Yes," Michelle said. "I'm sorry for your loss as well."

Mattie shook her head, obviously confused.

"I was with your son when he found your best friend. I think her name was Lulu."

Pink's mother seemed surprised and annoyed in the same instant. "I don't remember seeing you."

"I walked to the edge of the yard. I didn't want to interfere."

"Why were you there?"

"Your son was going to look at my property."

"I thought you owned Pink's cabin. Why would he have to look at that? He would know his own property."

"I didn't know it was his at the time," Michelle said.

"Of course, what was I thinking?" Mattie said.

The statement had sounded a bit sarcastic to Michelle.

"Do you know my son's wife, Isabelle?" Mattie continued.

"No, I never—"

"Why did you think she was dead?"

Michelle took a tissue from the box and wiped her nose, remembering the things she'd said to Pink at the Hilltop. Had Pink told his mother? Was that why she was here?

"I was not myself that night. I'm . . . I'm very sorry. I have been through a lot over the last year," Michelle said, suddenly feeling like Ms. Smith, piecing together a life from someone else's reality.

"Yes, I know. But what did you want with my son?"

"Uh . . . to sell my property . . . his cabin, my . . ."

Michelle couldn't assemble complete sentences, couldn't stop shaking. She felt like a fool, pleading with herself to pull it together. This was her chance to get answers.

Mrs. Souder stood to leave.

"No, please, stop. I want to talk with you," Michelle said, sitting up, pushing the tray holder away from her chest. "I want answers!"

"Answers? What answers could my son possibly have for you? He barely knows you."

Michelle thought a moment. "Answers to why . . . if . . . he killed his wife, Isabelle?"

Mattie glared at Michelle. The comment seemed to have torn the color from the old woman's face. She spun toward the doorway.

"Please, Mrs. Souder," Michelle pleaded. "I need your help . . . my daughter . . ."

Mrs. Souder paused at the white message board only long enough to pick up the blue marker and scrawl something in the upper corner. Michelle couldn't read it from across the room.

*****

Pink felt stupid sitting in front of the hospital, his motor running like a getaway car. He pictured Claire sleeping on the couch and wondered if he'd be able to coax her into the spare bedroom for the night, have her sleep with him. He couldn't remember the last time he'd actually slept next to a woman.

Pink leaned forward and turned the radio on, his eyes trained on the entrance to the hospital. What was taking her so damn long? The radio announcer talked about another snowstorm headed toward Ardenwood, one that could rival the "infamous" storm of '93. Pink wondered if a storm could be infamous. It sounded stupid to him.

Mattie jerked the door open and threw herself into the seat, slamming the door behind her.

"Another storm coming," Pink said, easing the shifter into Drive. "Supposed to hit tomorrow night. Said it might be worse than the infamous storm of '93."

"The what?"

"The storm of '93. You remember that one, don't you?"

"Let's go, Pink. I'm really tired. I want to go to bed."

"Well, what do you think I'm doing here?" he said. "Can't you see I'm driving?"

"Don't talk, Pink."

He hated being shut out, especially since he wanted to know what his mother had found out in Michelle's room, if she'd actually talked with Michelle, what Michelle had said. He wished he'd gone up with her—he'd like to see Michelle again, even if she was crazy. He could overlook insanity if a woman had a nice ass. And Mrs. Stage's ass was Olympic gold.

"Is this it?" Mattie said, holding out something shiny in her palm.

Pink glanced over, quickly taking his eyes back to the road. "I can't see what you're holding there, Mama. It's too dark."

"Turn on a light."

Pink twisted in the seat, guiding the Suburban with one hand, flipping the overhead switch with the other. His mother looked haggard and worn under the yellow light. Pink took his eyes to the pavement, righted the vehicle between the shoulder and yellow line then looked back at the object in his mother's hand. It appeared to be Isabelle's pentagram, the one he'd seen in Michelle's purse.

"Did you steal that, Mama?" Pink asked.

"Is it Isabelle's?"

"Well, Mama, you gave it to her. You should know."

"Why must you talk to me that way, Pink? Can't you just answer my question?"

"Well, you're the one weaving all the mystery, Mama. Why won't you tell me what you want with Michelle Stage? What's this 007 stuff all about? You won't tell me anything, and then . . ."

Mattie glared at Pink, then clenched her fingers over the necklace and shoved it back in her purse.

"Look, Mama, you don't have to get angry with me," Pink said. "I just want to know what's going on. How do you think you can help Mrs. Stage? You think you can bring her husband back from the dead?"

Pink was suddenly sorry he'd snapped at his mother, even sorrier when she slapped him across his face.

"Don't speak to me that way, Pink. Ever again!"

She had never hit him before. It hurt worse than he ever imagined, as if she had rejected some part of him, had broken off a chunk of his soul and tossed it out the window. His mother was the only person in the world who had ever accepted him completely. Not even Isabelle, who was probably his closest friend, could look at him without some trace of pity or irritation. But it never mattered, because it was his mother who held firm to his image, who upheld the highest reflection of who Pink could be, who he was, who he would like to be. She would never betray him, no matter what. That knowledge, he realized in this moment, his cheek stinging, was what made him resilient, confident, strong

She sighed, and Pink could tell she was sorry, but neither of them would say a word. By tomorrow, all would be forgotten. It was the same way with Isabelle when they argued, and Pink preferred it that way. There was no need for boiling it all down, sifting through the rubble of anger, offering foolish apologies wrapped in remorse. Even so, this felt different to Pink. He and his mother had argued plenty, but she had never hit him, and now she seemed to possess something crucial to his wellbeing, something he couldn't describe, but knew he needed desperately. And whatever it was, it seemed impossible to get back through silence. It was as if she had exposed some inferior part of him that had been hidden, as if his shame and vulnerability would now be obvious to the world.

The road to her house was slick. Pink put the Suburban in four-wheel drive and the tread found footing. Across the seat, his mother fingered her purse, as if her thoughts processed through her fingertips. Pink had never seen his mother so pensive, so distressed.

His mother's house was dark as he pulled up to her porch, the headlights reflecting like glowing eyes in her front windows.

"Mama . . ." Pink tried to apologize, but Mattie pushed the door open and jumped out before he could.

"Pink, do you know where Mrs. Stage might have gotten Isabelle's pendant?" His mother held the door open, a cold draft sweeping across the seat.

Pink shrugged. "What difference does it make? It's just a little damn piece of jewelry. It may not even be Isabelle's." But he was almost certain it was. "What do you care so much about it for? And why are you so—" Before Pink could finish, his mother slammed the door and hurried to the porch. She fumbled a moment with the doorknob then disappeared inside the house, not bothering to wave or acknowledge him in any way.

He drove home dumbfounded, the radio playing an elevator rendition of a Waylon Jennings song. Pink's house was dark when he arrived home. He really hadn't expected Claire to be up and was relieved she wasn't. He stepped softly through the living room, past the couch where Claire slept, and was almost to his bedroom when he heard Claire whisper, "Pink, come back here. I'm still awake if you ain't too tired from all that voodoo."

Pink hesitated a moment at his bedroom, then went in and closed the door behind him, pretending he hadn't heard her.

CHAPTER 29

Sunlight cut across Michelle's hospital bed and glistened off the white breakfast plate sitting on her food tray. Dr. Price, the resident psychiatrist, had been in earlier that morning, talked with her, and she was surprised to have fallen back to sleep after he left. Dr. Price had told her she would be released today, so long as it was agreeable with the sheriff.

She stretched her arms, her muscles aching from nonuse, as if she'd been laid up for weeks. Or maybe it was stress. Dr. Price had not given her Xanax when he'd visited earlier, wanting to see how she would do without it. Was Dr. Price aware of her personal history? That was such an odd concept now, personal history, her daughter's death, Cliff's cheating. It had always seemed to Michelle that she could have only one account of her past, and that everyone would agree on the facts of it. But that was not the case. Darcy remembered events differently than she did, even events they had experienced together. And Cliff was constantly negating her memory of things, as if her mind was a faulty contraption, incapable of accuracy. And now Dr. Price. What was his version?

"Bye, Michelle," someone said.

Michelle looked up to see her roommate, dressed and clutching a plastic Ardenwood Hospital bag with her clothes. Michelle figured the things in the bag were probably donations, and wondered where she was going, if she was being moved to another ward.

"They found me, Michelle. I'm Charlene House. They contacted my daughter in Chicago. She's flying here to get me. I was hiking the Appalachian Trail."

Even though the woman spoke with apparent relief and joy, there was a reserve of sadness beneath her words, the information coming from her lips like rehearsed sound bites on the evening news.

"Did you hear me get up last night?" Charlene asked Michelle, as if skeptical over details of her apparent good fortune.

"No, I didn't."

Charlene pointed to the white message board. "The nurse figured I must have sleep-walked to the board and written my name. Isn't that amazing?" But there was no amazement in Charlene's eyes or voice, only a residue of doubt and confusion. She looked more lost than the previous night when she had no idea who she was. Now that she'd been told she was someone named Charlene House, memories should have flooded back, but Michelle could tell they hadn't.

"You'll be okay," Michelle said, not sure where the encouragement had come from. It felt phony.

The woman nodded, then smiled, as if she were unable to connect the two gestures, as if they couldn't be linked. When the nurse brought in a wheelchair, Mrs. House guided herself backward into the seat and placed her feet on the metal rests, the plastic bag nestled in her lap. Michelle couldn't help but wonder what would happen to Charlene when she was safely back in Chicago, if she would remember why she'd left her home to hike the Appalachian Trail, if she'd been fleeing a stale life, a lonely existence, or seeking an adventure. When Michelle heard her assumptions about the woman playback through her head, she realized it was her own life she was examining not Charlene's.

A moment after the nurse wheeled Mrs. House from the room, Darcy came through the doorway, as if cued by the departure of Michelle's roommate.

"Hey, Darcy," Michelle said, ecstatic to see her sister, thankful there was no question about their relationship, about who they were to each other, and that no matter what happened, she knew Darcy would always be there for her. She hugged Darcy close and didn't want to let go.

"Are you okay?" Darcy said, holding Michelle's embrace.

Michelle wiped her eyes, releasing her sister. Darcy handed her the box of tissues. "You ready to go home?" Darcy asked.

"I am," she said.

She was. Then she wasn't. What would she go home to? Michelle found herself playing out the remainder of her life, something she'd always done with maddening regularity, picturing herself sitting alone in her big home in Atlanta, the blue pool growing green and spoiled with algae, the concrete cracking and crumbling, the roof leaking, the lawn choked with weeds, the electric lights failing and leaving her in darkness.

Michelle tried to shake the images, tried to see herself selling the house, living with Darcy for a while, working at the health food store, getting stronger, starting over. Wasn't that what she'd wanted all along—to start over? But not without Cassie. She had never reinvented her life without Cassie in it. Cassie was the thread that would hold the fabric of her new life together, the seed that would expand infinitely—children, grandchildren, great-grandchildren. Life would move forward in that way, circumvent the intolerable stasis of a solitary life—Mattie Souder. The name jumped into her head so quickly it startled her. She had forgotten about the strange visit from Pink's mother. The old woman asking her very pointed questions. Then stopping at the door, writing something on the whiteboard . . .

"You're shaking, Michelle," Darcy said, reaching out to touch her arm. "What's wrong?"

"I don't know." Michelle gathered her things and tried to stand but sat back down to steady herself. Darcy picked up the box of Cliff's belongings, the one the sheriff had left with her.

"Here, hold onto me," Darcy said. As they walked from the room, Michelle glanced at the whiteboard, at the name scrawled there: Charlene House.

CHAPTER 30

Pink felt rested when he arrived at the office, excited about his new scheme to get business percolating again. Clarence's Jeep sat out front, and Pink was surprised to see him at work so early, especially when there was the perfect excuse of a snowstorm to keep him home.

On the drive in, Pink couldn't stop thinking about Claire's crazy husband, Kenny, and Kenny's equally bizarre friend, Curly. But Pink had to hand it to him—Curly was a marketing genius. Pink couldn't believe he'd never thought of the scam himself. He was usually pretty good at those things. But Curly was the master.

"Clarence," Pink shouted as he opened the front door to the office. "I got an idea that's gonna set sales on fire!" Until this morning, when Pink had tiptoed past Claire sleeping on the sofa, he hadn't realized how well things had worked out from Kenny's little deed on the bridge. Because of that, Claire was afraid to go home, and with nowhere to go, Pink now had a full-time, live-in nursemaid to Isabelle, a cook, and a cleaning lady, and more than that, a little Barbie doll for himself. It was almost too perfect, and Pink thought about sending Kenny a thank-you note to show his appreciation.

"Clarence!" Pink shouted again. "Did you hear me? I've got a great idea."

Pink strolled into Clarence's office. Clarence was seated at his desk, a newspaper spread out before him, his feet propped up above some kind of small, humming machine.

"What the hell is that?" Pink asked.

"A dehumidifier. Doc said my feet are too moist too much of the time. He saw the beginnings of mushrooms growing between my toes. I thought this little gizmo might dry out the fungus. Val-U-Mart had 'em for nineteen dollars. Can you believe that?"

Pink was tired of Clarence's fungus, and especially disliked that Clarence was always barefoot in the office. "Does it ever make you wonder," Pink began, "that in the most prosperous time of real estate sales, our sales are actually worse than last year, maybe the worse they've ever been?"

"I suppose," Clarence said, turning the page of the newspaper, the crinkling noise slicing a corner off Pink's pleasant mood.

"Well, I've got an idea that's gonna change all that. It came to me this morning." Pink wasn't about to give Curly credit for the idea. Why should he? Clarence wouldn't know the difference anyway.

Clarence glanced up from his newspaper, scratched his neck, and turned the page. "Sounds good, Pink."

"I haven't told you yet."

"Well, you always have good ideas. I'm sure this one's a blue ribbon."

Oh, it was. Pink recalled Curly's sign out by Burtran Lake, the drawing of the sexy girl riding the Jet Ski, wishing there was some kind of award offered for the best ad campaign. Pink was sure he'd win.

"Are you listening? 'Cause I'm only gonna tell you once."

Clarence nodded, then toed the dehumidifier to change the direction of the flow.

"Okay, here it is. I hire a gorgeous tan model in one of those skimpy bikinis, something in white—no! In pink! Of course. Hot pink! Then we have her riding in a boat or something, on the lake, right? A close up so we see her from stomach to face . . . or maybe knees to face, so we see her crotch area."

"Hasn't that been done before?"

"That's not it yet, dammit. Listen to this." Pink took a deep breath, amazed at the machinations of his own mind. "I hire a couple of high school dropouts, maybe a couple of those kids that work over there at the Game Depot, to go up to my sign at night and paint nipples on the model in the photograph!"

Clarence squinted at Pink, his brain apparently chewing on the details.

"Don't you get it?" Pink said. "We'll have the only billboard around with a bare-breasted woman! The law can't say anything because vandals done it. They can make me clean it up, but I can drag my feet for weeks, maybe months before I do anything, complaining to Fisk and the county officials how the whole damn country's going in the shitter when kids can deface a man's advertising, his very livelihood! It's perfect!

"I'll have Fisk searching for those damn kids, while I'm calling him everyday whining about how expensive those billboards are, how much the model and photographer set me back, how much it will cost to fix. The whole time, folks from Georgia, Florida, and Alabama will be getting an eyeful of Pink Souder Real Estate. It's goddamn brilliant!"

"What do bare breasts have to do with real estate?" Clarence asked. "And they won't really be bare, right, just nipples painted over the swimsuit? Won't people see that?"

"Not from a distance. Christ, Clarence, you think they're gonna drive up and inspect the goddamn artwork? And who gives a shit anyway? By the time they figure out the titties ain't real, my name and phone number'll be seared into their memory. I mean, if you was courting some woman all night with whiskey shots and finger sandwiches, do you think you'd care if you finally got her in the sack and found out her titties weren't real? Hell no! Don't you get it?"

Clarence scratched between his toes, then the back of his neck.

"You're gonna have that fungus all over your damn body if you keep doing that," Pink said, frustrated he'd ever told Clarence his idea. Clarence had no vision, no imagination. It was no wonder business was so bad—Pink had to carry the entire company. Pink had to invent new sales techniques, had to handle the scheduling, man the phones, organize the appointments, woo the clients, handle all the puckering, and kiss all the ass. What did Clarence do besides pick his toes and read fishing magazines? He was supposed to make sure properties were fit to be shown, but since they had few properties to show, and even fewer folks to show them to, Clarence sat around nursing his fungus and drawing a fat paycheck.

Pink turned to go back to his office.

"Well, I'll be damned," Clarence said.

Pink was about to tell him he was *damned*, when Clarence started poking at the newspaper. "Looks like some crazy folks jumped off the bridge the other night over at Burtran," Clarence said. "Maybe it'll turn into some kind of Lover's Leap." Clarence leaned in closer to the photograph then glanced up at Pink. "If I ain't mistaken, this feller in the picture looks a lot like you."

CHAPTER 31

Leaving the hospital parking lot, Michelle asked Darcy to drive back up to the cabin.

"Why?" Darcy said.

"Let's just spend the night up there. We'll go home tomorrow. Or the next day. I can't go back to my house in Atlanta. It's too fucked up . . . with Cliff . . . Cassie . . . I can't ever go back there." Michelle grabbed the box of tissues from the glove compartment. She felt like she was being turned inside out.

"You'll stay at my place. Until you figure things out," Darcy said. "Or forever. I don't care." Darcy pulled the car to the shoulder. "Besides, won't the cabin freak you out? Shit, Cliff shot himself there. Jesus, that had to be fucking horrible finding him like that."

Michelle knew Darcy was right, but she had to go back. She knew the answers were there, with the cabin, Pink, Mattie Souder. But how could she stand to see the cabin again? The deck stained with Cliff's blood. His clothes in the closet. His stuff on the walls.

"Maybe we could just stay at the Comfort Inn or something," Michelle said. "I can't go back to Atlanta."

"You know I'm worried about you, right? And you know I want you to let go of all this . . ."

"Nonsense?" Michelle said.

"No, Chelle. All this stuff that keeps you stuck. I think you would do better if we were back in Atlanta, away from Ardenwood."

"You sound like Mom. You know that, right?" Michelle said, taking her gaze out the window. "I can't leave, Darce."

They sat in silence. Cars rushed by, rocking the Explorer as they passed. Darcy checked the rearview mirror, then glanced over at Michelle. Michelle met her eyes.

"Someone came to visit me last night in the hospital, Darcy," Michelle said. "Mattie Souder. Pink's mother. She asked me all kinds of questions. Why would she do that if there wasn't something going on?"

"What *something* do you think is *going on*?"

"Don't be sarcastic, okay?"

"All right. Sorry."

"Anyway, she asks me all these pointed questions, then just gets up to leave." Michelle turned in the seat to face Darcy. "So I asked her to stop . . . then I asked her if Pink killed his wife Isabelle. Mrs. Souder turned white as chalk."

Darcy looked away, then turned back and touched Michelle's wrist. "Chelle, you asked a woman if her son killed his wife who isn't even dead? Fuck, what did you expect her to do? The question is crazy. I'm sorry. It just is. I'm your biggest advocate, but I have to be honest with you."

Michelle wasn't sure she believed Darcy about being her *biggest advocate*. But she needed to get her sister onboard if she was going to convince her to stay in Ardenwood. Michelle needed to stay; she knew Mattie Souder had the answers.

"When she left my hospital room last night, she stopped and wrote Charlene House on the whiteboard," Michelle blurted out.

Darcy looked surprised then confused at the same time. "I don't have a clue what you're talking about. Who wrote Charlene House on the whiteboard, and who the hell is Charlene House?"

"Mattie Souder wrote Charlene House on the whiteboard."

"Okay. So who is Charlene House?"

"Charlene House was my roommate. Some hikers found her on the AT wandering around, lost, without shoes or food. Apparently, she was hiking the AT and . . . I don't know . . . got lost or something and couldn't remember who she was. The hospital wasn't sure if she fell or what happened to her.

Anyway, these hikers called the police who brought her into town, and the hospital psychiatrist had been working with her to bring back her memory. Charlene had no idea who she was or where she lived or anything about her life. They were calling her Connie Smith at the hospital."

"You said she was on the AT. What's that?"

"The Appalachian Trail or something."

"I've heard of that," Darcy said. "It's that trail that goes from Georgia to Maine, right?"

"I guess so. I don't know. That's not the point here."

"Yeah, I kind of forgot what the point was. And I'm confused about something. If the hospital staff knew her name was Charlene House, why were they calling her Connie Smith?"

"That's just it . . . they didn't know her real name until this morning. That's what Mrs. Souder wrote on the whiteboard."

Darcy shook her head lightly, obviously having trouble following the orbit of Michelle's explanation.

"I'm sorry, sis, but what does Charlene House have to do with Mattie Souder?" Darcy asked. "Does Mrs. Souder know Charlene House? Were they friends or something?"

"No! That's my point. Mattie Souder somehow knew Charlene House's real name, even though Charlene couldn't remember her own name. Don't you see, Mattie Souder knew this woman's name even though she had never met Charlene before. Don't you think that's odd?"

"So maybe she's psychic," Darcy said. "What does that prove?"

"Okay," Michelle said. "You win."

"This isn't a contest, Chelle. I'm not trying to beat you. I'm on your side. You know that, right?"

"Sure. I do. I know that," Michelle said.

"Well, you sound like you *know* it but still don't believe it," Darcy said.

Michelle sulked, feeling trapped in an endless loop.

A short while later Darcy pulled into a service station. Michelle got out to stretch her legs. The day had clouded up as night approached. "I think it's good we're heading back now," Darcy said, tilting her head back at the sky. "Looks like they're in for more snow up here."

Michelle looked up, then over at Darcy. Darcy had four-wheel drive and good tires. They wouldn't get stuck. Michelle wished Darcy would stop with the excuses. Michelle had let it drop and couldn't understand why her sister hadn't.

"Besides, I can't depend on Anna to manage things at the store for more than a few days," Darcy added.

"It's okay. Let it drop," Michelle said to Darcy, who was busy pumping gas. Michelle walked around to where Darcy was holding the pump handle, reminding her of Darcy's gun, the one Cliff used to kill himself. How could he have done that?

I have to go back, Michelle thought. *I have to go back one last time. After that, I never want to see the cabin again.*

Darcy finished with the gas, screwed the cap on, pushed the cover shut. She stared at the gas pump, at the receipt slot, waiting.

"This is my last chance, Darcy," Michelle said. "I have to go back. I have to face what Cliff did. I have to be there one last time."

Darcy ripped the receipt from the pump, spinning toward her. "What am I supposed to do, Michelle? Wait around until you take off again? Cliff called me the night he killed himself, Michelle. He told me everything you did, everything you said. When is this over?"

"Wow, how long have you been holding that in?" Michelle said. It was the first time Michelle had ever felt that her sister blamed her for what was happening, blamed her for everything. It was a shock, as Darcy had always been of the new age thought that blame was for victims, a game for the feeble-minded, serving no real purpose other than to keep one stuck in a hopeless cycle of powerlessness.

After stuffing the receipt in her purse, Darcy turned toward Michelle, her expression much softer. "Let's go home, Michelle. You can live at my place until you figure out what to do with the house. You can work at the store, reassemble your life. We'll face everything together. Just like growing up. This is me, Chelle. I love you. You have to trust me."

"I can't remember Cassie's death, Darcy. Do you have any idea what that's like? I don't want that to happen again. I don't want to forget what happened to Cliff. I want to keep it straight in my mind, then maybe . . ."

"Maybe what?"

"Then . . . I don't know . . . maybe everything about Cassie will come back." Michelle couldn't believe she'd spoken the words, wasn't sure if she believed them or if it was a ploy to coax Darcy into driving her back to the cabin. What scared her most was the small voice inside her saying it was true, that if she faced Cliff's death, she would remember Cassie's death as well. The notion weakened her knees, left her hollow. *You have to trust me.* Her sister's words lingered near the back of Michelle's eyes, as if at any moment she would be able to see the truth as some solid object with shape and dimension, something she could put in her pocket, and bring out when she needed reassurance. She recalled the pale fright in Charlene House's eyes; the truth had definitely not set *her* free. If anything, it had imprisoned Charlene more, forcing her mind to establish alien connections, accept them as fact, rebuild her life upon loose and shifting sand. Charlene had seemed more at ease not knowing who she was or where she belonged than trying to trick her mind into embracing a life that didn't feel like her own.

Michelle looked past Darcy to a Toyota Sequoia that pulled up to the pump.

"Do you want anything from inside?" Darcy asked, removing the keys from the ignition. "I have to pee."

Michelle shook her head. "I'm good." She hadn't missed that Darcy took her keys with her.

A Toyota with a mountain bike on the roof pulled in across from Darcy's Explorer. A young man in shorts and a bright yellow jacket slid his credit card into the reader and started pumping gas.

"Hi," Michelle said to the young man. "Are there good places to ride around here?"

"Yeah, for sure. The Tsali trail is awesome," the man glanced at his bike, then back at Michelle. "I wasn't riding today . . . just getting some work done on my bike. The snow has made it impossible to get to the trail right now, but it'll melt pretty fast this time of year."

"Hey . . . thanks for the info," Michelle said. "Uh . . . I was wondering, are you headed in the direction of Ardenwood right now?"

CHAPTER 32

Pink folded the newspaper at his desk, fuming at Ramsey for running such a dumb thing. Private humiliation was something Isabelle seemed immune to, but public humiliation was a different beast altogether. If Isabelle saw the photo and recognized Pink and Claire nearly naked on the bridge, she'd be angrier than a butt-shot bear. And then there was the part about the "anonymous witness" who took the picture, but couldn't leave his name because he was, "too disturbed and embarrassed." Disturbed and embarrassed my ass, Pink thought. How could Ramsey be so stupid? Was he taking a special vitamin for that? And goddamn Kenny! Where did he come up with such a plan? Or maybe it was Curly's idea. It had to be. Kenny didn't have enough sense to pull his foot out of dogshit, but Curly . . . that was a hell of an idea he'd had about the billboard. It was hard to be upset with Curly's caliber of genius.

The phone rang again. People Pink hadn't spoken to in three years were calling, asking if he was the one in the photo. Pink instructed Clarence to tell them he wasn't there, and that it wasn't him in the photo, that he had been out of town for the past week.

"You better take this one, Pink," Clarence yelled from the adjoining office.

"Somebody want to buy or sell property?" Pink said.

"No."

"Then tell 'em I'm not here."

"It's Loudon. He wants to talk to you. Says it's urgent."

Pink shot up from his desk and rushed into Clarence's office. "Did you tell him I was here?" Pink said, glaring down on Clarence.

"Not exactly. I told him you were in the crapper."

"Well . . . tell him I left, that I was in the crapper . . . and then I left."

"But, Pink, I . . ."

"Damn you, Clarence! You tell him right now!"

Pink stood over him making sure he didn't screw it up. Clarence's lies sounded less dumb than his truth, which made everything seem believable.

"He was in the bathroom, but I guess he left when he finished." Clarence nodded, then hung up and went back to his newspaper.

"Well, what did he say?"

"He said, 'Okay.'"

Pink sighed and went back to his office, wondering if Claire had seen the paper. She was terrible at secrets, would break down blubbering when she saw the photo. She might feel so bad she'd go in and show it to Isabelle, confess the whole damn thing. Pink didn't care if Isabelle suspected he had slept with Claire, long as she never knew for sure. That's when the trouble would commence. He wanted to call Claire, but didn't want to chance Isabelle picking up. He hustled back into Clarence's office and told him to phone the house.

"Only ask for Claire, and whatever you do, don't say who it is. You got that?"

"Of course, Pink. I ain't dimwitted."

Pink paced behind Clarence's chair.

"Hello," Clarence said. "Is this the lady of the house?"

Pink grimaced and shook his head. "Is it Claire?" he mouthed. "Hang up the dang phone if it ain't Claire."

Clarence nodded, holding his hand over the receiver.

"Give me that damn thing," Pink said, wrenching the phone from Clarence's hand. "What are you doing?"

"Who is this?" Claire said.

"Pink. Who the hell you think it is? What are you doing? Have you been out today?"

"Too damn cold. Where are you?"

"What's Isabelle doing?"

"She's taking a bath. She looks stronger today. I have to help her in and out, but—"

"Nobody been by?"

"Well, no, why?"

"Good. Keep it that way."

"That's easy for you to say, 'cause you ain't stuck in this damn house like a damn prisoner. And we're running low on groceries. They're supposed to be sending a boy up here, but I'll be damned if he's got here yet. He must be coming on a damn bicycle."

"What are you talking about?" Pink asked, motioning for Clarence to give up his chair so Pink could sit.

"Isabelle had me call for groceries."

"Did she ask for a newspaper?"

"No. But I did. Crossword puzzle comes out today. There ain't a damn thing to do in this house except watch TV. All my jigsaw puzzles are over with Kenny, and—"

Pink slammed the phone down. "Shit-fire-hell-and-damnation!" Pink cradled his head in his hands, wishing he had his gun with him so he could drive over and kill Kenny, then Ramsey, then . . .

"You never told me, Pink," Clarence said, sitting on a plastic file folder box across the room.

Pink glared over at him, thinking how stupid Clarence looked sitting on that box, his bare feet covered in white powder. "Told you what?"

"If that was you in the picture?"

When Pink stood to go back to his office, he heard the bell on the front door ring. "Go find out who that is," he told Clarence. "And don't tell 'em I'm here unless it's somebody who wants to buy some damn property. And put some damn shoes on!"

Clarence slipped on his orange Crocs and clopped into the foyer. Pink could hear men's voices, followed by the clapping of Clarence's plastic shoes on the linoleum floor.

"Did you get rid of—" Pink started to say, when he noticed Loudon behind Clarence.

"We need to talk," Loudon said.

Pink walked past Clarence, shaking his head. "Come on, then," he told Loudon.

Pink closed the door after Loudon stepped in and seated himself opposite Pink's desk. Pink sat down and leaned back. "So what can I do for you?"

Loudon slid a newspaper out from under his coat and spread it before Pink. "Now, Pink, before you start lying to me, I'm gonna tell you I don't care what the hell you were doing on that bridge. That's not why I'm here. But I need your help. I'm up to my ass in stranded retirees, cars skidded off back roads, and I even have a frostbite victim wanting to sue the weatherman. And if that's not enough, now I have to assemble a damn team of divers to muddle around the bottom of Burtran Lake. I need to know if this is you, Pink, so I don't have to spend thousands of dollars searching for two people that aren't there. Are you following me?"

Pink's office chair squeaked when he rocked backward. "What do you want from me?" Pink asked.

Loudon poked the photo, the paper crinkling each time his finger jabbed the smeared ink. "I know this is you. Just confirm it so I can call off this stupid search and get on with the real emergencies."

Pink folded his hands behind his head and rocked in his chair. "I don't know why you believe that's me. You think I'm the only chubby guy in Ardenwood who wears white BVDs?"

"Goddamn it, Pink, I don't have time for this. There's another storm hitting tonight, and this one's supposed to be ten times worse. Now help me out here, Pink. Do the right thing."

"Supposing it was me," Pink said. "How you going to handle it?"

"I'm gonna say we have it on reliable information that no one is at the bottom of Burtran Lake and all rescue plans have been postponed, that the photo was a hoax."

Pink popped forward in his chair, shuffling old contracts on his desk, ones he'd stacked there to make potential clients feel more at ease. "Well, all I can say is, I doubt very seriously there's any dead bodies at the bottom of Burtran Lake."

"Tell Mattie hello for me when you see her," Loudon said, putting on his hat.

The phone rang as Loudon was leaving the office. Pink heard Clarence answer it. "What else can happen?" Pink said to himself as he stood and grabbed his coat.

Maybe he'd drive to Dedmonson for lunch. No one knew him over there. He went into Clarence's office and was about to tell him that he was going out when Clarence looked up at him, his eyes pale and round. Pink could hear someone shouting through the phone. Clarence pointed at the other line for Pink to pick up. Pink gently lifted it from the cradle.

". . . and if I was well enough I'd come over to that office and kick your ass, Clarence. I know he's there, so you tell him he'd better call me in the next five minutes, or I'll find a way to get down there. You hear me Clarence?"

"Yes."

"I mean it, goddamn it! You tell him to call me. I'm done with this shit— and I'm done with your shit, you lying bastard! You're always covering for him, Clarence. Why is that? What is it Pink does for you? Do you owe him? I know he doesn't pay you for shit. Of course, you don't do shit, so the pay is right."

For a moment there was silence on the phone. Pink stared at Clarence. Clarence shrugged back, as if to say, "What do I do now?"

Pink motioned for him to hang up. Clarence was easing the phone into the cradle when the voice began again.

"Clarence! Don't sit there like a fungus! Say you understand. Say you'll have that fat bastard call me. I mean it, Clarence." Pink heard Isabelle sniffle, then cough. "Do you hear me?" He wondered if she was crying. A moment later he got his answer. She continued shouting at Clarence, but her words were unintelligible now, runny and drippy with sobbing, like someone arguing under water. Clarence looked over at Pink and shook his head, frowning, thrusting the phone at Pink. Pink shook back violently, mouthing the words, *no no no no no.*

There was silence when the bawling stopped. Pink heard Isabelle blow her nose, then she started speaking in a low, calm tone that was more disconcerting than the mewling of a moment earlier.

"Pink, I know you're listening on the extension," Isabelle said. "I'm not protecting you anymore, Pink. There's something you need to know, something you should have known a long time ago. I won't protect you anymore."

Click.

Pink held the phone close to his ear. Clarence laid the phone in the cradle then looked up at Pink. Pink hung up and pulled up the collar of his jacket around his neck.

"I'm going to lunch," Pink said. "I don't know when I'll be back."

Pink stepped from Clarence's office, expecting Clarence to say something or ask him to bring back a sandwich but Clarence said nothing. Pink could feel Clarence's eyes on the back of his neck.

What a hell of a morning, Pink thought, as he walked to the front door.

*****

After lunch, Pink couldn't go home, and he didn't want to go back to the office. He browsed the shops along Main Street in Dedmonson, bored out of his mind. Protect him? From what? He couldn't stop wheeling Isabelle's statement around in his head. Maybe Claire had some rare disease he could catch, one she'd failed to tell him about? Or maybe Isabelle's illness was contagious and the only reason he hadn't caught it was because she had been sneaking some antidote into his coffee and now she would withhold it? Or maybe the Mafia had contract killers stalking him, and she'd managed, each and every time, to thwart their attacks. Picturing Isabelle as some kind of martial arts expert, kicking and punching and spinning, made him chuckle. He stopped at a bakery and ordered coffee and a donut. All this thinking made him hungry.

Pink sat at a table and checked his cell phone. Five calls from Isabelle and some other numbers he didn't recognize, probably busybodies who'd seen the newspaper. He punched in the office number. Clarence answered.

"Any business?"

"Is that you, Pink?" Clarence asked.

"No, it's the IRS and we want to audit you as soon as you make some damn money. Christ, Clarence, who else calls and asks if there's any business?" Half-wits without an ounce of charisma were selling the entire country out from under the poor and middle-class, two and three times over, while Pink watched from the sidelines. Millions of dollars going to people who didn't deserve it near as much as he did, poor suckers who happened to be in the right place when no one was watching.

"Isabelle called again," said Clarence.

"Anybody else?"

"Yeah, lots of people," Clarence said. "None you'd want to talk to though."

"Only call me if somebody has property or wants property. I'm not coming back today. And if Isabelle calls, you tell her you haven't heard from me." Pink waited for Clarence to say something. "Hello? Are you there?"

"I'm here, Pink. You really should give her a call."

"And you should wear something other than plastic shoes, Clarence. Where'd you ever get the idea that plastic was good for your damn feet?"

"She was really upset the last time she called. It wouldn't hurt to talk to her."

"Did Claire call?" Pink asked, suddenly wondering what was going on with her. Silence again. It was starting to irk him. "Clarence?"

"Yeah, Claire called. I could hardly understand her for the blubbering."

"Where was she?"

"Home, I guess."

"My home?"

"No, her home. She wanted me to tell you she's back with Kenny. She wants you to call her."

Why in the hell did she go back to him? Pink wondered. "Call me on the cell if something important happens . . . like new business." Pink hung up and checked his messages again. Why weren't there any calls from Claire if she needed to talk to him so bad? He punched in her number, hoping Kenny didn't answer the phone. It rang at least ten times before Claire answered.

"What's wrong with you, Claire? You sound like shit? You got a cold or something?"

A second of silence before Claire's howling bellowed through the phone. Pink tried to quiet her down, but Claire wouldn't stop long enough to speak, each time choking, strained sounds as though she were hyperventilating. "Breathe into a dang bag, for Christ's sake," Pink said. "And why'd you go home to that maniac of a husband? He's the one started all this in the first place."

"She said . . . horrible . . . things. Horrible, dirty things."

"Who?"

"I can't . . . talk . . . right now . . . Pink," Claire said, sniffling and crying. Her voice trailed off in a slow, melting whine until the phone clicked and went dead. Pink clamped his cell shut and shoved it in his pocket.

"What the hell is going on?" Pink said to himself. "Have they both got some crazy gene that's kicked in?"

Pink couldn't stand another second window-shopping in Dedmonson. He knew of a strip club in Burryville, not far from the casino. It was an hour's drive, but he had nothing else to do. If he couldn't find a girl at the club to spend the night with, he figured he'd go back to his mama's house to sleep, give Isabelle time to cool off. By morning, everything would be back to normal.

CHAPTER 33

The young man backed his Toyota out of Michelle's driveway, then stopped on the road and rolled down his window. "Are you going to be okay, Michelle?" he asked, glancing toward her dark cabin.

"Sure," she said. "Thanks for the ride. Can I give you some money?"

"No way. Call me if you want to try mountain biking sometime." He waved as he drove off. She was glad he declined the money—she didn't have any.

This was not how Michelle imagined the evening unfolding, her driving off with some stranger, leaving Darcy behind to worry. Before she'd pulled away with the young man, she'd glanced back at the convenience store and saw Darcy standing in the middle of the parking lot, a brown paper sack in her hand, staring at Michelle. Her face had looked as blank as the bag she was holding.

Snow drifted outside the cabin while Michelle prepared supper in silence. She wondered where Darcy had gone, if she'd driven back to Atlanta alone, if her sister would ever speak to her again. Michelle hated running out on Darcy like that, but she couldn't leave. Cliff flashed through her mind, his body frozen under a foot of snow, the dark, ragged hole in his scalp. She would never bleach that image from her mind.

Michelle scooped spaghetti onto her plate and sat with her hand resting on the table, noodles wrapping her fork like a mummy. She couldn't eat, thinking about her sister, about Cliff, everything that had happened, or hadn't happened. It was maddening. She scraped her spaghetti into the trashcan.

Michelle didn't want to sleep, wasn't even sure she could. Her eyes kept searching out the window for Darcy's headlights. Snow was coming harder. She took her coat from the closet. Maybe if she stood outside in the cold, fatigue would overtake her, make it impossible to keep her eyes open.

When Michelle stepped onto the deck, snowflakes settled on her face. Living in Atlanta, she missed real winters like they'd had in Pennsylvania. She looked over the folding chair and wondered if Cliff had intended to kill himself when he positioned it near the railing or had the idea occurred to him later as he stared into the remote and deadening darkness where the light ends, as she was now doing? She felt disconnected from everything in front of her, everything that had happened, a queer crease in her life without time or emotion. She tightened her hands around the aluminum tubing of the chair, the cold biting through the thin flesh of her palms. She bent down and smelled the webbing, as if Cliff should still be lingering there, maybe Cliff from college, flushed and sweating from a wrestling match, or Cliff fresh from the shower, the scent of Irish Spring on his skin, the unimproved Cliff, before he needed that shimmering jolt of new love from another woman, returning home smelling of smoke-fouled perfume. Strange how none of that mattered now.

Michelle folded the chair and carried it to the far end of the deck, setting it under the overhanging roof. Fresh snow erased the blood-soaked snow and in a few hours, maybe less, the indentations from the chair would be gone as well.

Michelle walked back to the railing and let her eyes fall down the dark mountainside, into the inexhaustible geometry of pointy limbs and dusky trees. She could have abandoned her senses to the pattern, let it pull her into a sluggish sleep, had it not been for the tiny orange light flickering up at her like a fallen star burning in the snow. It was quite a distance off, maybe several hundred yards, maybe farther, and seemed to radiate pale heat. At first, she thought it might be the dusk-to-dawn light, but it was in the wrong place, its source more organic than electronic.

Michelle walked to the edge of the yard where the mountainside plunged into darkness. At least with snow covering the ground, she figured it would be easier to see, and picking her way down the slope should be much less difficult. Her theory was immediately quashed when her sneaker slipped on the loose leaves beneath the frozen powder, sending her sliding into sticker bushes and rhododendron. Lying on her back, Michelle looked up toward the cabin, half expecting to see Darcy at the railing shaking her head, disappointed. Michelle pulled herself up by a branch, brushed off her jeans, and stood a moment to steady her footing. The incline gave her a tenuous hold on gravity, her center not quite perpendicular to the earth. She waited until her lungs calmed before testing the hill again. She probably should have brought a flashlight.

The snow managed to gather enough light from the cloud-filled night sky and to Michelle's surprise, she had no trouble seeing. The trek down the mountain was invigorating. After several minutes, she felt a fresh momentum gathering in her chest, a kind of helium buoyancy. She figured it was from the cold. The temperature had dropped, but she felt warm, even tranquil. The orange light was closer now, maybe a hundred yards away, and it had a fluttering quality that seemed to indicate a fire of some sort, a campfire maybe, but small and manageable. A trace of apprehension crept in, but she pushed it away and kept moving.

Whatever fear Michelle may have felt a moment earlier vanished when she saw the house. It was Mattie Souder's place. She recognized the picket fence and shutters. Light from her backyard colored the trees and limbs in a flickering orange glow, the source partially blocked by the house. It was fire. Michelle hurried past the shrubs that lined the side of the house, expecting to find something ablaze that shouldn't be. Instead she saw a woman in a black-hooded cloak less than fifty yards from the house, her back to Michelle, her arms raised to the night sky, the flames partially blocked by her body. A ruddy peach smoke rose past her outstretched fingers. The woman stood in the center of a circle of exposed stones, the center oddly free of snow. Michelle crept toward the woman, angling slightly to the side to get a better look. The woman turned away and when she did Michelle saw the fire clearly, and the cauldron hanging above it.

The cauldron was not very large, maybe the size of a soup pot. Not even that big. But it was still strange, and Michelle had decided to leave, when the woman called out.

"Stop there. Who are you? What are you doing here?"

Michelle spun around to see a featureless silhouette, the hood of the woman's cloak concealing any indication of a face. The woman withdrew an object from the pocket of her cloak. Yellow light glinted along its metallic surface and Michelle knew it was a knife. She should have turned and fled up the mountain, tracked her own footprints through the snow back to her cabin, but she couldn't move, too mesmerized by what the woman did next. Standing beneath a trellis festooned with colored ribbons, the woman raised the knife against the night, and like a mime, cut a circle into thin air, starting well above her head, sweeping down past her feet, finishing above her head where she'd started. She bowed momentarily and the knife disappeared. Michelle had not seen where she put it. The woman stepped beneath the trellis and moved toward Michelle as if she floated on the snow, her black cloak gliding like a shadow cast from some missing object. Michelle watched her approach, and smelled the charred wood scent of the blaze, smoke twisting up through the limbs, evaporating into the night. When the woman threw back her hood, Michelle recognized her at once.

"Mrs. Stage?" Mrs. Souder said.

"I'm sorry to bother you," Michelle said.

"What are you doing here?"

Michelle put aside the lie she'd prepared and asked what she really wanted to know. "Why did you come to my hospital room the other night?"

With her back to the fire, Mrs. Souder's features appeared fragile, the grayish night light dusting her cheeks and chin, making her seem exhausted. Michelle held the woman's gaze, but Mrs. Souder's eyes slowly lost intensity, as if some mechanism inside her was spinning to a halt.

"I was . . ." Mrs. Souder said. "I'm sorry if I disturbed you. I knew the woman in the room with you."

"Yes, I know," Michelle said. "She was relieved that you did."

Mrs. Souder turned and walked up the hill toward the house, her cloak stirring up wisps of snow.

"Wait," Michelle said. "Why did you go through my locker?"

The woman stopped, pausing a moment before spinning toward Michelle. "What are you doing here?" the old woman said, the frustration in her voice giving her an edge of desperation. "Why did you come here tonight?"

"I followed the light down the hill."

"Followed the light? Weren't you afraid?"

"Not anymore," Michelle said. "Everything's so fucked up I think I've forgotten how to be afraid."

"You should try remembering, dear," she said, her eyes etching into Michelle's. "Fear can protect you."

"I lost my daughter," Michelle said. "Did you know I lost my daughter and I have no recollection of her dying? My friends and family all remember. My sister remembers. My husband drove me to her grave. It was very convincing, but somehow, I didn't believe it. They say she's been dead for over a year, and yet I spoke with her a week ago. Cassie's her name." Michelle was rambling but didn't care.

"She's fifteen and was voted captain of the swim team. She's not even a senior. Isn't that wonderful? She's an excellent swimmer. Cliff didn't even know she was voted captain. Before my daughter had a chance to tell him, he headed down this mountain"—Michelle turned to point—"looking for a dusk-to-dawn light and never came back. Isn't that crazy? Why would anyone go looking for a dusk-to-dawn light in the middle of the woods? But then I did the same thing. Can you believe that? Yeah, I followed the same light and when I found Cliff, he was missing a finger, and he told me our daughter was dead . . . and . . . and I had . . . my . . . life . . ." For a moment Michelle felt like she was lifting from the ground, weightless, floating.

"Are you all right, dear?" the old woman asked. "You don't look well."

Michelle closed her eyes, playing back everything she'd said, mortified by how stupid it must have sounded. She felt possessed, as if the words had originated somewhere else.

"I'm sorry," Michelle said. "I must have sounded insane. So much has happened lately." When Michelle realized the woman was holding her arm to steady her, Michelle pulled it back slowly. "I'm okay."

"You look pale," the old woman said. "Come up to the house. I'll make tea."

"No. Thank you. I have to go."

"No. I think you should stay."

Michelle was disturbed by Mrs. Souder's insistence. It had the ring of threat, even though her eyes seemed harmless, loving. Michelle followed her into the house, remembering how upset Pink had become when Michelle wandered into Mrs. Souder's private room. Michelle felt like a sneak not telling her she'd been in the house before, had actually been in her private altar space.

Michelle sat at the kitchen table, trying to rein in her discomfort, while Mrs. Souder held the teakettle under the faucet. The old woman swiveled toward the stove and slid the kettle onto the burner, then turned up the flame. Michelle couldn't help picturing her cauldron hanging over the fire, the queer otherworldliness of it, like something from a movie, or a cartoon.

Mrs. Souder sat down, opposite Michelle at the table, folding her hands in front of her. In the warm light of the kitchen, the woman's face appeared younger than it had outside, even though the lines at the corners of her eyes were creased deep with worry and concern.

"I have a strange story for you, Mrs. Stage," Mattie said. "One you may find difficult to believe.

CHAPTER 34

More titty bars and strip joints. That's what the country needed. Pink followed Paula down a corridor to a red curtain. When she parted the material, Pink walked through. In front of a mirrored wall sat three men in chairs, spaced about five feet apart, each man with his own writhing and nearly naked woman grinding her butt into his lap. Paula walked up beside Pink and took his hand. "This way," she said, cooing. "Paula has her own private boudoir."

The room was no bigger than a walk-in closet, all the walls mirrored except for the one behind the single chair, everything cast in red, though Pink could not discern the source of the light. Paula motioned for him to sit. He reached out for Paula's plump little fanny.

"Paula will take care of those hands for you."

"Long as you give them back when you're done," Pink said.

It was the first time he'd seen a smile from her that hadn't looked faked. She pulled two red scarves from a shelf behind the chair and tied his hands to the back.

Pink wished he'd rearranged his compass needle before Paula bound his hands. Now he'd have to suffer a southeast pointer instead of a more comfortable northern one. Paula turned her back to Pink and slowly slid the G-string down her thighs, letting it fall to the floor at her feet. She turned to face him, then bent down to check the knots in the scarves. "This way you won't be a naughty little pumpkin, will you?"

Paula eyed him, dropping her gaze to the lump in his trousers. "Paula can fix that." She gently maneuvered him upright, toggling him with the deft of a safe cracker. She lowered herself down onto his lap and swayed to the music. Pink leaned his face closer to her breasts and she met him halfway, arching her back. It was Paula who noticed the vibration in his pants.

"Do you need to get that?"

"Get what?" Pink said, burrowing into the swells of her bosom.

"Isn't that your phone?"

"It's nothing." Pink knew it was Isabelle. She would keep calling and leaving messages until the phone exploded in his pants.

"Paula likes," she said, straddling the device in Pink's pocket. Each time it vibrated, Paula cooed. Pink hoped Isabelle would stay true to form and keep calling every few minutes.

When it stopped, Paula grasped her breasts and mashed them into Pink's jowls.

Pink hated having Paula in his lap and Isabelle in his head. What was so goddamn important she had to keep calling? The calls were wrecking his concentration. The phone vibrated again. Paula warbled and Pink sighed. "Hells bells on wheels! Reach in my pocket and grab that dang phone for me, will you?" Pink asked Paula.

She slipped it out slowly, flipped it open. She pressed the talk button and held the phone to Pink's ear, leaning in close enough for Pink to smell her breasts—funnel cakes, he thought, or cotton candy. "Okay, Isabelle," Pink said, stretching his tongue toward the tender brown flesh of Paula's nipple. She arched her back slightly, pulling the prize out of Pink's reach. "What is so hell-fired important?" he said.

*****

The words *strange* and *difficult to believe* from Mattie's lips gave Michelle a surprising jolt of relief. Since the night she'd gone down the mountain looking for Cliff, her entire life had been strange and difficult to believe.

Mattie poured tea and set the cup in front of Michelle. For one fleeting second Michelle felt a peculiar caution, as if she should not drink or eat anything this woman had to offer. Michelle pushed away her concern and raised the cup to her lips

"I'm sorry about your husband," Mrs. Souder said. "Such a tragedy. He must have been young like you."

Michelle nodded, unwilling at the moment to grapple with the reality of Cliff's suicide. She needed to know what Mrs. Souder was going to tell her.

"The day after your husband's death, my Pink went to your cabin with Sheriff Fisk. Pink said he saw a pendant that belonged to you but looked a lot like one I had given his wife, Isabelle, when she was a young girl. That alone wouldn't have mattered much to me. After all, Pink's not much on details, and there are probably millions of pendants most people would mistake for Isabelle's. But it was something he told me, something you said to him, that started me wondering."

Michelle sipped her tea.

"He said you accused him of killing Isabelle. That seemed an odd thing to say given that Isabelle isn't dead. Did you know that Isabelle isn't dead?"

Michelle nodded, feeling like she was on trial and was about to be lectured instead of enlightened. She didn't appreciate the edge in Mrs. Souder's voice. For whatever reason—maybe Mattie's visit to the hospital or the concern on her face the day her friend Lulu died or just intuition—Michelle had hoped to find an ally in this peculiar woman.

"The thing that's troubled me most about all that was how you got here," Mrs. Souder said.

Michelle didn't know what she was talking about. Mrs. Souder was hard to read, her expression unflinching, unchanging, like a bird, or an animal. Michelle couldn't even tell the color of her eyes, as if her features were vulcanized against detection, a shape shifter.

"I'm not sure what you mean," Michelle said. "I came down the hill like—"

"We'll get to that in a moment. As I was saying, when Pink told me about the pendant, I started pulling things together." Mrs. Souder got up from the table and went to the living room, bringing her purse back. She dug down in the bag, looking over at Michelle, obviously intent on finding something. "I lied about why I came to your room that night," Mrs. Souder said, glancing back. "I didn't know your roommate, not until I saw the name on the board. Sometimes I have visions, impulses. I knew the name was wrong, so I wrote the correct one. But that wasn't why I was there."

Mrs. Souder emptied her purse one item at a time on the counter next to her. She was shaking her head now, as if frustrated, or anxious. The contents of the old woman's bag were sampled across the counter, plain, ordinary things no different than Michelle would carry in her own purse. When Mrs. Souder turned to face Michelle, her features tightened. She seemed confused.

"I'm sorry, Mrs. Stage," she said. "There's something I must confess. It's shameful." Mrs. Souder's eyes reddened, but she never moved from the counter. "I came to your room the other night to see the pendant. I took it from your handbag."

Michelle couldn't respond. She strangely didn't care the old woman had gone through her things. She felt too dazed by the uneven tumble of the evening. And she knew the old woman was wrong about the pendant. Michelle leaned to the side and wiggled her hand into the pocket of her jeans, withdrawing it. "This one?" Michelle asked.

"How did you . . . ? I took that from your locker."

"I don't know." Michelle felt sorry for the woman; she looked frightened. "It was in my jeans when I left the hospital," Michelle said.

Mrs. Souder came over and sat across from Michelle. "Lulu said these kinds of things could happen." Mrs. Souder brought her hands to her face, and it seemed she was crying. After a moment, she sniffed then wiped her eyes. "I'm sorry."

"You mentioned something earlier," Michelle said, "something about not knowing how I got here. I don't understand what you mean."

The old woman looked over, hurt coloring her eyes, a new severity drawing all the life from her features. She stared at Michelle as if constructing words into sentences, thoughts into tangible bits of conversation.

"You really don't know, do you?" the old woman said.

"I only know that when I went down the mountain to look for Cliff, my entire world changed and I don't know how to put it back. And so far, you're the only person who doesn't look at me like I'm from Mars when I say that."

Mrs. Souder wound the string around her tea bag and squeezed it against the spoon. "I'm a midwife," the old woman said, turning toward Michelle. "Years ago, I delivered my cousin Ida's child, a baby boy. She didn't want it. That's not exactly true. Her husband, Ruther didn't want children at the time. Of course, he wasn't her husband yet, and was embarrassed she was pregnant. He even blamed her, like it was her fault she'd gotten pregnant. So Ida left the child with me. I was barren, so I took the baby without hesitation. I didn't even ask my husband, Buck. He was away on a project for the Corps of Engineers. I told him over the phone, and he was less than thrilled, but I didn't care. By the time he came home I had already named the child. Pink."

Mrs. Souder paused a moment. "A few years later, when Ida and Ruther married, he decided he wanted to start a family. They had two girls. Isabelle and Claire."

"Isabelle?" Michelle said. "Pink's wife, Isabelle?"

"Yes," the old woman said, her fingers tugging at the skin of her jaw. "Pink's wife, Isabelle. Isabelle is Pink's sister. But he doesn't know that."

Michelle had no words, only questions spinning in her head, so many it was hard to verbalize even one of them. She waited for the old woman to speak, watching her lower lip tremble.

"Pink and Isabelle grew up believing they were second cousins. Ida and I had no idea how close they were growing."

Michelle remembered the path through the treetops, the old boards twisting and rickety now, strung together with rusty nails. But there was a time when the wood had been new and strong. She envisioned how it must have looked when Pink hauled it up the hill, how excited he must have been. She pictured Pink, a boy of seventeen, carrying the tools, climbing the trees, hammering the boards, building the miraculous trail without Isabelle's knowledge. Michelle could almost imagine Isabelle's surprise when Pink took Isabelle to the trail, helped her up the ladder, guided her between enormous pines, oaks, and poplars. Was it spring when Isabelle first saw the path? Were the dogwoods in bloom?

"They loved each other by then," Mrs. Souder said. "Pink and Isabelle decided to get married. But Ida wouldn't have it. She told the preacher that Pink and Isabelle were second cousins, but the preacher didn't see how that mattered—second cousins were hardly blood relatives, he'd told her. At that point, I couldn't talk to Isabelle anymore. She hated me."

"She hated you?" Michelle said. "Why?"

"Not just me. She hated Ida too. She hated both of us for our deception."

"Did Isabelle know Pink was her brother?" Michelle asked.

"When Isabelle was fifteen, same age as your daughter, Cassie, I told her. She never talked to me after that. I think that's why she was so set on it," Mrs. Souder continued, "like it would be a way to punish Ida and me for what we'd done. And it worked. Ida was so distraught . . . she killed herself."

The strangeness of the evening cloaked itself around Michelle, a queer tingle running through her blood. "What about your husband?" Michelle asked.

"Buck? Buck didn't hold with Pink and Isabelle being married. The shame overtook him. One night he called from Kentucky, where he was consulting on a project, and said he couldn't live with the dishonesty anymore. He didn't come home, and I never saw him again."

"And Pink? Does he know Isabelle is his sister?"

Mrs. Souder shifted her gaze toward Michelle and for a moment it seemed like a strange light came from the old woman's eyes, as if they glowed from within. Michelle had to look away for a moment to reset herself. When she looked back, Mrs. Souder was staring across the kitchen, her fingers absently wiping the tears from her cheek.

"That's why he killed her."

Michelle wasn't sure she heard right. "What?"

Mrs. Souder turned to Michelle. "That's why Pink killed her."

"But . . . I thought she was alive."

"Yes, she is, here," Mrs. Souder said, "but she wasn't before. I know Pink killed her."

Michelle didn't want to keep asking Mrs. Souder to explain, but she was having a difficult time following. Even so, Michelle felt a peculiar calm being with the old woman.

"I'm sorry, Mrs. Souder. I . . . I don't understand."

"How could you dear," the old woman said, as if returning from somewhere else. She looked over at Michelle.

"Pink went crazy when Isabelle told him."

"Isabelle told Pink?" Michelle asked. "Why?"

"Because Claire, Isabelle's sister, was having an affair with Pink. Claire didn't know she was Pink's sister. We only told Isabelle. Anyway, Isabelle got tired of it, especially when the affair became public. Isabelle didn't care what people thought of her, but the idea of town-folks knowing about Pink and Claire's affair was too much of an embarrassment and Isabelle wanted to punish him, the same way she wanted to punish Ida and me. The strange thing was, Pink never really believed Isabelle, but he couldn't understand why she'd say something so vicious."

Mrs. Souder folded her hands on the table.

"I finally told him the truth," Mrs. Souder said. "That's when he blew up, knocking things over, swearing, calling Isabelle a bitch, asking me how I could do such a thing. When he left here, I knew there would be trouble. I tried to make him stay, calm him down. It was the first time in my life he was deaf to me.

"After that night, I didn't hear from Pink for over three weeks. I called, went to their house. He hadn't been to the office. Clarence, Pink's friend, hadn't seen him either. Clarence was the one who found him." Mrs. Souder looked over at Michelle. "Pink was up there working on his cabin . . . your cabin. He was drunk, putting shingles on the roof wearing nothing but his BVDs, cowboy boots, and a tool belt. No one saw Isabelle again after that. Pink and Isabelle's neighbors had heard them arguing, and Claire reported Isabelle missing. Everyone was sure Pink had killed her because Isabelle would never have left Ardenwood. She would never have moved away. They called the police. Everyone searched for her. I asked Pink what happened. He wouldn't even talk to me."

"Why didn't they arrest Pink?" Michelle asked.

"They never found her body. They couldn't arrest him for murder without a body. Louden questioned him for days, but Pink would never own up to it. Finally, Louden had to just let him go. There was no proof a crime had even been committed." Mrs. Souder got up from the table and went to the kettle. "More tea?"

"No. Thank you," Michelle said.

Mrs. Souder filled her cup, adding milk and honey. She came back and smoothed the tablecloth with the flat of her hand. "Nearly a year went by, I had lost almost everything. Buck was gone. And Pink hadn't talked to me that whole time. I couldn't stand it anymore. That's when I asked Lulu for help.

"Lulu was a powerful witch, the seventh daughter of a seventh daughter—the most powerful. I asked her to make things right again. I couldn't stand losing Pink. I couldn't stand the thought he had killed Isabelle. I couldn't live if he cut me out of his life. He was all I had. Can you understand that, Mrs. Stage?"

Michelle understood perfectly.

"Lulu didn't want to do it," Mrs. Souder said. "She was afraid of the consequences. But I begged and begged, so she agreed. She always regretted it."

"What did she *do*?" Michelle asked.

CHAPTER 35

Michelle found it difficult parsing the story Mrs. Souder was sharing—infinite, fluid realities, portals to multiple existences, shapeshifting, immortality. Mrs. Souder brought out a book, a worn, leather-bound text that appeared to be handwritten. Michelle was reluctant to touch it for fear the pages would crumble. *The Philosophia Visita* was scribed on the cover. Mrs. Souder told Michelle about a man, an alchemist and sorcerer, who taught Lulu everything about the subtle body, spirit, traversing the gateways. "He was born in 1605," Mrs. Souder told Michelle.

"But . . . I don't understand how . . . how could he have taught your friend?"

"He knew how to cheat death." The statement was resolute, sending a chill through Michelle. "So did Lulu," Mrs. Souder added.

She must have read the skepticism in Michelle's eyes.

"Lulu is dead because she wanted to be. She was over 130 years old."

Michelle's rational mind was trying to piece this all together. For the first time since all of this started, Michelle could finally understand how perplexing it must have been for Cliff and Darcy listening to her own queer ramblings and rants. But the most disconcerting aspect of Mrs. Souder's story, the part not easily written off as the discourse of a mad woman, was the absolute certainty with which she related it. Her words were not freighted with doubt. This was not myth, or speculation, in the old woman's mind, but fact, which made Michelle squirm.

"Lulu explained to me that life was like a book, each page a different possibility, a different reality," Mrs. Souder said. "One must only know how to turn the page, Lulu had told me . . . but there could be consequences."

Mrs. Souder looked over at Michelle, tears brimming the bottom of the old woman's eyes. She cleared her throat. "Lulu opened up a gateway to another reality, one where Pink had not killed Isabelle. Then Pink and I came through it. To here. To now . . ."

A vortex spun through Michelle. Questions overlapped questions, coming with such speed as to cancel each other out. She could not grasp one thought and hold it long enough to give it form.

Mrs. Souder stood and took her cup to the sink, while Michelle sat staring at the curious book in front of her, its pages scribbled with Latin, drawings, formulas, and permutations, symbols not only foreign but unearthly.

"The night Pink and I were to pass through, I asked Lulu if she was coming." Mrs. Souder rinsed her cup in the sink. "I didn't want to go without her. She told me not to worry, that she would be there when we arrived. I didn't understand. She explained that reality is fluid, that the existence we believe is the one and only, is merely a single possibility, one choice in our life. She explained that she existed in every reality that I did, as long as we had met in that reality. She said that past and present were merely perceptions, they did not exist in the way we think of them. 'But what about me?' I had asked Lulu. 'What about Pink? Will we run into ourselves in this new reality? Will there be two of each of us in Ardenwood?' Lulu shook her head. 'No,' she said. 'By traversing the gateway, you are leaving this existence behind and entering a new one, a new choice, as if you had been there all along. Neither of you will remain behind in this reality. It will be as though you instantly vanished from the face of the earth.'"

Michelle recalled Sheriff Fisk saying how Mattie and Pink disappeared, never heard from again. Mrs. Souder came back to the table and sat, wiping her hands on the towel she'd brought with her.

"Lulu said there was one thing I had to understand though. She told me I would have to carry a talisman to take Pink through. No one could cross the gateway without it, unless they had a guide or helper."

"But I did," Michelle was quick to state. "I came through without a guide. So did Cliff."

"I can't speak for your husband," Mrs. Souder said, "but *you* did have a charm. That pentagram in your pocket."

Michelle reached into her jeans and brought it out again, remembering how it had been behind the toilet the night she'd gone to look for Cliff. "This?" she said to the old woman. "I found this in the cabin. No one gave it to me."

"Someone did," Mrs. Souder said. "Someone wanted you to have it."

"Someone? I don't . . ."

Mrs. Souder took the pendant from Michelle and held it in her palm. "This pentagram belonged to Isabelle years ago. She wanted to learn witchcraft, the way of Wicca, and I had given it to her. Unlike Pink, Isabelle was dedicated to the study, probably because her own mother was so opposed to it—Ida thought it was the work of the devil. Isabelle pursued anything, including Pink, that might upset Ida. Lulu and I worked with her. Isabelle read and listened and practiced the whole time she and Pink were falling in love. I should have done something much sooner, but by the time I allowed myself to accept what was happening, it was too late. Lulu had urged me to tell Pink the truth from the beginning, but I couldn't. Pink would never have understood what Ida and I had done. Lulu said I should at least tell Isabelle, that even though Isabelle would be devastated, she would be strong enough to handle it, and end the affair with Pink. The day I finally told Isabelle, she ripped the pentagram from her neck and threw it in my face. She never spoke to me after that. From that day forth, Isabelle tried to take everything from me, punish Ida and me for what we'd done. I couldn't blame her. Our deception was a travesty against nature, the very nature I live my life by."

Under the avalanche of information, Michelle was barely able to sort through her own questions, working to clarify the ones most pressing in her mind. What did any of this have to do with her? Or Cliff? And how had Cliff passed through this "gateway" if it was impossible without some special charm? Had he found an amulet and absentmindedly shoved it in his pocket the way she had? And now what? Was there a way back? And where was "back," and what would it be? Would Cassie be there? Alive?

Mrs. Souder picked up Isabelle's pentagram. The old woman's features were taut. "The thing I don't understand is, why your husband was so different from the way you remembered him? And why he didn't remember coming through the gateway."

"Does Pink remember?" Michelle asked.

"Of course not," she said. "Lulu gave him nothing to carry. She asked if I thought Pink could handle knowing. I knew he couldn't—it would drive him insane remembering that he'd killed Isabelle then finding her alive. Besides, if he remembered, then it would defeat the purpose of going through to begin with. He would still hate me for my deception, he would still know what Ida and I had done."

Mrs. Souder looked up at Michelle, sadness dulling her eyes. "It must be driving you insane as well," she said to Michelle. "I'm truly sorry."

"Then how did Pink come through? I don't understand."

Mrs. Souder reached across the table and took Michelle's hands, explaining how she and Lulu had tricked Pink into going with her through the woods. They'd waited until Pink was drunk, which he was every night at the cabin, and Mattie begged him to help her find Scout, her golden retriever, that he'd run off and she was afraid he'd tangle with a wild boar and get killed. Pink had initially refused to go, but she knew how much he loved Scout. Eventually he put on his jacket, grabbed his bottle of Jack Daniels, and followed her out the door.

"It was terrible," Mrs. Souder told Michelle. "Lulu tried to prepare me for what would happen to Pink when we journeyed through the opening between worlds, but nothing she said came close. Pink was just sick at first, vomiting. Then his legs went weak. He was barely able to walk."

Michelle recalled how the chopper pilot had taken sick when he hovered above the dusk-to-dawn light, but Sheriff Fisk and his deputy had seemed fine. But they had never seen the light when they drove down the road.

"I could handle the illness, but it got so I felt like I was pulling Pink through a meat grinder. He was refusing to get up off the ground, screaming he couldn't go on," Mrs. Souder said. "I was sure I was killing him, and was ready to turn back, but I realized I had no idea where we were, couldn't recognize anything. And that's when they came."

"They?" Michelle said.

Before Mrs. Souder could explain further, there was a noise from the front of the house. They both turned, the front door opening then slamming shut a moment later, followed by stomping, like someone trying to remove snow from their shoes.

"Mama?" a voice called through the house. Footfalls tracked down the hall until Pink appeared in the doorway to the kitchen, his features pained and agitated.

"Pink?" Mrs. Souder said, getting up from her chair.

Mrs. Souder brushed snow from Pink's shoulders, while Pink kept pushing her hands away. "Christ, Mama, it'll melt on its own." When Pink noticed Michelle, his expression went from irritation to concern.

"I thought you were in the hospital," Pink said, looking at his mother, then back at Michelle. "What have we got going on here?"

"Nothing," Mrs. Souder said.

Michelle got up to leave.

Mrs. Souder put herself between Michelle and the doorway. "You can't go."

Until that moment, Michelle had felt safe in the company of the old woman, but now Mrs. Souder appeared scornful, her brow tightened to thin ridges.

"I have to go," Michelle said, dread flowering in her stomach. "I'm leaving in the morning. Early. Going back to Atlanta."

Mrs. Souder came closer, her eyes watery, suddenly old, yellow. "You must stay," she said, speaking the words with emphasis, as if Michelle was supposed to decode some secret message from her intonation.

When Michelle turned to leave the kitchen, the old woman snagged her wrist, her grip surprisingly strong. "Don't go, child," she whispered, "or you will never be free."

"Christ, Mama, you're scaring the poor woman to death," Pink said. "I'll drive her home in a few minutes."

Michelle wrenched her wrist free from the old woman, unsettled by the red finger marks on her skin. What was this all about? Did the old woman feel she'd told Michelle too much and wasn't about to let her blab to Sheriff Fisk? It wouldn't matter anyway since Fisk would never believe the old woman's story any more than he'd believed hers. But Pink's mother was acting queer. Michelle felt safe with Pink there, but what if he left to go home?

"I'll take that ride, Pink," Michelle said. The old woman seemed to relax then, taking her seat at the kitchen table.

Pink talked about how strange his evening had gone and seemed to want to talk about Isabelle, bringing her up several times, saying how Isabelle had been calling him all night. Michelle felt like she was intruding. "She told me the damnedest thing tonight, Mama," Pink said. "It scares me to even repeat it. I'm afraid the white coats'll come haul her off yonder. Maybe the best thing for her is some time in a padded room though." Pink tried to laugh, but Michelle could tell he was troubled.

Michelle excused herself to the bathroom and stood at the sink. She splashed water on her face. Where was Darcy? She wished her sister were here. Darcy was the only sanity left in Michelle's life.

When Michelle returned, Pink's expression had turned dark, the room charged with a metallic hush. Neither Pink nor his mother said a word when she came in and sat down. Mrs. Souder stood, grabbed her cloak off the chair, and went out the back door. Burrito had been sleeping in his bed in the corner. He got up and whimpered where Mrs. Souder had departed. Pink sat staring at the table, his eyes lost in shadow. After a few minutes, he stood up, scratching his wrist.

"Mama says she can help you," Pink finally said.

"I don't need help. Are you going to drive me up to the cabin? Or I can just . . ."

"She wants to have a little ceremony for you. Out back."

No ceremonies. No nothing. Michelle was almost to the front door when Pink caught her from behind. "Let me go," she said.

"I will, but my mama . . . I don't know . . . she says she can help you. I don't know how she does it, but she does help some folks, rids them of ailments doctors can't even cure. She seems scary sometimes with all that talk of hers, the incantations and potions and such, but hell, she's harmless. What I mean is, she does seem to have powers, but she'd never use them to hurt anyone."

Michelle wasn't so sure. Pink obviously had no idea what his mother, or Isabelle, was capable of.

CHAPTER 36

Burning embers swirled and darted up through the falling snowflakes as Michelle slogged down the hill, her eyes on the distant fire. Pink followed a few steps behind. Mrs. Souder, cloaked entirely in black, with a hood concealing her head and face, stood near the flames in the center of the stone circle, as if she were peering into a trapdoor to hell, her figure straight and fixed as a charred post. Fresh snow collected atop the rounded stones of the circle. Hot, orange light from the blaze illuminated the branches and trees encircling Pink's mother. When Michelle glanced back at Pink for guidance as to where they were headed, he nodded forward, his eyes pointing her toward the ring.

Standing at the arbor, Michelle could hear Pink breathing hard from the trek down the slope. Mrs. Souder stood with her back to them, and Michelle wondered if she even knew they were there. Michelle analyzed the bizarre scene, the four small altars festooned with different colored cloths, each altar spaced ninety degrees apart from the other, within the rim of stones. The surface of each altar was adorned with various items: crystals, pinecones, candles. Some had little toy gnomes or mermaids, like something a child might create. Incense burned on one of the altars. There was also a bird's nest and a wooden bowl with dried leaves, ordinary items that could be found in anyone's home or yard.

Mrs. Souder turned to face Michelle and Pink, then stepped forward.

She raised her head and Michelle could see her eyes, blank stones in the old woman's featureless face.

Pink whispered to Michelle to step forward a few inches but not to pass under the arbor. Michelle considered what Pink had told her coming down the hill: "Just go with whatever happens." Michelle had thought she could do it, convincing herself she wasn't afraid. Now she wasn't sure, with Pink's mother staring into her eyes, unblinking, as if in a trance. A second later the old woman swept a knife out from under her cloak and held the point against Michelle's chest. Michelle's breath caught. She stumbled backward, her retreat halted by Pink's chest and stomach. She couldn't move. The point of the curved blade pushed against the material of her jacket. Pink pressed up behind her.

"Thee who approaches the veil between the worlds, the comfort earth of humankind, and the dread domains of the Lords of the Outer Realm, hast thou the courage to make the assay? For I say verily, thee would fare far better to rush onto my blade and perish than to put forth the effort with fear in thy heart," the old woman intoned, vapor coming from her mouth, as if she had recently swallowed fire.

Michelle stood fixed, the point glinting at her chest. Pink whispered to Michelle to repeat his words: "I come in perfect love and perfect trust." When Michelle recited the phrase, the old woman answered, "All blessed with perfection in love and trust shall be doubly welcome. I grant thee passage through this dread door."

Michelle couldn't move. "I can't do this. Please, just let me go."

Mrs. Souder gazed hard upon her, then leaned forward and whispered to her. "Don't you want to reunite with Cassie?"

Michelle drew a deep breath, trying to stiffen her resolve when Mrs. Souder withdrew the knife and stepped back from the arbor. Just then, Pink shoved Michelle from behind with his shoulder, knocking her into the circle. Michelle lost her footing, nearly falling, a dull pain between her shoulder blades where Pink had pushed her. Before Michelle could gain her equilibrium, the old woman rushed forward and kissed her on the lips, hugged her, then spun her three times where she stood. "And thus is every-one first brought into the circle," the old woman said.

Pink leaned in close and asked Michelle her sign. "What?" she said. "Your sign," Pink said softly. "You know, Scorpio, Sagittarius . . ."

"Virgo," she said.

Pink seemed to think a moment, until his mother said, "North, Pink."

"Yeah, that's right," he mumbled to himself, guiding Michelle toward the altar with the green cloth covered in pinecones and acorns. "I'm a Leo," he told her, placing her next to the small altar. "So I have to stand . . . let's see . . ."

"South," his mother said. Pink shuffled across the circle, opposite Michelle, wiping the residue of melted snowflakes from his cheeks.

Once Pink was in place, an interlude of silence followed where Michelle wasn't sure what to do with her hands. She watched Pink, who was stepping from foot to foot as if his toes were frozen.

Mrs. Souder raised her palms over the yellow altar to Michelle's left and spoke, her words rising against the cold air. "Ye Protectors of the Watchtower of the East, ye keepers of the Sky, of all creatures of wing and air, the Star-seeker, the Golden Hawk, the Soaring Sun. We summon you now to stir and rise, witness our rites, breathe safety into our circle. Join us this night, ye wind of life, and be with us now."

When the old woman fell silent, the branches above them clicked and rustled under a slight breeze. The old woman gestured with her hands, then turned toward the altar where Pink stood and raised her arms, reciting, "Ye Protectors of the Watchtower of the South, ye keepers of the Fire, the Fiery Dragon of Summer, the Scorching Disc of Noon, the ceaseless Flames of Earth's own Furnace. We summon you now . . ." Pink's mother continued, speaking to each direction, turning at last to face the altar where Michelle stood. "Ye Protectors of the Watchtower of the North, ye keepers of the Earth . . ."

When Michelle closed her eyes, the words entered her like a low current, thrumming beneath her skin. The drone of the old woman's voice bled through Michelle, into her chest, her stomach, floating her up, detached, as if suddenly unmoored from bone and muscle. Michelle felt a bristle of dread over opening her eyes, fearing that everything would be gone—the circle, Pink, his mother, the woods, her own body—nothing left of the world but a fine, pale mist. Everything fell silent. With her eyes shut tight, even the crackling of wood in the fire had fallen mute. It was then Michelle heard the anomalous timbre of the old woman's voice, her words seemingly without origin in the world.

"I call upon Thee, O Mighty Mother of all creatures, purveyor of all abundance—by vein and blood, water and air, through loving breath and beating heart do I invoke your presence, join the flesh of this, Thy loyal servant and priestess. Hail, Aradia! As I lowly bend before Thee with loving sacrifice and adoration, O Powerful One, that I too may rise like a wisp of smoke, who, without Thy very breath, like fire without air, I am forlorn."

Sounds rushed back to Michelle's ears as if a wave long held at sea had suddenly crashed to the shore. Michelle opened her eyes.

Mrs. Souder faced Michelle. The old woman's eyes were closed, vapor escaping her parted lips like the final breaths of a dying creature. Michelle glanced past her to Pink, who was blowing heat into his cupped hands, dancing his feet in place as if to conjure warmth from his own impatience.

"O darksome Mother, true and divine, to Thee I charge you in this sign, my blight of fear, five-pointed star, pure love and bliss."

Mrs. Souder withdrew her knife and pointed it toward the night sky, cutting a sign into the air in front of Michelle. Before Michelle could tell what the symbol was, Mrs. Souder spoke again, invoking the Great God Karnayna, asking Him to return to earth. Michelle shut her eyes and let the old woman's words sweep into her, overtake her. At once the air grew rarified and golden. Great pillows of clouds poured across a vast and vacant ocean. Mountains like pyramids rose slowly from the sea, exploding with green trees and velvety shrubs, cracking open with scorching yellow light. Michelle felt her breath strain, her heart winging from her chest and beating free in the exotic landscape.

The old woman's words took form, great herds of bleating goats, birds by the thousands wheeling above her, suspended structures swaying hundreds of feet above the ground, water cascading from shelves of clouds, steel-banded wooden doors with enormous bronze hinges.

"Open the door that hath no key, the door of dreams, only by wisdom shall man come to Thee, O Shepherd of Goats, answer unto me."

Blinding light rushed through the opening doors and Michelle felt herself falling backward. She opened her eyes to the piercing, glassy gaze of Mrs. Souder, radiant orbs glowing from her dark hood. Michelle blinked, startled, and the image vanished, leaving the image of the old woman speaking quietly to Pink, her back to Michelle. Michelle couldn't tell what was real and what wasn't. She wanted to speak, but her own tongue felt foreign and dead in her mouth.

Mrs. Souder gestured with her hands toward the heavens, saying Hail and Farewell. Hail and Farewell. Michelle had no idea how long they had been in the circle. In that moment, cold rushed back into her extremities, snow collecting on the shoulders of her coat. She tried to kick warmth into her feet by tapping them on the ground discreetly, so as not to disturb the old woman. Mrs. Souder spoke incantations to the four directions then used her curved knife to slice an imaginary opening in the space beneath the arbor.

"It's time to go," she told Michelle, pointing toward the exit. Pink yawned and followed Michelle out.

"How about some pork chops before I drive Mrs. Stage home?" Pink asked his mother, walking under the arbor. "I'm sure that little soirée of yours made her as hungry as it did me."

Mrs. Souder took a deep breath as if to calm herself. Michelle plodded up the hill to the house, still dizzy, her skin like damp cotton. She felt like she'd just stepped out of a hot tub, both cold and sweaty at the same time. Never had she been so aware of every cell and molecule in her body, as if she could feel the blood swabbing her veins, the marrow feeding her bones.

In the kitchen, Pink's mother fried pork chops in a skillet on the stove, smoke swirling up into the exhaust fan in the range hood. Pink excused himself to the bathroom. The clock read almost three in the morning. Michelle wasn't the least bit sleepy.

"Is that it?" Michelle asked, after Pink left the room.

"Is that what?" Mrs. Souder said, her back to Michelle, twisting to look over at her.

"Is that . . . I don't know . . . is that all there is? I mean . . . can I go

home now? Back to my old life, the way it was before? My daughter?"
Michelle's words felt clumsy and stilted in the wake of what she had just
experienced.

Mrs. Souder turned her spatula toward Michelle. "That's not what we
were doing," the old woman said. "I don't know how to tell you this, but
I can't open it. I don't have those kinds of powers." The old woman spun
back to the skillet as if Michelle should have assumed that all along.

"I don't understand . . . how . . . what can I . . . ." Michelle muttered,
confused by all the ceremonious rigmarole. What had that been about, the
chanting, the fire, the shiny blade at her chest?

"Lulu opened the portal for Pink and me," the old woman said over
the sizzling of the meat. "Then she closed it. I don't have the slightest
notion how she did it."

"But I thought that's what you were doing, the stuff about the door
and all? I saw light pouring through the opening doors."

"I was trying to understand what happened, why you ended up here,
trying to get answers from the Outer Realm, from Lulu."

"And?"

"Only one thing came to me," the old woman said, shoveling a pork
chop onto the waiting plate. "Isabelle."

"Isabelle?" Michelle asked.

Pink padded back into the kitchen.

Mrs. Souder slid her eyes toward her son, setting the plate down in
front of an empty chair. "Oh, I bet they can smell these chops all the way
over in Arkansas," Pink said, rubbing his palms together as he sidled up to
the plate. "Sure you don't want one, Mrs. Stage? Put iron in your blood."

Michelle shook her head, glancing over at Pink's mother, who was at
the sink drying dishes, her back to the table.

Pink finished both pork chops and sat a moment picking his teeth
before he asked Michelle if she was ready to go. Mrs. Souder had left the
kitchen and hadn't returned. Michelle had no idea where she was, thinking maybe she'd gone to bed.

"Mama, we're leaving," Pink called to the hallway.

A moment later Pink's mother appeared under the small archway to the kitchen in her bathrobe and slippers. "Why don't you go warm up your car first," she told Pink. "So Mrs. Stage won't get cold."

"Sure, but it ain't gonna do much good with the window broke out and all," Pink said, pushing himself up from the table. Mrs. Souder waited to hear the front door close before she spoke. "I suspect that you will be able to return to your previous life tonight if you're ready," she said to Michelle, "if that's what you want. But there is a catch."

Michelle waited, watching the old woman's colorless eyes.

"You will have to take Pink with you," Mrs. Souder said.

"Take Pink?"

"I am almost certain Isabelle opened the portal. Isabelle wants him back."

"But I thought Isabelle didn't practice witchcraft. And why would she—"

"Not the Isabelle that lives with Pink. The Isabelle Pink killed. Isabelle from the other realm. That's why you were given the pentacle."

Michelle was confused, trying to make sense of something that could not be reconstructed through reason.

"Horrible images came to me in the circle tonight," the old woman said. "Images I can't begin to explain, things I have never seen before. I fear Pink has done something unspeakable with Isabelle's body, something disgraceful to her spirit."

"How can I get Pink to come with me? He'll never agree."

"I'll take care of that," the old woman said.

"What about you?" Michelle said. "If Pink goes . . . you'll lose him forever."

The old woman pulled out the chair and sat. "I lost Pink the moment Ida and I deceived him. We should have told him who he was from the start. I have tried to change what has happened, and it's all gone terribly wrong. Now he must go back, or he'll kill Isabelle again. At least if he returns, I can try to help Isabelle get well, so she can live out her life."

Michelle wanted to say something to Mrs. Souder, but could not find any words that seemed to make sense.

"It was unforgivable what Ida and I did to those children." The old woman hung her head, curtains of gray hair falling forward, covering her cheeks. "What hurts the most is . . ." she added, raising her head, "knowing Pink will be alone. In his whole life, he's never been alone."

"I'll try to help him if I can," Michelle said.

The old woman stared up at Michelle through glossy eyes, using her bent fingers to push the hair from her face. "He won't know you, child," the old woman said. "Once you pass through, Pink will have no idea who you are."

Michelle could not fully grasp the implications of what the old woman was saying, or how Pink might react, or what she might find when she "passed through." She had no idea how much time had elapsed? Or how to explain Cliff's death to Cassie, if Cassie were even there? Wherever *there* was. She couldn't tell Cassie that her father shot himself—there would be no body, no funeral, just numerous unanswerable questions, impossible leaps of faith. Then another thought broke in: Where was Cliff's body? Was it still in Ardenwood or on the way back to Atlanta? If she left, who would take care of his remains? Michelle felt a dizzying sensation, close to what she'd experienced in the circle, except this one left her nauseous.

"You need to go now," the old woman said. "Don't be afraid, child. Isabelle only wants Pink back. She has no row with you."

Michelle felt a hollow opening in her chest, as if something had fallen out, leaving behind a flimsy space that could collapse at any moment. The emptiness spread to her stomach, her knees. She held her eyes on the old woman a second longer, trying to restore balance, then turned down the hallway toward the front door.

In the driveway, Pink's Suburban pumped a tower of billowing steam up into the night sky. Michelle cinched her collar around her neck and dashed toward the car, stepping high to traverse the deep snow. When she got in the Suburban, Pink slid out the other side.

"My mama wants something," Pink said, motioning toward the house. "I'll just be a second." He hitched up his trousers as he trod back toward the front porch. Michelle saw Pink's mother standing in the doorway, watching Pink approach, glancing occasionally in Michelle's direction. Snow fell heavier now, nearly erasing both Pink and his mother as he climbed the steps and disappeared inside.

CHAPTER 37

Pink shot a glance up the hall. "Aw, hell," he said. "Mama? I got to get going. Where'd you run off to?"

She came out of her private room.

"What is it you wanted, Mama?"

She walked past him and motioned for him to sit.

"Mama, I need to get going. My damn eyes are starting to feel like sand pits," he said, plopping down in the lounger. "And if that ain't enough, Isabelle's about to make me crazier than a sprayed roach. I ain't even had a chance to tell you her latest nonsense." Pink hadn't thought about Isabelle in the last couple hours, but now it seemed she was living rent-free in his head. What would make a woman say the crazy shit she'd told him? he wondered. How could she even conjure up such a notion? It was beyond him.

"Pink, I want you to do me a favor," his mother said.

"Sure, Mama, but I may need to stay here tonight. Isabelle's lost her mind. You know what she told me? I can't even believe I'm telling you this. She's been calling me all damn night to tell me—"

"Pink. I need your attention."

Pink crooked his arm over his other shoulder and scratched an itch at the center of his back. "Yeah, Mama, I'm listening."

"Don't repeat what I'm about to tell you."

Pink looked at her.

"Mrs. Stage . . ." his mother said. "Mrs. Stage is a very disturbed woman. I'm worried about her, Pink. I called Loudon's office and left a message while you were eating supper. I told him to come by in the morning to fetch her. She needs professional help. She shouldn't be in that cabin alone. I'm afraid she'll end up like her husband."

"She's got her own people, Mama, back in Atlanta. Let them handle her. We got our own nut logs to deal with . . . like Isabelle."

"Pink, listen to what I'm telling you. Mrs. Stage believes she followed a light in the woods and somehow ended up in some other dimension or something."

"Whew!" Pink said. "I should get her and Clarence together. He's in some other dimension too. They'd be happier than a three-legged dog in a ball-licking contest."

"Pink! Why do you say such things?"

"Sorry, Mama."

"Mrs. Stage experienced a terrible trauma with the death of her daughter . . . and now her husband. She's delusional. I'm not sure why they released her from the hospital."

"What's this got to do with us?"

"She came to us for answers. She came to us for help. We need to help her, Pink."

Pink shook his head. He didn't share his mama's altruism, and he didn't believe he was put here to save anybody. He saw folks out there trying to help other folks when they couldn't even help themselves. "Blind leading the blind," his daddy used to say. Pink felt he'd be lucky to save himself, much less anyone else.

"After you drive her back up to her cabin, I want you to go with her. Into the woods. Tonight. And I want you—"

"Tonight? In the damn snow? Mama, I can barely keep my brain working as it is, I'm so damn tired. I ain't going down no damn mountain in the middle of the damn night in no damn snowstorm!"

"Pink, go with her. Make sure she's doesn't hurt herself and bring her back here. Once she sees there is no strange light, no mysterious cabins—just a hill and my house down here—she'll have to accept reality."

"Then what?" Pink asked.

"Then she can sleep here, on the couch, till Loudon comes to fetch her in the morning."

Pink shot up from the chair, pulling his fingers into fists. "Where the hell will I sleep? I can't go home. You have no idea the shit I been through the past few days. I got Mrs. Stage telling me I killed my wife. I got crazy rednecks shooting holes in my upholstery, making me jump off bridges. I got Clarence spraying his damn toes with jock itch powder, and I got Isabelle calling me every damn three minutes to tell me I'm her damn blood brother! Now I know it was a full moon the other night, but right now my life's got more nuts in it than a squirrel's nest!"

Mattie sat back in the couch, her hands folded in her lap. "I need you to do this, Pink. I want you to go with her. Bring her back here safe."

Pink shot away from his mother and went to the window. He looked out at his Suburban in the driveway, wondering how much it was going to cost to fix his window. He'd never had to replace an electric one before.

"I don't know why I can't just take her back to her cabin and leave her," he said. "She's none of my business. Yours neither."

"Because I asked, Pink." His mother wrapped her arms around him at the window and hugged him. "I love you, Pink."

He scratched behind his ear. "Aw, hell, Mama, why do you have to get involved in other folks' business?" He turned in her arms and returned the hug, pulling her to his chest, planting a kiss on the top of her head. For a second he thought she was crying. "You okay, Mama?"

"Yes, baby. Maybe tomorrow, Pink, you can help me take down the circle, and I'll cook you a nice, big lunch."

CHAPTER 38

The drive to the cabin took longer than normal, the road hidden under more than a foot of snow. Michelle gripped the armrest when the Suburban's tires slipped, then caught, slipped again, then caught, the rear end shifting before the tread found traction, jerking the vehicle forward. A few times, the front end slid and Michelle thought they might crash into the trees lining the edge of the road. Pink kept the wheel steady as he crawled the big truck up the mountain, eyes straight ahead, not saying a word. Snow cut past the windshield. Pink's silence made her nervous. She didn't know him well, but she knew he liked to talk.

When they arrived at the cabin, Michelle was shocked to see Darcy's Explorer in the driveway. She felt a moment's relief that her sister hadn't abandoned her, followed by the dismay of knowing Darcy wouldn't approve of what Michelle was about to do.

When they got out, Pink knocked his fist on the hood of Darcy's vehicle as he walked past. "Looks like you have company," he said.

Michelle walked up on the deck. The cabin was dark, and Michelle wondered if Darcy was asleep, if she should wake her. Why? she thought. What would be the point? Michelle padded through the snow to the far railing. Pink followed.

"Mama says you got some business down there," he said, walking up beside her, brushing snow off the rail to rest his hands on the wood. "Wants me to go with you."

Michelle had no idea what Mrs. Souder had told him and didn't know quite what to do. She could tell by the flat tone of his voice that he was making fun of her, that he probably thought she was insane. She searched the blizzard for a light, tried to force her eyes past the fusion of snow and darkness—nothing. It was like trying to read a newspaper through a sweater. She heard the sliding door open behind her and turned to find Darcy in the doorway.

"What are you doing, Michelle? Who's that with you?"

Pink turned to look at Darcy then looked back at Michelle shaking his head, muttering something about squirrels. How could she explain who Pink was? "It's nobody," Michelle said. "Go back to bed."

"That's right, ma'am," Pink said, speaking to Darcy. "I'm nobody. Just one of those figments of your imagination. Like the tooth fairy."

"Darcy . . . this is Pink Souder," Michelle said. "Everything's going to be all right. Can you just go back to bed? Please? Just trust me."

Darcy started to protest. "Michelle, what the hell is going on . . . ?"

"That's a good idea," Pink said, turning to leave. "Let's all sleep on it tonight, and we'll all go to Shoney's in the morning for a big biscuits-and-gravy breakfast. My treat."

"Pink, no. Please don't leave," Michelle said, grabbing his arm.

"This is Pink?" Darcy said. "The real estate agent?"

"I see my reputation precedes me," Pink said. "Do you need a card?"

"Darcy," Michelle said. "Please, just go back inside."

"Michelle, what's going on?" Darcy said. "Can you just come in and tell me what's happening here? Alone, please?"

"Okay. I just need to speak with Pink for a minute then I'll be in. Why don't you put on some coffee? Maybe decaf? I'll tell you everything."

After sliding the door shut, Darcy disappeared into the darkness of the cabin. Michelle could tell her sister was disgusted with her, but none of that would matter. Not if this worked. *If* it worked? Michelle examined the words her mind had used, the little battles waged on a regular basis between fantasy and logic, denial, and acceptance. Then a new thought came, a tricky one. What would Darcy do in the morning when Michelle was gone? Michelle recalled the photos of missing children on boards in Post Offices and grocery stores, remembered stories she'd read about people who disappeared and were never heard from again. To Darcy, Michelle would be just that, a person gone missing. The notion distressed her.

"Let's go," Michelle said, trying to push away her discomfort.

"Where?" Pink asked, stopping at the head of the steps.

"Down there."

Pink swiveled his head toward the slope then back at her, his eyes sleepy and disinterested. "Thought there was supposed to be some kind of light or something?"

"We don't need it," she said, unsure if that was true, but it felt right. She was going on a *feeling*. A crazed and absurd leap into the unknown. There was no denying the tensile urgency in her chest, the sense of something waiting down the mountain, a searing gravity in every cell of muscle and bone.

"This is the most damn fool thing I ever done," Pink said, sweeping his head from side to side. He zipped up his coat and flipped up the collar to cover his ears, tucking his head down into the opening. "After you," he said, bowing, sweeping his hand away in a mock princely gesture.

*****

Trekking down through the woods, Michelle no longer saw the snow as a sparkling new surface on the world but more a disguise for the ice, loose leaves, and shifting soil that lay beneath it. The farther they traveled from the cabin, the more treacherous the footing became. Without warning, the ground would sweep out from under her feet and drop her in the snow. Each time Pink landed on his butt, he cursed, rolled over, and tried pushing himself back up, getting to both knees first, then one knee, sometimes falling again when he tried to stand. Snow powdered his clothes. Michelle brushed herself off each time she fell. Pink came up behind her once and slapped snow from her coat, proceeding down her backside until Michelle pulled away and said she'd be fine.

"Don't want you to catch pneumonia," he said.

"Yeah, thanks." she said.

After they'd gone a little farther, Michelle spun back to look toward the cabin, upset she'd forgotten to turn on the porch light. She couldn't see anything. Snow came so hard the air was like fog, and so cold it felt like the night could break apart.

"So how much farther?" Pink asked. "Seems like we're lost."

His comment was flippant and laced with ridicule. He'd probably never been lost in his life, she figured, especially in these woods. Michelle pictured him hunting every square inch of this mountain, knowing every clump of dirt, every stone, branch, fern, and snake hole.

"Should have brought us a quart of Lyman's lightning for our little rendezvous," Pink said. "Something to kill the chill."

In spite of his sarcasm and prurient innuendos, there was an allure about Pink, one that was oddly endearing and made Michelle feel safe and calm in his presence. Maybe it was his confidence and compassion, his cheery cynicism, or adolescent guile, or some unwavering concoction of all these traits. He wasn't a handsome man in the slick Hollywood sense, but under all his wayward cherubness was a rugged, undeniable charm.

Michelle was surprised to find herself thinking of Pink in this way, thinking of him at all. Faced with the cold and darkness, her mind had unknowingly swerved toward human contact, the unlikely attraction she felt toward this peculiar man. It wasn't sexual, but more like a sibling camaraderie, or the first flowering of a blissfully troubling friendship. If nothing else, Michelle admired his devotion. Even as he cheated on his wife, lied to his mother, and deceived everyone around him, it seemed there was nothing he wouldn't do for someone he cared about. Maybe, in some strange way, he reminded her of Cliff, the Cliff she'd fallen in love with over twenty years ago, the Cliff who drove by her house every day for a month holding a red rose out the window when she'd gotten grounded for staying out all night. Where had that Cliff gone?

"Why we stopping?" Pink asked, walking up beside Michelle.

She was lost, but didn't want to admit it. And cold. And scared. What was she doing on the side of a mountain in the middle of a snowstorm?

"We probably should go back," she said. She looked up the slope, then down, to the side, blizzard in every direction.

"Sure you don't want to go on?" Pink said.

Michelle wanted to know what Pink's mother had told him, how she'd persuaded him to come with her.

"I have no idea what we're doing," she finally said, blowing into her hands to warm them. Neither her nor Pink were dressed for this kind of weather.

"Can't go back," Pink said. "No way I'm climbing back up that hill. Let's go on. We're not far from my mama's house. About a mile or so."

"We'll never find it," she said, seeing something move beyond Pink. She hadn't realized the blizzard had eased, visibility improving as the moon bled through the thinner clouds. She pointed at the dark shape in the distance, its silhouette padding close to the snow. Pink turned and squinted, neither of them speaking.

"What is that?" she whispered.

"Too big for a bobcat," he said. "And sure ain't no deer or bear. Don't move right."

The creature skulked across the frozen terrain, its body close to the surface. It didn't look very big to Michelle, but it was still a ways off.

"Looks like a damn black panther," Pink said.

"Aren't those just in Africa or something?" she said.

"No. Panther's a mountain lion. Years ago, these parts were filled with 'em. Unusual to see a black one though. Never saw one before."

In a moment the animal was gone. Michelle hadn't even seen where it went, disappearing into the hemlocks and shadows.

"I don't know if we should feel privileged," Pink said, "or cursed. After all, it was a *black cat*." At this, Pink chuckled and slid his eyes toward Michelle. "Hope you're not superstitious."

Michelle never quite knew how to read Pink.

Before she could ponder his statement much longer, a bright light flashed and rippled through the dark sky beyond the trees, like an enormous electric eel twisting through the clouds, followed a minute later by low, rumbling thunder. Michelle looked at Pink. He shrugged. "I'll be damned," he said. "Never seen that before, either. Not in a damn snow-storm. Must be the Quickening."

Michelle had no idea what Pink was referring to, but he seemed amused by his own comment. Snow began to fall again, as if the light-ning had ripped open a massive cloud. Michelle resigned herself to going back to Mrs. Souder's house for the night. There seemed no point in going on—in search of a *gateway*—if there was no light guiding them. Michelle was surprised her vocabulary now included words like *gateway*.

Pink now led the way, using his arms to sweep limbs from his path, snow dumping from branches as he pushed them to the side. Michelle's attention shifted between Pink's footprints in the snow and the dark mate-rial of his coat. She stayed far enough back so the branches wouldn't whip her face. He looked like a bear making its fierce, undaunted trek through the woods and weather, as if Pink had been born in a moss-covered hollow log and possessed some special symbiosis with the outdoors.

They had traveled probably a hundred yards or so when Pink stopped in front of her, his hand resting against a tree, his shoulders suddenly and eerily without a head. The image startled Michelle, quashing her breath, until she realized he had his head bent forward. When she came closer, she could see he was exhausted.

"What's wrong?" Michelle asked, walking around to face him. He raised his eyes to her, as if lifting his skull was impossible, too heavy to bring upright. Pain creased his brow into tight accordion ridges.

"My stomach's full of firecrackers," Pink said. "I can't hardly move." He took a deep breath and tried to straighten. When he did, pain splashed across his face. He clutched his abdomen and collapsed on the snow.

"Pink!" Michelle shouted, dropping down next to him.

His mouth was a craggy, open hole, his eyes thin crevices in a hard-ened face. He rolled to his side, his knees springing to his chest as if he were reverting to his most primal remembrances. When he moaned, his legs shot out straight then folded back upon him until he was once again a tight ball in the snow. Between his weight and movement, the snow around him hollowed into a small cavern, as if he were inadvertently burying himself.

Michelle wiped the sweat from his brow with her palm. She searched her pockets for a tissue, but found only the pentagram, recalling how she'd come down the mountain looking for Cliff, free of incidents other than falling and cutting herself. But those seemed like the normal kinds of things that would happen to someone trying to blaze a trail down a dark mountainside on a bleak, rainy night. Michelle remembered what Mrs. Souder had said about the amulet, how it protected its owner. She removed the pentagram from her pocket and placed it into Pink's palm until his features relaxed. As the skin of his face slackened, she felt her insides tighten, her stomach sparking little fires. She felt herself getting dizzy, the cramping growing worse. She opened Pink's fingers and pressed the pentagram against his palm with hers, weaving her fingers through his to hold the pendant firmly, their hands clamped together like the pages of a book pressing a fresh rose. Her pain subsided.

She craned her head, searching the slurry of snow and darkness, unsure where they were, how far they were from the house. She considered going the rest of the way holding hands with Pink, sharing the protection of the pentagram, but she wasn't sure which was worse: The physical pain, or the emotional torment of myriad realities, the strain that information placed on logic, on one's own mental stability. "It would drive him insane," Pink's mother had said. Maybe insanity was better. Not the torture she was experiencing, not the slow erosion of facts, but true insanity, where all consciousness of who you are, where you are, melts to a seamless dream. Pink stirred, and Michelle tried to help him up to a sitting position, not releasing his hand until Pink took curious notice of their fingers entwined. She cupped the pentagram into her palm and slid it back into her pocket.

"Ain't sure I can stand," he said. "I must have me a damn flu bug or something." He surveyed the area as if it had been familiar at one time but wasn't now. He took Michelle's hand and she helped him up. She asked if he was okay when she noticed how unsteady he looked brushing snow from his trousers. Pink shivered, holding himself in a bear hug.

"I'm freezing to death," he said, his face blistered with sweat. He looked around, then at his shoes wet with snow.

"I'm sorry, Pink," Michelle said.

"Don't be sorry. Let's get to my mama's house so I can warm up."

They picked their way down the slope, holding to saplings, bracing against tree trunks, Michelle leading a few yards in front. They both stopped when they saw the light.

"What the heck . . . ?" Pink said, doubling over before he could finish, falling to the snow.

"Pink!"

He grimaced and cupped his hands over his face, his elbows tucked into his stomach, and kicked his legs, once again writhing in the snow, convulsing. Michelle took the pendant from her pocket again and held it against the back of Pink's neck until he stopped moving. Blood rushed back to his face, his features growing calm.

"Pink?" she whispered, kneeling next to him. "Pink?"

He opened his eyes and held them on Michelle, panic shifting across his face. "What's happening?" he said. "Can you hear that?" He wiggled his body toward Michelle, pushing his weight against her knees.

"What? What do you hear?"

"Voices," he said. "People mumbling, groaning. Can't you hear them?" His head swiveled on his shoulders, his eyes wide, his fingers digging into Michelle's leg. "They're everywhere. Can't you hear them?"

Michelle couldn't hear anything but the low grumble of thunder in the distance. "It's thunder, Pink," she said. "That's what you're hearing." He squeezed her tighter, wedging his shoulder against her thigh. She wove her arms around him and held the pendant against his flesh until his body relaxed.

"Pink, we need to get up and run as fast as we can toward that light. Then we'll be safe." It felt like a lie. She wasn't sure what would happen to Pink when they reached it, if they even could.

Pink stared up at her, his eyes hollow, glazed. She was helping him to his feet when she caught movement off to her left. The ground trembled. The branches above them knocked together, though the air was dead still.

Michelle set her gaze toward the thick hemlocks fifty yards beyond an old stump and saw something drift between the shaggy bows. Each time she caught sight of it her breath snagged. For a moment she thought it might be the panther again, but it was too tall. Whatever it was, it walked upright. That's when it appeared in the opening between the hemlocks and came toward them. The figure was dark, moving unimpeded by snow or obstacles. Pink was shivering again, his face nestled against Michelle's abdomen. She felt Pink jerk and was fairly certain he had yet to notice the apparition.

It moved closer, but now there were more of them, floating among the trees, shifting shadows. Michelle tried to convince herself that that's what they were, just shadows of clouds and tree trunks tossed there by the moon.

"Get up, Pink, we need to go."

Pink wouldn't release her legs. She pulled the pendant from his neck and felt his hold on her tighten. The figures moved closer, and as they did, it seemed the snow began to disappear. Not melting but vanishing.

"Pink. Get up. Please."

Pink held his hands over his ears, as if trying to block out some deafening noise, but there was nothing, no sound at all. The snow was gone, the ground dry, as if it were the middle of summer.

The figures stopped thirty yards away, figures that appeared wavy in the light-starved bracken. One came forward, a woman, moonlight flashing across her features as she drifted between the branches. Pink had rolled himself into a ball, his hands covering his ears. "Stop!" he yelled, scooting closer to Michelle, his body fully against her now.

"Come on, Pink," Michelle said. "Get up."

The woman came within a few feet of Michelle and looked at her, then down at Pink. She was young, beautiful. Her lavender nightgown was damp and clung to her body, revealing her breasts and the flesh of her tummy. Pink took his hands away from his ears and looked at the woman.

"Isabelle? What the hell?" Pink said.

Pink seemed to be listening to the woman, though her lips never moved. Now the other figures moved toward them. As they came closer, Michelle could not make out what they were doing. It appeared as though they were approaching backward; she could see no facial features. At first, she figured it was a trick of light, some undependable offering of the moon. But when they were too close for Michelle to deny what she was seeing, she had to look away. Their skin was craggy and wrinkled, but they had no faces. Michelle could not look back at them. When she tried, her chest tightened, the queasy current in her stomach pulsing. The woman Pink had called Isabelle turned and moved away through the shadows of the trees and was gone. Michelle couldn't even tell if she had feet. It was as if Michelle were witnessing the scene through some restricted lens where peripheral detail would not register in her brain.

When the other figures surrounded Pink, he backed up toward Michelle. "What the hell is this?" he said to her. "Is this a damn nightmare?"

"Come on, Pink," she said, grabbing his hand in hers, the pendant trapped in the nest of their pressed palms. "Move." She pulled him forward. He stumbled at first, as if his legs would not function, but then fell into a trot behind her, telling her to slow down. Michelle fell into the rhythm of a skipping gallop to hop over fallen trees, using her free hand to swat branches from her face, the other hand holding fast to Pink. His grip grew stronger, not as if he was struggling to keep up, but more that he was gaining strength himself, until his pace finally matched hers. The light was in front of them, but still appeared as far away as when they'd fled the queer beings. She wasn't sure if they were following, too afraid to look back and check. Pink ran beside her now, until he tripped over a decaying log, dragging her down with him. She flew headfirst and rolled, leaves and sticks crunching until she slammed into a tree trunk. Her ribs burned, sending a fire through her torso, into her shoulders. Michelle pushed up on one arm trying to tune her breathing, make it regular again, but she felt sick to her stomach, as if her organs were expanding, cutting off her air. That's when she heard noises—a low keening, groaning. She tried to convince herself it was Pink, but there were too many voices. It seemed the rhododendron had come to life, all the leaves moving, rustling, in the perfect stillness. The ground shifted beneath her. She grabbed at the dirt, trying to hold on. Then she heard someone walking. "Is that you, Pink?"

She tried to get up, but her muscles were tight, constricted, like they were being twisted off the bone. A whining shriek rose in the woods, distant sounding at first, eventually growing so loud Michelle had to cover her ears. Even with her palms pressed to the sides of her skull, the noise felt like a torch cutting through her hands, burning into her brain. That's when she realized she'd lost the pentacle.

She groped the ground, the piercing trill like the sustained scream of a hundred sirens. She had no idea where Pink was. The faceless beings appeared from behind trees, forming a circle around her, coming closer. She could barely move, her stomach rising into her throat, her arms, legs, and chest congealing into one lumped mass. She scratched her fingernails through the dirt and dead leaves. The smell of something spoiled and moldy and dead rose from the earth. Her bones tingled, growing numb, as if dissolving. Her throat closed when one of the beings touched her shoulder. Another grabbed her ankle. She couldn't breathe, then felt the grip of another, their touch like cold gel. A high-pitched tone emanated from the center of her forehead, burrowing deep into her neck, her back. Michelle clawed the ground, grit and mud catching beneath her fingernails—then something hard and cold. She closed her fingers on it. It didn't register at first. The pendant. Michelle felt something grip her shoulder, grab her foot, begin to drag her away. She squeezed the pendant into her palm and held it tight, shutting her eyes. The nausea dissipated slowly, the ache leaving her arms and legs, until the buzz was gone from her head.

When she opened her eyes, the beings had formed a circle around Pink. Pink was contorted into an impossible shape, screaming, as if his body were hot steel being forged into a peculiar torus. Michelle got up and stumbled past the faceless beings, falling next to Pink. In the throes of a seizure, Pink convulsed, his face like oil, queer iridescent colors swirling through his skin. Michelle pressed the pendant against his leg, his flesh queerly rough, furrowed as tree bark.

After several moments, Pink's writhing eased, but even through the material of his trousers, his skin felt cold. She wondered if he was dead. "Pink? Pink?"

The beings dispersed slowly, moving away in rays of yellow light, dissolving the circle, until they finally disappeared. Michelle held Pink's wrist, trying to find a pulse. Nothing. "Pink?"

CHAPTER 39

The sky beyond the rim of mountains turned deep blue, bleeding though the tangle of black branches. Morning approached, but nothing looked familiar. The dusk-to-dawn light had vanished.

Michelle felt as if she were waking, but could not remember falling asleep. Pink lay next to her on the ground. He looked dead. She tried to stir him. She didn't want to leave Pink, but there was no way to move him.

She surveyed the area, deciding to go in the direction she'd last seen the light. After picking down the slope for almost twenty minutes, she saw her and Cliff's cabin. She looked back in the direction of Pink, but could see nothing, the underbrush so thick visibility was less than twenty feet. Michelle was sorry she hadn't marked the trees in some way when she'd left Pink, traced some kind of path with rocks or broken branches. Now she had no way of finding him again.

With the cabin in sight, she jogged toward the front porch, checking the driveway for Pink's Suburban, Darcy's Explorer. Nothing. When she found the glass sliding doors locked, she went around to the front. That door was locked too. She grabbed a walkway stone and smashed the glass, then reached inside and undid the latch. For the first time in twenty-four hours, fatigue slogged through her veins.

The cabin was different, the way it had been before Cliff disappeared, the way it was when Cassie was still alive. The sudden relief weakened her knees, caused her to fall to the floor. Rays of sunlight cut bright shafts across the carpet. Her mind went to Pink, the faceless beings, the woman in the lavender gown. She wondered if the apparitions had come back for Pink after she'd left him. Maybe that's why they were there, to claim his dead body.

Michelle shifted between consciousness and vague, restless dreams. Something crossed the back deck, interrupting the sunlight. She tried to push up, exhaustion keeping her down. A moment later, a silhouette pressed against the glass door. When she focused the figure, she saw it was Pink, his hands cupped against the glass.

"Michelle?" he said. "You in there?"

For a moment she was relieved that Pink was all right, then her heart sank. If Pink knew who she was, then nothing had changed. But the cabin? It was different. Even so, Pink's mother had said he wouldn't remember her, wouldn't remember anything from the previous evening or his previous life. He would only remember the life where he had never met Michelle, the life where he had killed Isabelle.

He rapped on the glass with his wedding ring then tried the slider, the door rattling against the lock. "Michelle?"

Michelle pushed up and went to the door, flipping the latch, jerking it open.

"Whew," Pink said, walking past her. "That was the strangest damn dream I ever had in my life. No more pork chops before bedtime."

He remembered everything from the previous evening. Nothing was different. Had she dreamed the woman in the lavender nightgown, the faceless spirits, the burning in her bones?

"I was happy I woke up when I did," he said. "There was a mangy damn coyote sniffing around me."

"You feel okay?" Michelle asked.

"Yeah, except I don't recollect how I came to be out in them woods in the first place. Plenty of times I been drunk and woke up in possum shit, but I didn't drink that much last night."

Pink found the couch and plopped down in the cushions, the foam rubber exhaling a whoosh. Michelle sat in the chair opposite him, wondering where Darcy had gone. Nothing felt right. She looked over at Pink. His expression was gloomy, his eyes receding into dark slits. He seemed to be ruminating on difficult subjects, as if his head were filled with sharp, pointy objects.

"What happened to the damn snowstorm?" he finally said. "And my Suburban?" He looked over at Michelle, then down at his own clothes, studying the rips and stains, poking his finger through the hole in the knee of his trousers. "What happened to me? And what the hell happened to you?" His eyes went to her hair, and Michelle's hand instinctively followed his gaze, her fingers finding a tangle of leaves and sticks at the side of her scalp. She combed them out with her fingertips, inspecting the detritus momentarily before dropping it on the coffee table.

"What happened to all the snow?" he asked again.

"It disappeared," she said, too weary to concoct a meaningful lie.

"Like one of them chinooks?" Pink said.

Michelle didn't get his meaning. "What?"

"Clarence told me about 'em," Pink said. "A rogue wind that blows warm air that melts all the snow. Indians called them 'Snow Eaters.' Clarence knows the damnedest things."

How resourceful the mind was, Michelle thought, grabbing information from one phenomenon to patch over another much-less-palatable one. There had been no wind, no mysterious snow-eating zephyr from the gods, only faceless creatures and a woman in a lavender gown.

"It's my Suburban I can't figure out," Pink said. "Where that is. Any chance your sister had it towed?"

"No," Michelle answered.

"Got a phone?" Pink asked. Michelle pointed toward the desk.

Michelle watched Pink dial, feeling frazzled, jittery. She tried to think when she'd eaten last. She got up and stood at the sliding glass door, letting her eyes drift over the gentle repeat of valleys and mountains. Everything looked beautiful, yet nothing felt right. She stepped out on the deck. The air was thin, and for one brief moment she felt free.

She heard the slider open. Pink stood beside her, his hands on the railing. "Every damn phone number I called's been disconnected. Even my own damn office. Recording said the number's no longer in service. I couldn't raise Isabelle, Claire, or my mama. All the damn numbers are out of service. Can you beat that? Even Clarence's number is changed, but they wouldn't give it out. Hell, the only person in Ardenwood's got the same number is Lyman. He's coming to fetch me." Pink looked troubled and confused. Michelle remembered Lyman from the Hilltop Club.

"You know what Lyman said to me?" Pink continued. "He told me he was glad I was back, said everybody wondered where I ran off to. I asked him what the hell he was talking about."

Michelle turned toward him, finally realizing what had happened.

"I didn't leave anywhere," Pink said. "I have no idea what he's talking about. Do you know what else he said?"

"I have to make a phone call," Michelle said, hurrying inside.

Pink stood by the railing, unmoving. She felt sorry for him, felt terrible that she had brought him through the way she had, the pentagram pressed between their palms. He had no idea where he was.

She picked up the phone, her fingers trembling as she pushed the buttons. The phone rang several times before someone answered.

"Hello?"

"Cassie?" Michelle asked.

A hollow silence. Michelle wondered if the person was still there.

"Mom? Is that you?" Cassie said.

"Cassie! Cassie!" Michelle said.

Cassie shrieked, then cried. They talked in excited bursts, not waiting for one to finish before the other spoke, conversing in questions and disjointed statements, voice over voice, elation, tears, laughing, shock.

"My god, Mom, I can't believe it. Dad will be blown away!"

"What?"

"He never gave up on finding you," Cassie said. "He stayed up at the cabin by himself, hunting the woods, phoning the police, organizing search parties. Aunt Darcy stayed with me."

"Your father . . . where is he now?" Michelle asked.

"At the dealership, but I'm going to call him as soon as I get off the phone."

Michelle was about to tell Cassie that she would call him, but decided against it. "Okay." She needed time to figure things out before she spoke to Cliff. "Cassie . . . I'm so glad you're in my life."

"Me too. I love you. Now don't you leave that cabin."

Cassie couldn't stop asking questions, wanting to know everything that had happened, making Michelle promise to not leave the cabin.

"I'll be here," Michelle said. "Cassie?"

"Yeah, Mom?"

"Don't hang up yet. Tell me how the swim team is doing."

Michelle listened to the tender resonance of Cassie's voice, the excited consonants, the rich, eloquent vowels. Michelle could picture Cassie's mouth, her lips forming the words, the silky skin of her chin and cheeks. Michelle pictured Cassie in the pool, water sheeting from her arms and legs as she climbed up the ladder, her face shiny and wet, a sparkle of sun at her cheeks. Michelle couldn't wait to be home.

Michelle hung up after Cassie did without saying goodbye. She never wanted to say goodbye to Cassie again.

Pink walked into the cabin with Lyman. Lyman introduced himself and she could tell he didn't remember her. Pink reminded him he'd danced with her a couple nights ago at the Hilltop. Pink said, "You act like you never seen her before."

Lyman said he hadn't. "And the Hilltop . . . that burned down a year ago, Pink."

The two men stared at each other as if they had suddenly become strangers. "Is the whole damn town on drugs?" Pink shook his head and looked back at Michelle.

"Need a ride into town?" Pink asked.

"No. Thanks," Michelle said. "I have someone picking me up."

Lyman kept glancing over at Pink as if Pink were some kind of phantom. Pink didn't seem to notice.

"Well, Mrs. Stage," Pink said. "I hope you find what you're looking for. Call me if you ever want me to list this cabin for you." He handed Michelle a card. "This is a solid place, you know. Built it myself."

What would happen to Pink when he found that the people he loved were gone, everything he knew had vanished? She wondered if Claire still lived in Ardenwood. And what would Clarence tell him—how would he react to Pink's reemergence? Michelle felt responsible for the grief Pink would most certainly endure when he found he was living a life that wasn't the one he remembered from the day before.

"I'm so sorry, Pink," she said, going to the desk and grabbing a pen. She scribbled on the back of the card he had given her and handed it back to him, telling him to call if he ever needed to talk.

He looked surprised. "Well, I can always use a new friend," he said. "Let's go, Lyman."

The house fell quiet after they left. Michelle went to the fridge to see if there was anything to eat, finding a bagel and a partial loaf of bread. How could Cliff still be alive, she wondered? In her mind, she could see the red snow around his chair, the pistol locked in his hand. She saw the dark hole at the top of his head. She remembered Cliff's missing finger, the scar on his forehead, Cliff telling her how Cassie had been killed when the Cherokee flipped. Had she glimpsed one possibility, something that had happened in a different version of their lives? What determined which one you lived?

The phone rang. Michelle caught it on the second ring. It was Cliff, gushing into the phone, crying. She was hardly able to understand him.

She assured him she was okay. It had been a long time since she'd felt comforted by the sound of his voice.

"I can't wait to see you," Cliff said, sniffling. "I thought I'd lost you forever. I couldn't think. I couldn't . . ."

"I'm here," Michelle said. He wanted to know where she'd been the past few weeks, if she'd been hurt, how she'd survived, if someone had found her, if she'd been alone, scared.

"I'll tell you everything when I see you," she said, knowing that whatever she told him wouldn't be the truth.

The afternoon dragged. Michelle couldn't wait to see Cassie, to get back to Atlanta. She was resting on the couch when the phone rang. She figured it was Cliff with an update on their ETA.

"Mrs. Stage?" the man said. "This is Sheriff Fisk. Remember me?"

"Yes, of course," she said.

There was a pause. "Glad to know you're back," he said. "At some point we'd like to get your story, everything that happened. Helps us when folks go missing, to know where to look, what to expect. But that's not exactly why I'm calling."

Michelle closed her eyes. There was no way to explain what happened without sounding crazy.

"Mrs. Stage?" the sheriff said. "You still there?"

"Yes. Yes, I'm here."

"I understand you met Pink Souder?"

What was this about? She wanted Cliff and Cassie to show up, wanted to go back to Atlanta and forget everything.

"I'd like to drive up there with Pink," the sheriff said. "Just ask you a few questions. Promise we won't stay long."

How could she sit across from Pink and deny Pink's account of the last few days? Or corroborate everything? It was impossible.

"This is probably not . . ."

"Pink's in a pretty bad way. Keeps saying crazy things. He's confused and upset. I thought it might help to get your side."

It won't help, Michelle thought. *It won't help anyone.* She thought about what Mrs. Souder had told her: It would drive Pink insane. There seemed nothing Michelle could do to stop it.

"Sure, that would be fine." Michelle was already sorry she hadn't said no.

When Sheriff Fisk arrived, Pink wasted no time getting to the point. "Tell Fisk about going to the Hilltop, about coming to my mama's house, about us hiking down through the damn woods in the middle of a damn snowstorm!" Pink appeared distressed, his features vague and faulty, as if some life-sustaining armature had been removed from his body.

Michelle motioned for them to sit, but Pink refused, pacing across the braided rug. He spun toward Michelle, his eyes flashing. An uneasy heat spread through Michelle.

"I don't know what to say," she told Sheriff Fisk. "There's so much I can't recall."

Sheriff Fisk suggested talking about the events of the last week.

"To hell with that, Loudon!" Pink said, pumping his hands into fists at his sides. "I'm drowning in madness here and you want to stroll down memory lane." Pink looked over at Michelle. "Tell him what happened last night, dammit! Tell him about the last two days."

What could she say that could possibly help?

"Tell Loudon about the ceremony my mama performed," Pink said. "Tell him about the damn snow! I know you remember that."

Fisk tried to settle Pink.

"How am I supposed to calm down, Loudon? I don't have a home, business, or pot to piss in. Hell, I don't even have a damn car! Where the hell did it all go, Loudon? If you can tell me that, I'll calm right down. Hell, I'll be calm as a bluetick hound with a neck bone."

Sheriff Fisk looked at Michelle with apologetic eyes, then down at his shoes. His hands were wound into a bony knot in his lap. He leaned forward and studied his knuckles.

"Maybe you wouldn't be so calm if you saw my mama's house," Pink said to Michelle, standing near her chair now, angling his face to catch her eyes. "Maybe we should take a little drive down there. Then you might feel a . . ."

"I've seen it Pink," she said.

"Not like this you haven't," he said.

"Yes, I have. The gate is hanging by one hinge. The paint is peeling. The window to the right of the front door is broken out. The place is a shambles."

Pink stepped back and stared down at her, then glowered at Sheriff Fisk as if accusing him of collusion with Michelle. Fisk only half-shrugged and shook his head.

"What the hell is going on here?" Pink said.

Michelle looked up at him, wanted to talk to him in private, pull him aside and explain everything. Not that he would believe her. But if she framed it in witchcraft, maybe it would help. Just then a car pulled in the driveway. This was not how she imagined her homecoming. She wasn't sure she could lie to Pink and the sheriff in front of Cassie.

Cliff was halfway up the walk when Michelle ran out to meet them.

Michelle felt an instant peace anticipating her reunion with her daughter. But Cassie wasn't with him. Michelle's eyes searched frantically, looking around him toward the car.

"Where is she! Where's Cassie?" Michelle blurted out.

"She had a swim meet," Cliff said. "She was so bummed. She really wanted to come. She's captain of the swim team now. Did you know that?"

Michelle's heart fell, followed by a moment of relief. Maybe it was best she hadn't come. She didn't want Cassie to witness this scenario.

"Is everything okay?" Cliff asked, turning his eyes toward the sheriff's car.

"Pretty much," Michelle said. "They have a few questions."

"Isn't it enough you're back?" Cliff said. "Can't they leave you alone for two minutes?"

"It's okay. None of that matters now." Michelle studied Cliff, his forehead, his hands.

"What?" Cliff asked, apparently noticing her intense survey.

No scar. All his fingers. Everything she already knew but wanted visual proof of. She wanted Pink to have proof as well, some confirmation that he had not imagined everything. Could anything do that now? Could Michelle's account possibly stitch together Pink's two disparate worlds? She decided to tell Fisk about everything, the ceremony, the snowstorm, coming down the mountain, the dusk-to-dawn light. Validate Pink's experience and at the same time, feel no responsibility for explaining it.

"Cliff, everything you're about to hear is going to sound strange," she told him. "Just don't freak out on me."

"Sure." Cliff followed her into the house. Fisk stood and shook Cliff's hand.

"We're thankful your wife is back," Sheriff Fisk said to Cliff. Pink stared at Cliff, his face leached of life.

"You!" Pink said. "You . . . you're dead!"

Cliff glanced at Michelle then at the sheriff. "Excuse me?" Cliff said.

Pink trembled, moving in a wide arc around Cliff, knocking a picture from the wall as he scooted past him, giving Cliff wide berth. "You're dead!" Pink looked over at Fisk. "Christ, Loudon, don't you remember? You pried the damn gun from his hand, remember?"

Cliff looked shocked, glancing toward Michelle then back to Pink, the sheriff.

Pink implored the sheriff to remember, recounting the details of Cliff's suicide, detailing the blood, the snow. Fisk urged Pink to stop.

"Let's go, Pink," the sheriff said. "Sorry for the disturbance, folks."

Pink refused to go. Fisk grabbed him by the arm and led him toward the door.

"Dammit, Loudon. I want some answers," Pink said, jerking his arm free. "She knows what's going on. Make her tell you!"

"Not today, Pink," Fisk said. "Let's go."

The sheriff pushed Pink out onto the deck then led him down the stairs. The two men argued in the driveway for a few minutes before Michelle finally heard car doors slam. She looked over at Cliff.

"What the hell was that about?" Cliff said.

"Let's go home," Michelle said. "I can't wait to see Cassie."

CHAPTER 40

Pink sat in Fisk's office trying to find the thread of his life. Fisk fired questions at him that made no sense. Pink bristled in the chair, annoyed. Elmer looked on from the doorway. Pink felt he was purposely blocking it, in case Pink tried to leave.

"Pink, I need to know where Isabelle is?" Fisk said.

"What the hell is going on here, Louden? She's probably at home like I've told you a hundred times. Let's drive up there. You'll see."

"Pink . . . she's not there. Trust me. I need to know—"

"What the hell's wrong with you, Louden? Christ, let's drive up there. Have you called Claire? She can clear all of this up. Let's call Claire."

Fisk looked over at Elmer. "Let's just leave Claire out of this for now. Besides, we spoke with her after Isabelle disappeared. She had no idea where you were. All she could tell us was you and Isabelle had a big blowup the night before . . . Hell, Pink, we've already been through all this years ago."

Pink shot up from his chair and swung his arm across Fisk's desk, knocking the lamp to the floor. "We ain't been through nothing, Louden! I don't have one goddamn clue what the hell you're talking about!"

Elmer bolted toward Pink to restrain him. Pink elbowed Elmer, catching him under the chin. When Elmer regained his balance, he drew his weapon.

"Okay, okay now, everybody grab hold of your senses, here," Fisk shouted, jumping up from his chair. "Elmer, put that away. Pink, sit back down."

"What the hell you gonna do with that, Elmer? The way I recollect it, you couldn't hit a bull's ass with a bass fiddle!"

"Okay, Pink. Enough," Fisk said. "We're making no headway here. Elmer, get your coat. We're taking a ride."

Elmer followed behind Pink. He reached to open the back door of the police car for Pink. Pink stopped.

"You ride back there. I'll ride up front with Louden," Pink said, and he reached for the front door handle.

"No, Pink. I need you in the back," Fisk said. "Don't make this difficult."

When Pink was seated, Elmer closed the door and slid into the front seat.

They drove in silence, the radio bleating out garbled noises. Pink looked at his hands, his trousers. The bleeding had stopped, but he still hadn't had a chance to clean up. His pants were stained and ripped. His fingers and palms were covered in small cuts and abrasions. He suddenly felt dizzy and thought he might need Fisk to pull over. Just then, he was visited by a strange image: a woman in a lavender nightgown, wet and dark, imploring him toward her. The image vanished too quickly for him to be sure, but she almost looked like Isabelle.

"Pink, now don't go crazy on me here," Fisk said as he pulled into Pink's driveway.

Pink looked up and couldn't believe his eyes. His house was fully engulfed in kudzu. Leafy vines writhed up the siding and along the roof, covering the gutters like some insidious green predator. Windows were broken out. The porch was rotted away. Light fixtures were missing and loose wires dangling from ragged holes.

Pink reached for the handle, but there was none, and he was unable to release himself from the back seat. "Goddamn it, Elmer, open this fucking door!"

Elmer looked over at the sheriff, then got out of the car and jerked the door open. Pink sprung from the car and darted toward the house.

He stopped dead and stared at it for a few seconds before spinning back toward Fisk. "What the fuck is going on here, Fisk?"

Pink stood motionless, his mouth open, his arms limp at his sides. A moment later, his large frame listed to the left, his eyes rolling back in his head. Before Fisk could reach him, Pink was down.

CHAPTER 41

On the drive back to Atlanta, Cliff apologized to Michelle, taking full responsibility for her getting lost, saying that if he hadn't gone searching for the light, she would never have gone looking for him. He explained about going down the mountainside, losing sight of the cabin and the light, and getting sick. He said it was like the flu or something, then he passed out. When he woke the next morning, he was lost. He was weak and wandered most of the day, resting often, finding refuge that night under a hemlock. He used his jacket to cover himself. The next morning, he felt better and found a dirt road where an old man with a chainsaw was cutting firewood.

"He felt sorry for me," Cliff said. "Gave me a sandwich and insisted on driving me all the way home. I don't know how, but I had ended up almost twenty miles from the cabin."

Cliff never went through the gateway! The realization hit Michelle like a punch. If she had just waited another day, Michelle thought, an old man would have pulled into the driveway and Cliff would have gotten out, come into the cabin and taken a shower, telling her about the rain, being sick and lost in the woods. And that would have been the end of it.

*****

Back in Atlanta, Cassie wanted to know about Michelle's experience. Michelle fabricated details surrounding her absence, invented scenarios of amnesia and isolation. Using memories of Charlene House, Michelle pieced together a story of falling and forgetting who she was, claiming to have been found and cared for by an old woman secluded away in the woods. She even called the old woman Charlene House. Michelle told Cassie and Cliff that Mrs. House had no phone, no car, no connection to town. In the evenings, Mrs. House would return to the cabin with a possum or coon to make into a stew.

"You ate a raccoon?" Cassie asked.

The day her memory returned, Michelle told Cassie, Mrs. House escorted her through the woods to within a hundred yards of the highway, where Michelle could hear the traffic, could see the colored flashes of metal rush past beyond the trees.

"Probably the raccoon made you remember," Cassie said, chuckling. "Your brain probably figured it better recall something quick before you had to eat a skunk." Cassie seemed content with Michelle's story. Michelle wasn't sure it convinced Cliff though.

"I'm just so glad to be home, baby," Michelle said, hugging Cassie to her.

*****

The days spun off routinely with swim meets, meals, and homework. Cliff talked about selling the dealership, moving back to Maine, working for his brother selling suits. "Remember how you loved Maine?" Cliff said one morning at breakfast. Michelle recalled it perfectly—the shiny expanse of ocean, the snow in winter, always alive, always new.

"Cassie would never go for it," she said.

"Yes, she will. We already talked about it," Cliff said. "I told Cassie I couldn't stay in the house without you, that I wanted to go back to Maine. Cassie agreed, but she told me not to give up on finding you. And I hadn't. But I was scared."

Michelle wasn't sure about the plan—or Cliff.

*****

On Mondays and Thursdays Michelle helped Darcy at the store. Michelle told her sister the same story she'd told Cliff and Cassie. She wondered if the knot would always tighten in her chest when she recounted the lie. Or would the story eventually feel like truth?

One afternoon Michelle was reading by the pool. Cassie stepped out onto the patio in her yellow bathing suit, a Coke can in one hand, the cordless phone in the other. "Mom, for you."

Michelle didn't want to answer any more questions. A reporter from the *Atlanta Globe* called several times a day wanting Michelle's story. "People love to read about stories of survival," the woman told Michelle. "It gives them hope." Cliff handled most of the calls, dismissing them with promises of future interviews.

"They'll forget about it by the end of the week, when the next big story breaks," Cliff had assured her. She hoped he was right.

Michelle took the phone from Cassie. "Hello?"

The woman on the other end introduced herself as Lulu Martin. Michelle got up and went into the house, leaving Cassie on the patio. Michelle hurried into the dining room and sat in one of the chairs. Lulu said she was calling because of Pink Souder, explaining that she was his mother's best friend.

"I know who you are," Michelle said.

She could hear Lulu's breathing, but the woman fell silent.

"Pink is in the hospital," she finally told Michelle. "He had a nervous breakdown."

Lulu asked Michelle to recount everything that happened so that maybe she could help Pink. Michelle told her every detail she could recall, from the moment Cliff went down the mountain in search of the light to the evening of the snowstorm; the faceless people, Pink showing up at the cabin with the sheriff, and about Pink seeing Cliff—who was supposed to be dead.

"I'm sorry," Michelle said. "Mrs. Souder warned me, but I couldn't stand to see him suffer that night. It was awful."

Lulu assured her it wasn't her fault. "If anybody's to blame, it's Mattie, Ida, and me. But there is nothing to be done about that now. I'm sorry you were involved."

Lulu gave Michelle her phone number and told her to call if she needed to talk and apologized for any trouble it may have caused Michelle's family.

"Is Pink going to be okay?" Michelle asked.

"He's doing better . . . but he's still confused. I'm picking him up from the hospital in the morning. He's going to stay with me for a while. He has no family here anymore."

"Lulu," Michelle said, uncomfortable with what she was about to share with the old woman. "I don't know how to tell you . . . you're dead in Pink's reality. He won't . . ."

"We've already been through that," she said. "It set off another episode for Pink, but he seems okay with it now . . . maybe because he knows they'll release him from the hospital if he can accept it."

After hanging up, Michelle stared at the floor, the events of the past week wheeling through her, a dizzying spin of emotions and images.

"Mom?" Cassie said.

Michelle turned to see Cassie standing in the doorway to the dining room. She didn't know how long Cassie had been standing there, but her arms were folded across her chest as if she were cold and her eyes were caught beneath a swell of tears.

"Hey, baby, are you okay?" Michelle stood to hug her daughter.

"Is it true? What you told that woman on the phone?"

The buoyancy Michelle had felt a moment earlier relaying everything to Lulu flattened under a surge of humiliation. Her skin tingled.

Michelle hugged her closer. Cassie felt like clay in her arms, no bones in her body.

"I can't explain it, Cassie," Michelle said. "I only know what I *think* happened. Do you understand? I don't know if any of it is true. That's what scares me."

Cassie held her tighter.

"Does Dad know?" Cassie asked.

"No."

CHAPTER 42

A week later, amidst a maelstrom of fears, nightmares, and anxieties, Michelle called Cliff and told him she wanted to sell the cabin. She was having difficulty focusing—her dreams and memories shaping every waking thought. The energy of the cabin pulled at her constantly, a nagging and persistent thread running through each and every day. Even sleep provided no solace. Her dreams spewed up ghastly images of people shot through the head, or buried up to their neck in snow, or frozen to death. Or the reoccurring figure in black, its face hidden by the shadow of a large hood, coming toward her like death itself. She awoke crying out, sweating, afraid to drift back into sleep. Perhaps by severing all ties with their mountain retreat, she might orient herself back in her own existence.

Cliff agreed without hesitation to selling the cabin. He could not see going back up there either. "Too many ghosts," he said. He'd meant it metaphorically, but for Michelle, the ghosts were real, always there.

"Michelle, I don't want to push you . . . but . . . could we talk about us this weekend?"

Michelle was relieved Cliff hadn't fought her when she'd suggested he find his own apartment for a while, but he brought up their marriage every time they spoke. "I need time, Cliff," Michelle said. "It would be so helpful if you could just not bring it up for now."

That night, the woman in the lavender gown came in Michelle's dreams, her lips moving. Michelle strained to hear what she was saying, but there was no sound. Some nights a black panther stalked Michelle, moving ever closer, Michelle and the animal linked on some tangential plane of existence, revolving against a stationary landscape, changing, fading, aging. She woke up screaming.

"Mom," Cassie said, shaking her. "It's just a dream."

Just a dream. Michelle trembled. She thought her eyes were open, but for a few seconds, even though she knew she was in bed, she could see only the panther. She looked at the clock. Three thirty-three in the morning. It was black outside. They sat quietly, Cassie with her arms around Michelle's shoulders. Her breathing came back slowly, sinking into her lungs like something foreign, slipping deeper until rooted once again in her diaphragm, filling, emptying, a million near-deaths a day.

"Is everything okay?" Cliff asked, when they talked on the phone the next day.

"When can we go?" Michelle asked.

"Go?" Cliff said.

"To the cabin. I want to sell it as soon as possible."

*****

When Cassie fell asleep on the drive up to the cabin, Cliff brought up the old woman who had found Michelle. He told Michelle that there had been a Charlene House in the newspapers a few weeks earlier. Some hikers had found her dead on the Appalachian Trail, several miles from her tent and sleeping bag. She had died of exposure.

Michelle recalled Charlene's glacier-blue eyes, both hopeful and skeptical, the day the old woman had left the hospital. Dead in the woods? Michelle thought. One of many possibilities. How queer it all felt.

"That's odd, isn't it? That she would have the same name as the woman who found you?" Cliff said. "She died in the big snowstorm over a week ago. While you were missing. You must remember that?"

Michelle didn't know what to say. So there had been a snowstorm, she thought, just earlier than the one she'd experienced.

"Look," Cliff said. "I didn't tell you that to make you uncomfortable, and I certainly don't want to give you reasons to lie to me, even though I know I don't deserve honesty. I just want us to start over. No lies. No bullshit."

She looked over at him, surprised he hadn't pressed her on Pink and his ravings. Maybe he'd forgotten, but she doubted it.

"Here's the thing, Cliff," she said. "I don't know exactly what happened. It was . . . queer. So, for now . . . I hope you can accept what I've told you."

CHAPTER 43

They arrived at the cabin before noon. Bright green buds sprinkled the tree branches. Daffodils lined the driveway, the sky polished to deep blue. Michelle could hardly believe this was the same place from a few weeks earlier.

Cassie was the first one from the car, asking for the key, saying she needed to use the bathroom. She bounded up the front walk with her overnight bag and schoolbooks.

Cliff assured Michelle it shouldn't take more than a day to put everything in order, get the listing set up, pack the Cherokee. They might spend the night, but they'd spend it in town at the Hampton Inn.

Michelle was halfway up the steps when she heard Cassie scream. She dropped her bag and ran for the door. Cassie was in the living room, dancing from foot to foot—part laughing, part hysterical—the cuffs of her jeans pulled up to her knees. "Get Dad! The toilet's gone berserk! There's water everywhere."

Michelle ran into the bathroom and knelt by the toilet, turning off the valve behind the tank until the water stopped flowing over the rim of the bowl. Water soaked her jeans and she half-expected to see the pentacle lying there, the way it had the night she'd gone looking for Cliff. Nothing but a cobweb in the corner. She wasn't even sure what she'd done with the thing, where she'd left it.

Cassie stood in the doorway on her tiptoes. "It wasn't like there was anything gross in there," Cassie said. "Except this ugly black and red bug. I flushed it before I sat down because it was disgusting."

Cliff appeared in the doorway and put his arm around Cassie's shoulder.

"Did you break the cabin? If you break it, you buy it," Cliff joked with Cassie.

Michelle appreciated Cliff's easy manner, the way the sharp corners of his intensity were seemingly rounded off.

"Yeah, I broke the whole cabin. Here's a dollar," Cassie said, handing him a wrinkled bill from her pocket.

"Hey, is this my change from the gas station?" he said, studying the money. "I forgot about that. Where's the rest? I gave you a twenty."

The familiarity of Cassie and Cliff's banter was both reassuring and heartbreaking, since Michelle's own feelings for Cliff were so different now.

Cassie returned with a mop and bucket and swabbed the water from the floor. Michelle changed into a spare pair of jeans. Cliff called a plumber, then suggested having lunch before they got too carried away with packing.

Michelle and Cassie drove into Ardenwood and ordered lunch from Thai Mountain. After picking up the food, they passed the converted house on Main that had been Pink's office. Michelle hardly recognized it. It was now an ice cream parlor called Sprinkles and Cream.

Cliff was packing canned food from the pantry when they came in. Michelle placed the take-out on the kitchen counter, and Cliff came over behind her and put his hands on her waist. The caress surprised her. Since she'd been back, they slept in the same bed but hadn't touched each other. After he moved out, she hadn't even thought about it, their lack of intimacy over the past few years having become routine. She thought about them making love that one afternoon upon returning from the cemetery. But that was a different Cliff, the man missing a finger. She was quick to remind herself that that wasn't part of this reality, and Cliff would have no knowledge of that afternoon.

Michelle pulled his change from her pocket and laid it on the kitchen counter, surprised to see the pentagram among the nickels and dimes. She picked it up. Maybe these were the jeans she'd been wearing that night with Pink, the pentagram making it through a wash and dry cycle at home. She didn't want it, still unsure how to dispose of it. Cliff saw it in her hand.

"Is that Cassie's?"

Michelle looked up. "This? No."

Cliff pulled plates down from the cabinet, and then tore off paper towels to use as napkins. They ate out on the deck. They had just finished eating when the plumbers arrived, two men wearing blue shirts and jeans, both with name patches. Cassie and Michelle went out on the deck while the men checked the bathroom pipes, the drains in the laundry room, the kitchen. Cliff came out on the deck a while later and told Michelle and Cassie they might want to come watch.

"The plumbers?" Cassie said.

"Yeah, they have a video camera like surgeons use for laparoscopic surgery. I mean it's bigger and clunkier, but it's amazing."

"Ughh, no thanks," Cassie said. "I don't want the guided tour of our sewer system."

"You'd have something to share with your friends," Cliff said, laughing.

"Yeah, right. That's the kind of thing we always talk about."

Even though Michelle was glad that Cliff's relationship with Cassie was intact, Michelle felt like she was trapped behind two-inch thick bulletproof glass. She wanted some of the lightness Cassie and Cliff enjoyed, to be part of the jokes they tossed between each other. Had it always been this way, them laughing, joking, and her on the periphery watching in silence?

"Do you want to go for a walk?" Michelle asked Cassie.

"Let's see," Cassie said, mugging an inquisitive look. "A walk amid the mountain laurel and fresh air . . . or a dark, dismal journey to the center of the septic tank? This is tough. Let's go, Mom. Sorry, Dad."

"We won't be gone long," Michelle said. "We can start packing when we get back."

"Just remember, Dad, Mom said that, not me."

Michelle and Cassie walked up the road in silence, the smell of fresh pine in the air. Michelle took Cassie to the pathway Pink had built through the trees. When they reached the gnarled poplar tree, Michelle was first to climb the worn, wooden planks nailed to its trunk.

"Wow, Mom," Cassie said. "That looks a little dangerous."

"Come on," Michelle said. "Just be careful."

When Cassie reached the top, she walked past Michelle, holding the railing, and looked out over the varied green hues of rhododendron, mountain laurel, and conifers. Michelle told Cassie about Pink, how he'd built the path for Isabelle. When she finished the story, she took the pentacle from her pocket and lashed it to the railing.

"Why are you doing that?" Cassie asked.

Michelle explained that she'd found it in the house, that it was Isabelle's. "This is where it belongs now."

"Mom," Cassie said, "I've been thinking about what I heard you tell that woman on the phone the other day, that Lulu woman."

"I'm sorry you had to hear that."

"No, it's okay," Cassie said. "It's not freaking me out or anything. Actually, it made me think about something that happened last year with Chloe. I mean, it's not anything like what happened to you, but it was kind of weird.

"Chloe had this beautiful necklace she let me borrow," Cassie said. "A week or so later I gave it back to her. Then two weeks after that, Chloe asked for her necklace. I told her I gave it to her already, at Ginny's Halloween party. Chloe told me that was impossible because she hadn't been at the Halloween party, that her parents hadn't let her go. It was too weird, because she *was* at the party. I remember."

Michelle was surprised by her own desire to offer Cassie a logical explanation. In spite of all she had experienced, her mind hungrily craved the comfort of a predictable universe, quantifiable reality, irrefutable laws of nature.

"Are you ready to head back?" Michelle said.

Cassie kicked rocks as they walked along the macadam road toward the cabin. A hawk drew a quick shadow across the pavement in front of them, causing them both to look up. But it was the blue and red flashing lights splashing through the trees that caught their attention.

When they reached the cabin, they saw two police cars blocking the driveway. Cliff was on the deck, his hands on the railing, his eyes on the riff of distant mountains. He didn't turn until Michelle called his name.

"Are you okay? What's going on?"

His face was white.

"Daddy, what's wrong?" Cassie asked, her eyes darting between the house and her father.

"They found a skeleton," Cliff said.

"What are you talking about?" Michelle said, shifting her gaze between the opened door and Cliff. Two officers stood inside the house, one of them speaking into the microphone attached to his collar. With his tan uniform, he looked like a state policeman.

Cliff explained that the plumbers checked all the pipes with the video scope and found no problem then checked the pipe leading to the septic tank. "It was unbelievable," Cliff said. "The skull looking back . . ."

"In the septic tank?" Michelle said. "They found a skeleton in the septic tank? But how . . . I don't understand."

Sheriff Fisk walked out onto the deck with Deputy Bogan following. The sheriff shook his head, his eyes fixed on Michelle.

"Been a hell of a time for you folks," he said, "with Mr. Stage gone missing, then you, Mrs. Stage, disappearing like that. Now this."

"What's going on?" Michelle said.

Sheriff Fisk took off his hat and ran a hand through his hair. "Don't know for sure, but I'd say that's probably Isabelle Souder in that tank. We suspected he'd buried her here at the cabin, but never thought to look there. Who would, you know? I'm not a gambling man, but I'd wager that's Pink's wife. State boys'll sort it out. In the meantime, we got to go get Pink." He riveted his gaze on Michelle, as if trying to pull up vital information from the deep green of her eyes. "He's a pretty bad mess."

Michelle couldn't look at Sheriff Fisk.

"You folks mind if I have a word with Mrs. Stage alone," Sheriff Fisk asked, his question pointed at Cliff and Cassie.

Cliff wrapped his arm around Cassie's shoulder and guided her toward the driveway. Michelle wondered if this would ever be over.

"A few years back I bought my wife a blouse for her birthday," Sheriff Fisk said. "The day before I was to give it to her, she saw a woman in the grocery store wearing the same blouse and turned to me and told me how ugly it was. Well, I took the blouse back to the store and exchanged it for bath oil beads and little soaps I knew she liked. So I'm a strong believer in serendipity. But Pink showing up after all these years, then a few days later we find Isabelle's remains? Well, it strains all credibility, if you follow me. Now, I know you been through a lot, but I really need to know what happened between you and Pink, especially with this new wrinkle."

Michelle repeated the lie that when she'd made it to the highway, she hitchhiked into town and saw Pink's office and stopped there because she remembered the sheriff telling her Pink had built the cabin. And she thought she could use the phone to call Cliff. "I don't remember much else."

The sheriff regarded her a long moment, a mild ripple of disgust tightening the straight line of his mouth. "Ma'am, Pink don't have him an office. Hasn't had one in years. Not here in Ardenwood. Do you mind telling me where you two happened to link up?"

Michelle stared into the sheriff's eyes. Deputy Bogan stood beside him, both men awaiting the answer.

"It's a blur," Michelle said. "Isn't that obvious? I can't remember anything clearly."

Fisk continued to wait for a more adequate answer until a heavy truck rumbled up the road and pulled in behind the squad cars.

The sheriff put his hat on, screwing it slowly from side to side until it fit just right. "I already explained to your husband that you folks won't be able to stay here tonight, being a crime scene and all. State boys won't want evidence spoiled. But I don't think we've had our last talk, Mrs. Stage. Lot of folks are wondering where Pink's been, and Pink keeps saying he's been in Ardenwood all along, says we're all crazy and throws a fit. But chances are, Pink's going to trial for Isabelle's murder—and when that happens, prosecutor's going to want to know what you know. You understand, Mrs. Stage? You're the first person to see Pink in years. And he talks like you and him are old friends. State boys might even get it in their mind you've been hiding him all these years, that maybe you had something to do with this, if those bones turn out to be Isabelle's."

The two men who brought the backhoe came up on the deck and asked the sheriff where to dig. Deputy Bogan escorted them around the side of the house.

Sheriff Fisk looked back at Michelle. "Hell of a thing, all this new technology. They run a cable fixed with a camera and light no bigger than a dang pencil down the pipe. Even has a sensor on it that ol' Andy there can follow with that contraption he's holding, lead him right to the tank. They'll pull out them bones and check 'em with all their fancy equipment, find out exactly who that is in there. Hell of a thing, isn't it?"

The backhoe fired up and sputtered under a large plume of blue smoke. It rattled loudly across the yard.

Michelle said nothing, unconvinced the sheriff could really believe she had anything to do with the skeleton, with any of what was happening. But he could subpoena her back to Ardenwood for Pink's trial, force her to perjure herself before judge and jury. She could tell the truth and test the limits of incredulity, risk insulting the judge and judicial system with her preposterous story. And what about Pink? He would have no idea about the murder. In the version of his life he was living, he had not killed anyone. He could probably pass a lie detector test without a problem, a lot easier than Michelle could.

"Can I go?" Michelle asked. "We're going to head back to Atlanta today."

"Sure thing," Sheriff Fisk said. "I gave the state boys all your contact information. Someone from the prosecutor's office'll probably be getting in touch with you."

"You can't possibly believe I had anything to do with this?" Michelle said.

"Not directly, but you and Pink have one heck of a vexing story. It just doesn't jibe, ma'am. And that puts an itch in my sheriff's brain I just can't scratch." The sheriff tweaked the brim of his hat and headed in the direction of the men with the backhoe, down the back stairs off the deck. She heard the crisp slice of metal into dirt, followed by the sound of clumped mud and rock tumbling through the weeds as the backhoe dumped its take from the fresh hole.

*****

Cassie asked questions from the back seat. Michelle didn't want to talk, her mind a whorl of intangibles, roads going nowhere, travelers without destinations, night without end. She wanted it to be over.

They drove back to Atlanta in silence, Michelle incapable of unplugging from the lies she'd told Sheriff Fisk, how embarrassing they were, how stupid they'd sounded. She'd seen that Pink's office was an ice cream shop—why did she stay with that lie? It seemed impossible to construct a believable truth from what she knew, all the facets of reality she'd seen, how the pieces should all fit.

Cassie slept on the trip back. Cliff turned on the radio. "The real estate agent didn't say anything about skeletons in the septic system," Cliff said.

Michelle looked at him, unable to grasp his meaning.

"It was a joke. You know, real estate agents are supposed to—never mind. It was a bad joke. Why don't you close your eyes and rest?"

Michelle curled against the seat, the woman in the lavender gown coming in her dream.

CHAPTER 44

When Lulu opened the door, she was surprised Pink wasn't sitting on the couch watching television. That's where he'd spent nearly every waking hour since she'd picked him up from the hospital, there or in the fridge looking for something to eat. Most nights he didn't even sleep in the spare bedroom she'd set up for him, just dozed off in his boxers on the couch, the television playing all night.

Burrito ran over to her, jumping up and down, propping himself up with one paw on her shin. She leaned over and rubbed his head, then got some dog food and poured it in his dish. "You're supposed to make sure Pink doesn't sleep all day," she said to the dog.

Lulu set the sacks of groceries on the kitchen table. Pink had hardly spoken to her the last couple of days, ever since she'd told him the story of Mattie and Ida and what they had done. Maybe it was a mistake telling him, she thought, but he needed to know if Fisk came for him. She knew Fisk had questioned him in town and hadn't arrested him. Lulu wanted to ask Pink what he had done with Isabelle's body but she didn't have the courage.

She put the lettuce and cucumber in the vegetable crisper and closed the refrigerator door, remembering how Pink had first reacted when she came to the hospital after his breakdown. She'd come in the evening, after visiting hours, hoping to avoid making a scene. Evelyn, the night nurse, had let her in.

"Lulu?" he'd said, seemingly still trying to pull himself from sleep. "What the hell! Lulu, you're dead—"

Lulu had clamped her palm over his mouth. "Quiet, Pink."

He had tried to wrestle free of her grip. When he settled down, she drew back her hand.

"There must be hell to pay if I'm seeing you, Lulu!" Pink had said, wiping his mouth. "Damn, I helped Mama spread your ashes!"

A few days later, Lulu picked Pink up at the hospital and brought him to her house. He was groggy from medication, so she waited a few days to tell him about Mattie and Ida—and Isabelle.

He'd been napping in front of the television.

"Pink" she'd said, shaking his arm.

"Uh, oh, Lulu," Pink had said, rubbing his eyes. "What is it? Supper?"

"Pink." Lulu had switched the television off. "I have something unsettling to tell you and I need you to listen."

Lulu had tried to frame the story in terms Pink could deal with, but she could tell he'd been flummoxed by the account. "That's just batshit crazy!" he'd shouted, pushing himself off her couch. "How could Isabelle be my sister?" he said. "And how could I have killed her?" he said. "That's one whopper of a yarn, Lulu."

"I'm so sorry, Pink," she'd said. "But you need to know."

"Why would I need to know something like that?" he'd shouted. "Hell's bells, Lulu, I'll never get that damn story out of my head. Why would you concoct a tale like that? Hell, you should've been in the damn hospital, not me."

Pink had gone to his bedroom, and Lulu had heard the television in his room come on. The next few days had been tense. Pink was impossible to talk to. He took his plate to his room, and she'd see it in the sink in the morning when she got up to make coffee. Every time she spoke to him, he'd fly into a tirade. "Everybody in this whole damn town's crazier than a hornet on a bug strip." Then he'd slam his bedroom door.

Lulu filled a pot with water and set it on the stove. She turned the

burner on and remembered the railing on the porch needed some attention, feeling it would be good for Pink to busy himself with something
other than police shows and horror movies.

"Pink," she called. She went down the hall to the bathroom, but it
was empty. She could see his bedroom door was closed. "Pink, are you
awake?" she waited a moment, then rapped lightly on the door. "Pink, are
you awake? I need some help with something."

Knowing how stubborn Pink could be and actually having to deal
with it were two different things. Lulu had never had children of her own,
and she didn't know how Mattie had managed with Pink all those years.
She twisted the doorknob and pushed it open. "Pink, are you awake?" She
walked to the bed, to the roll of blankets. He wasn't there.

Burrito followed as Lulu walked to the back porch and surveyed
the yard, the trees at the edge of her property, the mountains painting a
bluish-gray backdrop to her view. She checked with a couple of her neighbors, but no one knew anything.

Standing in the front yard, Lulu let her eyes rove the gravel driveway
leading up to her place, the field just beyond her front gate, the flashing
lights turning off the county road heading her way. It was then she heard
the sirens. Two cars. She watched as they came closer.

She picked up Burrito. The dog licked her cheek, her neck, wriggling
in her arms.

"Pink, where have you gone?"

CHAPTER 45

"Well ain't you a sight for sore eyes," Pink said, getting into Claire's car. "I thought you'd never come get me. Hell, Lulu told me she didn't know where you were. I told her I just saw you a few days ago, but that old woman's crazier than a woodpecker with a neck brace.

Pink looked over at Claire, placing his hand on her shoulder. Claire's sour expression gave him a start. Claire turned onto the county road, heading for the highway.

"Pink, I ain't seen you in almost five years," she said. "I don't know what the hell you're talking about."

"What?" Pink said. "We just watched that crazy damn video last week, the one where those fishermen all drown in a hurricane."

"*The Perfect Storm*?" Claire said. "Is that the movie you're talking about? I can't even remember when I watched that. Hell, Pink, what did they do to you in that damn hospital? I heard you'd gone bonkers, but shit . . . I'm worried for you."

"You telling me we didn't see that damn movie last week?" Pink said. "Well, which one was it then?"

Claire pulled the car into a deserted gravel parking lot off the highway.

"Pink, baby," she said. "We didn't watch any movie last week, or last month, or last year! I haven't seen you since . . . you know . . . Isabelle."

Pink searched his pockets for the pills the hospital had given him until he realized he'd left them in the bathroom at Lulu's. He needed them now. The tingling had come back, like he was hooked up to some low voltage car battery. He hated the disorientation, the vertigo.

"Pink, you okay?" Claire said. "You don't look so good, baby."

Pink threw open the door and stepped out into the fresh air. He took his eyes to the mountains beyond, to the leaves on the trees, the sky, things familiar and able to bring him back to the world. He filled his lungs with fresh air. Even so, he still felt like he might get sick.

A hawk flew above him, its shrill call echoing through the valley below. Pink felt a hand on his back. "I've never seen you like this, Pink," Claire said. "Come on, I know where we can go. It's not safe here."

In twenty minutes they were sitting near an old gravel boat ramp, the lake calm and beautiful beyond the windshield. Pink had dozed off. Sleep had always been a hobby for him, but since he'd been in the hospital it had become a full-time job. A drip of water woke him.

Claire was crying, holding Pink to her chest, staring out at the water. Pink sat up, but she never turned to look at him. He reached across the seat and took her hand in his. "What's this?" he asked, referring to her wedding ring. "I thought you pawned this after you left Kenny."

Claire shot him a confused look and started crying harder, her head slumped toward the steering wheel. "Pink, don't do this to me."

He didn't know what she was talking about. "Claire, remember that night at Burtran Lake after your crazy husband, Kenny, made us jump off that damn bridge. Remember how we stayed warm that night, how we made love in the front—"

Claire pushed his hand away. "How could you even suggest such a thing, Pink. You're my damn brother. What we did was a sin against nature, against all things holy. We're gonna burn in hell for what we did."

Pink had no way to relate to this newfound narrative. Why did everyone, even Claire, think they were siblings? It made no sense. Pink started to get out of the car when Claire snagged his wrist.

"Pink, we've got a problem," she said, her eyes marshaled by fear.

"What the hell, Claire?" Pink drew back from her, but she dug her nails into his skin.

"Look, Pink, you need to listen closely. I hope for both our sakes you can do that."

Claire's makeup ran from her left eye like a muddy creek. Pink pulled the door closed. He wasn't sure how much of this he could take. Something in his head had gone off-plumb and was spinning haphazardly, making him dizzy.

Claire spun the wedding ring on her finger. "I married Elmer a couple of years ago," she started.

"Bogan?" Pink said. "You . . . married Bogan? How could you . . . when . . . ?"

"Pink, this will go a lot easier if you just let me talk."

Pink wasn't sure he could do that.

"Anyway, after you left . . ." she said, putting her hand to his lips to thwart his interruption. "After you left, I went back to Kenny. I was so messed up and I had no one to talk to about what had happened. Then when Kenny drove himself off that mountain all drunk and coked up, I nearly fell apart. I was so alone. Elmer came to the house to give me the news about Kenny. He came day after day, bringing me food, cooking dinner for me. I fell in love with him, Pink. He was the only thing in my life that made sense."

"Well then you're about the luckiest damn person in the world," Pink said. "Cause nothing makes a bit of damn sense in my life. But Bogan, Claire? Don't you remember how we always made jokes about him?"

"He's a good man, Pink. Good and kind . . . and he loves me so much. I'm pregnant with our first child."

Pink looked at her stomach and saw no signs of life there.

"It's only two months, Pink. But that's not what we're talking about here," she said. "Anyway, several months after Kenny's accident, I thought I might like to try getting a job. Elmer said there was an opening at the sheriff's office, and we weren't sure how that would work out, him being a deputy and me a . . . well . . . assistant, I guess. But I took it. Eventually we told Louden about our relationship, and he didn't seem to care that we were seeing each other and all."

Pink couldn't understand how she could see anything in Elmer. They were different as a beaver and boll weevil. "I was in Louden's office the other day and I didn't see you there."

"Yeah, I know. Elmer called me from the squad car and told me they were bringing you into the station," she said. "I . . . I didn't want to see you."

"Why?"

"Too many bad memories . . . you know, with Isabelle and all. Then there was all the talk about . . . you know, incest and all, and all the looks at the damn grocery store. And Kenny, he rode me all the time about fucking my own brother. He'd try to use it against me. He'd say, 'Well, hell, Claire, why not try some anal? Christ, you slept with your own damn brother. I'd think you'd be up for some experimentation.' The way Kenny talked to me was just . . . cruel. But Elmer didn't care about any of the talk and rumors and bullshit."

Claire wiped her eyes, and Pink felt like he was caught up in one of them reality shows he hated so much.

"But when the call came in today that they found a skeleton up at your old place, I knew there was going to be trouble."

"What?" Pink said. "A damn skeleton? Well, I'll be damned." What was even more disturbing than the thought of a skeleton at his old cabin was the look of fear on Claire's face.

"Pink, you said they'd never find her."

Pink jerked back like he'd been slapped. "What the hell are you talking about?"

"Don't do this, Pink! You know what I'm talking about. Isabelle's body. You said you put it where no one would ever find it! Well they did . . . and . . ."

"This is crazy shit . . . Claire . . . what is everybody drinking around here? Lulu told me the same damn thing. I never killed Isabelle . . . and I never did anything with her body!"

Claire's face registered shock, then disbelief. "You really don't remember, do you?" she said.

"No, that's what I been trying to tell you, for Christ's sake. This is all apeshit crazy talk. I never killed Isabelle!"

Claire paused a moment before she spoke. "I know you didn't, Pink. I did. You just said you'd hide the body."

Pink felt himself swirling on some lopsided axis, as if it could spin right off into the lake. "What do you mean you killed Isabelle? Why? I don't understand any of this." Pink said.

Claire tried to explain about the night Isabelle had called her into the bedroom, yelling at her about sleeping with Pink, about Pink's birth and Ida, how they were siblings.

"It crushed me hearing her say those things," Claire said. "I was so ashamed. Then Isabelle lit into me again, commenced to calling me a whore and a tramp, and she said, 'If Pink turns you into a family woman, you'll give birth to a bastard double-cousin. Then where will you be?' And, Pink, I was so hurt and so angry, and Isabelle sat there with her damn sickly eyes and that smug face, judging me, demeaning me . . . and . . . and all the while she knew, Pink, she knew and never said a word . . . never said a word about you being my brother . . . just let me carry on and I . . . I just lost control . . . I went into her room after she fell asleep with her potions and her oils and her high-brow-better-than-anyone-else bullshit, and I pushed that damn pillow into her ugly face until she stopped moving."

Claire fell against the steering wheel crying, pounding the dashboard with her fist. Pink tried to console her, but she wasn't the same person he had been with only a week earlier. After several minutes, Claire regained composure. She sniffled and looked at Pink, her eyes so red Pink couldn't find the color there anymore. "You came back to the house that night," she said, sniffling, wiping her nose. "I have no idea why. The next morning when I woke up, Isabelle's body was gone. Some of that is still a blur, but a couple of days after that, you told me to call Louden and tell him that Isabelle was missing. You told me to tell Louden that you and Isabelle had a huge row the night before, and that I hadn't seen Isabelle since. I don't know why you were so willing to take the blame for what I'd done, but I loved you for being there for me. And I've never forgotten." She reached across and touched Pink's cheek. Tears came again.

Pink placed his hand over hers.

"They're coming for you now, Pink, and I don't want you punished for what I done. So you need to go to the station with me, and we'll tell them I killed Isabelle and hid her body at your cabin."

Pink was trying to parse all this information, all of it so foreign to his ears his mind was going cattywompus on him. He recalled everything Lulu had told him, all of it sounding like the rant of the criminally insane a few nights ago. Now he wasn't so sure. Claire was convinced that these events had taken place. Maybe they had. Maybe Isabelle was dead. Was that her skeleton they'd found at his cabin? He thought about Michelle Stage, her troublesome questions about Isabelle. Her accusations about him killing Isabelle. Where had she gotten that notion? Things were adding up but made no sense. Something was off-kilter, that was for sure. But Claire's fear was real and serious, and there was no doubt there.

"That will never work, Claire. Nobody's ever gonna believe you could haul Isabelle's body to my cabin and bury it," Pink said. "Besides, you don't even know where I put her. Hell, if you don't know that, they're never gonna buy one word of your story."

"Elmer'll tell me where they found the body, Pink. He'll believe me."

"No, Claire. I'll tell Elmer exactly where the body was found, before you even have a chance to ask him, and your story won't amount to a hill of beans. And if you tell him you killed Isabelle, well, that's just stupid—there's no reason for both of us going down for her murder. They'll arrest me anyway for—I don't know what they call it—but for burying the body. I'd be an accomplice. Besides, Isabelle's deception was eating her alive. Hell, you probably done her a favor," Pink said, then kissed her cheek. "I love you, Cuddle Cakes."

"You know I still hate that name, don't you?" Claire said, showing a faint smile and wiping her cheek.

"I know," Pink said. Pink wasn't sure about much of anything anymore, but one thing was sure—he loved her.

"Pink, you can't . . ."

"Claire, now don't grab the wrong end of the poker on this, I mean it. You let Louden and his boys try to hunt me down. Hell, I know

Louden, he's a terrible damn hunter—no instincts—he ain't never gonna catch up to me."

Pink opened the door and got out of the car. "I mean it, Claire. You take care of that baby and keep your mouth shut. If you have guilt over Isabelle's death, you're just gonna have to bear it. Can you do that, Claire? Can you just bear it? For Elmer? For that baby inside you?"

"Pink . . ."

"Look, now, don't do anything stupid. Promise me. You don't want to ruin Elmer's life, do you? And you sure as hell don't want to ruin that baby's life. If you need penance for what you done to Isabelle, then be the best damn mother you know how to be. That's your penance, Claire."

Pink swung the door shut and loped off into the woods. Out of breath after only a few minutes, he stood on a small knoll overlooking Burtran Lake, his chest heaving, watching Claire's car from behind some pines. After a few minutes, her car pulled away slowly, moving along the gravel road until it disappeared behind the trees.

CHAPTER 46

Reporters called day and night, some camping for hours on the sidewalk in front of Michelle's home in Atlanta, hoping for an interview. A television anchorman reported that the skeletal remains had been found at the Stage's cabin. The reporter then reiterated the story of Michelle's disappearance only weeks earlier, openly speculating on a possible link between the two events.

One evening after dinner, Cassie called Michelle to the living room. "Mom, come see this."

A CNN anchor was talking about Pink Souder, the story of his disappearance and the bones found on his property. The segment was accompanied by photos of Pink Souder, some old photos of his real estate office space in Ardenwood, as well as pictures of Isabelle Souder as a young, attractive woman.

"A statewide search for Pink Souder continues after he fled the home of Lulu Martin, where he was rumored to have been convalescing after a nervous breakdown," the announcer said. "Details are sketchy, but what we've learned is that police had driven to the house to arrest him, but when they arrived, he had already fled Mrs. Martin's home. Authorities are combing the area aided by neighboring law enforcement. He is believed to be armed and dangerous. This is considered to be the region's largest manhunt since the search for the abortion clinic bomber, Earl Borden."

Armed and dangerous. Michelle was seized by conflicting emotions. She realized Pink had killed Isabelle in one reality, based on everything Mattie had told her, yet the Pink Souder Michelle knew hadn't killed or hurt anyone. That was the only Pink she knew. She pictured the path he had built in the trees for Isabelle, how Mattie spoke of them as kids, how much Pink must have loved Isabelle. And now Pink was running for his life, unaware of the crime he was being hunted for, unaware of the reality he now found himself in.

CHAPTER 47

Pink scrambled down the hill, pulling himself through the thick rhododendron. He dropped the shotgun when he slipped on the loose dirt. The gun slid down the culvert and into a shallow draw. "Oh, fuck it all to hell!"

The sun was bright through the trees, and he figured it was close to noon. Even so, the day held a chill not uncommon for this time of year. He pulled the shotgun from the creek then scooped clear water to his mouth. He gulped down several palmfuls, then sat a moment, allowing his thoughts to ramble unimpeded over Lulu's story and Claire's account of things. There was much overlap, and Pink was fairly certain Lulu had actually pulled off something supernatural. But he couldn't wrap his brain around any of it.

"Crazy as a trapped bat, that old woman is," he said to himself. The sound of barking hounds snapped him back to the present. He'd managed to stay ahead of Fisk for two days, but they'd found him now.

It was Claire that most troubled him. What she lacked in brains she made up double in heart. Pink hoped she'd bought his bluff about Isabelle's body and where it was buried. Pink had no idea where Isabelle was buried and until Lulu told him the story, he hadn't even known she was supposed to be dead. He hoped Claire wouldn't say anything to cast doubt about Pink's guilt in Isabelle's murder, hoping she'd keep her mouth shut. There was no way she could stand up to a Fisk interrogation. Fisk would ask her two questions, and she'd breakdown and confess to every murder that had ever happened in Ardenwood.

"Uhhh, shit, Louden. The fucking dogs? You brought them dogs down on me?" Pink got up and started running again, but he knew he could never outpace the hounds. Fisk knew him too well, knew where Pink hunted, knew every cave and hollow tree, just like Pink. He'd lied to Claire about that as well. They'd hunted bear and boar together. They walked these woods all their lives. And Louden was one of the best damn trackers he'd ever met. Pink knew it was a death sentence with Louden tracking him, but he didn't care anymore. Pink felt like he was wearing someone else's life, and everything felt wrong and unfixable.

The dogs were getting closer. Pink had run another couple of miles, but was out of gas, partly from not having eaten much since he'd left Claire, but mostly from being out of shape. He had to sit down against a tree. His breathing was strained and shallow. His chest pounded. Why Michelle Stage entered his mind he didn't know. "I guess that's why she acted like she hardly knew me," Pink said to himself. Things were adding up but only if he could accept the premise of some alternate reality that Lulu had gone on about. "Alternate reality," Pink said, smiling to himself. "Where's that alternate reality where I live at the Playboy Mansion?"

The dogs howled louder, clearly on his tracks. Pink hunted enough coon to know the high-pitched wail of a hound on a hot lead. He couldn't go on. He'd probably covered ten miles this morning alone, but it was barely noon and he was already on empty. He pushed himself up to his feet using the butt of the shotgun. He'd gone by Clarence's trailer early in the morning while it was still dark. He knew Clarence kept a shotgun in his pickup truck and a nice stash of peanut butter crackers in his glove box to curb his hypoglycemia. But Pink hadn't bothered to check if Clarence's shotgun was even loaded. Pink shook his head. He cracked it open—two dark, empty chambers—then clapped it shut.

"Hell, Clarence. You're just a damn pumpkin roller after all." Didn't matter, Pink wasn't planning to shoot anyone, but a loaded gun might be nice to give them hounds a scare, he thought. "Hate to get all bit up before I die."

A squirrel ran down the tree and stopped ten feet away from Pink.

"Come to watch the show?" Pink said to the animal. Its tail twitched. "Well, it ought to be one hell of an event. I'm too fat to keep running and too wore out for prison. I got me an empty shotgun and no prospects for the future. Don't that beat all." Pink laughed a little, his head drooping. "Them folks chasing me think I killed Isabelle. No sense disappointing them." Pink wiped his eye, picturing how beautiful she'd been before she took ill. "You ever killed anyone, Mr. Squirrel? Of course not. I could never have killed Isabelle either, even though that ill-conditioned woman had grown to hate me. And her sister, Claire. That girl made me crazier than a peach-orchard pig. I loved them both. Those girls were the most precious things I ever laid eyes on."

Pink looked at the ground, wondering what it would have been like to grow up in the same house with Isabelle and Claire as his sisters. But his mind lacked the nimbleness to embrace that thought for long. It was too hard to erase how Claire felt in his arms, how her hair smelled of honey, how she cried when they watched sappy movies, her warm breath in his ear when they made love. And Isabelle's smile, her laugh when Pink said stupid things, her patience when he did stupid things. Pink had always been clever, but Isabelle was smart. And the first time they made love. She was fifteen, and he had never been with a girl before.

All Pink had now were memories. The world he knew was gone.

The dogs were running full-out, snapping twigs beneath their paws, leaves crackling under their speed. Pink could almost see their tongues flapping, teeth flashing white, ropes of saliva swinging from their mouths.

"Been one hell of a week, Mr. Squirrel," Pink said, thinking about Isabelle, Lulu, Claire and her baby, Mrs. Stage. His mother. He wished he could have seen her one more time. He wiped his cheek.

The dogs were closer now. Sounded like five or six of them, Pink reckoned.

"Well, Mr. Squirrel, seems like this is the last button on Gabe's coat. Wish I had a little corn squeeze for the occasion." The squirrel ran up the tree and disappeared into the canopy above.

Pink shook his head. The dogs were within fifty feet.

"Louden, call 'em off!" Pink shouted from behind the tree. "I don't want to shoot them mongrels."

Someone yelled, calling the hounds back. One of the dogs rounded the tree, snarling at Pink, barking. Saliva hung from its black lips as it growled at Pink, lunging at his leg. Pink butted the dog firmly in the head with the shotgun. Not enough to kill it, but to stave it off. The dog whimpered, backing up, then ran in circles. Someone whistled the dog back, and it scampered away.

"Pink, I know you have Clarence's shotgun. He called me this morning. You need to throw it out. Then you need to come out, hands on your head."

Pink knew Fisk's voice and felt the woods start to spin and tilt, the earth beneath his feet begin to loosen. Pink figured he probably should have stolen Clarence's truck instead of the damn gun. Maybe he'd be halfway to Kentucky by now.

"Hey, Louden, I know why you don't remember that Stage fella with his head blown half off," Pink shouted. "Lulu told me one hell of a story the other day." Pink was sweating through his shirt, yet he was chilled and shivering. "You didn't even flinch when Mr. Stage walked into that cabin the other day live as a stripper at the Katty Klub Room. Now I know why." Pink laughed and swayed, leaning against the tree for support.

"Pink, I need you to throw out that weapon. You hear me?"

A helicopter cut across the trees above Pink. Men moved in the bushes and trees around him, partially hidden, but Pink still saw them; he could spot a deer in a thicket from a hundred yards. Pink knew he was surrounded. How did this happen? How did everything go to shit overnight? What a strange world, he thought.

Pink stepped out from the tree. He heard the unmistakable clatter of rifles and pistols being cocked and readied to fire.

"Pink, drop the shotgun!"

"Louden, it's too bad you don't remember breaking that feller's fingers to get that pistol out of his frozen hand." Pink chuckled. "Hell, I'll never forget that. You called it a 'death grip' if memory serves."

"Pink, you gotta drop that gun! Now!"

Pink shook his head, laughing. "That was some crazy shit, wasn't it, Louden? I'll never forget that . . ." Pink brought the shotgun up. ". . . for as long as I—"

"Pink! Don't . . ."

Gunfire rang from every direction, ripping leaves and brush and bark. Pink's body took the bullets, his limbs flailing in a strange rhythm to the explosions around him. He kept his feet for almost a full ten seconds before slowly sinking to his knees, his torso and arms jerking under the constant barrage of lead and brass. When he finally settled to the ground, steam rose from his body, like a spirit too-long trapped. The gunfire stopped. An errant breeze stirred the leaves around him for just a moment, and the woods fell silent and still.

CHAPTER 48

Michelle stepped from the pool and dried herself with the towel then grabbed her cell phone from the glass table. "Hello?"

"Hello, Mrs. Stage. Sheriff Fisk . . . from Ardenwood."

"Hello, Sheriff," Michelle said.

"I'm sorry to bother you. Not sure if you heard, but . . . we verified that the skeleton we found in your septic was indeed Isabelle Souder, Pink's wife.

"I heard it on the news," she said.

"Also . . . Pink's dead."

"Yes, I know," Michelle said. She tried to imagine the level of Pink's rage, enough to kill Isabelle, to dispose of her body in such a horrible and demeaning way.

"Yeah, sad deal, Pink and Isabelle," Fisk said. "Not sure how much you knew about them two, but it was . . . uh . . . well, just a sad deal from the beginning."

"No, I didn't really know Pink. I had just met . . . you know . . . very briefly . . ."

Cassie had come outside and was standing next to Michelle, listening. Michelle smiled at her.

Fisk was quiet for a moment then cleared his throat before he spoke. "You remember that day you called me to your cabin, Mrs. Stage?"

"Yes, of course," she said. "I really appreciate all your help. I should have just waited for you to return . . . it was stupid . . ."

"I'm just glad you and your husband are both safe," he said. "But there are still some questions I have . . . you know. Some things that still confound me."

"Like what?" Michelle asked.

"Well, that night we drove down the road and Dell said he could see that house from his chopper . . . until he turned his light on, and then the house disappeared. Well that has been weighing on my mind. And Dell stands by his story. Then Pink told me some crazy stuff about the night he showed back up in Ardenwood. With you."

Michelle sat down on one of the chairs. Cassie stood next to her, touching her shoulder.

"Pink had all kinds of wild ramblings about faceless creatures and noises and beings and a woman in a nightgown and feeling sick, and snow melting, and I pretty much discounted everything he said, 'cause Pink's no stranger to corn liquor, but then he mentioned something that gave me pause."

Michelle listened.

"He said you had been at his *mama's* house the night before," Fisk said. "And Mattie told him you had psychological problems. That you had experienced a terrible trauma with the death of your daughter. Don't you think that's odd?"

"Well, sure. I mean clearly my daughter is fine . . ." she said.

"Yes, of course," Fisk said. "But that's not what bothered me."

Michelle waited for him to speak.

"How could Pink know you had a daughter?" Fisk finally said. "Supposedly he had just driven you back to your cabin and left? It's vexing. How could he know that?"

Michelle was rewinding the story she'd told Fisk, trying to stack the lies together into a believable pile. "I . . . I don't know . . . I think maybe I might have mentioned it on the drive up."

"Yeah, I thought about that too. But how could Pink's mother, Mattie Souder, know you had a daughter? When could you have possibly met

Mattie? She's been gone from Ardenwood for years. Do you know Mattie? Where did you two have this conversation about your daughter?"

"I don't know why Pink would say that . . . you know . . . about his mother."

"Well, let's talk about that ride Pink gave you. You said you happened upon his office in Ardenwood. And he gave you a ride up to the cabin. Is that about right?"

"Yes, but it's all kind of vague now . . ."

"I'm talking about the ride he gave you from his office . . . the office that no longer exists. You see, Pink hadn't been in Ardenwood for a long spell. There's no office anymore, Mrs. Stage. It's an ice cream shop now and has been for three years."

Michelle fell silent. Cassie must have sensed her discomfort and held her.

"There was no ride, was there, Mrs. Stage?"

Michelle wiped her eyes. Cassie leaned in close and put her head on Michelle's shoulder.

"Mrs. Stage?"

Would this ever be completely over? "I don't know what to say, Sheriff Fisk. I wish I could give you more answers, but . . . I don't . . ."

"Well, I don't mean to upset you," Sheriff Fisk said. "I would love to get a hold of Mattie. Have any thoughts on that . . . how I might get in touch with her?"

"No, I really don't."

"I'd like to contact her, tell her about Pink," Fisk said. "That boy was everything to her."

Michelle imagined Mattie sitting at her table alone, sipping tea, no one left in her life.

"Did you hear how Pink died?" Fisk asked.

"No . . . no I never got the details."

"Me and about ten law enforcement officials tracked him down near Miller Ridge. The dogs was howling, and Pink just walked out from behind a tree with a gun . . . we shot him to death. It was horrendous. His shotgun wasn't even loaded. It was almost like he wanted to die. That wasn't Pink's way."

"I'm so sorry," Michelle said, picturing Pink, smiling, laughing at the Hilltop.

"Me too," Sheriff Fisk said. "Pink was a friend of mine. Vexing at times, but a friend nonetheless. So was Isabelle. Shame how both those kids died."

Michelle reached out and brought Cassie to her lap. She was glad Cassie knew everything that had happened. Cassie was the only person she had no secrets from.

"I'm very sorry, Sheriff. I really am," Michelle said.

"I suppose you don't know Lulu Martin either, do you?"

"No, sorry." Michelle pictured Lulu being wheeled out on the gurney the day Pink and she'd driven to Lulu's house.

"Hmm. That's curious, because somehow she knew you. She told me the most outrageous yarn about Mattie and her, and some kind of black magic . . . gateways to alternate universes—which I don't even know what them's supposed to be—and Pink not even knowing he killed Isabelle in this reality, and you taking Pink back through some portal in the dark woods down the mountain from your cabin into another reality with a pentagram or something, and hell, it near give me a headache listening to her rattle on about such ridiculous things. Where on God's green earth would that woman get such a notion, do you figure?"

Michelle couldn't respond. What did Fisk want? Why was he so willing to share all of this with her, seemingly unconcerned what she might think?

"Yeah," the sheriff continued. "A downright bewildering story, isn't it, Mrs. Stage. You're still there, aren't you?"

"Yes, of course," Michelle said, wiping her eyes again.

"Lulu died this morning. A heart attack. Ain't that a coincidence, dying the day after Pink? She was Pink's godmother. Of course, I didn't believe her story at all. How could I, but it would have been nice to learn more, don't you think? About them gateways and alternative universes? Guess we'll never know now, will we? Unless Mattie shows up next."

Michelle gently moved Cassie from her lap and stood, anxious, weighing the consequences of what she was about to share. She walked to the edge of the pool, glancing back at Cassie.

"Sheriff . . ." Michelle said, "maybe we can't always understand everything about our world. Maybe there are things we just don't comprehend, and that Lulu . . . well . . . maybe she and Pink's mother had insights into things that most of us can't fathom. You know? Like . . . I mean, all those things Lulu told you . . . they may be very foreign to you and me and most people . . . but maybe there's something to what she said . . ." Michelle paused, unsure if it was wise to share with Fisk what she was about to tell him. "Sheriff, I didn't know how to tell you before, but . . . that day we met, when you came to look for my husband, and I went down the mountainside . . ."

"Well, Mrs. Stage, I can tell you're tired, and your family's been through some trying events these past few weeks. I don't want to take any more of your time. Give my best to your husband and daughter," Fisk said. "And you take care of yourself, ma'am."

Fisk hung up before she could say goodbye. Michelle clicked the phone off and set it on the table. She hugged Cassie to her, trying to hold back tears, still trapped in the strange conversation. Was Fisk looking for some kind of closure? Did he want Michelle to give him an alternative story that was more palatable to his beliefs? Or did he just need to talk, so perplexed by the events of the past few weeks, just as Michelle was? But maybe it was something more, a kind of search for a vague validation of Lulu's narrative, one that would explain the unexplainable, yet remain just ambiguous enough to allow his mind to deny the possibility.

"Mom, you okay?" Cassie asked, when Michelle came back to the table.

"Sure, I'm fine," Michelle said, pulling Cassie to her chest. "I love you so much, baby."

"I love you too."

"Is your father taking you to the music festival this weekend?" Michelle said.

"No, this weekend is . . . ugh . . . the car auction. You want to come with? It would be more fun if you came. We always go for pizza after," Cassie said.

Michelle chuckled, "No, I've been to enough of those."

"Yeah, pretty boring," Cassie said. "Well . . . how about a swim, then?"

"How about three laps," Michelle said. "Loser cooks dinner."

"You're on," Cassie said. "What are you making?"

ACKNOWLEDGMENTS

A special thanks to Nancy Reeder, Lianna Costantino, Jubal Tiner, Susan Snowden, Louise Fury, and Peggy Hageman.